Dear Reader,

We are almost three-~~~~~~~~~~~~~~~~~~~~~ another
year and I hope that you have been enjoying the *Scarlet*
titles I have chosen for you so far. The response to our first
hardback, *Dark Desire*, has been overwhelming, and I hope
that you will write and let me know what you thought of it.

This month, in *Mix and Match* by Tegan James, rich,
charming, easy-going yachtsman Jet Diamond is unique.
Or so Aberdeen thinks when she falls in love with him. But
that's before she meets his twin brother, film-maker Jasper
Diamond. Identical in looks but with very different
personalities, the Diamond twins bring double trouble to
the women in their lives. So what does that mean for
Aberdeen? In Stacy Brown's regency novel, *Heaven
Sent*, rebellious bluestocking Celeste Wentworth is determined to escape from the dreary life that her stern grandfather is planning for her – a suitable marriage and a
family. She resolves to be 'ruined' and falls for notorious
rake Simon Barclay, the Earl of Dragonwood. As their
relationship develops, they become caught up in the
strange web of a secret society responsible for the corruption of society girls, including Simon's own stepsister.

Don't forget that the second *Scarlet* hardback, *Finding
Gold* by Tammy Hilz, will be available next month. To
reserve your copy, send us your details now!

Till next month,

Sally Cooper

SALLY COOPER,
Editor-in-Chief – *Scarlet*

STACY BROWN

HEAVEN SENT

Enquiries to:
Robinson Publishing Ltd
7 Kensington Church Court
London W8 4SP

First published in the UK by Scarlet, 1998

A copy of the British Library Cataloguing in
Publication data is available from the British Library

ISBN 1–85487–569–8

Printed and bound in the EC

10 9 8 7 6 5 4 3 2 1

CHAPTER 1

England, 1820

'Are you quite sure you truly wish to do this?' Lady Joy Carmichael whispered fiercely in her younger sister's ear, glancing nervously over her shoulder at the nearby group of babbling debutantes to make certain they were not eavesdropping. Gathered by the rhododendron bushes bursting with pink blossoms, the giggling group was engaged in an avid search for potential husbands and took no notice of anything out of the ordinary. Each of them had attended this weekend party in the hope of attracting the interest of an eligible male under the age of forty.

'Of course I'm sure I want to go through with it,' Celeste snapped, letting her gaze survey the myriad guests milling about Lord Holmes's perfectly manicured gardens.

Very shortly now, the enormous ballroom would bubble over with enthusiastic guests who, doubtless, would later enjoy a hearty meal in Holmes's glittering dining room. Celeste wondered how many of the two hundred guests were planning to spend the weekend? Having heard rumors of the wicked liaisons that often took place on such occasions, she wondered with titillation if she might be privy to anything as exciting.

As she watched the liveried servants carry torches to illuminate the balcony and gardens, she realized with a surge of triumph that the defining moment of her life had finally arrived. In a few hours, her grandfather would be thoroughly disgusted with her. He might banish her to the country. A smile played around the edges of her mouth. Who knows, she might even be sent away to the continent. She sighed with glee. The far-reaching ramifications of tonight's actions were simply too wonderful to contemplate.

'I fear it's too risky,' Joy complained tersely under her breath, 'even for you. Heaven knows, you dare more than the law allows,' she added, her face pinched with displeasure.

'Nonsense.' Celeste's voice rang with impatience. But she managed to essay a bright smile in acknowledgment of Lord Whitehead's impertinent perusal. Inclining her riotous curly head, she made a mental note of his attention. He might come in handy if the Earl of Dragonwood failed to perform. 'You only say that because it has never been done before,' Celeste told her nerve-racked sister quite calmly.

'Oh, it's been done,' Joy muttered and caught sight of Whitehead's searing gaze. Fixing the audacious rake with a stern frown, she grabbed Celeste by the arm and propelled her down the balcony steps. She traversed the sprawling gardens – disgruntled sister in tow – in search of a secluded spot.

'You have chosen to overlook one small, highly relevant factor, however,' she imparted with irritation as they trotted across the plush green lawn.

Celeste blinked at her sister. 'What factor?' she asked, her brow wrinkling.

A white stone bench flanked by two towering hedges came into view. Joy steered her younger sister, none too gently, in that direction.

'No one actually wants it to happen,' Joy averred, her mien cool, 'and they certainly never go out of their way to *make* it happen,' she added fiercely under her breath.

'Well,' Celeste replied, snatching her arm free at last, 'more fool them.'

Joy gave her sister a disapproving look and sank down on the white stone bench, welcoming the brief respite. 'Really, Celeste, I must protest,' she cried, throwing her arms up in frustration. 'Your intended course is entirely deplorable,' she insisted in the harshest elder-sister voice she could muster. 'You must stop this folly. Immediately.' She bit her lip and gazed imploringly at her intractable sibling. 'I-it is not too late to change your mind.' Her voice rang with desperation.

Celeste rolled her eyes heavenward. 'You are wasting your breath,' she replied with bold imprudence. 'I have no intentions of changing my mind.'

Joy clutched at her recalcitrant sister's arm. 'I implore you, do not allow your emotions to rule your head. I beg of you, consider your future, dearest.'

'I am thinking of my future,' Celeste fired back and wriggled her arm free. 'I know exactly what I am doing.'

Joy hung her blonde head. 'I am glad one of us does,' she groaned. 'I do wish Anthony was here. I know he'd find a way to stop you.'

Seeing her poor sister's harassed face, Celeste's mood softened. She sat down beside her and patted her slumped shoulders. 'Don't carry on so. It's not the end of the world. Everything will turn out for the best. You'll see.'

Two enormous hazel eyes peered over the top of Joy's hands. 'That's what you think. I can well imagine what Grandfather is going to say. As your elder, married sister, I am supposed to look out for your welfare. It is quite vexing the way you always manage it the other way around,' she grumbled churlishly.

Celeste donned a wide-eyed innocent look that never failed to soften her sister's heart. 'That's because you are much sweeter than I,' she countered, adopting a demure façade.

Joy's eyes narrowed contemptuously. 'Flattery will not help you on this occasion. What sort of a peagoose do you take me for?,' she snapped with startling vehemence. 'You know as well as I that Grandfather never would have consented to this ridiculous weekend party if *I* hadn't persuaded him. You would never have managed an appearance without the benefit of my escort, you know it's true. Admit it.'

Celeste indolently shrugged her shoulder. 'Very well, I admit it,' she said with an air of indifference that further heightened her sister's anxiety. 'And I thank you from the bottom of my heart. I don't know how I would have effected it without you.' Joy paled considerably at that admission. 'But I won't let on what an invaluable help you've been to another living soul,' Celeste hastened to add. 'Besides, given what an obdurate, defiant nature I have,' she averred in her best baritone grandfather rendition, 'I am quite sure you will be exonerated post haste.'

Joy did not look much encouraged. 'He'll blame me, I just know it,' she moaned and clutched her forehead.

'Nonsense, he knows you have no control over me.'

Celeste's lips twisted. For that matter, neither did her grandfather – regardless of the power his controlling nature wielded most of the time. Tonight, she planned to prove to that narrow-minded, domineering old goat that she was her own woman. She'd make him regret his implacable overbearingness dearly. On this occasion, no amount of bread and water while closeted in her room would bring her to heel.

'Aren't you the least bit concerned?,' Joy's voice was laced with trepidation.

Celeste shook her head, sending her dishevelled locks dancing in different directions. 'I cannot think why I should be. I've everything to gain. And very little to lose.'

Joy winced at her brave younger sister's attitude, for she was also behaving like a cavalier fool. 'Grandfather can be very persuasive, you know.

Have you thought of what this evening might mean? The reckoning you will face?'

Celeste turned on her sister. 'How can you ask me that?,' she cried, her clear blue eyes clouding with emotion. 'You know *exactly* why I am doing this. I shall never forgive him. If I don't take action now,' she declared, her voice wavering, 'I shall go mad. I just know it.'

Joy was instantly contrite. 'Of course, dearest,' she said patting her sister's arm with care, 'I know. But surely there is another way to achieve your objective?'

It was Celeste's turn to sigh. 'I don't see how.'

Joy's face brightened for the first time since her sister formulated this outrageous scheme. 'I am sure if we just put our minds to the problem at hand –'

'Don't,' Celeste snapped the word. 'Must you always be such a coward? Just because you never dared take a chance in your entire life doesn't mean I have to allow other people to make my decisions. I, for one, have a mind of my own. I am going through with this. Nothing you say or do will stop me.'

Joy clasped her sister's hand tightly. 'Celeste, for once in your life, pray think before you act,' she implored.

Celeste snatched her hand away. 'We have gone over this a thousand times. It is the best and only course of action.' She got to her feet. 'If you cannot bear to watch, then I suggest you don't.' Without allowing her poor bedraggled sister the benefit of a reply, she turned on her heel and trudged down the expansive lawn in search of the notorious Dragon. She dearly hoped he, at least, would not disappoint.

Simon Barclay, Earl of Dragonwood, retrieved Lady Declaire's slender arms from around his neck. Removing the crisp white linen handkerchief from his breast pocket, he wiped it across his mouth, removing the wet evidence of her clinging, aggressive kisses. It was little surprise Lord Declaire had died last year of a stroke, Simon thought with a rueful smirk. The old man clearly lacked the stamina to satisfy his wife.

The object of his thoughts giggled and twined her arms around his neck. 'I simply cannot wait,' she breathed, grinding her hips against his suggestively, 'to lie beneath you.'

Simon grimaced and pushed her gently away. She had seemed eminently more kissable and, for that matter, beddable, a fortnight ago when he'd initially expressed interest in her. Looking at her pinched narrow face now, he wondered if he ought not to give up drinking brandy, for under its influence his judgement was woefully inadequate. 'Let's not rush our fences, my dear. It's early yet.'

She pulled a petulant frown. 'You certainly do not live up to your reputation, my lord. I expected, from all accounts, to be exhausted by morning.' She ran her eager palms over his chest. 'You've barely touched me and it's nearly dark.' She glanced over her shoulder at the shadowed shrubbery maze. 'You could take me right here and now,' she suggested, breathless with lust.

7

He frowned. Subtle she was not. Where was her sense of decorum? Everyone knew the proper way of approaching a midnight tryst. One did not blurt out their expectations in graphic detail. Nor did they refer to past illicit liaisons as a sort of sexual endorsement. And the lady in question should never make overt sexual demands. At least, not unless she was already in bed.

'You know, my dear,' he drawled with dry mockery, 'there is a great deal to be said for subtlety. Or, at least, the vague appearance of it. Have you never considered the coy approach?'

She shrugged and flashed a provocative smile. 'Who has time to wait? I see something I want – I go after it,' she assured him, letting her hands slide lower. 'And I want you.'

Suddenly, revolted by the woman before him and the entire sordid event, he snatched her hands from his waistband and held them firmly against her chest. He wasn't sure what disgusted him more, her or the fact that he'd played this part before.

It was always meaningless.

Always empty.

And utterly boring.

Was this all there was to life? he wondered with irritation. Just a series of shallow exchanges between two uncaring people? At the ripe old age of two-and-thirty, he found he no longer had the stomach for it.

'No,' he said sharply, furious with himself as much as with her. 'You've overplayed your hand, my lady.'

Evidently rejection was something new to Lady Declaire, for she stared at him, her vulgar mouth gaping wide. 'You scoundre... ...dare you spurn me?'

He inclined his dark head in ... 'My apologies, madam – consider i... if you like. We can enjoy a passiona... somewhere more private, at a more conve...

'When?,' she asked, running her tongue ... ...er lips with lascivious anticipation.

'How does the twelve of never sound?'

Her face fell. 'Why, you –,' she snarled and raised her hand to slap his face.

But he caught her hand before it flew to his cheek. 'Oh, no,' he muttered and squeezed her bony wrist between his thumb and forefinger. 'No, my dear. That pleasure is reserved for a lady whose honor has been insulted.' He let out a derisive chuckle. 'You and I both know that you have none. Now,' he said in no uncertain terms as he released her gruffly, 'be a good girl and go away. Or I'll have our esteemed host throw you out.'

'You haven't heard the last of Harriet Declaire,' she said through her teeth before she disappeared in a huff of garish gold silk.

He shook his head. 'I sincerely hope I have,' he muttered to himself and raked his hand through his thick raven hair.

Distant laughter, echoing against the backdrop of the orchestra playing a Mozart concerto, beckoned his weary bones. It was high time he joined the party. This evening had the earmarks of a total disaster and it hadn't even begun yet.

* * *

tally preparing her witty introduc-
ught sight of the Dragon emerging
om the dimly-lit shrubbery maze. A current of
excitement ran through her. Excellent! He was
alone. A tiny smile ruffled her mouth. If Dragonwood was everything she'd heard, her troubles would
soon be over.

She tugged as hard as she could at the modest lace
neckline of her pink muslin gown, in an effort to bare
a small amount of what she hoped would be enticing
cleavage. Picking up her hem, she hurried along the
outside hedgerow in search of a good spot to intercept
her prey. She ducked through the break in the hedge
and plonked herself down on a small round bronze
bench that vaguely resembled a mushroom top.

She drew a deep breath and waited, hearing the
tiny white pebbles crunch beneath his immaculate
shiny black Hessian boots. Any minute now they'd
meet. She could barely suppress her smile or contain
the exhilaration that coursed through her veins. This
was easier than she had imagined. Her plan was
working splendidly. Had she really worried it would
be a challenge to garner an introduction? Silly girl.

As he drew near, she glanced up at him beneath
what she believed were coquettish lashes. Her eager
gaze slid over the length of him. Her pulse quickened. My, he certainly did not disappoint. He was
taller. And *much* bigger than she imagined. And
startlingly . . . older, more sophisticated than any
imagining could have been. And she'd devoted a
considerable amount of time envisioning this particular rogue.

Why, he looked *at least* thirty. The perfect age for her purposes. She needed an experienced, mature man who knew how to get the job done. He was dressed impeccably, as she knew he would be. His valet must be as patient as the devil, for the neat, intricate folds and tucks in his cravat were awe-inspiring. Not to mention the delicate, flawless fabric of his cambric shirt and enviable wrist frills. She estimated he'd paid a fortune for that soft blue velvet cut-away with clawhammer tails and satin-embroidered waistcoat that fit his formidable chest like a second skin. A wave of dizzy excitement overtook her.

In that instant, she knew exactly why he'd earned the reputation of notorious rakehell. He was beautiful. A Greek Adonis to be sure, she allowed, as her hungry gaze devoured all six feet something of him. Could those buff-colored buckskin breeches fit his muscular thighs any better? she wondered with a surge of warmth. Were there ever such well-made shoulders? Or finely chiselled features?

A slight smile touched his lips, softening the normally forbidding lines around his mouth. He inclined his raven head in her direction.

Now, here was a man who'd sampled all the world had to offer and found it mildly boring. His carriage, his countenance, everything about the man fairly oozed arrogance and self-assurance. To her surprise, she found that extremely – unbelievably – alluring.

She donned her sweetest smile, lowered her lashes demurely and waited for him to fall at her feet.

And waited.

And waited.

Her head snapped up. She found herself staring helplessly at his broad-shouldered back. She blinked. He hadn't stopped. He'd walked right past her. Her mouth fell open. He wasn't even *remotely* tempted. She bit her lip in frustration. So much for her well-laid plans. What on earth was she going to do now?

Self-recriminations were a waste of time for, if her eyes did not deceive her, the Dragon was getting away. And she was no closer to achieving her goal. She hopped to her feet. Hauling her elegant dress above her knees, she ran after him, looking very much like the hoyden her grandfather accused her of being.

'M-my lord,' she cried. 'Wait!'

At the sound of her voice, he stopped and swivelled around to face her. Even in the purplish twilight glow she could see – no, actually *feel* his gaze on her. His blatant perusal lingered for a moment on her bared legs as he savored her shapely calves before his ebony brows hiked up in silent query.

Colour flooded her cheeks. So – *that's* what a pair of bedroom eyes looked like. She dropped her skirt. No wonder the man was considered England's premiere rake. She felt an unfamiliar rush of heat overtake her and all he'd done was look at her.

'May I be of some assistance?' His deep silky voice swirled around her in seductive enquiry.

It was a wonderful voice. Deep and rich and sensual.

'Oh . . . yes,' she managed on a sigh. What was the matter with her? She could barely catch her breath. She hadn't run that far or that fast. 'You certainly may,' she told him, breathless with excitement. 'I'd like you to ruin me, if you please.'

He must have stared at her for a full minute before the impact of what she'd just said sank in. Piercing grey eyes narrowed into silver slits. 'I beg your pardon. *What* did you say?'

'You know, ruin me. Make me ineligible for balls, marriage or, for that matter, any decent society at all.' She smiled up at him brightly. 'I should very much like to be firmly installed on the shelf. And I think you are just the man to do it.'

'I know what it means,' he almost snapped at her. 'What eludes me at the moment is – *why*?' he asked, his tone decidedly cool.

Her back stiffened. What ailed the man? He was supposed to suggest a more secluded spot, not question her motives. 'I have my reasons,' she imparted with stiff civility. 'Would you like to ruin me or not?'

He looked at her askance. This was by far the most bizarre exchange in recent memory. And he'd had quite a few. Amused, and more than little baffled by the fetching sight before him, he decided to play along. 'With such a generous offer,' he drawled softly, 'how could any man refuse?'

She breathed a sigh of relief. 'I was hoping you'd feel that way,' she replied, grinning from ear to ear.

'I am afraid you have the advantage of me. I don't believe I have had the pleasure of making your

13

acquaintance. And you seem to know me rather well.' He looked down at her with an indulgent tilt to his lips. 'That doesn't seem quite fair, now, does it?'

She hesitated for a moment before she stuck her hand out. 'My name is . . . Juliet.'

The warmth of his large hand enveloped her much smaller one. He raised an ebony brow. 'Juliet? As in *Romeo and Juliet*?,' he clarified, his tone faintly mocking. He knew she was lying, of course. But why? She was either an incurable romantic. Or a naïve twit. To his surprise, he discovered he had a marked preference for the former.

She donned a puckish grin. 'Naturally.'

Glancing down, he realized he was still clasping her hand and promptly released it. 'I think,' he said with a hint of derision, 'as you've approached me with your *very* tempting offer, you should explain why you wish to throw away what I presume is, at present, a perfectly good reputation.'

She squared her shoulders. 'I have no need of a pristine reputation,' she told him in curt tones, her chin arched in defiance.

'Indeed.' He crossed his arms over his chest and appraised her with keen interest. 'You must be the first and only member of your gender to feel that way.'

She giggled at that remark. 'What good has it ever gotten any woman? Save for landing her in the dreaded Marriage Mart,' she muttered with obvious disgust for that unfortunate state. 'Besides, I have asked you to ruin me, my lord. Not court me. The less we know about each other, the better.'

He bit back a smile. Her guileless nature was utterly charming. That she was a refreshing change from the Lady Declaires of his acquaintance there could be no doubt. Besides, it did his jaded heart good to find innocence was alive and well and talking to him.

'I see your point,' he murmured thoughtfully. 'And I appreciate the difference,' he added with a sardonic grin. 'Still, I am curious. If I am to be the man to do the deed, I must know why a charming young girl such as yourself would deliberately seek to ruin herself?'

She expelled an irritated sigh. 'I cannot see what difference my reasons could possibly make to you,' she snapped, her impatience mounting. 'You are either willing, or you are not.'

He studied her for a long moment, his hooded, languid gaze roaming over her. She looked all of twelve years old. Bold as brass, she practically demanded he tarnish her fine reputation on the spot. 'You understand, of course, the gravity of what you ask?'

'Oh, yes,' she replied, clearly enamoured of a state considered by most members of her sex as tragic. 'It is my understanding that there are three traditional ways to achieve total ruin,' she added in a flourish of barely-contained excitement.

'I can think of several,' he muttered with sarcasm.

'Oh, good,' she said, a gleam of anticipation in her eye. 'I felt certain you would know the most efficient way. I want to be totally ruined, mind you.'

'Irrevocably?,' he queried with amused tolerance.

She nodded her curly head. 'Completely. Let there be not a shred of decency left to my name.'

His forehead crinkled in speculation. 'What makes you think I am your man?'

She glanced up at him in surprise. 'Why, given your outrageous reputation, you are exactly the sort of man I require.'

He inclined his raven head. 'I am flattered.'

'Think nothing of it. Any man who could . . . could . . .,' her voice trailed off. Two blotches of bright red stained her cheeks.

One dark brow drifted upward. 'Could?,' he prompted.

Her pert little nose wrinkled and she leaned forward to whisper, 'Well . . . *you* know.'

He shook his head. 'No. I don't.' He folded his arms over his broad chest and gazed down at her. 'Why don't *you* tell *me*?'

She swallowed audibly. 'Suffice to say,' she replied, clearing her throat to conceal her awkwardness, 'I shall not be the first debutante to fall from grace.'

'Nor the last,' he snorted with derision. This charade had gone on long enough. It was time to set the impetuous little miss straight. 'I hate to disillusion you, but I make it a rule never to prey on young innocents.'

Her eyes went wide. 'Never?' she asked, crestfallen.

'Never,' he added firmly.

Her gaze turned forlorn. 'I see.' She bit her lip and pondered her situation. 'What if . . . I were willing to

16

pay you?' she asked, glancing up at him beneath speculative lashes.

To his credit he did not laugh. 'You're that desperate, eh?'

She pulled a miserable frown. 'I am afraid so,' she muttered on a restless sigh. 'I simply must destroy my reputation.'

'Mmm,' he murmured indulgently, 'that is quite a vexing problem. But I sincerely doubt you could afford me,' he drawled with barely-cloaked sarcasm. 'And, in any event, I couldn't possible accept your money. Just for future reference,' he advised in a sage whisper, 'it is usually the other way around.'

'Oh.' She sounded utterly dejected. Her forehead creased in thought. 'I was given to understand it worked both ways.'

He shook his head to the contrary. 'I am afraid not.'

'Oh, very well.' She shrugged off her misunderstanding. 'Still, I do wish you'd reconsider, my lord. Could you not make an exception in my case? Just this once?,' she practically begged him.

She was unlike any woman of his acquaintance – in, or out, of the bedroom. Nothing short of temporary insanity, however, could induce him to shatter her chaste existence, no matter how tempting a morsel she was.

'No,' he said at length, 'I do not think I will.'

'Why ever not? Surely,' she sputtered, her tone harsh with frustration, 'I am eminently worthy of ruin?'

He inclined his dark head in agreement. 'Eminently.'

Her eyes narrowed on his faintly-amused face. 'See here, you *are* Lord Barclay,' she asked, rancour sharpening her tone, 'known over half of London as the Dragon, are you not?'

His lips curled slightly. 'I have heard that unfortunate euphemism used to describe me, yes.'

She slapped her hands on her narrow hips. 'Then, it is true that you've charmed more women than you can count out of their virtue and husbands cleave to their wives the moment you enter a room?' she demanded hotly.

He winced. By Jove, was his reputation as bad as that? 'Do they?,' he asked on a bored sigh.

Exasperated and clearly at the end of her tether, she burst out, 'I cannot credit how a man capable of unholy wickedness with his own stepsister will not grant me one insignificant favour.'

His jaw turned to granite. So, the vile gossip-mongers were still whispering about poor sweet Emily. No one dared suggest the child was his – publicly. They did not have the mettle to meet him on the field at dawn. But they'd damned well hypothesize in private. It sickened him to hear of it.

'That episode,' he ground out, 'of which you so cavalierly speak, is not founded in a shred of truth.'

Two delicately arched brows shot upward. 'Not a smidgeon?,' she asked, clearly amazed by the discovery.

Devil take it! The little chit actually sounded disappointed. 'Not a one,' he told her, his voice like ice. 'It is, however, a painful subject for me and my family as a whole. Something I do not wish to discuss.'

By God, if he could lay his hands on the black-guard responsible for his stepsister's decline he'd make him pay. He'd scoured Emily's possessions for some evidence as to the scoundrel's name, but he had found nothing more than a love letter and an insignia ring. Not much to go on. But he was determined to seek retribution. If it took him years, he'd make the blackguard pay for destroying his beautiful stepsister.

'I . . . apologize,' she managed to get out. 'But I can hardly be responsible for tales of your disreputable past, however exaggerated. Believe me,' she complained, crossing her arms over her chest, 'it comes as no small disappointment to me. Am I to assume that episode on the Thames last month is also pure fiction?'

His lips twitched ever so slightly. 'No. But the lady in question was fully clothed at the time.'

She arched an inquisitive brow.

'Her aquatic abilities were woefully lacking,' he went on to explain. 'I had no choice but to jump in after her.'

'I see.' Deep worry lines marred her otherwise perfect forehead. 'In that case, my lord, I simply cannot understand why you have refused my offer. What's wrong with me?' she asked, gazing up at him with guileless blue eyes.

His slow gaze slid over her, lazily assessing the creamy expanse of her neck, her nicely rounded shoulders, her soft supple breasts. His hooded gaze lingered on the neckline of her simple garb. 'Nothing that the next few years won't remedy,' he drawled out.

She gawked at him. 'Are you suggesting,' she asked, bristling from the top of her curly head to the tip of her tiny toes, 'I am too young?'

'Precisely.' He took her by the shoulders, turned her around and patted her on the bottom. 'Now, why don't you go back to the nursery where you belong, before you get yourself into some real trouble?'

'Go back to the nursery!' She spun around to face him, hands balled into fists. 'I'll have you know,' she averred, nearly bursting with indignation, 'I've acquired a wealth of experience well beyond my eighteen years.'

'I've no doubt you have,' he imparted with dry sarcasm. 'Being ruined by me, however,' he told her, a note of warning in his voice, 'shall not be one of them.'

'I must say,' she sputtered angrily, 'you certainly do not live up to your reputation. You, sir, are clearly not the notorious scoundrel I hoped. In fact,' she added with bristling contempt, 'you are not a whit like the man of whom I have heard so much.'

He shook his head. That made twice. He really needed to do something about his reputation. Whatever happened to a man sowing his oats? And the sanctity of the boudoir? Perhaps his father was right. If Simon continue on his current course, no reputable family would admit him. Either he decided to live up to his wickedness or marry before it was too late to acquire a bride worth having.

'Sorry to disappoint you,' he uttered with a cool smile, 'but my answer is final.'

Her spine straightened. 'Obviously,' she said with as much dignity as she could summon under the mortifying circumstances, 'I misjudged you.'

'Obviously,' he concurred with a nod of his perfectly groomed head.

Dozens of unruly fiery red ringlets bounced every which way as she haughtily tossed her head back and said with an imperious air, 'I see no reason to continue our brief acquaintance.'

'Nor do I.' He etched a mocked bow. 'Good evening, my dear.'

'Good bye, Lord Rakehell,' she barked huffily and hurried past the uncooperative rogue.

Her legs could not carry her down the narrow garden path fast enough. She'd never been more insulted in her life! Back to the nursery, indeed. She'd like to send him back to school to learn some manners.

Humiliation mingled with outrage. Her cheeks burned. How dare he spank her like a child? She pressed her cool palms against her hot cheeks. What utter embarrassment!

Tonight was a perfectly ghastly affair. Nothing was working out as she had planned. She hadn't considered he might be selective. A rake was a rake. Any woman would do. Wouldn't she?

Her mouth twisted. Apparently not. He may cut the most impressive figure of man she'd ever encountered, but that did not give him licence to be rude. The man was beyond contempt.

'Oh, bother!' She snatched a blossom from the nearby peony bush and tugged at the soft white petals. She had to come up with a replacement for that offensive boor. Fast. At this rate, she'd never get ruined.

CHAPTER 2

Simon managed to slip into the crowded ballroom without encountering any more female interlopers. Gad! What a strange evening this has turned out to be, he thought, channelling his way through the swarm of popinjay suitors and frivolous females. He was in no mood to dance the quadrille and make idle small talk with some helplessly unattractive wallflower looking to get legshackled. A game of cards and a stiff drink was what he needed.

Up until an hour ago, he'd have wagered he had heard it all. Precious little could shock him. The outrageous baggage in the juvenile pink gown, however, was something he'd never yet encountered.

He shook his head and smiled to himself. She was quite an adorable little thing. At least, what he could make of her in the dim light. Nice legs too. Pity he wasn't sufficiently ignoble to accept her offer. Just the same, he couldn't help wondering who she was.

He was about to see how much money he could lose in a friendly game of commerce when yet another woman intercepted him. This one was tall, blonde and slim. And she looked extremely distraught.

Devil take it, was he to be accosted by distressed females all night long? He glanced longingly at the mahogany tables, the deck of gleaming crisp cards, and the betting chips that beckoned. He drew a weary sigh and looked away. Forcing a polite smile to his lips, he asked the beautiful blonde in his path, 'Madam, are you unwell?'

'Indeed I am, my lord.' She wet her lips nervously. 'We are not formally acquainted. But I wonder if I might not impose on your good nature to assist me?' she asked in a soft undertone.

He frowned with displeasure. Damn and blast. Not again. 'Of course,' he managed with a stiff civility, 'what is it that troubles you?'

'You are,' she whispered, 'I believe, familiar with my husband, Anthony Carmichael?'

'Tony?' He breathed sigh of relief. Lady Carmichael would scarcely be interested in a turn in the bushes. Or total ruin. 'Of course. We fought on the Peninsula together. I'm afraid I haven't seen him in ages. How is he?'

Lady Carmichael appeared visibly relieved. 'He spoke so fondly of you, I was hoping you might recall.'

Simon glanced around the densely populated ballroom. 'Is he in attendance this evening?'

'Unfortunately, no. His father is ill. He could not come away just now. I am here with my younger sister.'

'I see. I hope you and your sister are enjoying yourselves?'

'Tolerably well.' She hesitated for a moment before she asked, 'Might I impose on your friendship and take you into my confidence on a rather grievous family matter?'

Tony had saved his neck more times than he could recall. No matter how much he wanted to lose himself in a bottle of brandy and a good card game, Simon could hardly abandoned Lady Carmichael in her hour of need.

'If there is anything I can do to alleviate your discomfort, I would gladly do it,' he assured her.

She cleared her throat. 'The matter which weighs so heavily on my mind concerns my sister. She has recently come out. Have you perhaps made her acquaintance?' She looked positively ill as she explained 'I fear she would not be easy to forget. She has . . . a rather singular request.'

His lips twitched. *That* was an understatement. So, the little scamp had an older and, he hoped, wiser sister. 'I believe I have had that pleasure.'

She gulped. 'You did not comply with her –'

His eyebrow lifted. 'Request?' He shook his head. 'I should sooner rob the cradle, madam.'

She released the breath she'd been holding and splayed her hand over her chest. 'Thank heaven.'

His lips curled ever so slightly. 'I take it her name is not Juliet?'

Lady Carmichael's forehead creased. 'No. It's Celeste.'

'Celeste?,' he echoed incredulously. 'That is a misnomer, if ever I heard one. Allow me to venture a guess.' His lips quirked with poorly-concealed mirth. 'Your exalted mother could only have been christened Angelica?'

'No.' She shook her head. 'Divina.'

'Ah. I should have known. Doubtless, your esteemed father was Michael?'

'No. His name was Gabriel.'

'Why am I surprised?,' came his soft condescending murmur. 'With such a wild daughter, I shouldn't wonder.'

She shot him a queer look. 'Why did you believe her name to be Juliet?'

He chuckled softly. 'For the simple reason that I was cast in the role of Romeo.'

Her face turned a whiter shade of pale. 'Oh, dear. How embarrassing for you. I must apologize for my sister – she is younger than her years, due perhaps to the fact that she has led a completely sheltered life and has an unfortunate headstrong streak.'

'Think nothing of it,' he replied with an amicable smile.

She looked visibly assuaged and managed a smile for the first time. 'I felt sure you were a man of honor, that is why I suggested she approach you.'

A deep crevice marred his forehead. '*You* suggested?' Was the entire family eccentric?

Her smile blossomed. 'As you must have noticed, my sister is bound and determined to destroy herself. I could think of nothing else save offering a man whom I believed would not –'

'Accept her offer?,' he interjected archly.

'Exactly.' She glanced at him tentatively. 'You are not . . . angry, I hope?'

Was he angry? Diverted was a better word. His brief encounter with the little baggage was sure to be one of this evening's highlights.

'Not in the least. Although,' he muttered dryly, 'I cannot say the same for your sister.'

'That's what worries me.' She caught her lower lip between her teeth. 'I feel certain she will approach someone less honorable. What then?'

He smiled to himself – at least one woman still believed him worthy of esteem. Perhaps his tainted character was salvageable after all.

A rueful expression touched Lady Carmichael's lips. 'I cannot very well continually intercept her invitations and beg abstention, my lord.'

'Quite,' he murmured pensively. 'I see your dilemma.'

'What am I to do?' She gazed up at him with enormous miserable doe eyes, and he knew he could not refuse her aid.

'Allow me to assist you, Lady Carmichael. Rest assured, your sister shall come to no harm this evening.'

Relief flooded her features. 'I felt certain you would help us,' she said, clutching his hand. 'I cannot thank you enough for your kindness. I know Tony will be eternally grateful when he hears of your kind intercession.'

'Think nothing of it.' He bowed politely over her hand. 'It will be my very great pleasure to assist you in any way that I can.'

He told himself it was because he owed an old friend a favor. And that he was helping a beautiful damsel in distress. He even thought of poor dear Emily so brutally wronged. He dared imagined himself as a saviour, halting a foolish innocent's leap into utter misery.

Whatever the reason, he found himself in search of the damned chit with an aim to protect her. The Dragon, who had graced more matronly thresholds than he cared to remember, was off to save an innocent from ruin. If it wasn't so damned ironic, it would be hilarious.

It did not take long to find her. She was in a secluded alcove, batting her eyelashes at Lord Whitehead whose wolfish tendencies were legendary. An irritated frown touched Simon's lips. What on earth women saw in the man, he could not fathom. He was blonde, pale, taller than a bean pole, and twice as spindly. He found himself wondering if the effete Whitehead had accepted the little chit's outlandish offer. A black scowl crossed his face. His gait quickened.

'Ah, there you are,' a deep voice uttered softly against her ear. Celeste looked up. Her gaze collided with the sultriest pair of roguish eyes she'd ever seen. Her breath caught in her throat.

'Dragon!'

Her eyes widened owlishly at his lazy sensual smile. It was far too warm. The way he was looking at her reminded her of Grandfather's hounds licking their chops before a good meal.

He etched a mocked bow. 'None other. I wondered where you'd got to.'

'You did?,' she gulped.

'I've been looking for you everywhere,' he murmured and pressed a kiss to her hand.

Her mouth dropped open. 'You have?'

He inclined his head imperceptibly in Whitehead's direction. 'Forgive me,' he drawled, an icy edge to his voice, 'but the lady promised this dance to me.'

Whitehead arched a dubious brow. 'Did she, indeed?'

A dangerous glint shone in Simon's eye. 'Are you perchance suggesting I have mistaken the matter?'

Whitehead looked taken aback. 'O-of course not.'

Simon bared his teeth in a predatorial smile. 'Good. I shouldn't like to have to call you out. It is so damp and chilly at dawn.'

Whitehead's scrawny adam's apple bobbed up and down. He bowed his head in a curt farewell. 'Good evening, Barclay.'

Obviously, Celeste was not worth fighting over. She could do no more than stand helplessly by while Whitehead mumbled something about it being a pleasure to meet her and disappeared with his tail between his legs.

Her furious blue gaze collided with Simon's indolent silver orbs. 'I never promised you anything,' she hissed under her breath, 'least of all the next dance.'

He ignored her censure, clasped her by the hand and dragged her towards the dance floor.

'See here,' she cried, struggling to keep pace with his long strides, 'who do you think you are, barging in where you are not wanted?'

'Think of me –,' he pulled her into his arms and gathered her close '– as Romeo.'

She scowled up at him. 'Very amusing, my lord. Kindly leave me. I have no intention of dancing.'

'That's too bad,' he countered with icy determination, 'because you are going to dance, with me, right now.'

Thoroughly annoyed with the meddling man, she glared up at him and dug her heels mulishly into the floor. 'No,' she countered firmly through clenched teeth, 'I am not.'

Heedless of her objections, he placed one large masterful hand on her waist and drew her flush against him. Before she could utter an objection, he'd whisked her small frame on to the dance floor. As the music sent the couples twirling around the enormous ballroom, she felt her feet leave the floor. Her lips thinned with displeasure. Another domineering beast – he and Grandfather would get on famously.

His strong, masculine grip grated on her. She detested the hot flourish of pleasure that threatened to consume her. It was entirely due to the uncooperative rogue's proximity.

'Has anyone ever told you,' she whispered in a fierce under-breath, 'you are a brute?'

'You're the first.' He whirled her around as if she weighed less than a feather.

The unnerving warmth of his hand seeped through her thin dress, searing her flesh. Her discomfort increased tenfold. 'Doubtless,' she grumbled with irritation, 'I shall not be the last.'

'I cannot tell you how heavily that weighs on my mind,' he drawled, his voice laced with mockery.

She glanced up at him beneath beetled brows. 'You are a vexing man. I was doing rather well before you interrupted.

'Mmm. I noticed.' He glanced down at her up-turned petulant face. 'Just what the devil did you think you were doing back there?' he asked roughly.

'Throwing myself at Whitehead. What did it look like?,' she muttered testily.

His jaw clenched. 'That's what I was afraid of.'

'You can hardly blame me, my lord,' she said, an irritated edge to her voice. 'What choice did I have? Besides being the only other rake I could find on such short notice, he was available. And interested.'

'I wager he was,' he snorted with derision.

She gave him a mulish look. 'This is all your fault, I hope you realize. If you hadn't been so stingy with your favors, I'd be well on my way to achieving my goal.'

'My fault?,' he repeated, agog at her temerity. 'In case you have misunderstood,' he growled against her ear, 'I just rescued you from the lion's den.'

'Oh, pish-posh!'

Pish-posh? What the devil did pish-posh mean?

'You must see in what an impossible position your lack of cooperation places me.'

'I am afraid to ask what position that might be?'

She expelled a deep sigh. 'Now I shall have to move down the list. Approach someone new. Make another introduction. And I sincerely hope *he* will be a rake worthy of his reputation.'

'The list?,' he echoed incredulously. 'You have a list?' His face darkened. 'What blasted list?'

'Naturally I have a list,' she snapped. 'What do you take me for? I'll have you know I've researched the subject thoroughly. You were my first choice, of course. But as you are unwilling to oblige and you've seen fit to interfere where you do not belong,' she reminded him tersely, 'I have no other option but to pursue Lord Carew.'

Momentarily stupefied, he gazed down at her. 'By God,' he breathed, 'you are a most singular girl.'

'Thank you,' she replied primly. 'But I think you miss the enormity of my current predicament. I've lost valuable time. Worse yet,' she said, exasperated, 'I do not know what Carew looks like.'

His arms tightened around her, crushing her delicate frame against his hard lean body. 'Listen to me,' he growled, fully intending to pound some sense into her addled brain. 'You little fool! This is not a game. Do you have any idea what could happen to you if you offer yourself to every stranger you meet?'

His breath was warm against her temple. A tingle of excitement ran down her spine. 'I was not offering myself, as you put it,' she muttered, wriggling to no avail against his hard muscular chest. It was most disconcerting to be pressed against a warm wall of manly flesh. 'I merely want to be ruined.'

He snorted, tightening his grip on her small waist. 'It amounts to the same thing to a man like Carew.'

An unbidden current of pleasure swept over her, causing her mind to draw a momentary blank. 'Yes

. . . well . . . as you are not going to be involved,' she replied, clearing her throat, 'kindly unhand me, and let me go about my business.'

'No.'

She quit struggling and looked up at him. 'No?' Her eyes searched his handsome face for some clue to his intentions. 'What do you mean, no?' She eyed him with suspicion. 'What are you about, my lord? Have you perchance . . . reconsidered?' she asked, breathless with longing.

He cast a dark look in her direction. Devil take it! No, he had not reconsidered. What kind of imp ran around offering herself to men without the slightest idea what her offer actually entailed?

He ought to leave the little chit right where she stood. Let her learn her lesson the hard way. What was she to him? Nothing. Just another foolish hen-wit. London was full of them this time of year.

His mouth thinned with anger. Confound it, how had he gotten dragged into this ridiculous situation in the first place? It was rather like asking the wolf to mind the sheep. He smirked and glanced down at the headstrong bundle in his arms; an innocent, wayward little lamb, more like. Painful memories of his step-sister's folly tugged at his heart, softening him. Emily was roughly the same age when she made her grand *faux pas*. If only she'd had a dark angel to guide her.

His critical gaze swept over Celeste's face. It struck him suddenly that she was quite a beauty. Not in the traditional sense, of course. Most would not appreciate her untamed red hair, which curled about her face in reckless disarray. Or the sprinkle of freckles across her nose, which should have been doused with lemon juice. But she had a wild, unvarnished innocence that was strangely engaging. Those enormous blue eyes fairly sparkled every time she smiled at him, as she was doing right now. And she had dimples. The cutest pair of dimples he'd seen in a long, long time. Oh, yes, she was very appealing.

'I might be persuaded,' he told her softly. His gaze slid over her flushed face and settled on her soft, supple lips. Another man might be tempted to taste that tempting little mouth. *Only a dishonorable cur* came a harsh mental reminder. He tore his gaze from her soft parted lips. They were far too inviting. What the deuce was wrong with him? She was a mere child, completely naïve to the ways of the world.

'Might you be?,' she asked, all eagerness and excitement.

'Naturally, I will require full participation on your part,' he told her in a low husky voice. 'That is absolutely necessary to achieve total ruin.'

'I assumed as much.' She craned her neck back to look him squarely in the eye. 'You do understand, of course, time is critical?'

'Trust me.' His silky voice held a sardonic note. 'What I have in mind won't take long.'

'Oh, good,' she said, bubbling over with enthusiasm, 'I must say, I am pleased that you are the one to do the deed.'

He fixed her with a curious gaze. 'Why?'

'If you're going to be ruined, my lord, who better to do it than a man who is the envy of every woman in town? You are considered by far the most handsome rake of the season,' she told him in the blunt manner of which he was growing fond.

He stared down at the adorable chit and managed to utter a dry, 'Thank you.'

'Don't mention it. Lead on, my lord,' she instructed, waving her arm in the air indicating her full cooperation. 'I am ready and willing.'

He shot her a rueful look. 'I am glad you are so eager,' he murmured softly. 'I hope you won't be disappointed when you find out what I've planned for you.'

'Oh,' she replied in heartfelt earnest, 'I feel certain I shall not be.'

Those huge artless eyes of hers tugged at his conscience. What the devil was the matter with him? He wasn't actually lamenting his decision, was he? Devil take it, no. But he didn't have the heart to disappoint her either. She looked so deuced eager, standing there like a willing victim in his arms. Devilish tempting too. The least he could do was give her something to remember and giggle about with the rest of the debutantes of her acquaintance. Taking her petite gloved hand in his, he weaved a way through the hordes of guests and led her from the dance floor across the marbled foyer.

'Where are you taking me?,' she asked, barely able to contain herself as she trotted along behind him down the long hallway.

'In here,' he told her and opened the door to what appeared to be Lord Holmes's library, for the walls were covered with countless volumes of leather-bound books.

Closing the door, he swung her around and pulled her into his arms. Gasping in surprise, her eyes flew wide. He bent his head to press a kiss to her lips. His mouth was a mere hair's-breadth from her own. He did something he had never had occasion to do before – he hesitated. And found himself gazing into the most gorgeous pair of blue eyes he'd ever beheld. Two innocent, startling blue eyes searched his. It was more than the striking color, he realized. It was the expression. He knew exactly what she was thinking. Or very nearly. She was undeniably startled and a little apprehensive. But what struck him most was the trust shining up at him. A frown crossed his face. It made him feel a real cad. No woman had ever looked at him that way. He reckoned he did not deserve to be trusted.

Her softly-parted lips were a stronger temptation than he would have liked.

'What are you doing?,' she whispered.

His hands slid up her arms, drawing her closer against him. 'I am going to kiss you.'

She wrinkled her brow. 'Why should you want to do that? And in the library of all places?'

He stared down at her for a moment. He'd never met a woman who talked so much. 'I prefer to sample the merchandise before buying, so to speak,' he imparted dryly.

Her mouth formed the word 'Oh.'

She did not appear the least bit excited by the prospect.

He arched one dark brow. 'I presume you have no objections?'

'No. None at all,' she replied. 'You may kiss me if you like.'

An easy grin played around his lips. 'I am so glad you approve.'

Closing her eyes, she lifted her dainty little chin and offered her closed mouth to receive his kiss. He wondered if he were not a debauched cad, for this was the most endearing sight he'd ever witnessed. Slowly, he covered her soft enticing mouth in a tender kiss, pressing his lips gently against hers. He lifted his head and waited for her to swoon.

She did not swoon.

She frowned.

'Is something wrong?,' he asked, his ego slightly deflated.

'Oh, no,' she replied politely, but her expression was all disappointment.

'Apparently, my expertise is lacking,' he averred with a sardonic smirk.

'Well, it was not what I was given to understand it would be,' she allowed.

Mildly insulted, his lips twisted with displeasure. 'Am I to assume your first kiss was not everything you hoped?'

'No,' she told him frankly. 'But it was not my first kiss.'

He blinked in astonishment. Devil take it. His jaw clenched. What the hell did she mean, not her first kiss? She's a child barely out of the school room. His brow darkened. 'Who's kissed you?,' he demanded, his tone brisk.

'I was kissed by Jeremy, our stable boy, two years ago. I must confess,' she went on to say, 'he put a bit more effort into it than you, my lord. It was a rather wet and sloppy, but infinitely more exciting than what just passed between us.'

Impertinent chit! Infinitely more exciting. The devil it was. Since when did stable boys go around kissing ladies of the manor? He'd never been so piqued in all his days. The little baggage thought he fell short of the local help. 'I am sorry to hear it,' he muttered in a churlish tone.

'I don't mean to complain,' she rushed out, 'and I am more grateful than I can say for your cooperation. But –'

'But what?' Irritation made his voice grate.

'Well,' she said, wetting her lips in an enticing manner, 'it strikes me that you chose a rather inopportune moment.'

She never ceased to amaze him. First, she criticized his technique. Then she argued over his timing. Something could be said for jaded women – ironically, they were much easier to please.

His temper flared. 'How's that?,' he asked her roughly.

'If you were planning to kiss me, might it not have been better to do it earlier, for the benefit of the other guests?'

He gave her a speculative glance. 'Possibly. But I have something else in mind for you. Provided, of course, you still want to be completely ruined.'

'I do hope it is more exciting than kissing,' she remarked with a disappointed pout.

He smirked at that remark. 'I'll try not to disappoint you.' Smarting from the little imp's setdown, he suggested amicably, 'Perhaps if you gave me another chance, I might garner higher praise than a common stable boy?'

She shrugged one slender shoulder. 'If you like. But quite honestly,' she imparted on a bored sigh, 'I cannot understand what all the fuss is about.'

'You will,' he vowed in a low growl and slid his arms around her small waist, pressing her close enough to feel the pounding of her heart. 'I promise,' he whispered against her mouth.

Her soft curves moulded to the masculine contours of his muscular body. He felt her tremble. A smile of male satisfaction spread over his lips. She was not wholly unaffected. As his mouth lowered to devour her sweet, supple lips, he realized with a jolt that he was far from immune.

The moment his lips brushed against hers – caressing, melding her lips beneath his – he knew his mistake. She gave herself up to the kiss, opening like a budding flower. Soft, sweet and eager. She was like a perfect rose, delicate and full of exquisite promise. As his mouth, warm and wet, opened to taste her fully, his arms, strong and sure, tightened around her. One hand slid down her back and settle in the soft indent. His palm splayed against the small of her back, pressing her closer.

Her ardent response surprised him. And his first taste of her left him wanting more. Much more. The kiss turned fervent, hungry. His mouth twisted and turned over hers, devouring her as if he'd been starving for years.

Celeste had never experienced anything quite like the Dragon's kiss. The touch of his lips seemed to set her aflame. Every inch of her body awakened to his caress. A warm wave of pleasure engulfed her, rendering her incapable of rational thought. Floating adrift a sensual, soft cloud, she let her arms creep around his neck. The feel of his soft persuasive mouth – hot, wet, and overwhelmingly sweet – made her quiver. She leaned into him, desperate for more of this delicious ambrosia. Currents of desire rippled through her. Clutching at his hard muscular arms for support, she met his fervour, welcoming her foray into the sensual world.

His expert hands moved in a slow caress over her soft enticing body, caressing her firm, round breasts, small waist and narrow hips with sensual precision that elicited a soft moan of pleasure. She twined her fingers through his ebony hair and met the deep, erotic thrusts of his tongue with equal pleasure.

She was an apt pupil. And that pleased him more than he cared to admit. She followed his passionate lead with remarkable finesse, savouring every sweet, tantalizing, provocative movement which served to heighten his pleasure. In fact, in no time at all, she'd turned his seductive skill on him! Her tongue was doing the most unbelievable things to him. Those sexy little half-sighs and half-moans of pleasure threatened to stretch the boundary of his self-restraint. And the way her fingertips caressed his ears and the nape of his neck was driving him mad. Her instinctive, uninhibited response was nearly his undoing.

To his stunned disbelief, he acknowledged he was losing control. If he did not end the kiss, he'd end up obliging the little chit. She'd be irrevocably ruined on Holmes's library floor.

When at last he tore his mouth from hers and came up for air, she expelled a deep dreamy sigh and, to his surprise, nestled against him as if she never wanted to leave the succour of his embrace.

'That was very pleasant indeed, my lord,' she whispered, in awe of what had just transpired, and rubbing her cheek against his broad chest. 'I never knew kissing could be quite so . . . wonderful,' she said on a breathless sigh.

It most surely was! What the devil had just happened, anyway? he wondered with a frown. How could this little slip of girl affect him so? It was damned disturbing. He was old enough to be her father. Well, not quite. An elder brother, at the worst.

She buried her face in his neck. 'I feel so strange,' she murmured in a soft, warm breath against his throat.

Devil take it, so did he. His arms closed around her. He rested his cheek against her soft vibrant red tresses and drew a deep breath. She smelled wonderful, like a fresh summer's day. And the way she felt in his arms – nothing had felt this right in a long, long time.

He shuddered at the direction to which his thoughts turned. He was depraved. He had to be.

She was fourteen years his junior, a mere girl . . . a girl with a woman's body. And a deeply passionate nature. If he did not release her luscious little body, right this minute, he'd be tempted to drink more deeply from that sweet fountain of tempestuous youth.

'Meet me outside the front entrance in fifteen minutes,' he murmured in a warm breath against her mouth and abruptly set her away from the serenity of his embrace.

She opened her mouth to object, but before she could utter a single word, he quit the library. Heavens, she thought on a wistful sigh, she dearly hoped his plan involved more demonstrations of his rakish expertise. She'd be severely disappointed if it did not.

Celeste could barely contain her excitement as she bounced down the stone horseshoe steps and waited for the instrument of her ruin to appear. It was truly going to happen. Total ruin. And at the hands of a notorious rake. The Dragon would see to it that not a shred of decency was attached to her name.

The thrill of it all made her dizzy. She had no idea in what way he hoped to achieve his ends. But she found herself extremely curious to experience whatever it was he had in mind. If it was anything like the way he had just kissed her, she was bound to reel. One thing was for certain, she thought, rocking on her heels with delight, Grandfather will be livid.

A sleek black carriage rounded the drive and came to a halt where she stood. She smiled to herself. How clever he was! By tomorrow morning, she'd be well and duly ruined. And what fun she'd have tonight. A tingle of excitement rushed over her. This was more fortuitous than she ever dreamed. She had to admit her judgement was excellent – the Dragon was *extremely* provocative!

She'd have to come up with a way to show her gratitude for all he'd done for her. Or was about to do, as the case may be. To think, earlier this evening she'd imagined he was the most vile sort of person. And now, here he was, gallantly coming to her aid. And kissing her. Soundly. Passionately. Deliciously. She drew a dreamy sigh. Life certainly had odd twists of fate. And she was never as glad of anything in all her born days.

The object of her admiration jumped down from the carriage. She smiled up at him with warmth. 'My lord, I cannot thank you enough for what you are about to do,' she gushed.

His lips twitched. 'You may not always think so highly of me.'

She clutched his arm. 'Oh, but you are wrong.' She gazed up at him with artless eyes. 'I could never form a dim view of your character. Not now.'

He frowned slightly. It was about time she learned a rogue's kiss meant nothing. He just did not like being the cad to teach her that bitter lesson. Regardless of how pleasurable he found the dalliance, after tonight, he'd never see this adorable little hellion again. He'd discovered intoxicating innocence was a bit too tempting, even for a seasoned rake like him, to resist entirely. He removed her hand from his velvet sleeve.

'I shall bear that in mind.'

'Where are you taking me?,' she asked, jubilant with anticipation.

'Home,' came his curt retort. He tugged open the black lacquered door and motioned for her to climb in.

Her brows snapped together. 'Is your estate nearby?'

He shook his head and uttered a decisive 'No.'

A gurgle of laughter escaped her throat. 'I hope you don't plan to abduct me and demand ransom,' she teased lightly. 'I doubt Grandfather would pay a farthing for me.'

His eyes turned a dark slate gray. 'Don't underestimate yourself,' he snapped at her.

She smiled a little ruefully. 'I'm not. I know exactly what I am worth in his eyes. Still,' she said, her smile turning impish, 'it might be fun to be kidnapped. Is that what you are planning?'

He laughed and shook his head at her. 'Nothing nearly as exciting. Now, get in.'

She lifted her hem, baring two lovely ankles, and climbed into the carriage. Two things struck her almost immediately. First, his carriage was quite elegant, with purple satin walls and velvet swab seats. Second, her sister Joy was sitting exactly in the middle of those comfy seats!

Her brows knitted in confusion. 'Joy? What on earth –?'

'It's for your own good, dearest,' Joy insisted, reaching over to give her hand a sisterly pat.

Celeste pieced the scenario together with lightning speed. The Dragon never intended to ruin her. Joy, her so-called loyal, devoted sister, had conspired with the blackguard from the start. No wonder she'd plied Celeste with wicked stories prior to their arrival this evening. Her despicable scheme was now patently clear. It was insulting. It was hurtful. It was mortifying.

Fixing her sister with a wrathful look, Celeste burst out, 'How could you?'

Joy smiled at her sister's wounded expression. 'Some day you'll thank me and this kind gentleman, too, for saving you.'

'Saving me!' Celeste looked askance at her sister. 'Kind!' Vile rogue more like.

He'd tricked her.

And he'd used her.

She should never have trusted him. And she definitely shouldn't have kissed him. It rankled her most to know Joy had enlisted *his* help. Her own sister! These days a girl could not trust her own flesh and blood. It was deplorable.

She opened her mouth to issue a resounding setdown, but was deprived of that pleasure by the wretched rogue.

He slammed the carriage door shut. Without so much as a sideways glance in her direction, he instructed Joy in a curt tone, 'See she gets home safely. Next time, she might not be so fortunate.'

His hateful voice rang with condescension in Celeste's ears. She gnashed her teeth. One burning desire consumed her. She wanted to murder her sister. Slowly.

'I cannot thank you enough, my lord,' Joy's insipid voice grated against Celeste's ears.

'I am only to happy to be of service, Lady Carmichael,' came his disgustingly polite rejoinder.

How could she have clung to him like that without at least some guarantee of ruin? Heat crept into Celeste's cheeks as she recalled their torrid kiss. Amid her self-recriminations, a thought occurred to her. She could still achieve ruin. All was not lost. A slow devious smile crept across her lips. She'd give this arrogant interloper the setdown he so dearly deserved.

A gleam of mischief lit her eyes as she remarked with brazen cheek, 'I am sure my dear sister would love to hear all that just transpired in the library, my lord.'

Piercing grey eyes glinted dangerously into amused blue. The air fairly crackled with tension. Her mouth broadened into a triumphant smirk. She'd cornered him rather nicely.

Joy glanced from one to the other. 'In the library?,' she queried in dismay.

'Pray, do tell, my lord. I, for one,' Celeste chimed in, verbally tweaking his arrogant nose, 'am dying to hear your explanation.'

Joy turned the full force of her questioning gaze toward his lordship. 'My lord?'

His furious gaze locked with Celeste's. 'A momentary diversion,' he imparted on a bored sigh. 'Nothing more. Your sister is young and has a flair for the dramatic. I fear her imagination is overactive. Where she cannot find scandal,' he added with a nonchalant shrug, 'she invents it. A foolish and childish game,' he intoned with a meaningful glint in his eye.

Celeste glowered at him, outrage lurking in her furious gaze. He crossed his arms over his chest and leaned one shoulder against the carriage door. He had the audacity to smile.

'As you must know,' he told her sister with maddening composure, 'such a circumstance leads to embarrassment for the lady's family and little more than an imposition for the gentleman.'

'I am relieved beyond measure to hear that was all there was to it,' Joy replied with a sigh.

Celeste gave her sister a dubious look. How she could swallow that rogue's Banbury tale, like an empty-headed twit, was beyond her. The man was as slippery as a snake, and twice as as dangerous. No wonder he was notorious. He avoided culpability with amazing deftness. God help the woman who tried to snare him.

Ignoring the repellent bounder, she gave her sister a forsaken look. 'I thought C.C. Dunhill was as important to you as he is to me,' she blurted out, hurt written all over her face.

'Oh, he is,' Joy insisted with what struck Celeste as poorly-feigned earnest. 'Truly.'

'You know how important this is to me. How could you?'

'Please, Celeste,' Joy urged with a furtive glance at his lordship, 'don't fly up in the boughs.'

'I shall never forgive you,' Celeste replied with strong conviction.

She felt the Dragon's gaze flick over her. 'Oh, I think you'll recover sooner than you think. Good night, fair Juliet –,' his deep masculine voice was heavy with hateful mockery, '– it's been an education.'

Celeste's head snapped up. Blue shards of ice impaled him. 'May you rot in hell, Romeo,' she imparted with a frigid smile.

Joy drew in a shocked breath. '*Celeste!*'

His smile broadened into a roguish grin. 'Possibly. Just make sure I don't meet you there, my impetuous little one.'

Disgusted with herself for being so gullible, she fired back, 'No need to fear, my lord. I sincerely hope I shall never have the misfortune to set eyes on the likes of you again.'

He threw back his raven head and gave a shout of laughter. 'That is one wish I will happily grant you.' He hit the roof of the conveyance with his palm. 'Drive on,' he commanded and stepped back.

Simon watched the carriage creak along the gravel drive until the dark of night eclipsed its shadowy form, then shook his head and started up the steps. A smiled tugged at the corner of his lips. He could not credit the way that outrageous hoyden had just tried to entrap him. She was more resourceful than he had given her credit for.

An unfamiliar twinge of regret gnawed at him. What fun it would have been to soil that precocious imp's reputation. Who the devil was C.C. Dunhill? And why did that blasted name seem oddly familiar?

CHAPTER 3

A fortnight later, Simon drew his pensive gaze from the prowling caged animal in the menagerie at the Tower of London. With a critical eye, he examined the woebegone-looking Bow Street Runner he'd hired. He'd been eager to take his leave of the country and return to London in the hopes that Mr Crawford would have good news. But what the Runner had to report was worse than Simon had imagined.

'What you are saying,' Simon said in a lethal tone, 'is that you've taken my money but provided none of the information I sought.'

Crawford raised his hands in self-defence. 'Now, 'old on a minute. I done like y'asked. T'ain't me fault naught came of it, now is it, milord?'

Simon sneered at the scruffy-looking man. 'No, it isn't. The fact remains, however, I am no closer to learning the identity of the blackguard who led Emily to her ruin. You have your fee, regardless.'

The Runner cleared his throat. 'That ain't strictly true, milord. I done some pokin' 'bout.'

He dug into his pocket and retrieved a tattered handkerchief. Carefully, he unfolded the material to reveal a gold signet ring. 'Dunno know what the insignia means yet. But I do know, t'was crafted at a shop on Bond Street. The craftsman remembered casting several rings. His last customer was a fellow by the name o' Paine. Canno' say I remember anyone o' that name among your stepsister's acquaintances, though.'

'Several rings, you say?,' Simon remarked, examining the ring thoughtfully. It was an ugly piece. The significance of a snake wrapped around a naked maiden evaded him. Why would anyone sport such a hideous piece on his finger?

'Find this man Paine,' he said with harsh impatience and flung the ring into Crawford's grimy paw. 'I want him found. He may know the name of the other owners. I don't care what methods you employ. I want the man responsible for Emily's downfall. Do I make myself clear?'

'Aye, milord, that you do,' Crawford said with a confident nod and slipped the ring back into his frayed pocket. He lifted his shoulders in a defeated shrug. 'Don't mind tellin' ye,' he muttered, scratching his balding head, ' 'tis a strange case, this one. I've looked into all her dalliances –'

'My stepsister did not have dalliances,' Simon corrected him bitingly. He refused to accept that notion. Whoever destroyed his stepsister led her astray, of that he was certain. Emily's character was above reproach. Her one flaw was that she trusted too easily. And, for that trait, she'd paid dearly.

The Runner dragged his red bulbous nose along his sleeve. 'Beggin' yer pardon, milord,' he said with a gruff snort. 'I meant no offence. Simple fact is, I canno' find nothin' out o' the ordinary.'

'Mmm,' Simon intoned. He hadn't been able to unearth any incriminating details of Emily's life either. A sombre expression overtook him. 'I suppose a signet ring and a love letter are not much to go on.' He heaved a sigh. 'Keep at it. Someone must have seen her with the blackguard. Let me know as soon as you come up with something.'

Mr Crawford donned his shabby cap. 'Right you are, milord,' he replied and tipped his brim in farewell.

As he departed the Tower of London, Simon's mood was understandably foul. He was not a bit closer to solving the mystery of his stepsister's ruin. He'd searched for six long months. Half a blasted year. Tirelessly, he'd probed for some clue, some inkling of the scoundrel who'd taken her under his spell.

His mouth curled downward. Obviously, he wasn't looking in the right places. For the first time since little Annabelle's birth, he wondered if he'd ever discover the identity of her father.

His mouth twisted with contempt. What sort of man would leave a woman to fend for herself and her child without any means of support? Even the most nefarious rakes of his acquaintance paid for their byblows. He winced at the thought of dear Emily involved in such a circumstance. How could the sweet, innocent girl he knew and loved more dearly than anyone in the world have become involved with that ilk of person?

Guilt consumed him. Perhaps his father was right. Bad blood did run in the family. It was little wonder Simon's unheralded return from Italy after nine months with a newborn baby girl in his arms was steeped in controversy. It was difficult to find anyone among the *tonnish* elite who did not believe him capable of such corruption. The fact that Emily had married an obscure Italian Count, and her daughter was a Contessa, assuaged the vicious rumors not at all.

Simon's fingers tightened around his walking stick. In retrospect, he wished he'd squelched his fierce temper rather than endlessly berating poor Emily for the blackguard's name. Clearly, she had been afraid of Simon's punitive reaction; frightened that he, like their father, would judge her actions. No wonder she'd refused to offer any explanation for her condition, let alone name the miscreant responsible. Simon's constant badgering for details during her confinement must have confirmed her worst fears.

Simon drew a heartfelt sigh. How she must have longed for a confidant, but found an interrogator. It is a wonder she had not grown to despise him over those long difficult months. No matter how well-intentioned, he knew he'd behaved badly. It haunted him.

He stabbed in frustration at the cobblestones with his walking stick and swore under his breath. He despised feeling powerless. One thing he'd make damn sure of, Annabelle would never know she'd

51

been born on the wrong side of the blanket. He'd kill the first person who suggested it.

'I think it only fair to tell you,' Joy Carmichael told her sister when the two were alone in the rose salon at Morely House on Berkeley Square, 'I have written to the Earl of Dragonwood and thanked him for his intercession.'

Celeste sprang to her feet. 'You did *what*?'

Joy gave her sister a stern look. 'I thought someone should.'

Celeste expelled a miserable sigh and plopped back down in the chair beside her sister's escritoire. She knew her sister's note would be a source of amusement for the cad. Thank him! Thus far, the wretch had kissed her, in a most unseemly – albeit wickedly exciting – fashion, and tricked her in a most dishonorable manner. The scoundrel was hardly worthy of gratitude.

'How can you harbor the slightest regard for that vile man?,' she asked tersely. 'You know Barclay has caused me no end of misery,' she muttered and threw her leg over the arm of the chair in a most unladylike manner. 'It is extremely disloyal of you to be kind to him.'

'It is *Lord* Barclay. And he is not a vile man,' Joy replied, preoccupied with the arduous task of penning responses to dozens of social invitations. 'Tony is very fond of him. I told him how obliging Lord Barclay was in helping us to avoid total social disaster; he was so grateful. As we all should be,' she averred with a reproachful look in her impertinent sibling's direction.

Celeste was not green enough to miss the pointed reminder. Tony had been livid when he learned of Celeste's quest for total ruin. She received the customary lecture on her wild, impulsive nature. Worse yet, he had vowed to put an end to her association with C.C. Dunhill should she ever try anything so foolish again.

She was still smarting from his vile pledge – she knew he would make good on his threat. She had no choice but to abandon her scheme – her hopes of a quiet life in the country were well and truly ruined.

'Lord Barclay has promised to be as silent as the grave. We owe him a debt of sincere gratitude. If you are embarrassed by the unfortunate incident, you have no one to blame save yourself,' Joy remarked, unmoved by her sister's plight.

Celeste pouted, for it was patently obvious Joy was firmly entrenched on the enemy's side. 'I am not embarrassed in the slightest,' she remarked and raised her chin a notch. 'Why should I be?'

Joy laughed softly. 'I can think of several reasons, dearest.'

Celeste's lips thinned. While her conduct verged on unconventional, it could hardly compare to the shocking liberty that rogue had taken. She chose to overlook the salient fact that she'd enjoyed his kiss thoroughly. In the recesses of her mind, she wondered if she'd ever meet the dark and dangerous Dragon again. A small smile tugged at her lips. That encounter promised to be interesting, to say the least. Of course, she would rather die than admit it to another living soul.

'I am amazed he has the nerve to speak to Tony after the way he conducted himself,' she intoned with a scowl. 'His manners are not at all agreeable, to my way of thinking.'

'As I recollect,' Joy remarked with poorly disguised mirth, 'It was *you* who approached *him*. He can have no reason to be ashamed. If memory serves, he refused you outright.'

Celeste blanched at the reminder. 'You were instrumental in his decision, to be sure,' she said bitterly. 'I seriously question the wisdom of speaking to you again after your horrid betrayal.'

Joy flashed an indulgent smile and pushed back her chair. 'Yes, dearest,' she murmured as her slippered feet padded across the deep rose-colored Aubusson carpet, 'and I was so pleased you changed your mind.' She tugged the tapestry bell-pull beside the fireplace.

Joy's inexplicable loyalty to the man vexed Celeste. Wasn't blood supposed to be thicker than water? 'I do not know what you find to admire about the man,' she complained, swinging her half-bare calf to and fro with ire. 'He's unbearable. Arrogant. Conceited. A hateful man. Truly.'

A small smile touched Joy's lips. 'Oh, I don't know. Perhaps it was his very great kindness toward us,' she intoned with a meaningful glint in her eye.

Celeste scoffed at that remark. 'You're my sister. You are supposed to support me –'

But Joy spoke over her. 'Not when you behave like a headstrong fool.'

Pulling a face, Celeste looked away and pouted. 'All you ever do is criticize my judgement,' she grumbled.

'When you demonstrate to me that you have a level head on your shoulders, I should be very happy to pay you the compliment of trusting your judgement.'

Frowning, Joy lifted her sister's leg off the arm of the Queen Anne chair. 'At some point, dearest, I should very much like to see you comport yourself like a lady for more than one hour at a time.' She took in her sister's dishevelled appearance and sighed unhappily at the sight. 'You are scarcely the epitome of manners. You are always the last down to dinner. And you are lucky if your dress is ironed and buttoned,' she lamented with dry humour.

Nettled by the reproof, Celeste tossed an irritated glare in her sister's direction. It was, of course, true. Garbed in a pleated brown silk gown with mameluke sleeves and triple shoulder ruffles, Joy was the epitome of fashion. How she could be remotely comfortable exercised the mind. Celeste's wrinkled light blue muslin gown, however, paled in comparison. No hope for it. Celeste simply was not a proper lady. Nor did she have any wish to be.

Loosely translated, feminine demeanour equated silent complacency. But that would never do. With so many different thoughts and feelings rolling about inside her, threatening at any moment to burst forth, how could she ever hope to squelch them all?

She could not.

Still, she thought with a sigh, it was vexing to live among people who required total submission of her spirit. How could she ever hope to attain the proper female state? It was useless to try. Her mind was simply too occupied with intellectual quests to trifle with inconsequential details such as whether or not her dress was ironed.

'Is it my fault I was born with a natural inclination toward intellectual pursuits?,' Celeste asked her sister.

'No. It is not your fault. But you don't have to slouch in your chair, use outrageous slang and act like a man when you clearly are not.'

A knock sounded at the door, cutting Joy's lecture mercifully short. 'Ah, Alfred,' she said, handing the pristine pile of ivory parchment missives to the butler, 'see these are delivered.'

'His lordship's afternoon paper has arrived, my lady. Shall I leave it with you?'

She smiled and accepted the freshly ironed newspaper from the silver tray. 'How well you know my sister's habits, Alfred.'

He inclined his salt and pepper head in tacit agreement. 'Will that be all, my lady?'

'Yes. Thank you.'

Sketching a dutiful bow, he closed the door, leaving the two sisters alone once more.

'Your paper.' Joy tossed the coveted item on the table beside the porcelain tea set and tempting cakes.

Celeste's mood brightened. 'Thank heavens.' She rushed over to peruse the latest edition. 'Something interesting to occupy my time, instead of fancy work. It is beyond my comprehension,' she remarked and unfolded the newspaper to pore over the articles, 'how you manage to produce scads of those wretched things when all I ever end up with is lumps and knots.'

Joy gave her sister a dubious look. 'It's an acquired art,' she remarked dryly. A mischievous glint came into her eye. She sank down on the rose velvet settee beside her sister. 'Celeste, I can scarcely believe you hold no affection whatsoever for our magnanimous Earl. I think you are withholding something.'

'He is not *our* Earl, Joy,' came Celeste's curt rejoinder from behind a wall of newspaper print. 'I don't suppose such a man could ever really belong to anyone.'

'Oh, I don't know,' Joy sighed dreamily. 'I must confess, I rather thought Lord Barclay cut a fine figure of a man.' She poured a liberal amount of piping hot tea into two porcelain cups etched with tiny pink roses. 'That he is uniformly charming, intelligent and exceedingly wealthy there can no doubt.' She placed a slice of cake on a plate. 'Kindly remove your nose from the paper and drink your tea,' she said in an irritated tone as she handed her petulant sibling the tea and cake. 'What more could a lady ask of a gentleman?,' she asked, savoring a bite of the buttery treat. 'I, for one, find him exceedingly agreeable, good-looking and a gentleman. How you cannot agree is a mystery to me.'

Having heard more than enough on the subject, Celeste decided to set her nauseatingly smitten sister straight. Once she knew what a vile cad the Dragon was, she'd leave her alone.

Celeste placed her cup on the table with a loud clatter. 'It just so happens,' she imparted hotly, 'that

57

hateful rogue, whom you seem to regard as an honorable gentleman, kissed me in the most improper fashion in the library.'

Joy arched a golden brow. 'Did he, indeed? I suspected as much,' she murmured with a conspiratorial smile. 'Was it wonderful?,' she asked, her eyes dancing with devilment.

Celeste gazed at her sister in blank surprise. 'Are you not shocked? I think you should be shocked,' she said, nonplussed. 'Or, at the very least, outraged.'

Joy paid no heed to her sister's dismay. 'I've heard tell,' she said, a wicked gleam in her eye, 'Lord Barclay has been known to leave women swooning.'

'I did not swoon,' Celeste countered sharply and snapped open the newspaper to conceal the color that had crept into her cheeks, for she very nearly had! 'Really, Joy, your curiosity is most unbecoming – you are a married woman, after all. Remember yourself. What would Tony say?'

'I am not dead, dearest,' Joy retorted in a dry tone. A slow smile spread across her face. 'I should think Tony would be mildly diverted.'

'I don't see why you are interested in Barclay's overtures,' Celeste snapped, growing impatient with her sister's preoccupation. She found the topic unnerving. She did not like to dwell on the vexing Dragon. It was an impossible circumstance. She turned the page and perused an advertisement for leather vamp boots. 'I assure you,' she averred, giving what she hoped sounded like a banal sigh and placing her feet on the table top, 'he bored me to tears. I doubt if the man is serious half the time.'

Joy swept Celeste's feet off the table. 'Come now,' she remarked over the rim of her cup, 'even a blue-stocking like you cannot be wholly unaffected by a man like him. Confess to me, you harbour feelings for him,' she coaxed with a sly grin.

'He is an amusing diversion, nothing more,' Celeste mumbled in a failed attempt to appear preoccupied with the paper.

'Are you possibly in love, do you think?'

Celeste refused to dignify that question with a reply. She shot her sister a quelling glance over the corner of the newspaper, and was rewarded with an amused chuckle. Her mouth turned downward. Was there no way to deter her meddling sister? She had never noticed before what a stubborn, deter-mined nature Joy possessed.

Reaching over, Joy turned down the edge of the newspaper. 'Are you listening to a word I am saying? I asked you if you thought you were in love. And you offered no reply. That simply cannot be normal,' she muttered with a frown.

Celeste glared at her sister and resumed her feigned reading.

'Why can you not be more docile and malleable like the other debutantes your age?,' Joy asked with a miserable sigh.

'Because they are insipid and annoyingly dim-witted,' came Celeste's nonchalant rejoinder from behind the crisp newspaper. 'A dreadful combina-tion guaranteed to produce a perennial headache, Tony always says.'

'Yes, but could you not try for a modicum of

normalcy? Most would be thrilled by the mere thought of a man like Barclay expressing interest.'

Her sister's suggestion gave Celeste pause. Expressed interest? She caught her lower lip between her teeth. Had he expressed interest?

It was preposterous. Certainly, he was not interested in her. Her forehead creased.

Or . . . was he?

A man like that simply did not have the inclination to marry. She frowned slightly.

Or . . . did he?

Her breath caught in her throat. Could it be?

No. She shook her head. It was unconscionable. He simply was not the marrying sort. Of course, being his mistress was no dull prospect either.

A warm flush swept over her. How would it feel to be courted by the Dragon? The idea was undeniably exhilarating. He could provide an extensive sensual education, bar none. That was definitely an alluring quality in any man. Particularly if one had to suffer marriage.

She knew he would never understand her attachment to C.C. Dunhill and that greatly diminished his appeal in her eyes. Doubtless he would force her to give up her intellectual pursuits. She could never do that. A rueful smile ruffled her lips. Well, it was a nice reverie while it lasted.

Shaking off her fanciful thoughts as empty-headed romantic notions, she mentally chastised herself for being as foolish as her fanciful sister.

'Must we discuss this?,' she demanded with barely-cloaked irritation.

'Dearest, you act as though you never hope to fall in love.' Joy's voice was nearly shrill with frustration.

Rolling her eyes heavenward, Celeste lowered the paper to her lap. 'How you contrive to think about nothing else but love from morning till night I do not know?'

Joy tilted her blonde head to one side. 'I don't suppose I can help it, really. It is in my nature to be romantic. Just as it is in yours to evade the issue,' she replied with a knowing smile.

'I am not evading it,' Celeste denied fiercely. 'I simply have no desire to discuss Lord Barclay.'

'Why on earth not?,' Joy asked, clearly astounded by the mere idea that any woman would not warm to the subject of the Dragon.

Celeste opened her mouth to verbally lambast her meddling sister when a tap sounded at the door. Alfred appeared.

'I beg your pardon, my lady, but Lady Merryweather is waiting to see you.'

Joy and Celeste exchanged a look of blank surprise.

Constance Merryweather was a middle-aged woman who had a well-earned reputation for knowing, or instigating, the most scandalous pieces of gossip in all London. Other people's lives and what conjectures could be made about them were meat and drink to her.

'What can Lady Merryweather want with us?,' Joy asked her sister.

Celeste shrugged her shoulders and tossed the newspaper aside. 'Whatever it is, we shall shortly discover.'

'Show Lady Merryweather in, Alfred,' Joy instructed.

A second later, the plump, grey-haired woman floated into the sitting room on a sea of voluminous lavender silk.

'Oh, my dears,' she exclaimed breathless with excitement. 'I simply had to come. I must tell you. You will never believe it when you hear.'

Joy glanced at her sister and frowned slightly. 'Pray, be seated, Lady Merryweather, you look overset.'

Lady Merryweather collapsed on the rose velvet settee in an exhausted heap. 'I am exhausted. It has been such a morning.' She waved her pudgy hands in the air. 'You will scarcely believe it when I tell you.'

Joy's forehead creased with worry. 'What is it that has made you ill?'

Lady Merryweather mopped her brow with her white lace handkerchief. Her eyes fluttered shut. 'There's been a terrible . . . murder,' she said with a shudder.

Joy looked stunned.

Celeste was stupefied. In general, people of her acquaintance were not murdered.

'A murder?,' the two sisters echoed in unison.

'It was grisly,' Lady Merryweather said with a sob of horror.

A shiver ran over Celeste as the elderly woman recited the hideous details.

'The victim – you will never believe it, my dears,' she said, her eyes wide with fascination, 'was a young woman of some means. They found her body early this morning, in Cheapside. She had been strangled, and her body tossed in the river,' she exclaimed, throwing her plump arms in the air.

Joy drew in her breath in shock. 'Who would have done such a thing?' she asked, abhorred by the violent crime.

Before Lady Merryweather could impart further details, Celeste spoke up. 'Well, don't keep us in suspense – who was she?,' she demanded with a mixture of excitement and morbid curiosity.

Joy shook her head at her sister.

But Lady Merryweather was just as eager to impart the gruesome details as Celeste was to hear them.

'Lady Jane Greenly, a debutante like yourself. You might even be acquainted with her family, as I myself am. Her father is the Earl of Bellingham,' she cackled. 'A highly respected family to be sure. She'd come up for the Season from Essex. We all had great hopes for her to make a suitable match.' She clutched at her breast. 'When I reflect that she was at Almack's just last Wednesday. Lady Jersey greeted her in person. Imagine how bright her future would have been. And now . . . this!' Her eyelashes fluttered shut. 'It is unfathomable.'

'I should say so,' Joy mumbled, dazed by the news.

'I know Jane,' Celeste remarked with pensive air. 'Or knew her. Not more than a fortnight ago we were chatting about the appalling food at Almack's. The lemonade was horribly tepid and the cakes were as stale as last week's bread. And now . . . she's dead.'

Joy gave her sister a forbidding look.

63

But Celeste paid no heed. 'Poor Jane,' she whispered softly. 'She was a quiet, shy girl. Certainly not the sort you'd expect to end up –'

'You are correct, Lady Merryweather,' Joy interjected. 'We are acquainted with the poor unfortunate girl – she and my sister came out together. They were presented at court on the same day, I do believe.'

'Yes, we were. I liked her exceptionally well,' Celeste added with a forlorn sigh.

The grey ringlets bobbed to and for as Lady Merryweather nodded her head. 'I suspected as much.'

'What is being done?,' Celeste asked pointedly.

Lady Merryweather shrugged her portly shoulders. 'What is to be done? The poor girl is dead. The family is beside themselves with grief, that I can tell you.' She wagged her sausage-like finger for emphasis.

'It is little wonder,' Celeste remarked, eliciting a censorious look from her sister.

'Who could have done such a heinous deed?,' Joy asked, hugging her arms around her.

'Who, indeed?,' Lady Merryweather clutched her handkerchief to her mouth in abject distress. 'It is unthinkable.'

'But what is being done?,' Celeste demanded. 'Certainly inquiries will be made to discover who perpetrated such a vile crime?'

Lady Merryweather blinked at Celeste over the top of her frilly handkerchief. 'I've not the slightest notion. Such matters are best left to the men, my dear,' she said with a dismissive wave of her corpulent hand.

'That is the wisest course, naturally,' Joy chimed in, fixing her wayward sibling with a quelling glance.

Celeste scowled, but fell silent.

'You are quite unwell, Lady Merryweather, as we all are upon hearing such news. Is there something we might offer you to bring you some relief? Tea, perhaps?,' Joy inquired politely.

'Gracious, no,' the rotund matron said and struggled to heave her great bulk from the narrow settee. 'I must be off, my dears. I must extend my sympathies to Lady Jane's father this very day.'

A concerned Joy walked with the enormous matron downstairs.

As soon as Celeste was alone, she snatched up the paper. Her eyes could not move fast enough over the black print.

'Whatever are you doing?,' Joy asked upon her return.

'Reading about the murder,' Celeste replied, her hungry gaze devouring the contents of the article.

'Your avid curiosity is abominable. Really,' Joy scolded, 'I think it shows the poorest taste.'

Celeste shot her sister a withering glance. 'Oh, do come along, Joy. Stop being such a ninnyhammer. Come and have a look at what it says.'

'Very well, if you insist.' Joy scurried across the room and snuggled on the settee beside her sister. 'What else does it say?'

Celeste bit her lower lip. 'Not much more than Lady Merryweather explained. But I am sure they know more than they are printing. They must. I could find out more . . . if C.C. Dunhill were to write to Mr Hammersmith at *The Chronicle*. He might be able to make some inquires.'

'Are you mad?,' Joy burst out. 'Tony would be shocked to know we read the story, let alone intended to snoop about for gruesome details.'

'*We* won't,' Celeste replied calmly. She folded the irrevocably wrinkled newspaper and placed it on the table. 'C.C. Dunhill will. Tony cannot possibly have any objections.'

'Oh, no.' Joy shook her head in grave disapproval. 'It is out of the question. You know as well as I, that he would never approve.'

'Well,' Celeste wheedled beneath mischievous brows, 'what Tony doesn't know cannot hurt him.'

Joy affected a prim and proper posture that was all too familiar to her disobedient younger sister. 'What you suggest is grossly underhanded. It speaks rather badly of your character,' she admonished sharply.

'I am merely suggesting it would perhaps be better if he did not know everything all the time,' Celeste replied evenly. 'I do hate to see Tony overwrought.'

'You don't care a whit about Tony's nerves,' her sister fired back. 'Or mine for that matter. You are thinking of yourself. As is your custom, I hasten to add.'

Celeste looked peevish. 'You are just as curious as I to hear more about it. You know you are. It is merely your strict sense of propriety that prevents you from admitting it. Someone murdered Jane Greenly, a woman with whom we were both acquainted. I happened to like her quite well. We cannot just sit back like docile idiots and pretend it hasn't happened. Besides, as young women living in this city, we should know, if only for our own protection.'

'If you would cease to cavort about without a proper escort you would need not fear for your safety,' Joy snapped crossly.

'If there is a madman roaming the streets,' Celeste tossed back tartly, 'I for one would very much like to know about it. If only to allow for caution on my part. Someone has to find out who killed poor Jane. If it were me, I would want you to care enough to discover the perpetrator – at the very least, enlist the help of someone who could.'

Joy heaved a weary sigh. 'Why do I feel myself being drawn into another one of your outrageous schemes?' she groaned, rubbing her temples.

A slow smile of satisfaction crept across Celeste's face. She knew her sister was weakening. Constrained as she was by her strong sense of decorum, curiosity was eating at her.

'I am not asking you to lie,' Celeste cajoled, 'just . . . omit the more incriminating portions.'

'Oh, very well,' Joy said in a harassed voice. 'I'll see what can be done. But, this time, if you get yourself into a spot of trouble, I won't come to your rescue,' she imparted strictly.

Celeste shrieked with delight and threw her arms around her sister.

'Do be careful,' Joy whispered, hugging Celeste tightly. 'This entire episode has chilled my blood.'

'I confess that it has me unnerved as well. But you mustn't worry. I am always the epitome of caution.'

Except where the Dragon was concerned, an irritating voice whispered in her head. She chose to ignore that voice. At the moment, the Dragon was the very least of her concerns. She could ill afford to waste precious time and energy on a mere man – particularly not one who was unattainable at best. Not that she wanted to attain him, or any man for that matter. She did not.

Regardless of how incredibly attractive he was, she had far more important things to contemplate. How on earth she planned to investigate that ghoulish murder was a far more formidable challenge. It promised to be quite a feat, even for her.

CHAPTER 4

As the clock in the hallway of Simon's elegant Upper Brook Street townhouse struck midnight, the master of the house settled comfortably before the fireplace in a large winged-back chair. Tugging at his cravat until the knot gave way, he placed his black polished Hessians on the ottoman. Taking a sip of the pleasantly warm amber liquid from the crystal balloon glass cradled in his palm, he laid back his head and expelled a tired sigh.

His frustration was boundless. This evening's meeting with Mr Crawford had not yielded any news. Lord Paine had proved a trifle uncooperative. After a week of surveillance, all Simon knew about the elusive man was that he had a marked preference for base and corrupt pastimes, which would land him very shortly in a debtor's prison.

Simon yanked his cravat from around his neck and tossed it over the arm of the chair. Irritated fingers fumbled with the buttons at the neck of his linen shirt. He couldn't dwell on the paucity of information. Not tonight. He needed to find some measure of relaxation or he'd go mad.

He was about to delve into Walter Scott's latest adventure novel *Ivanhoe* when he heard commotion in the front hallway beyond the dark mahogany library door. As the argument grew louder, he scowled and threw the book down on the ottoman.

Was he never to have a moment's peace? He was seriously considering spending a month in the country despite the appalling society. A little foxhunting could be just thing he needed to rejuvenate his blood. At least in Derbyshire he held some hope to find something vaguely resembling tranquillity.

Crossing the darkened library in three angry strides, he yanked open the door and demanded of his elderly butler in a disgruntled growl, 'What the deuce is going on out here, Evans?'

The butler straightened his crisp white collar and cleared his throat. 'My lord, this . . . *woman*,' he muttered looking down his gargantuan nose at the petite female shrouded in a hooded black redingote, 'is demanding to speak to you. She *claims* it is urgent. I told her that you were not to be disturbed. But she is very persistent.'

The intruder who was standing in the middle of the dimly-lit foyer removed the hood from her head to reveal a mass of golden tresses.

Simon stared at the woman in mute confusion. His piercing grey eyes narrowed on her face. 'Lady Carmichael?,' he asked, stupefied.

A smile softened the worried look on her face. 'My lord, I was hoping you would agree to see me.' She rushed forward to clasp his hands in greeting. 'I would not have come were I not in desperate need of your help.'

Her hands were like ice, he noticed with a pensive frown. 'What on earth possessed you to venture out on such a night? And at this ungodly hour?'

She glanced furtively over her shoulder at the butler who was firmly entrenched by the door, a look of contempt on his forbidding face.

'That will be all, Evans.' Simon's voice held a note of curt dismissal.

The butler cast a disapproving glance in Lady Carmichael's direction. 'Very good, my lord.' He turned on his heel and disappeared down the dark hall.

Lady Carmichael heaved a sigh of relief. 'Oh, my lord,' she whispered and closed her eyes, 'you are good, to be sure.'

His lips twisted. Good was not a word that leapt to most people's minds where he was concerned.

'How this must look,' she muttered with a miserable groan. 'What you must think of me.'

His concerned gaze drifted over Lady Carmichael's drawn countenance. She looked ill indeed. He could scarcely turn her out.

'Come, warm yourself by the fire,' he commanded, dismissing her trepidation. He led her into the library. When she was sitting comfortably before the warmth of the firelight's glow, he said, 'Tell me what has brought you here?'

She was wringing her hands. 'I did not know to whom I should turn.' Her voice was agitated.

'Could your husband not be of some help?,' he prompted, wondering where the devil Tony was whenever his wife needed him.

She shook her head. 'I left him asleep in his bed.'

Simon felt a twinge from the hairs on the back of his neck. He dearly hoped Tony was not a jealous husband, for his skill with a duelling pistol was formidable. Simon would hate to wound his friend over a silly misunderstanding.

Mystified by a seemingly happily-married woman throwing herself at his mercy in the middle of the night, he asked bluntly, 'Why should you want to do that?'

'I had no choice. You see –,' she looked away, '– something . . . untoward has occurred.' Her voice climbed an octave as she explained, 'I am at my wits' end. I have not the slightest idea what to do. Given the current predicament, I had nowhere else to go. I regret imposing on your kind nature –'

'Calm yourself,' he interjected with some force, 'and tell me what has happened.'

Trepidation ruffled her brow. 'It's . . . Celeste. I couldn't go to Tony,' she rushed on. 'After that débâcle at Lord Holmes's party, he vowed to punish her most grievously and tell Grandfather if she ever did anything stupidly foolish again which . . . I am very much afraid she has.'

He expelled an irritated breath. Somehow he knew the impertinent little baggage was behind her sister's distress.

Getting to his feet, he demanded in a voice that rang with curt impatience, 'What has she done now?'

Her gaze fell to her lap. 'She has attended Lord Hobson's house party under false pretences,' she said, her voice horribly small. 'Her conduct verges on infamous most of the time. I am persuaded, tonight, her behavior is beyond the pale. I am grieved indeed to impart such shocking news. You see, she has not been invited.'

Simon's jaw clenched. 'I see.'

Apparently, near ruin was not sufficient excitement for the little hellion. She'd moved on to more intriguing surroundings. So much for heeding his sage advice. Damned chit was bound and determined to get herself in trouble.

He glanced at Lady Carmichael's blonde head hung in shame. He'd been down this road once before and had no intentions of bailing the headstrong hoyden out of another mishap.

'Why come to me?,' he queried with his back to her while he filled his glass with brandy.

'You must realize, under the circumstances, you are the only person I can turn to for assistance.'

Uttering a scornful chuckle, he tossed the brandy down his throat. 'Happily, I haven't seen your sister since she demanded I ruin her reputation. Allow me to assure you,' he imparted with heavy sarcasm, 'I am not eager for another encounter.'

Lady Carmichael's eyes widened in dismay. 'Y-you must see the indecency of her behavior.'

He nodded sagely. 'Indeed. But what has it to do with me?,' he asked and dropped lightly into the chair opposite the fire.

She cast him a look of reproach. 'I cannot believe

you truly intend to stand by and allow my sister to fling herself into another scandal, my lord. Not after the way you interceded so gallantly at Holmes's party. You will never convince me to the contrary.'

His mouth set in annoyance. The woman had a knack for employing compliments to her advantage. No amount of flattery would induce him to rescue that ungrateful little wench. Not this time.

'She is by nature headstrong and rash. I fear she may be in grave peril. Please, my lord, I beg of you, will you not help?,' she beseeched him.

He looked away and gazed pensively at the fire. His lips thinned. The devil only knew the trouble that silly chit could get herself into with her reckless antics. He still hadn't fully recovered from her outrageous request that he ruin her on the garden path.

He scowled at the flickering flames. Oh, confound it. He'd do it. Against his better judgement, he'd save her. One last time. But he would not touch her. No matter what the inducement.

'What *exactly* do you think she is planning to do?,' he asked with ill-concealed rancour.

'I believe she has gone to do some investigating regarding that ghastly murder.'

'Murder?' He almost fell off his chair. A mantle of furious color spread over his taut features. 'What murder?,' he bit out.

'That poor unfortunate who was thrown in the Thames.'

'Good Lord.' He vaulted to his feet and paced the room. 'That was in Cheapside, was it not?' His ebony brows slanted in a frown. 'What the devil does she hope to find sneaking about in Hobson's home?'

Lady Carmichael heaved a woeful sigh. 'One can only imagine. I am afraid my sister is endowed with a rather singular character. Anything is possible.'

'Madam, you have a gift for understatement,' he uttered coolly.

'What are we to do?,' she asked her voice anxious.

'You,' he intoned meaningfully, 'will do nothing.'

Relief flooded her features. 'Oh, my lord –,' she clasped her hands together, '– you are a saint. I knew you would not disappoint me.'

He gave her a dubious look. 'I sincerely doubt that I am saint, madam. But I will help you find your recalcitrant sister.'

'How do you intend to fetch her without creating further scandal?,' she asked with concern. 'Have you, perhaps, an invitation?'

He gave her a sideways glance that told her he did not. 'I will manage. Somehow. Are you capable of returning safely home on your own?' he asked as he escorted her to the dark green marbled foyer.

A smile graced her tired countenance. 'Perfectly. Given the delicacy of the situation, my lord, I believe it would better if I showed myself out. My carriage is waiting near the corner.' She raised her black hood, concealing her identity once more. 'I shall slip back inside without anyone noticing I was ever gone.'

'Excellent. Never fear. I'll return your sister safe and sound by morning light.'

He opened the front door and met a gust of cold night air that sobered him better than cold water could. His lips curled ruefully. Once again, he found himself racing after the wild hoyden in the middle of the night.

He couldn't quite believe it himself. On this occasion, he couldn't use the excuse that he owed Tony a debt of gratitude. In fact, he couldn't produce any rational reason for his actions at all.

Lady Carmichael squeezed his hand. 'We are forever in your debt, my lord.' She wet her lips nervously and cast him a furtive glance. 'There is just one more matter that bears mentioning, although I hesitate to mention it . . .'

The chilly night air swirled around him and stung his cheeks with icy mockery. He wondered what possessed him to agree to this ridiculous adventure. He longed to be nestled comfortably in his library. Damn and blast! When he found the headstrong little urchin he fully intended to give her a good spanking.

'Yes?,' he prompted, his irritation waxing by the minute.

'This unfortunate incident must remain between ourselves. It would not do for Grandfather to catch wind of her escapades. He is not the understanding sort. Only consider what happened when he discovered her manuscript.'

Simon gave her a look of staggering disbelief. 'Her manuscript?' His mouth set in a tight line. 'Are you telling me she actually penned a manuscript?'

Lady Carmichael merely nodded as if it was the most normal thing in the world. 'Lord knows what he'd do if he found out about her latest pursuit.'

'On what topic?,' he ventured to ask.

'What? Oh, the madness of King George.'

'The *what*?,' he exploded in shock. The King's madness was whispered about in certain circles, but no one dared write a book on the subject. No one except the unconventional Miss Wentworth, that is.

'Grandfather shared your outrage. It was most distressing. Of course, I sincerely doubt he would have been pleased on any account. I shall never forget the day he discovered her work,' she shuddered.

'What happened?,' Simon asked pointedly.

She gave him a blank look. 'Did she not relate the horrid circumstance to you?' Her brow furrowed. 'I felt certain she must have told you.'

His jaw tightened. 'She was far too engaged in seeking total ruin to offer an explanation.'

Lady Carmichael shook her head. 'I cannot think why she'd omit something as important as her manuscript. It was her motivation for seeking ruin.'

'She hedged a bit on that minor point,' he replied in a terse tone.

'How very odd,' she murmured thoughtfully. 'I would have thought she'd have told you.'

'What *was* the reason?,' he prompted, his impatience mounting.

'Grandfather found out about her singular pastime, ransacked her room and tossed her entire manuscript in the fire.'

A dark expression overtook Simon's features. To say the old man was strict was an understatement. From all accounts, he was a heartless brute. No wonder the chit was wild. Anyone with an ounce of spirit would rebel against such a heavy yoke. Celeste had more spunk than the law allowed. A condition with which he was all too familiar.

'I suppose he hoped to put an end to her unnatural intellectual pursuits once and for all.'

Lady Carmichael nodded. 'Two years' worth of work went up in flames. It was devastating for the poor dear,' she said with a doleful sigh. 'All that research gone.'

He frowned sympathetically. 'I can well imagine how she must have felt.'

'Celeste, poor dear, was beside herself. My sister and I are devoted to one another – I simply could not bear to see her miserable.'

'I am still at a loss. Why precisely did she wish to be ruined? It seems to me she had little to gain from being shunned by society.' He knew all too well the hurtful consequence of total disgrace.

'I very much fear she would do just about anything to be free of our domineering grandfather. As long as she is able to pursue her intellectual interests, my sister would be content to live quietly in the country, permanently installed on the shelf.'

'She fancies herself an intellectual, does she?' Simon asked, stroking his chin in thought.

She lifted her eyes heavenward. 'You've no conception. To be frank, I do not always understand her. Her behavior is scandalous. Not at all proper for a young well-bred lady.' She released a weary sigh. 'I suppose it is left to us to conceal the undesirable truth at all costs.'

His lips twitched slightly. 'I quite agree.'

She etched a smile. 'I thought you might. Heaven knows what would happen should your involvement came to light. Grandfather would undoubtedly take a dim view.' She glanced up at him beneath sly lashes. 'He might even call you out. Or at the very least disown her, were he to catch wind of her antics. Is that not true, my lord?'

Staring at the woman before him, Simon tried to fathom what she could mean by such an odd comment.

'Indubitably,' he murmured with a nod of his head. 'Never fear, madam. You may rely on me to be the soul of discretion.'

'Thank you, my lord.'

Tony would have to be told at some point. Simon did not feel right keeping a midnight visit with his friend's wife a secret. But he needed to find the scandalous little hoyden first. He was itching to pound some sense into her addled brain.

He waited in the bone-chilling dead of night until he was certain Lady Carmichael was safely deposited in her carriage.

She leaned out the window. 'I knew you were trustworthy. I shall await the safe return of my sister with bated breath.'

As he closed the door, he shook his head. His mouth curved into an unconscious smile. Women as a rule did not trust him. And with good reason. It was pleasant to encounter one who thought him worthy of esteem.

Forty-five minutes later, a tired and thoroughly vexed Simon disembarked from his carriage behind Hobson's garden wall.

'Wait here,' he told his beleaguered driver.

'Right you are, milord,' the driver replied and hugged his collar around his neck to ward off the night's chill.

As Simon tramped across the shadowy thicket towards the estate he shook his head. 'I am definitely getting too old for this,' he growled under his breath. Never before had he attempted to slip into a ballroom uninvited. In fact, to his knowledge, it simply was not done. At least, not until this evening.

As he hoisted himself over the marble balustrade and landed with a hard thud on Hobson's deserted balcony, he told himself there was a first time for everything.

Fortunately, the scores of guests were so engaged in idle gossip and in romantic conspiracies that they took no notice of him as he strode from the dimly-lit balcony and mingled with the swarming crowd. He managed, to his great relief, to traverse the mobbed dance floor without being accosted by droves of giggling women looking for their next dance-card entry.

It shouldn't prove terribly difficult to locate the headstrong chit, given that she was the only woman of his acquaintance with vibrant red hair. With any luck, he'd whisk her from the premises before she caused any more trouble. Of course, the fact that the room was packed did little to aid his search.

Simon was beginning to worry that he would not find her by daybreak. A remote possibility existed; the foolish chit might have completed her outlandish investigation and be safely tucked in her bed where she belonged.

His lips twisted. The other possibility, of course, was that she'd finally gone too far and landed herself in a circumstance well beyond her capabilities. She was such a delicate little morsel. It was entirely possible that one of Hobson's guests might have taken a liking to her. Simon himself could plead guilty to having engaged in a momentary dalliance with the enticing creature. As much as he longed to see her get what was coming to her for behaving so foolishly, the thought of any real harm coming to her was decidedly unpalatable.

Celeste adjusted her pearl choker for the tenth time and tugged her white gloves over her elbow. She glanced down at her pale green silk dress and worried that it was too simple compared with the gowns of the other members of the *ton* present this evening. She did not wish to look out of place for fear of calling attention to her presence. Drawing a deep calming breath, she wondered why her nerves were overset.

Her pulse was throbbing like a wild thing for the simple reason that, in very short order, she was going to slink from the throng, creep upstairs and search her host's bedchamber for damning evidence. She was not at all certain she was prepared for what she might find.

Ghoulish details of poor Jane being strangled flooded her mind. She took another sip of watery lemonade and wondered if the stress of the evening was too much for her. If her eyes did not deceive her, the notorious, undeniably gorgeous Dragon was standing not ten feet from her.

Her breath caught in her throat. Gracious heavens. This was no illusion. He was real. He looked more beautiful than a man should. Occupied in conversation with a helplessly unattractive, clinging widow, he had not taken notice of Celeste as yet, which gave her the golden opportunity to admire him brazenly.

She took full advantage of the situation. As much as she hated herself for it, a thrill never failed to overtake her at the mere sight of the ominous wickedly dangerous man.

My, he was wonderfully tall, dark and handsomely forbidding, she thought with a sigh of appreciation. That is, when compared with the only other man under the age of forty whom she knew – her brother-in-law Tony.

Tony was fair and amicable. She had once regarded him as the most striking man of her acquaintance. Now she knew better.

The Dragon's shoulders were much broader and he was a good three inches taller than Tony. His well-defined muscles, accentuated by his snug black velvet cutaway, had her gazing with admiration.

She bit her lip and sighed remembering exactly how it felt to run her hands over his rock-hard chest and strong virile arms. It was pure nirvana.

It was then that he saw her. His grey tempestuous gaze drifted over every inch of her with excruciating thoroughness. Her pulse soared. She watched with blatant relish as he managed to disengage himself from the widow's clutches and to cross the room to where Celeste stood.

A thrill of excitement rippled through her as he sauntered purposefully towards her. Why, the man behaved as if *he* was the lord of the manor. But that was what made him so alluring, she acknowledged with a surge of warmth, he was always in command of any situation. A quality she found utterly irresistible. Oh, yes, Dragon suited him as a nickname, she decided, for it was not difficult to imagine him devouring anyone who got in his way.

He inclined his dark head in greeting. 'The honorable Miss Wentworth, I do believe,' he said, his tone sharp.

A rush of pleasure washed over her. Not in the least put out by his brusque manner, she quickly forgot about her nefarious mission and dropped into a polite curtsy that would have made even her stodgy grandfather proud. 'My lord.'

Silver eyes gazed deeply into blue. He clasped her slender hand in his and pressed his lips to her skin. Tingling currents of raw attraction ran up her arm.

'It is a delightful surprise to see you again,' he said in a voice smoother than velvet. 'Our last encounter was quite . . . unique. I wonder what you have planned to charm me senseless this evening?'

Good gracious. She could practically feel his heat. The sensual promise his hooded grey eyes conveyed made her knees turn weak. Her heart slammed against her ribs. 'You are too kind, my lord,' she demurred.

'Indeed, I am. I have been scouring the ballroom for you for the last half-hour,' he said in a curt undertone that belied his anger.

She pulled a frown. So much for another romantic interlude. She should have realized he gazed at every woman with equal hunger. 'What on earth brings *you* here of all places?' she whispered tersely.

'I'm saving your foolish neck,' he fired back. 'You ought to know it is considered outrageously bad conduct to go where you are not invited.'

She glared at him. 'You are being absurd, my lord. No one knows I wasn't invited.'

'Keep your voice down,' he hissed, 'or everyone will know we're *both* here uninvited.' His breath was warm against her ear. She hated herself for quivering all over.

'If you'll be so kind as to go away,' she whispered crossly, 'no one need know.'

'As much as I'd care to,' he told her sarcastically, 'I am afraid I am not at liberty to oblige you.'

Her mouth pursed. 'Why is it, my lord, that I continually encounter your unwanted presence at the worst possible moments? Have you nothing better to do than poke your nose into other people's private affairs?'

'As it happens,' he drawled with chilling curtness. 'I would be enjoying all the comforts of home were it not for the ramshackle existence *you* lead.'

She gave him a petulant glare. 'My life is not in the least ramshackle,' she flung at him. 'I do not desire your intervention and would do quite nicely without it.'

'It grieves me to hear it,' he muttered dryly, 'at the moment, however, we need to connive a way out of here. I am persuaded your poor sister must be

84

fretting excessively by now. If I do not get you home before the dawn, there will be the devil to pay.'

'I might have known Joy was behind your sudden appearance,' she fumed angrily. 'We used to be utterly devoted to one another. Marriage has done dreadful things to her. She's lost all sense of loyalty.'

A sardonic smirk touched his lips. 'I do believe it has an ill effect on most people. Now, why don't you and I slip away before we are noticed, shall we? And forget this unfortunate experience like a bad dream?'

'You are all kindness, my lord,' she imparted with biting sarcasm. 'But I have no intention of leaving here without getting what I came for.'

His eyes turned a dark slate grey. 'You,' he said through his teeth, 'are a naïve, dangerous child with a penchant for getting yourself into trouble.' He raked his hand through his hair and expelled an irritated sigh. 'I'm the damned fool who constantly seems to get you out of it.'

'I never asked for your help,' she barked back, oddly hurt by his disgust of her.

He regarded her as a childish nuisance. Nothing more. She regarded him as . . . as – as what?

She wasn't sure of anything at the moment, except for the currents of excitement that raced through her whenever he was near. She couldn't think why. Now, however, was not the time to delve into her feelings. The Dragon was a formidable opponent. She needed all her wits about her.

'No,' he replied coldly, 'you haven't the sense. Thank goodness your sister has a level head on her shoulders.'

Celeste could well imagine the impression Joy had given his lordship. Headstrong. Impetuous. Foolish.

'Come, my little hoyden,' his voice rang with maddening command, 'you are going home to bed where you belong.'

Shooing him away with her hands, she told him, 'Just . . . take yourself off.'

'Not possible,' came his acid retort.

She stamped her slippered foot in frustration. 'You are spoiling everything.'

His eyes narrowed on her determined upturned face. 'Exactly *what* am I spoiling?'

'My investigation, if you must know.' Her tone was decidedly peevish.

Simon drew an irritated breath and prayed for patience. And self-control. He needed self-control. Desperately. The desire to take the damned gel over his knee and smack her soundly very nearly overpowered him. Even more disturbing were the group of disapproving onlookers interested in the heated discourse.

A disgruntled frown touched his lips. 'Are you in the habit of creating scenes everywhere you go?' he growled against her ear. 'You look overly warm,' he averred with admirable civility and extended his arm in polite invitation. 'Allow me to escort you on to the balcony.'

She glared down at his arm with disdain. Short of causing a scene, however, she could do nothing else but accept his invitation. The wretch was relying on it.

'Oh, bother,' she grumbled. 'Must you make every circumstance work to your advantage?' she gritted under her breath as he led her toward the double doors that opened on to the secluded balcony and private gardens.

Oh, bother? He bit back a smile. She sounded older than his childhood nanny.

'Do I manage all that well?,' he murmured. The warmth of his breath against her ear made her shiver with unwanted pleasure. 'I was under the impression that was your penchant, dear heart.'

'Fustian,' she snapped and stepped back from his overwhelming presence. 'I am no slowtop. I know what you are about, why you connived your way on to the balcony.'

His lips quirked. 'Do you?'

She looked up at him, her gaze soft and languid. 'You are planning to kiss me again, are you not?' she breathed with ill-concealed anticipation.

He cocked a dubious brow. 'In full view of Hobson's guests? No.' He shook his head decisively. 'I am not.'

Embarrassed heat flooded her cheeks. She averted her gaze in an effort to hide her disappointment.

'Oh,' she said in a small voice. 'I cannot tell you what a relief it is to know your intentions are, at last, honorable,' she added with brusque sarcasm.

He smiled down at her with an indulgence she detested. 'As I told you once before, I am not in the habit of ravishing young innocents.'

That was a lie. He'd like nothing more than to offer her a stylish townhouse, expensive wardrobe, lavish jewels, and his protection in exchange for just one night of passionate lovemaking. What he wouldn't give to hear her call out his name on a breathless moan of pleasure.

A fierce frown marred his face. What the deuce ailed him of late? He was definitely not the sort to lose his head over a woman. Especially not one with the mind of a child and a desire for scandal.

His burning gaze drifted over the fetching creature at his side with lazy precision. She was a delight. She was a hellion. Quite the most unusual person he'd ever met.

'Do not be disagreeable, Celeste,' he coaxed her gently. 'You know as well as I you'd best slip away before our esteemed host finds out about your peculiar lack of protocol and you find yourself in trouble.' He inclined his raven head toward the ballroom. 'I dare say dear old Hobson would take a dim view of our being here without the benefit of an invitation.'

She crossed her arms under her bosom. 'If you wish to leave, you may. I am staying.'

He vacillated between the urge to throttle the little baggage and to kiss her soundly. 'The devil you are!'

'The devil I am,' she tossed right back at him. To her chagrin, she had to step back from his hard, tense maleness. 'Stop . . . interfering in my private affairs. You've no right.' Acutely aware of his overwhelming masculinity, she swallowed and willed her stomach to cease its somersaults.

His searing gaze raked over her. 'By God,' he breathed, 'you are an outrageous hellion.'

Her frosty glare drifted over him. 'I cannot credit your concern for my well-being. As I collect, my lord, you forfeited the opportunity to assist me in my moment of need.'

A sardonic smirk touched his lips. 'Disappointed, were you?'

She wet her lips. Oh dear, his hard, lean body was intimidating beyond belief. Craven coward that she was, she had to quell the urge to scurry back inside. 'Verily, my lord,' her voice quivered horribly, 'it seems rakes are not to be trusted. In, or out, of the library.'

He smiled at that. 'Ah, yes,' he said in soft dulcet tones that had her tingling right down to her toes, 'the library.' His hand reached out and caressed a soft tendril of coppery red hair that had fallen haphazardly down her ivory neck. 'How could I forget?'

One look in those sultry grey eyes and she knew he had not forgotten. Not one single solitary moment. Neither had she. Heaven help her. He was remembering their all-too-fleeting moment of wild, abandoned passion with obvious relish. Good gracious. She was too.

Wetting her suddenly parched lips, she forced her gaze lower. That was a mistake. She found herself staring at his sensual, full mouth. She knew she was in serious peril of being kissed.

He reached out, drawing her against his dangerous heat. Bending his head, he pressed his soft, parted lips against hers and kissed her fully on her quivering mouth. Liking the riotous sensations pulsating through her, she grew bold and touched her tongue to his. A muffled sound escaped his throat. His arms tightened around her. He pulled her against him, devouring her lips with savage hunger.

His mouth trailed hot, wet kisses down her neck. Tilting her head, she basked in the delicious sensations his searing touch evoked. A tiny sigh of exquisite pleasure escaped her throat. Her fingers tightened around his shoulders, clutching him for support, for her legs felt suddenly too weak to hold her.

He captured her mouth, smothering her moist lips in a slow, drugging kiss. His hand slid up her waist and covered her full, impudent breast. Cupping the round soft mound, he teased her sensitive nipple with the pad of his thumb. Pleased by her beautiful uninhibited response, he smiled with satisfaction as her breast peaked beneath his touch.

'*My lord*,' she gasped.

He chuckled at her use of formality in the very informal circumstances. He felt rather like a lord of the manor seducing an innocent governess. But he wouldn't think about that just now.

It might be madness, but it was also the sweetest pleasure he'd found in ages. His open mouth captured hers, moving with startling ardour over her pliant, sweet lips.

She returned his kiss with equal longing. Her lips intoxicated his senses. Her incredibly soft, supple body was more than any hot-blooded man could resist. With a concerted effort he managed to tear his mouth away from the enticing feast.

He thought the first time he'd kissed her was an aberration. Now he knew it was not. They were beautifully matched. Their compatibility was undeniable.

Sexually.

In all other ways, the impetuous little miss drove him closer to committing murder than anyone he'd ever met.

Breathless and weak, she pressed her cheek against his chest and clung to him. She felt his lips brush her hair and smiled to herself. The pounding of his heart beneath her ear pleased her. It spoke of his passion for her. Her hand slid over his chest and she pressed her palm against his thundering heart.

He lifted her chin to stare down at her. His gaze swept over her passion-flushed face. His chiselled face darkened into an angry scowl. 'Stop looking at me like that,' he snapped at her.

'Like what?,' she asked, gazing up at him with a dreamy smile on her soft ruby lips, which were moist from his torrid kisses.

His frown turned sardonic. 'As though I'm your dream lover and you're madly in love with me,' he said cruelly.

She stepped out the warmth of his embrace. 'I was not aware that I was looking at you in any particular fashion. And I am most certainly not madly in love with you.'

He sneered at that remark. 'I'd hate to see how you kiss a man when your feelings are involved,' he drawled with sarcasm as he ran his knuckles over her flushed cheek. 'I doubt he'd survive.'

Jerking her face away, she lifted her chin defiantly. 'I've not the slightest notion what you are talking about,' she told him curtly. 'You provide little more than a passing amusement for me, my lord. As an avid student of life, I regard our encounters as merely experiential. Every woman should be kissed by a rake at least once in her life. But you may believe me when I say that my feelings could never be involved where you are concerned.'

'Good.' The encroaching sounds of couples conversing wafted through the night air. He dropped his hand to his side and quickly stepped a respectable distance away from her. 'Let's keep it that way, shall we?'

She blinked at him in all innocence and confusion. 'I cannot imagine how else it could be.'

'I deuced well can,' he growled.

Her ingenuous gaze searched his face. 'Whatever do you mean?,' she asked him wide-eyed.

He shook his head at her. 'Never mind. I'll save that lesson for another time, my dear young lady.'

Her expression soured. 'My lord,' she imparted in a crisp tone, 'you appear to be under a grave misapprehension. Allow me to make my feelings patently clear. I desire nothing from you, much less, as you put it, another lesson.'

'I sincerely doubt that,' he snorted with a sardonic edge. 'At present, you may satisfy me with an explanation. What the devil do you think you are doing slipping into Hobson's ballroom in the middle of the night?'

CHAPTER 5

His imperious tone rankled Celeste to the core. She turned away from him and leaned against the stone balustrade to gaze up at the diamond-scattered night sky.

'Surely,' she said, resentment making her tone bitter, 'my distraught sister wasted no time in relating the circumstances which precipitated my appearance here tonight.'

His hand slipped around her upper arm; the warmth of his touch singed her bare skin. He turned her to face him. 'I should very much like to hear your explanation.' His gaze flickered over her face. One end of his mouth curved slightly. 'I am persuaded it will be quite colorful.'

She drew a deep impatient breath. 'Very well, my lord. As you appear to be bent on ruining everything except me for a second time, you leave me no choice. I must take you into my confidence. I am a journalist.'

His dark brows snapped together. 'A journalist?' he repeated, dumbfounded. 'The devil you say! I don't believe it. You're having me on?'

'It is all perfectly true,' she replied coolly. 'I am a journalist, my lord.'

He gave her a dubious glance. 'What Banbury tale is this?'

'It is no Banbury tale,' she countered firmly.

He scoffed at her. 'No reputable newspaper would employ a woman.'

'I never laid claim to being employed by a newspaper. You merely assumed it.'

He gave her a disparaging look. 'Then pray,' he asked pointedly, 'how do you write articles?'

'Tony visits the office on my behalf.'

He looked startled. 'Tony?,' he echoed in amazement.

'Most of the time. If he is too busy, he gives my articles to his secretary, Mr Bridges, who delivers them to *The Chronicle* newspaper office on Fleet Street.'

Simon went dead still. 'Not *The London Chronicle*?,' he asked, shock mingling with incredulity.

'Yes. Are you familiar with it?,' she asked brightly.

'Vaguely,' he muttered pensively. Why was he shocked? Nothing about this wayward changeling should surprise him. This, however, he had not expected.

'Perhaps you have read some of my articles on fossils and nature?' she asked, eager for his opinion.

'What?,' he mumbled, his thoughts preoccupied.

'Have you read them? My articles, I mean.'

'Er, no –,' he shook his head, '– I haven't.'

'Oh,' she said, dejected. 'Well, they are quite good. Some of them.'

'I'll bear that in mind,' he retorted, an acerbic edge to his voice.

'I am particularly proud of the account of my visit to the Royal Stables,' she was saying.

He pulled a frown. 'Royal Stables? I was given to understand women wrote about fashions from France or, at the very worst, the latest *on-dits*?'

She gave him a crushing look. 'As far as I am concerned, horseflesh is far superior to fashions, my lord.'

He raised his eyebrows. 'Ah, I see. How the devil did you manage to get yourself hired?'

She shrugged. 'It wasn't terribly difficult. Tony was immensely helpful in securing the position.'

Simon rubbed his chin thoughtfully. 'He must have been very persuasive to convince the proprietor.'

'I don't think I could have done it without his kind intervention. Not that I lack talent,' she hastened to add, 'but it is a very competitive field. As you know, women are barred from anything interesting altogether.'

'Somehow,' he replied with dry indulgence, 'I am not the least surprised you feel that way. Tell me, what does your precious C.C. Dunhill think about this unconventional pastime of yours?' he asked, his silver gaze gently mocking her.

She laughed out loud. 'He is quite devoted to it.'

Simon's jaw tightened. Her devotion to that miscreant infuriated him. Devil take it! He wasn't jealous, was he? Of an infantile twit who had a positive knack for getting herself into compromising situations? Hardly. 'Is that so? How convenient,' he muttered.

'Yes, it is, rather.'

'You are saving yourself for him, I take it?' he asked, observing her with a keen gaze.

She hesitated for a moment. Her lips curled slyly. 'In a manner of speaking,' she allowed, 'I suppose I am.'

One brow arched in mild inquiry. 'Marriage, I assume, is out the question?'

She wrinkled up her nose. 'Suffice to say, it is not welcomed.'

His lips thinned. Obviously the blackguard was a married man who preyed on naïve innocents. 'He sounds like a charming fellow,' he averred with scorn. 'Your future husband may not take kindly to your avid preoccupation – what then?'

Her eyes widened to the size of china saucers. '*Future husband*?' she spluttered and burst into gales of laughter. 'Oh, my lord,' she managed to say, her shoulders shaking with mirth 'you are under a grave misapprehension.'

'What, may I ask, is so diverting?' His voice held a distinct chill.

'I fear you have misunderstood the circumstance entirely,' she told him, struggling to maintain a straight face.

His eyes narrowed on her bemused countenance. 'And what circumstance might that be?' He liked being at a disadvantage about as much as he enjoyed being the object of laughter.

'It is quite simple. There is no such person.'

His intent gaze searched her face. 'What do you mean, no such person?,' he barked. 'I was given to understand that you were in love with the cad.'

A gurgle of incorrigible laughter escaped her throat. 'In love? I don't see how that is possible.'

Unamused, he asked roughly, 'And why not?'

'C.C. Dunhill does not exist. Well,' she amended, serious at last, 'not in the flesh.'

The fact that the little chit had misled him – deliberately – and he'd fallen for it, irked him no small degree.

'What the devil do you mean,' he snapped, angry at himself for believing her wild amorous tale in the first place, 'he does not exist?'

'I created C.C. Dunhill as a pen name.'

'You did what?,' he practically roared at her.

'I made him up,' she said with pride. 'He enables me to write my articles. Very helpful fellow, don't you think?'

'Mmm,' he muttered, 'quite.' No wonder the blasted name, Dunhill, had been oddly familiar to him. He'd probably seen it countless times and never made the connection.

'As you so aptly pointed out, I couldn't very well use my real name.'

'No. You couldn't.' He flashed an approving smile. She was more clever than he'd imagined. Resourceful too. In spite of his firm conviction that she was a headstrong fool, he could not help but admire her tenacity. He was right about her. She was an original.

'Dashed clever of you. I don't suppose the newspaper proprietor has any inkling?' he asked archly.

She gave him a forbidding look. 'Heavens no. It would not do for him to learn of it. I hope I may rely on you to remain silent?'

'I think I can manage that,' he said, his tone exceedingly dry.

'Thank you, my lord,' she said with an obvious rush of relief. She cocked her curly head to one side and smiled at him. 'For a notorious rake you have proven to be exceptionally discreet.'

He returned her scampish smirk with a crooked grin of his own. 'And for an untried schoolgirl, you, my lovely, are full of surprises. What lurid information are you in hot pursuit of at the moment?'

'It just so happens,' she explained, warming to her subject, 'I knew that poor unfortunate girl who was murdered. Her name was Lady Jane Greenly. She was the debutante daughter of the Earl of Bellingham, who has suffered a serious attack upon hearing the grievous news. No one seems to be doing anything to catch the killer. So,' she said on a shrug, 'I decided to take action.'

He cocked an intrigued brow. 'Oh, you did, did you?' Shaking his head at her, he crossed his arms over his chest and leaned back against the balustrade. 'I expect I should have my head examined. For the moment, you have my attention. Proceed.'

'Whose company do you suppose she was keeping most recently?,' she asked with titillating suspense.

'Hobson.'

'You are quite adept at this, my lord,' she mocked lightly. 'Jane was last seen alive at a party given by Hobson himself.'

He gave her a quelling look. 'I presume you've come to the ludicrous conclusion, based on their brief association, that Hobson killed her?'

She shrugged. 'I haven't the foggiest idea. Three other men have danced attendance at her side over the last few months as well. Notably, Lord Everly, Lord Grimes and Viscount Lindsey. All three were present the night she disappeared. I think each warrants further scrutiny, do you not agree?'

Simon shook his head. What the devil had come over him of late? Was he actually giving credence to this preposterous theory?

'No. I do not. Just because a gentleman dances the cotillion with a lady does not necessarily mean he's strangled her.'

She stiffened at his harsh rebuke. 'I did not say it did,' she replied, her tone crisp. 'I merely suggested it was worthy of further inspection.'

'For an intelligent woman,' he snorted derisively, 'you are remarkably naïve.'

'Why do you say that?,' she asked peevishly.

'For the simple reason, dear heart –' his voice was laced with acrimony ' – no one cares about that poor, unfortunate girl. Members of the *ton* do not care to read about murder and mayhem.' He paused to snicker. 'In fact, they rather prefer to ignore it altogether.'

Greatly distressed by his cavalier attitude, she imparted crossly, 'I don't know how you can be so callous. Do you not care a whit about poor Jane?'

He dragged his hand through his hair. 'With your penchant for brotherly love,' he remarked dryly, 'why didn't you join a religious order?'

She looked slightly taken aback. 'I scarcely think I am a proper candidate for a religious order, my lord.'

'I collect you are right,' he drawled with heavy sarcasm. 'You lack the self-discipline.'

She chafed at his condescending tone. 'You really are a heartless brute,' she snapped.

He flashed a rakish grin. 'Quite right, my dear. A rogue and a cur.' He etched a mocked bow. 'I plead guilty to both counts.'

She pursed her lips with displeasure. 'I cannot credit a man of your intellect and experience blatantly disregarding the tenuous future of your own country. Have you not read the papers? They are full of nothing else these days but a call for reform. Parliament's Six Acts are an outrage. It is small wonder we can bear such oppression.'

He wasn't quite sure what surprised him more; the fact that a woman had read the newspaper or that she dared to voice her opinion. Either way, he could not resist the urge to enter the fray. He had to admit, he admired her pluck. But she was entirely mistaken.

'That kind of parliamentary reform is too extreme for the more moderate masses to accept,' he murmured with satirical haughtiness.

'On the contrary,' she countered hotly, 'William Cobbett and others like him are precisely the kind of journalist this country requires. Reform is a must. We should be shouting it from the rooftops.'

He crossed his arms over his chest and fixed her with a cynical look. No wonder she'd expressed resentment towards the current Cabinet. The third of the Six Acts passed last December inflicted a stamp duty on all newspapers. It was widely considered a blow to the more radical journalist. It must have infuriated her to no small degree given her firm conviction that she was a bona fide journalist.

'Surely you are not advocating radical reform? Or are you one of those who favours the dissolution of the Cabinet altogether?,' he asked before he could stop himself.

He frowned slightly. How the devil had he gotten drawn into a political discussion with a feckless female on a balcony in the middle of a ball he was not meant to attend? Good Lord, she was the most unconventional creature he'd ever met.

She looked at him askance. 'You cannot mean to say you agree with Parliament's newest repressive code? They've no right to curtail public meetings yet again. Why, the newspaper stamp duty is an outrage.'

'An outrage that pales in comparison to your insipid notion that an article in the paper could affect social standards,' he countered with thinly veiled ridicule.

'Can you not imagine what it would mean to me to have the opportunity to prove myself both as a woman and a journalist?,' she asked, youthful exuberance etched on her face.

He eyed her sceptically. 'It means that much to you, does it? You actually fancy yourself as a serious journalist?'

'My work is the most significant part of my life,' she told him solemnly.

To his credit, he managed to keep a straight face.

'More important than you can ever imagine. I would give anything to be able to write serious stories. Something more interesting than the Rosetta Stone and Lord Elgin's Grecian marble statues at the British Museum.'

'I see. Well, in that case, perhaps you ought to pursue a really intriguing story for the paper. It might not be as outlandish as murder, but it would garner C.C. Dunhill the respect you seek. Say, something on Thomas Brown. He is giving a lecture this week on "Philosophy of the Human Mind". You might attend and summarize his discussion for the paper.'

She gazed up at him, her clear blue eyes brimming with admiration. 'Do you honestly believe such an article would secure me a foothold among serious journalists?'

He flashed a complaisant smile. 'It is a start. And certainly well worth a try. He is well-respected among his peers. I think you'll find his theories rather interesting. Such an article will go a long way towards proving you a capable writer.'

'I do hope so, my lord,' her soft, breathless voice rang with longing.

His gaze drifted over her sparkling eyes and rosy cheeks and captured her languid blue depths. Of its own volition, his hand reached out and caressed her cheek. The pad of his thumb traced her cheekbone. Her full moist lips, parted in warm invitation, were too strong a temptation. Dragging air into his lungs, he summoned his self-control and dropped his hand to his side.

'At the moment, I think it imperative that I get you home before you get yourself into a situation beyond your capabilities.'

She blinked at him in astonishment. 'I've yet to undertake my inquiries,' she sputtered in dismay.

His voice brooked no disagreement as he told her, 'You won't do anything. Let me assure you, my dear girl, this story of yours will never grace the pages of any newspaper. Ever.'

Squaring her shoulders, she tossed back tartly, 'Anything is possible.'

'Verily,' he growled, 'it might snow in summer. But that doesn't mean you'll ever get to write that blasted story.'

Her chin lifted a notch. 'Murder should be a matter for public concern. Whoever committed this heinous crime is obviously a desperate, undesirable sort who attacked a helpless young woman. He might strike again.'

'Rubbish,' Simon barked, 'it was an isolated event. A simple case of a poor unfortunate girl being in the wrong place at the wrong time. Where do you come up with these ill-conceived notions of yours?'

Her fiery blue eyes sparkled with temper. 'They are not ridiculous. My theory is every bit as plausible as your explanation.'

'Perhaps you should confine your pursuits to more feminine issues,' he imparted with an infuriating air of superiority. 'I do believe it is best to stick to what one knows.'

Slapping her hands on her hips, she flung at him, 'Next, I suppose you'll be claiming that my constitution is too delicate to delve into such things.'

'As a matter of fact –'

'Poppycock!' she blustered angrily.

Simon seriously questioned the wisdom of conversing with someone who used the expression *poppycock*.

'If I had been tossed into the river, I'd want someone to care enough to find out who'd done it,' she cried with energy.

He heaved a weary sigh. Wasn't that precisely his rationale for pursuing Emily's malefactor? His lips thinned. Dash it all. She had him on that point.

'What the devil do you hope to find poking about Hobson's estate?,' he demanded roughly.

She gave him a petulant glare. 'Clues, naturally,' she muttered dryly.

He shook his head at her. 'Forget it. You, my headstrong little hoyden, will gather nothing. Least of all clues. Henceforth, you will confine your powers of investigation to the mundane. I, for one, would sleep a lot better. It is high time we were on our way. I've had enough of your foolishness.'

She heaved a frustrated sigh. 'Have you not heard a word I've said? I cannot leave now. I may be close to uncovering some very important information.'

'I don't give a damn,' he muttered in a low terse tone. He reached out and took her roughly by the arm.

She dug her heels in. 'If you think to drag me from the premises,' she intoned sharply, 'I warn you, you will regret it. I will scream. Loudly. And I will cause the most outrageous scene you have ever witnessed. Do you fancy a scandal, my lord?' she taunted him.

His dark angry gaze threatened to impale her. 'You little . . . witch,' he breathed.

She flashed a puckish grin. 'I thought you'd see things my way,' she said, retrieving her arm from his clutches. 'Now that you have arrived,' she remarked, adjusting her long white gloves, 'you might prove useful. I do believe you are the perfect choice to aid in my investigation.'

The muscle leapt in his cheek. 'Why is that?' he bit out.

She cocked a raised brow. 'Who better to connive his way to an upstairs bedchamber than a notorious rake?' she tossed back saucily.

He gave her a hard, menacing look.

A few minutes later, the pair slipped from the packed ballroom into the front hall, which was blessedly empty, save for two footmen who flanked the front door. It was with relative ease that the two sleuths managed to pad unobtrusively up the winding staircase.

A quick visual inspection down the long hallway confirmed Simon's worst fears. Damned place was probably lousy with inner and outer corridors, not too mention adjoining rooms, he thought, uttering a string of oaths that would have put a sailor to the blush.

'My lord,' Celeste gasped in dismay, 'I am shocked at you.' Her brow knitted slightly. 'And not at all certain I know what you mean by those words, precisely.'

He dismissed her shock with an icy glare. 'Has it occurred to you,' he asked through gritted teeth, 'that we may well have to search all of the bedrooms? It could take half the night to locate Hobson's room.'

Gazing about her, she chewed pensively on her lower lip. 'Mmm, quite.'

But she was not daunted by the prospect. Oh, no. Wild horses would not keep her from her moral quest.

'We'd best get started. You take the left side and I'll take the right.'

Grunting his assent, Simon trudged down the hall to make a cursory inspection of the first room which he dearly hoped was vacant. Twenty minutes later, a frown of consternation touched his lips. He'd searched three different bedrooms with no success. Sooner or later, he was bound to stumble upon an occupied room. What then?

Devil take it! Creeping around Hobson's home in the middle of the night was utterly insupportable. How the deuce had he gotten into this outrageous situation? He not did relish the notion of being caught in one of Hobson's bedrooms. He raked his hand through his hair. This had gone far enough. He'd find the damned wench and toss her over his shoulder if need be. But they were leaving.

He opened the door to the next bedroom and froze. Someone was inside. Lord, he hoped it was his little hellion and not some unsuspecting guest preparing for bed. He strained to get a good look at the occupant's face through the crack in the doorway. His view was partially obstructed by the back of the door. It was definitely a woman. As she got down on her haunches to rifle through some papers, his gaze ran over the narrow waist and nicely rounded bottom.

Titling her head to one side, her profile came into his view. A slow smile spread across his face. Only one person of his acquaintance had an adorable upturned nose and blazing red hair. Unless he was greatly mistaken, the silly chit had actually stumbled upon Hobson's bedchamber.

Simon slipped inside the room and quietly eased the door shut. Creeping on tip toes, his arm snaked out and snatched her against him. She let out a shriek and fought her would-be assailant, kicking and squirming towards freedom. Her heel connected painfully with his shin bone. He let out a strangled groan. He clamped his hand over her mouth.

'Hush,' he snarled angrily against her ear. 'It's me, you little fool.' She stopped squirming.

'May I assume you have found Hobson's bed-chamber?,' he whispered softly against her cheek.

She quickly stepped away from his treacherous warmth. 'Indeed I have,' she said clearing her throat. 'Look what I have discovered,' she exclaimed with pride, holding up a gold signet ring with a snake coiled around a naked maiden.

Simon's dark brows snapped together. 'Where did you get that?,' he demanded, snatching the object from her fingers.

'It obviously belongs to Hobson. Does it appear familiar to you, my lord?,' she asked studying Simon's pensive frown.

He glanced at her. 'Why do you ask?,' he queried with trepidation.

She shrugged. 'Unless I am greatly mistaken, I thought I saw a light of recognition in your eyes.'

'Did you?,' he asked nonchalantly and handed the ornate gold piece back to her.

She examined the ring with curiosity. 'It is a perfectly hideous piece, I must say,' she murmured rhetorically. 'Is it of significance, do you suppose?'

He shook his head. 'I doubt it.'

An impish smile tugged at her lips. 'Well, you'd be mistaken. What would you say, my lord, if I told you that a gold medallion with the same insignia was found clutched in Jane Greenly's hand?'

Momentarily stunned, Simon quickly recovered himself. 'I'd say you have an overactive imagination.'

Reluctantly, Simon admitted tonight was not a complete loss after all. He'd stumbled on to a very important element in his quest for Emily's malefactor – or rather his wild, impetuous hoyden had. His initial assumption that the ring was an important link was entirely correct. Apparently, signet rings like the one in his possession were not as rare as he had once believed. The snake and the maiden were obviously a symbol. But of what?

No wonder Paine resisted being questioned. One woman was dead and another disgraced and abandoned. The ring must signify something untoward.

Quite an interesting development in the case, one about which Mr Crawford would shortly hear. Of course, Simon had no intention of telling the wayward chit the truth. The last thing the little hellion needed was encouragement.

'Well,' she said on a sigh, 'I doubt it was Hobson who killed poor Jane. He'd scarcely have a ring and a medallion with the same hideous insignia. What *do* you think the snake coiled around the maiden is meant to signify?' she asked, examining the disgusting piece with a critical eye. 'Why would two separate men wear the same emblem? It is no coincidence. The symbol is some sort of link between the two, it must be.'

'I have no idea. Put the ring back. Let's get out of here before someone takes exception to this lamentable interest of yours.'

She looked at him as if he had suddenly sprouted six heads. 'We cannot leave now, just when we've stumbled onto something valuable. Hobson may not have killed Jane. But you can be certain he knows who did. For all we know, other rings or medallions like this one exist.'

Simon was impressed. She was clever and resourceful and playing with fire. 'Possibly,' he imparted, his tone curt, 'but I, for one, have no wish to be waylaid by one of the guests and forced to issue what promises to be an exceedingly embarrassing explanation for our presence.'

'We've got to find the owner of the medallion,' Celeste affirmed, her voice determined. 'Who do you suppose it is?,' she asked almost to herself. 'Everly, Lindsey or Grimes?'

'At the moment,' Simon grumbled irritably, 'I don't suppose anything save for the fact that we are treading on perilous territory. We are in grave danger of scandal.' Grabbing her by the hand, he threaded his fingers through hers and dragged her towards the door. 'With any luck, we can slip out down the back stairs and no one will be the wiser.' He opened the door a crack and peered out into the hallway.

Their hasty departure was interrupted by the untimely arrival of a lively group of lords and ladies meandering up the stairs to seek their beds.

'Damnation!,' he spat under his breath. Ducking out into the hall, they sneaked into what Simon prayed was a deserted bedchamber and closed the door.

He crossed the darkened room to inspect the way down through the window. It was far too high to jump without breaking a leg.

'Thanks to your damned foolishness,' he tossed over his shoulder, 'we're stuck here for the moment, if not the night.'

At seeing his dark angry scowl, Celeste blanched. 'There must be some way out?,' she offered in a panicked voice, the enormity of their predicament sinking in at last.

He eyed her coolly. 'Nothing leaps to mind. What do you suggest?'

'I –'

'Hush,' he snapped, silencing her effectively. 'Someone is coming.'

Muffled sounds of conversation drew closer. Footsteps shuffled along the carpet beyond the door and came to a standstill. He could hear feminine laughter and the hushed murmurings of voices.

Darting a glance around the room in search of somewhere to hide, his gaze came to rest on the mahogany armoire. He shook his head. 'First place they'd think to look.'

She gave him a startled look. Planting her hands on her slender hips, she asked, 'Precisely how many times have you been faced with this particular dilemma, my lord?'

He slanted her a dark frown. 'Get under the bed.'

'Under the bed!' She recoiled in disgust at the mere idea. 'It is dark and dusty under there. I – I'll get filthy. And I'd ruin my best gown.'

He emitted a furious growl. They were about to discovered alone in a bedchamber and she was worried about soiling her damned dress!

'Over here.' His fingers bit into her wrist as he dragged her across the room toward the enormous trunk against the far wall.

'What on earth are you doing?,' she whispered fiercely.

He threw open the top. 'Saving your honor and what is left of my reputation,' he replied and shoved her none too gently into a sea of silk and satin dresses.

Her face sank into a billowing satin gown that threatened to suffocate her. Gracious, she thought, struggling to disengage a whalebone stay from her rib cage, this investigative work was decidedly unglamourous.

'Squeeze in,' he hissed and pushed her further into the satin abyss.

'I cannot breathe!,' she squealed.

He slammed the lid shut behind her, but it would not close.

'Damnation,' he growled and yanked her out of the encroaching fabrics that threatened to suffocate her.

'Where should we try next?,' she asked, sputtering feathers that seemed to have invaded her mouth.

His glance shot quickly around the dimly-lit room. 'The curtains,' he said, propelling her towards the large casement windows.

'What about you?,' she cried, casting a nervous glance over her shoulder at the door that was about to spring open.

'Don't fret,' he said and shoved her behind the green velvet curtains, 'I'll think of something.'

She opened her mouth to protest, but he silenced her and pulled the curtains shut.

The click of the bedroom door latch found Simon without a place to hide. Casually, he leaned his palm against the window ledge and essayed an indolent pose.

'Simon Barclay?' A shrill, horribly coarse, vaguely familiar female voice pealed through the dimly-lit room.

He shut his eyes for a moment, hoping the obscene creature was an aberration. She was not. He swore under his breath and cursed his bad luck.

Of all the bedchambers to get caught in, why did it have to be Harriet Declaire's? Never before had he lamented the small, intimate social circle to which he belonged.

She flashed a wicked smile. 'I don't believe it. Is it really you?' A derisive chuckle rent the air. 'I thought I saw your head duck into my bedchamber. But I wasn't sure. It is you, is it not?'

Curiosity got the best of Celeste. She edged the velvet curtains apart and peered around Simon's shoulder. Gracious heavens! Bedecked in the most ostentatious purple and pink silk gown, the woman fairly wounded the eye.

'Who is *that*?,' Celeste whispered, appalled by the obstreperous creature cannoning toward them.

'That,' he bit out under his breath and snapped the curtain shut, 'is Harriet Declaire.'

'Of course it is, darling,' the object of his disgust remarked. She drifted across the shadowy room to where he stood guard before the bulging drape.

'Who were you expecting?' Lady Declaire asked with a leer as she ran the tip of her ivory fan over his muscular, broad shoulder. 'How clever of you to slip inside when no one was looking. I had no idea you were here tonight,' she mused, her hungry gaze sliding over him with licentious delight.

The muscle in his jaw clenched. 'Nor I you,' he retorted with a tight smile. He couldn't quite believe his ill luck. The last place he wanted to get cornered was in Harriet Declaire's bedroom. How the devil was he going to emerge unscathed from this débâcle?

She pouted playfully. 'You will tease me, you wretched man. But I don't mind. I do like surprises. We both know why you sneaked up here. Let's not pretend.'

'I hoped you'd understand,' he murmured non-committally as he racked his brain for an escape route.

Her lips curled licentiously. 'I knew you could never resist a night in my arms. You won't regret it, I

113

promise you,' she crooned, running her palms over his chest.

Simon's face set in stone. He might have known the crass woman would jump at the chance to eradicate the dent to her otherwise colossal ego. How the devil was he going to escape without obliging her ferocious appetite?

'Be rough with me, Simon, I like it hard and fast,' she moaned and pressed a kiss to his mouth.

A squeal of shock emanated from behind the curtains.

Lady Declaire reeled back. 'What was that?' she asked, a suspicious gleam in her eye.

Simon crossed his arms over his chest. 'What was what?,' he asked blandly.

'I heard a noise. It was coming from behind the curtains.'

'Oh, that. It was nothing,' he prevaricated badly. 'Probably just a field mouse.'

She fixed him with a dubious look. 'Mice? This close to London?'

He shrugged. 'A rat, perhaps?' he offered lamely.

'In Lord Hobson's guest chamber?' She shook her head. 'I think not. You're hiding a woman behind there.'

'Don't be ridiculous,' Simon scoffed at her. 'You said it yourself, I came up here to be with you.'

Her eyes narrowed contemptuously on his guile-less façade. 'I think you slipped in here looking for a bed and I surprised you. Don't look so innocent – it's been done before.'

'Has it?,' he asked in poorly-feigned ignorance.

'Move out of my way,' she snarled.

'Now, Harriet calm yourself. I am sure we can –'

'I'll alert the whole house,' she vowed acidly. 'We wouldn't want that, now, would we?'

Simon expelled a defeated sigh and stepped aside. Lady Declaire tore back the curtains. Celeste etched an embarrassed half-smile.

'I knew it!,' Lady Declaire shrieked. 'You vile scoundrel!' She turned on Simon, her fists clenched. 'How dare you use my room to bed a cheap tart?'

Celeste blinked at the vulgar woman in shock. She turned her stunned gaze toward Simon. 'Is she suggesting –'

'Yes,' came his curt reply. 'She is.'

'That is the most insulting thing I've ever heard,' Celeste declared, the picture of righteous indignation. 'For your information,' she imparted in a huff, 'we are not on intimate terms. Well,' she amended, 'at least, not in the manner *you* suggest.'

Simon's eyes drifted shut. He stroked the bridge of his nose with his thumb and forefinger. He dearly wished she'd stop while she was ahead. Flattered as he was by her attempt to save him from total disgrace, the situation was rapidly deteriorating into total mayhem. A timely exit was imperative.

Lady Declaire eyed the impertinent chit with keen interest. 'I know you,' she snarled, her face pinched with loathing. 'You're the strumpet he was with at Holmes's garden party when he might have had me.'

Simon emitted a miserable groan and rolled his eyes heavenward. At this rate, he'd be lucky if Lady Declaire did not rouse the house with her shrewish ranting. News of his sneaking into Hobson's ballroom and cavorting with Celeste Wentworth in an upstairs bedchamber would be just the sort of thing to put his reputation over the edge.

And Harriet Declaire was just the sort of woman who'd do it. If this evening's scandal ever reached his family's ears, Simon would be banished from the single familial event he was welcome to attend – Christmas dinner.

Simon's arm slid around Celeste's waist. 'Time to leave.'

But she did not look inclined to heed him. Her statue-like stance could best be described as horrified. Apparently, scenes like this were something of a novelty for girls who lead sheltered lives. Damnation! It was not exactly a normal occurrence for him either.

'*She* called *me* a strumpet!,' she spluttered in shocked dismay.

'I know. I heard,' came his clipped reply.

Before Celeste knew what he was about, his arm slipped under her knees and he swept her off the ground. As if she weighed little more than a feather, he cradled her against his chest.

Flabbergasted, she cried, 'My lord, put me down right this instant.'

Seething, Lady Declaire watched as the object of her fantasies whisked the infantile tart off her feet.

Ignoring the squirming bundle in his arms, Simon addressed the irate Lady Declaire in a remarkably calm voice, given the outrageous circumstance,

'Good evening, madam, I apologize for the misunderstanding.' With that he marched from the room, Celeste securely nestled in his arms.

'This is the second time you've refused me, Simon Barclay,' Lady Declaire screeched and threw a pillow at the door through which he'd escaped her clutches.

Her fisted hands flexed with rage at her sides. It was too much to be borne. She'd make him pay.

Her fingers drilled a tattoo against her upper arm. As she paced the room in a furious prowl, a scheme took root in her mind. She knew exactly how to fix that rogue. A wicked smile spread across her feline face – he'd be sorry he ever insulted Harriet Declaire.

CHAPTER 6

Celeste objected strenuously to the vice-like grips intimately clamped over her rib cage and thighs. It was most disconcerting to be pressed against a brick wall of pure masculinity. He smelled wonderfully male – like soap and a hint of lemon, she noticed with a rush of warmth. Disconcerted by how much she enjoyed her current position, she wriggled with energy to be set free.

But it was of little consequence, for his iron fingers dug into her flesh with renewed energy.

'I suggest you act the part of the damsel in distress if you wish to avoid a confrontation with our un-doubtedly dismayed host,' came Simon's lethal warning against her ear.

His breath was warm and soft against her neck. She gulped. 'Oh, dear.' Her eyes grew round, 'I see your point.'

'I thought you might,' he murmured, his tone dry.

Her arm swooped through the air in a wide half-circle. She clutched her forehead in a melodramatic fashion and uttered a painful moan.

'*Ooh*, I am in agony, my lord,' she groaned and winced with mock pain. 'I shan't be able to manage on my own. How kind you are to lend me aid.'

'Much better,' he said for her ears only. His voice was husky and low. And she found herself enjoying the moment far more than was proper under the mortifying circumstances. 'I do believe London's premiere actresses would be pea green with envy, my dear.'

Simon hurried down the hallway past the crowd of astonished guests towards what he hoped were the back stairs. He emerged inside the bustling kitchen. The servants all stopped what they were doing and stared at the finely-clad gentleman hoisting a lady in his arms.

'Sprained ankle,' he explained as he headed for the servants' entrance.

'Ooh!,' Celeste moaned and let her eyes drift shut in agony, 'I shall never walk again.'

As soon as they reached the garden entrance, her performance drew to a close.

'You may now release me, my lord,' she instructed in a prim voice. She was far more affected by his proximity than she showed. It was unseemly to be held by a man who was not a lady's brother, or the very least, her husband. It was also wildly exciting. The last time she'd felt so deliciously wicked was, not surprisingly, in Lord Holmes's library.

Simon's carriage was waiting in the dark sheltered foliage of Hobson's trees. Yanking open the door, he dropped the rambunctious bundle down on the black leather seat. Before she had the chance to reprimand him for his outrageous conduct, he disappeared. Her mouth snapped shut.

Scrambling to set herself to rights, she heard his voice firing unintelligible orders at his driver.

Mortification consumed her. Gracious, had he actually swept her off her feet and tramped through the house with her like a sack of potatoes? He had. She bit her lower lip. My, it was quite a disturbing feeling to be manhandled.

'Just what gives you the right,' she blazed when he appeared at last, 'to parade through Hobson's home treating me like a wrapped parcel from Bond Street?'

He crossed his arms over his massive chest and regarded her with a cynical smirk. 'Age, wisdom, experience and the undying conviction that a scandal must be avoided at all costs despite the fact that a wealthy spoiled brat like you is out for a perverse, cheap adventure,' came his scathing retort.

His caustic remark wounded her to the core. She was glad the carriage was dark, it concealed her red, hot cheeks. Had the excitement of the challenge overtaken her senses completely? No. Certainly not. How like the Dragon to overlook the salient facts. She'd made a great discovery this evening. Hobson was somehow involved with the villain responsible for poor Jane's death.

She turned away from his haughty countenance. 'I scarcely know what to say in the face of such utter humiliation.'

'Now that is an occasion, to be sure,' he drawled out.

'Was it strictly necessary for you carry me from the house?'

120

His eyes glinted dangerously. 'How else did you suggest I extricate the two of us from a potentially disastrous circumstance?,' he gritted.

Before she could utter a response, the conveyance hit a deep rut in the road. Her shoulders slammed against the black leather squabs. She heard him chuckle at her efforts to stay upright. His lordship, she noted with irritation, had scarcely moved a smidgen. She glared at him.

'No gentleman would have dared.'

He turned the full force of his piercing grey gaze on her. 'I've told you before,' he said his tone ominous, 'I am not a gentleman.'

She was too annoyed to heed the subtle warning he'd issued. 'So I've noticed,' she flung at him. 'I've never been so mortified in all my life!'

Unruffled, he muttered in an exceedingly dry tone, 'I find that very hard to believe,' and settled back comfortably on the seat across from her.

She crossed her arms over her chest and fixed him with a mute look of burning contempt.

'Is this all the thanks I get for saving you?,' he queried with mild sarcasm. 'You really are going to have to do something about your manners. They are deplorable.'

'I do not know how you have the nerve to speak to me of manners when you keep such lovely company yourself, my lord,' she commented on a derisive snicker. 'Who was that horrid creature?'

He shrugged his broad shoulders slightly. 'No one of consequence. At least,' he murmured with a pensive air, 'not before tonight.'

She blinked at him. What did he mean by that cryptic remark? 'I am all astonishment, my lord. That *woman*,' she averred with disdain, 'insulted your honor and thoroughly offended my sense of decency. If she were a man, you'd have called her out, would you not?'

He flashed a sardonic smirk that conveyed his opinion. 'No. I would not. In any event, she is not a man; in fact, she is not even a lady. Let's just forget the entire sordid event, shall we?'

'Very well, my lord, if that is the way you feel about it. But I must say, I am surprised you are not more enraged.'

'May I remind you –,' his voice held a barbed note, '– if you hadn't been argumentative, that charming scenario could have been avoided entirely.'

'I am not argumentative,' she tossed back tartly. 'Your arrival caused that unholy scene.'

'I beg to differ,' he countered coolly.

It was dreadfully late. She was exhausted and lacked the energy to launch into recriminations. She peered out the window at the dark, misty, abandoned city street.

'Where are you taking me?,' she asked with a sleepy yawn.

'Home,' he told her, his tone like ice.

Closing her tired eyes, she laid her head back to rest. 'Good,' she said crisply, 'I should like to be dropped off around the back near the gardens, I've left a window open in the servants' quarters. My maid, Fanny, will be waiting for me –'

'Your sister's home,' he interjected curtly.

'Oh.'

Then it struck her. *Her sister's home*! She sat bolt upright. She could never explain her disappearance in the middle of the night when she was supposedly tucked in her bed at Grosvenor Square.

'Stop this carriage immediately. I have no intentions of going to Morely House. Fanny will be worried sick. To say nothing of what Grandfather will say.'

Simon's soft derisive chuckle cut through the darkness. 'That is your dilemma. Perhaps in the future you will consider your actions before behaving so rashly.'

'I am not going –,' she began in a fury, but he leaned forward and pinned her against the seat. Sandwiched between the leather squabs and a wall of pure male muscle, her heart fluttered around in her chest.

'I –' Her startled blue gaze collided with that of the virile, strikingly handsome man looming over her. Her voice died in her throat.

'I will brook no argument from you, little one. I cannot risk being seen with you in the dead of night.' He flashed a crocked smile. 'Seeing you to the garden entrance, servants' quarters or the front door is definitely not an option. I promised your sister I'd return you safe and sound. And I intend to do just that. It's quite a nice ride back to town,' he said in a voice like steel cloaked with black velvet. 'We will have plenty of time to have a nice cosy little chat, you and I. I am eager for you to satisfy my curiosity.'

Her temper ignited. How dare he order her about like a child? Who gave him the right to whisk her off

123

in the middle of the night without so much as a by your leave?

'Well, then, by all means,' she said, her voice dripping with sarcasm, 'ask your fill. Obviously, I am completely at your disposal.'

He smirked at that remark. 'So you are.' His dark hooded gaze slid over her with seductive slowness. Her pulse soared. 'Why did you lead me to believe you were Dunhill's lover?,' he asked, his voice low and husky.

Her eyes widened slightly. *Dunhill's lover*! Heavens, he was direct. And improper. Most improper. But that did not deter the tingle of excitement in the pit of her stomach.

'I did nothing of the sort,' she fired back.

'Oh, yes, you did.' His soft seductive tone swirled about her like a satin caress, all soft and wicked. Her heart lurched madly. She pressed back against the seat.

'You quite led me on,' he murmured huskily, his dark penetrating gaze holding her captive. 'Why?'

The smouldering flame lurking in his silvery depths made her heart jolt. 'I – I did no such thing. I am scarcely responsible for any erroneous conclusions you drew about my character,' she said with a hard swallow and eased, to no avail, away from the encroaching figure of overpowering, raw sensuality.

'You went out of your way to put me off, didn't you?' he asked, leaning closer.

Heavens. She could feel the warmth of his breath tickle her cheek. 'I – I did nothing of the sort,' she stammered, her senses careening.

He planted his palms on either side of her, trapping her between his arms. 'Was it because you were afraid I might decide I rather enjoyed our previous assignation and pursue you?' he asked, a seductive glint in his eye.

Telltale color crept into her cheeks. 'No, I never –'

'Never what?,' he asked, his sinfully provocative gaze flickering over her flushed face as he leaned over her. 'Imagined I'd want a girl like you?'

She wet her lips. 'Why would you?' she asked on a soft sigh of anticipation.

He smiled and dipped his raven head. 'My wicked perverse nature, I guess,' he murmured before he covered her mouth with his.

The hardness of his lips, strong and sure, made her quiver. With a soft groan of surrender she gave herself freely to his savage kiss. Mindless to everything but the feel of his mouth slanting over hers, she wiggled closer to his hard chest and kissed him back.

His hands caressed her hips and thighs and slipped beneath her hem to caress her bare legs. Easing her hem over her knees, his palms slid over her hips, caressed her thighs and in between. She trembled. His lips slanted against hers; hard and searching and deeply passionate while his roving hand stroked her inner thighs and grazed over her soft feminine core. Tilting her hips, eager for his roving caress, she met the sensual invasion of his tongue with her own, twisting, stroking, loving. His hands tightened on her thighs and he dragged her across the seat, pinning her against him. She gasped at the feel of his hard arousal against her.

His mouth grazed her earlobe. 'See what you do to me?,' he whispered thickly.

An involuntary tremor of desire washed over her. Arching her neck back, her eyes fluttered shut. She sighed. She could not understand what was happening to her, but she never wanted this moment of exquisite pleasure to end. He pressed her down on the seat and bent his head to kiss the hollow of her neck. She angled her neck, welcoming his hot wet mouth against her burning skin.

'I want to touch you,' he whispered hoarsely. She expelled a breathless half-moan, half-sigh and arched against him. His fingers fumbled with the buttons on the back of her gown. Yanking her bodice loose, he tore at the soft barrier that concealed her soft ivory globes.

His tortuous palm caressed the soft breast barely concealed by the filmy cotton of her chemise. Gently, he kneaded her soft mound until she nearly ached from the sensation. She felt herself peak beneath his roving hands.

Completely taken under his sensual spell, she could do no more than stare at him, longing mirrored in her torpid blue eyes.

'Kiss me,' he whispered, his voice rough with emotion. 'Kiss me,' he urged her thickly, his mouth hovering above hers.

Her arms wound around his neck. She lifted her face to his. As if they had a mind of their own, her lips found his. Her softly-parted moist lips pressed against his. Groaning, he crushed her to him, devouring the sweetness she offered him. A muffled sound escaped his throat. He deepened the kiss.

126

As his open mouth trailed hot, wet kisses down her neck, she clutched at his shoulders, desperate for more. Tilting her head, she basked in the delicious sensations his searing touch evoked. His hand moved down the length of her back, pressing her against his warm pulsing body.

'Simon . . . Simon,' she whispered breathlessly and covered his mouth with her own. Her soft, supple lips parted to receive his kiss. He covered her burning lips with his, devouring her mouth with bruising hunger. She met the strokes of his tongue, welcomed the sensual invasion and thrust deep into the soft recesses of his mouth.

The soft fabric of her chemise gave way, the warmth of his mouth covered her soft, creamy orbs. His tongue teased and laved the rosy taut marble. Her fingers dug into his hair. She arched against him, convinced she'd go mad from pleasure. When his mouth closed and sucked hard, desire overrode all reason.

She was on fire. Waves of ecstasy throbbed through her, radiating from his hot, wet mouth suckling at her breast, culminating in a dull ache in her soft, feminine core where the hard evidence of his burning desire pulsed against her.

She moved against his tormenting thrusts with some primal need she could not identify or understand. She thought she'd die if he ever stopped touching her. His hand tugged at the thin cotton barrier until the material gave way. He found her honeyed warmth with his probing fingers.

'*Simon*,' she breathed against his mouth. As her body responded to his tormenting strokes, she let out a cry of ecstasy and was carried away by the waves of pure rapture his touch created deep inside her.

His mouth found hers once more for a savage kiss. He parted her legs with his hard muscular thigh. Her eyelashes fluttered open; she gazed up at his passion-flushed face looming above her.

Their eyes met. Time stood still. She could hear their ragged, uneven breathing. Dark, penetrating shards of silver stared down at her, searching her soul. Then he pulled back, leaving her suddenly devoid of his warmth. He raked his hand through his hair. Taking a deep breath, he closed his eyes and shuddered.

'Get up,' he said, his tone cold and strangely taut with anger.

Staring at him in stunned disbelief, hurt written all over her face, she pushed herself up on the seat. 'W-what's the matter?' she stammered in a hurt whisper. 'What have I done?'

He turned on her, baring his teeth in a furious snarl. 'Cover yourself.'

'But I –'

'Cover yourself,' he gritted and drove his hands through his tussled black hair.

Numbly, she sat all the way up and tugged at the hem of her dress, dragging it over her legs. Clumsy fingers fumbled with her chemise. She felt as if she had ten thumbs.

The carriage was silent, save for the uneven creaking of the wheels against the furrowed road.

She did not dart so much as a glance in his direction. Oh, God. Lord, God. She wanted to die, to crawl out of the carriage and die. Simply die. Hurriedly, she straightened her bodice.

It was horrible. Every fibre in her body screamed out for his touch. Her breasts hurt. Her normally soft cotton chemise stung against her hard, achy nipples still moist from his hot searing mouth. The dull throbbing ache between her legs had not subsided. And she had the most mortifying urge to burst into tears.

The carriage mercifully ground to a halt. Without a word, he reached out and thrust the carriage door open. He looked at her as if he hated her. 'Get out.'

She managed to jump down from the carriage. How, she wasn't quite sure – her legs felt like lemon pudding. She heard the door close with a resounding click behind her. The carriage wheels creaked forward. The sound of the driver cracking his whip penetrated her addled brain like a hard slap of reality.

Her breathing settled down to a more even beat. Slowly, her mind returned to some semblance of sanity. He'd warned her that he was no gentleman. Tonight he'd proven it. Tears of shame rolled down her cheeks. She couldn't blame him entirely. She was shocked and humiliated by her body's eager response to his scandalizing touch. She should be thankful he'd put an end to it when he did, for she'd lost the ability to think clearly long ago. She'd slipped into that beautiful sensual haze where all that mattered was lover touching lover. Of course, it wasn't beautiful. And they weren't lovers. They were virtually strangers.

She sobbed even harder. Had she actually lain back in his carriage and let him do those things to her? Let him touch her intimately? Kiss her passionately? She had. The memory burned indelibly in her mind. She'd revelled in every moment of it.

What hurt most was his absolute disgust of her. The look of contempt on his face made her heart ache. She drew a ragged sigh and sniffled. On the other hand, she realized that she despised him. At least, she told herself she had every reason to.

She took a deep, steadying breath. Scrubbing away the tears that stained her cheeks with her palms, she swallowed the painful lump in her throat. Slowly, she pushed open the wrought-iron gate and crossed the darkened courtyard that led to the sleepy Morely House.

She must not be seen like this. Joy would have an attack of the vapours if she knew what had transpired this evening. Celeste had to get hold of herself. But how could she? She couldn't seem to stop shaking. Nor could she stem the wellspring of tears.

It was hardly surprising, she thought. She'd been compromised. Severely so. And in a carriage, no less! So much for life's experiences, she thought tearfully. She was a wreck. And it was just another night in the sinfully debauched existence of the Dragon.

Simon expelled a furious growl and smashed his first against the carriage wall. Damn her! How could he have lost all control over an innocent young chit? Resting his elbows on his knees, he dug both hands into his hair and squeezed his skull between his palms. What was wrong with him? Had he really come that close to having his way with her on the seat of his carriage? What the devil possessed him to act so rashly? He, who had brought his mistresses to the peak of excitement without ever losing control, had been consumed with mindless lust. Never in his entire life had he been so carried away by the woman in his arms that he'd lost his ability to reason. He'd never experienced such overwhelming passion, such all-consuming desire. Thank God he'd come to his senses.

Furious with himself, he pounded the leather seat with his fists. Squeezing his eyes shut, he swore under his breath. How could he have been so damned stupid? He never made mistakes. Not ever. At least, not where women were concerned.

Except for tonight. Another moment, and he'd have made the biggest mistake of his life. He'd have plunged inside her soft, wet, tight welcoming sheath and lost himself completely – the mere thought had him aroused. Her navy blue eyes brimming with unbridled passion, her soft wet lips eagerly parting to receive his kiss and her luxurious, fiery red hair spread across the dark carriage seat had all beckoned him into the sensual fray. And he'd gone. Eagerly. Unable to resist tasting her, touching her, the burning need to possess her had nearly overwhelmed him. In his haste, he'd forgotten her age and inexperience.

The only thing that kept him from making violent love to the little baggage were thoughts of dear Emily seduced and abandoned. He would not wish such an ill fate on Celeste. He chafed at the memory of looking down into those deep blue artless eyes, slumberous with desire, in awe of what were undoubtedly new sensations. Suddenly, he had seen the willing, eager woman in his arms as the beautiful, trusting, young innocent she was. And it stopped him. Cold.

He massaged his forehead. Celeste. Oh, she was aptly named – he'd never experienced such heavenly passion. She could teach *him* a few things about seduction.

It was hard for him to believe that the woman he had cradled in his arms, who'd burned with desire, was a complete novice. As a rule, he'd never paid any attention to virtuous women, never come close to deflowering a virgin. Now he knew why.

It would not do for Tony to catch wind of Simon's pathetic bad judgement, to say nothing of his embarrassing lack of self-restraint. Simon knew all too well what a disclosure would mean. A rendezvous at dawn on the field of honor. One of them would emerge with a bullet through his chest. The very last thing he wanted to do was kill Tony, or be maimed himself, over something as dashed stupid as pure, unmitigated lust.

A firm conviction took hold in his mind. He must never see Celeste Wentworth again. He must never be alone with her. He could not trust himself. He winced at his admission. A fair slip of a girl, a complete innocent, tempted him like no other woman he'd ever known.

CHAPTER 7

It lacked a few minutes before the hour of ten o'clock the following morning when Simon received his unexpected caller. Prying his eyes open, he instructed Evans to send Mr Crawford into the dining room. Clad in his navy brocade dressing-gown, Simon sat sipping a cup of strong, black coffee, and tried, with little success, to wake up.

By the time he'd finally got that damned silly chit out of his system and found sanctuary in sleep, it was around five. He'd fallen into bed and would probably still be there if not for Mr Crawford's arrival. The blasted man had better have a good reason for hauling Simon out of the depths of much-needed slumber. He expelled a lusty yawn. He wasn't feeling at all the thing this morning and was in no mood for another useless discussion. Particularly not when he was paying handsomely for the privilege.

'Mr Crawford, my lord,' Evans announced with stiff displeasure.

'Ah, Crawford,' Simon said and motioned to the chair on his right. 'Sit.'

Evans's eyes threatened to pop out of his head. He cleared his throat and extended his hand for the offensive man's tattered cap. The nervous Mr Crawford chose to clutch the mangy object between his fingers instead. A look of barely-concealed awe crossed his face as he looked around the elegant room. Evans dropped his hand and case a disdainful glance at the man who was ogling with envy the gold candelabras perched on either end of the walnut sideboard.

'Tell me, what has brought you here at this ungodly hour?,' Simon asked, rubbing the sleep from his tired eyes.

The Runner dragged his gaze from the plush surroundings and frowned a bit. 'It's near eleven, my lord,' he mumbled, shifting from foot to foot. 'I thought you'd be up by now.'

Simon flashed a humourless smile. 'Did you? Well, you were obviously wrong. I do hope your powers of observation are better than your judgement.' He yawned hugely. 'But you'd better take a seat and tell me what you've come to say. Your visit is not inauspicious, as I myself have some developments in the case to relate.'

Clearing his throat, Mr Crawford bumbled his way into the expansive dining room and pulled back the richly carved walnut chair. Evans watched in horror as the short stocky visitor slid – grimy, torn pants and all – on to the gold velvet seat.

Simon shook his head at his outraged butler. 'That will be all, Evans. I doubt Mr Crawford intends to abscond with the Barclay silver. It would scarcely be a sound endorsement for future clients,' he drawled dryly.

Evans cleared his throat and etched a stiff, dutiful bow. 'As you wish, my lord.'

'It's right nice of you to offer me a cup o' coffee, my lord,' the Runner said when they were alone.

Imbibing a large gulp of hot coffee, Simon muttered over the rim of his fine white porcelain cup, 'Get to the point.'

'Lady Jane Greenly were that girl we found floatin' in th' Thames not too long ago.'

Celeste would be pleased, Simon thought with a slight smile, at least Bow Street was interested in her dear departed friend. 'Go on.'

'Guess what's so special 'bout 'er case?'

Simon rested his elbows on the table, slowly sipping his coffee. 'I am not certain, but I've a feeling you are about to tell me she was murdered by a man who is fond of wearing a certain gold symbol of a naked maiden and a snake.'

Scatching his balding head Crawford sat back and stared blankly at his employer. 'How'd y'know that?' he asked, astounded.

'For the simple reason she was found clutching a gold medallion with that disgusting insignia.' Yawning hugely, Simon muttered testily, 'I do hope you have something relevant to relate.'

'As a matter o' fact, I 'ave. I think I am on to somthin' important,' Mr Crawford said, slurping his coffee. Doused with four lumps of sugar and an ample slopping of heavy cream, the concoction looked revolting.

Simon's eyes narrowed on the man's crooked toothless grin. 'Well, what is it?'

'Night afore last, our man Paine went to some meetin' at a fancy-lookin' place owned by a certain Lord Everly.'

Frowning pensively, Simon traced the edge of his coffee cup with his forefinger. Everly was one of the names on Celeste's list. How very interesting. 'And?'

'There were five other men who'd gone too. I could see from the street they was havin' a terrible row, 'bout somethin'. Paine was none too popular with the likes of 'em, I can tell you.'

Simon's brow drifted upward in surprise. 'Five men, you say? Were you able to ascertain their identities?'

'Just Paine and Everly. I'm still working on the rest.'

'Everly warrants further scrutiny, I should think. He may well have done away with the Greenly girl.'

'What makes y'say that, milord?'

Simon shrugged his shoulder. 'Consider it a hunch. Am I correct in assuming a stout, grey-haired gentleman was among the group of men you saw?'

The Runner look astonished. 'Right you are, my lord. He was sittin' back watchin' the proceedin's.'

'Mmm. That would be Hobson.'

Mr Crawford blinked at Simon. 'Now, how'd y'know that, milord?'

A slight smile tugged at the corner of his mouth. 'I paid an unexpected visit to his home last evening. He was in possession of a certain ring that I have seen once before.'

'So,' the Runner murmured thoughtfully, 'he's in on it too. That was right smart o' you, my lord.'

Simon uttered a dry, 'Thank you.' Truth be told, he could not actually take credit for the discovery. His feisty little accomplice was definitely on to something. Of course, it was far too dangerous for her to pursue. Still, he could not help but admire her intellect. She was a most unusual sort of girl, he mused.

'Milord?,' Mr. Crawford asked his wistful employer. 'Shall I tell you what 'appened next?'

Simon dragged his thoughts back to the present. 'By all means. Proceed.' He frowned slightly and took another gulp of coffee – the deuced gel occupied too much of his thoughts.

'I climbed up in the tree beside the house to get a better look at the goin's on. Paine was right angry, he was. He tore something off his finger, threw it down on the table and stormed from the place. Now, what do you think that might have been?'

'The signet ring.'

'Aye, my lord. I expect so,' he remarked, helping himself to another cup of coffee, heaps of sugar and a generous portion of cream.

'This sounds interesting,' Simon remarked. 'What did the others do?'

'The rest o' 'em stayed talkin' for hours. I waited and crept in after they'd left to do some pokin' about.' He shivered. 'Somewhat evil is going on up there, my lord, that I can tell you.'

Simon's brow furrowed. 'Evil? What do you mean, evil?'

'I went into the room and couldna believe me eyes. The whole place was covered in shrouds of black and deep purple.'

Simon nearly choked on his coffee. 'The devil you say?'

The Runner nodded. 'T'was downright peculiar. Decorated purposeful like. The walls were black. Eerie place it was, I can tell you. But I kept on lookin',' he boasted with a proud posture, 'coz I always do me job no matter what the perils.'

Simon nodded slightly. 'So you do. I am sure there will be a bonus in it for the risk you took.'

'Thank ye, milord.' Mr Crawford's gratified grin was followed by another loud gulp of the sicky sweet creamy contents in his cup. 'So, now,' he muttered, 'where was I?'

'The room was black and eerie,' Simon supplied with a sigh.

'Ah, yes. What I found next sent a shiver down me spine, let me tell you. Manacles, chains, whips and several large ropes laying about.'

'Sounds delightful,' Simon drawled in disgust.

'It was not,' Mr Crawford countered with an ominous air. 'Y'know the sort of place I'm describing.'

'Yes,' Simon said with a pensive frown, 'I know the sort of place. What else did you find in this dark, forbidding room?'

'Ain't that enough?' Mr Crawford exclaimed, incredulous.

Simon sat back and contemplated what he'd just heard. 'It is not much more than a bizarre occurrence. What does it actually tell us?'

'There's a group o' men who wear them there rings, that's what.'

Simon refilled his cup with much-needed coffee. 'I've already deduced that. It is hardly significant,' he said with a dismissive wave of his hand. 'We still do not know which one was involved with Emily.'

'I'm workin' on it, milord.'

'Not fast enough,' Simon snapped, his patience wearing thin.

'What about that there book?,' the Runner queried with pride in his discovery. 'That's worth me fee, surely.'

Simon's eyes narrowed on the man's weathered face. 'What book?'

'Almost like a bible, it was, lyin' open on a pulpit, draped in purple satin, like a shrine o' sorts. Someone 'ad been makin' an entry just afore I come.'

Simon frowned pensively. 'What was in this nasty little book?'

'Names, like the bettin' book you might find at Whites.'

'Yes, well, I doubt the members of this particular club are in peril of parting with their much-coveted honor.'

'You ain't heard the worst of it. Your stepsister's name was in it. And quite a hefty bet was placed on her, I don't mind tellin' you. O' course, I dunno who did the deed, just how much blunt he got for it.'

Simon's face contorted with rage. '*Emily's* name?' he exploded and slammed his cup down hard enough to smash its saucer. 'Who the devil would put my stepsister's name in such a vulgar book?'

'Aven't got the foggiest.' Crawford shrugged and filled his cup for a third time, repeating the nauseating cream and sugar ritual. 'But I've a feeling I know why.'

'Unfortunately,' Simon gritted his brow darkening, 'so have I.' What the devil had his sweet Emily got herself into?

'Caw,' Mr. Crawford went on to say, 'I shudder to think what goes on in such a vile sort of place.'

'Mmm,' Simon sighed, drumming his fingers on the table. 'Torture, I should think. Or perhaps something even worse,' he said to himself. He slapped his napkin on the table and got to his feet. 'I want to know which one of these men put Emily's name in that damned book.'

The Runner was quick to slurp down the remainder of his coffee and hastily got to his feet. Simon glanced at the now-empty sugar bowl and creamer. It was little wonder the man lacked a full set of teeth.

'Find out all you can about this nefarious group of men, especially the last two,' Simon ordered sharply. 'I should very much like to make their acquaintance.' *And plant my fist in the blackguard's face who dared enter Emily's name into such a disgusting sort of book*, he added silently.

'Aye, my lord,' Mr. Crawford replied, slapping his cap on his slightly balding head. 'That I will.'

Simon rubbed his stubbled chin with his hand. He needed a hot bath and a shave.

A knock sounded at the door. Inside the ornate dressing room, which boasted four cheval mirrors and a plush red velvet settee, the tall blond man standing before a mahogany highboy called out, 'Come.'

His dark brown eyes caught sight of Lord St John Everly in the mirror. He frowned slightly and dismissed his valet with an impatient wave of his hand. Gazing in the mirror, he adjusted his neck cloth to perfection, heedless of his friend's obvious agitation.

'How can you be so calm?,' Everly demanded in a fierce undertone as he approached the spot where the man stood fussing over his neck cloth.

The blond man shrugged his shoulder. 'I see no reason to panic.'

'You know, of course, *he* was at Hobson's last night? Just barged right in without an invitation,' Everly blustered, waving his pudgy arms in the air. 'The nerve of the man. It simply isn't done. But he did it.'

'Who?' the man asked, gazing into the mirror as he smoothed his blond hair with his palms.

'Barclay, of course,' Everly snapped.

He turned to face the room. 'Tut, tut, St John. You promised not to mention that name to me,' the man replied, his voice deceptively calm.

'What do you think he was doing there?,' Everly asked, ringing his sweat-soaked palms. 'He doesn't even know Hobson socially. You realize he could cause a lot of trouble for us,' he moaned, pacing to and fro like a frightened hound.

The blond man shrugged his olive green superfine coat over his shoulders and tugged the ruffled cambric shirt sleeves over his wrists. 'What trouble can he cause?'

'You know as well as I do what kind of trouble he can cause,' Everly snarled, his hands fisted at his side. 'Don't forget, you're responsible for Barclay's sister's death. If you hadn't gotten her with child, none of this would be –'

Before Everly could finish his sentence the tall man's hand snaked out and tightened around his throat. 'I told you,' he hissed through his teeth, 'never mention that name to me again.' He tightened the flesh and bone noose around Everly's neck. 'I won't be shouted at by the likes of you. You're not fit to wipe my boots,' he added with a vicious sneer. 'I've twenty-six maidens to my name. How many have you?'

Everly's face was beet red. He tried to choke out a reply, but to no avail. His beefy fingers clawed at the iron clamp around his throat that threatened to crush his wind pipe. He issued a pathetic plea for his life. Filled with disgust, the man released him. Everly collapsed on the settee in a heap. Gasping for air, he rubbed his sore neck and tried to catch his breath.

The man adjusted his ruffled sleeves. 'Women find me irresistible. There isn't a woman born I cannot seduce.' A smile graced his flawlessly handsome face. 'Where is the sport in that, I ask you?'

Everly was incapable of speech.

'Modest maidens are more challenging than hot, panting widows. The majority of the men in our circle frequent brothels, don't you know? Who wants to plough a well-worn path, I ask you? I must confess,' he said, splaying his hand across his chest, 'Emily was different from the rest of my conquests. I allowed myself to indulge in a momentary diversion with her. I must be even more potent than I realized,' he said, a proud smile touching his lips. 'She was breeding after a mere few weeks in my bed. Of course, then she was useless to me.' He waved his hand in the air dismissively. 'I had to rid myself of the clinging chit. Such a nuisance. All that muttering about love. Of course, I never imagined the damned chit would die birthing the babe. That was another thing entirely.'

'What are you going to do about that deuced Runner?,' Everly asked at last, still gulping for air. 'Paine insists he's after you.'

He tucked his gold watch and chain into his pink and green brocade waistcoat. 'Does he? How very flattering.'

'You know as well as I who is behind all this.' Everly coughed and tugged at his neckcloth. 'If he discovers the truth, we'll all be in for it.'

'You killed the girl.'

The color drained from Everly's paunchy face. 'You – you promised not to say anything about that!'

The man flashed a cool smile in the face of his friend's hysteria. 'So I did. I cannot think why I should. Unless, of course,' he said with a dark, menacing glare, 'you continue to annoy me. As to the other, all our clandestine meetings are held in that disgusting room of yours.'

'The girl's the least of it. You founded the damned society.'

'Mmm,' he replied and leaned closer to the mirror to scrub a spot on his pearly white teeth with his thumbnail. 'And you took to the notion quite well, as I recall. I must say, you surprised me with your assorted perversions. You'll soon have all the members using manacles.' He glanced at Everly sceptically. 'I do wonder why I ever let you in. Deflowering virgins takes skill, St John. I have my doubts about you. Still,' he said with a bored sigh, 'you are good for your losses and pay promptly on all my completions.' He slipped the gold insignia ring on his third finger. 'But you worry overmuch. Why should anyone assume I am guilty of anything?' he asked, glancing with admiration at his reflection in the mirror. 'No law against seduction. And it is so much more amusing to have a club where one can discuss and benefit so fittingly from one's conquests. If a stupid gel gets herself ruined that's her own fault, isn't it?' he asked, meeting his ignoble associate's stricken expression in the mirror.

'There is one person who may not feel that way,' Everly pointed out, his voice wavering with trepidation.

The other man tsk-tsked. 'Leave Barclay to me.'

Everly hung his head. 'Very well, if you insist. But I warn you, he is a dangerous man bent on finding you –'

'You, warn me?,' the tall man interjected with a sneer.

Everly gulped audibly. 'I . . . I only meant you should be careful. A-as we all should. Do you think it was wise to excommunicate Paine?' he asked,

144

nervously chewing on his fingernails. 'He's been one of us since the beginning. It doesn't seem quite fair.'

The lean masculine figure plucked at an imaginary piece of lint on his sleeve. 'Of course we should have done. He's been a problem from the first. Far too flamboyant for my taste. I don't like indiscriminate Corinthians belonging to the club. He attracts too much attention. He is the source of all your anxiety, I dare say. What with that inquisitive Runner on his tail, he's a liability none of us can afford, least of all you,' he remarked pointedly in the face of his friend's distress.

'I don't know why you say that to me. I am not the only one guilty of wrongdoing.'

The blond man uttered a satirical laugh. 'You are the only one fretting, old boy.'

'I – I think we should all stick together,' Everly whined, running his pudgy fingers through his thinning hair. 'We should operate like other societies do. As a-a brotherhood.'

One sardonic brow elevated slightly. 'Brotherhood? Come, come now, St John, you are scarcely *my* brother. Ours is a secret organization. Not exactly like a missionary society.'

'That may be, but we've got to be careful, protect each other's identity. You must agree.'

'But of course, a secret club is, by definition, secret.'

'Paine might talk. He's in a bad way.'

One blond brow cocked. 'And say what? That you killed a girl and tossed her naked body into the Thames?'

145

Everly's normally fish-belly face turned a whiter shade of pale. 'It was an accident. I didn't expect her to fight me. She shouldn't have. I wasn't planning to hurt her. Had she let me have my way with her, she'd still be alive.'

The blond man shrugged. 'They all fight you, St John. Perhaps you lack charm. Or does it give you some sort of a thrill to tie them down?'

'We cannot all be endowed with your good looks and charm,' Everly grunted with resentment.

The man sighed and admired his profile in the cheval mirror. 'True, St John, quite true. Leave everything to me.' He smiled at the man's tortured reflection in the mirror. 'Trust me. I know what I am about. Now,' he remarked, the picture of calm placidity, 'let's not have any more talk about Emily Barclay or her meddling stepbrother, shall we?'

The black carriage with the gold and red Carmichael crest gleaming on the door practically flew through the city streets of London. Anthony Carmichael sat inside, contemplating murder. He still couldn't believe what he had heard an hour ago when he'd stood in the house his wife had once made her home and listened to her grandfather's tirade.

As the carriage ground to a halt outside the stylish brick townhouse on Upper Brook Street, Tony did not wait for the footman. He threw himself down from the carriage and marched up the stone steps. Angry fists pounded against the door, dispensing with the customary bronze lion's head knocker.

146

The door swung open. 'Is his lordship at home?,'
Tony demanded to know.

Evans looked slightly taken aback. Obviously his
lordship was not in the habit of receiving callers
before the noon hour.

'His lordship is bathing and does not wish to be
disturbed,' Evans replied, easing the door shut.

Tony would have none of it. He wedged his booted
foot between the door and the casement. 'That is
indeed unfortunate,' he said through his teeth,
'because I intend to disturb his lordship, presently.'

Evans cleared his throat. Seeing no other avenue,
he opened the door to the large encroaching figure.
'Whom shall I say is calling?,' he asked with stiff
civility.

Tony shoved the door wide and stormed into the
foyer. He strode passed the stunned butler and
started up the front stairs.

'B-but, my lord, you must be announced!,' the
outraged Evans cried and scurried after the intruder.

Tony glanced down the hallway. Hearing the
muffled sound of male voices to his right, he trudged
down the hall. Not waiting to be admitted, he threw
open the door to Simon Barclay's private sanctuary.

Reclining in a large copper tub, the master of the
house was relaxing in a hot steamy bath. His valet
danced attendance at his side. As the door swung
open, Simon looked up in surprise.

'Tony? What the devil are you doing here?,' he
asked and motioned for his valet to get his robe.

Getting out of the tub, he wrapped the full-length
robe around his naked glistening body and caught

147

sight of his friend's dark scowl. 'Is something amiss?,' he asked and dismissed his astonished valet who happily took his leave.

Wordlessly, Tony marched up to the man he once considered a friend and planted his fist in his jaw. Taken completely unawares, Simon fell backward and landed in the middle of the floor. He blinked up at the ferocious man looming over him.

'You *bastard*,' Tony hissed, his fists balled in anger. 'Get to your feet.'

'I would be happy to do so, if I knew why the devil you just tried to break my jaw,' Simon countered coolly as he took himself off the floor, his pride damaged in no small degree.

'As if you didn't know,' Tony scoffed. 'You just couldn't keep your hands off her, could you?'

'Who?,' Simon asked, dreading the answer he knew was to come. His preoccupation with the fiery redheaded trouble-maker had mercifully been eclipsed by Mr Crawford's disturbing report earlier this morning. Naturally, he presumed he could rely on her to remain silent. He was mistaken.

He'd misjudged the damned chit. Her quest for ruin was at last realized. He might have known that she would divulge his foolhardy indiscretion. Unless he missed his guess, she'd chosen to omit her willing response. Not that it signified. In such matters, the man was ultimately responsible and, therefore, culpable.

Talons of dread clutched at his heart. Precisely what portion of their torrid encounter had she related? Not . . . all of it? He hoped not. This could prove to be a scandal he'd not easily weather.

'Celeste. Damn you! My sister-in-law. The complete innocent you ravaged last night.'

Simon's jaw clenched. 'I did not ravage her,' he bit out.

'Are you going to deny you were caught with my sister-in-law in one of Hobson's guest bedchambers last night?' Tony thundered. 'To add insult to injury, you saw her home in your private carriage? Alone?'

'No,' Simon snapped, his tone low and controlled. 'I do not deny that I rescued her – in the nick of time, I might add – from another one of her hapless plots. My propitious intervention was also at *your* wife's bidding.'

'I am aware of my wife's foolish entreaty. I apologize for it,' Tony retorted with curt civility. 'It was not Joy, however, who beseeched you to seduce her sister in the middle of the night!'

Simon winced. Even to his prejudicial ears he'd comported himself like a dishonorable cad. Taking a deep breath, he tried to retrieve his character from the brink of moral disaster. 'Upon my honor, the last thing I wanted was another encounter with that headstrong little minx.'

'Do not dare mention honor to me,' Tony replied with venom.

'If you must know,' Simon said, testing the damage done to his jaw, 'I vowed never to see her again. She is far more trouble than she is worth.'

Not in the least persuaded, Tony crossed his arms over his chest and regarded Simon with a cynical smirk. 'But you just couldn't resist taking full advantage of the fact that she is a total innocent who is infatuated with you, could you?'

Simon laughed harshly. 'Infatuated? I sincerely doubt it. Your outrageous sister-in-law is an avid student of life, didn't you know?' he averred sarcastically. 'Such persons do not suffer from infatuations.'

'You are not in a position to mock me, Barclay,' Tony gritted, hands clenched at his sides. 'I am closer than I ever thought I would be to calling you out. I've heard the ugly rumors circulating around your name, but I refused to believe them. I judged you an honorable, decent man incapable of siring a child on his own stepsister. Evidently, I was mistaken. It was a grave error, for it has brought disaster upon those I love most. The gossips have etched an accurate portrait of your character. It would seem you enjoy preying on young innocents.'

'You were not mistaken to bestow your good opinion upon me,' Simon replied, his tone cold as a winter's morning. 'I do not prey on virtuous women. In general,' he muttered with contempt, 'I avoid them like the plague.' That was the truth. He dearly wished he'd clung more firmly to his habits of old.

Of course, he'd never met a wild, bewitching creature like Celeste. Most virtuous women of his acquaintance were plain, shy creatures. Hardly the sort to make him burn. But she had. With a vengeance.

'I await your assurances that this was all a terrible misunderstanding and you will make immediate retribution.'

Simon opened his mouth to refute the accusations and frowned slightly. What the devil could he say? He hadn't laid a hand on her? When his hands and mouth had been all over her? He ploughed his hand through his midnight hair. He'd better make a clean breast of it.

One objective burned clearly in his mind; he was going to enjoy beating the little baggage senseless for the trouble she'd caused him. If she had not displayed such pathetic lack of judgement in going to Hobson's in the first place, he would not be facing the dreaded parson's trap. The fact that he was equally to blame, he dismissed as irrelevant. He was never particularly rational when he was angry. Right now, he was livid.

He cleared his throat and stood tall in the face of utter ignominy. 'I can only say that while her virtue is intact, her honor, I fear, has been badly tarnished.'

Tony gave him a scornful glare. 'That is putting it mildly.'

Undaunted, Simon continued, 'You, of course, are free to name your seconds. But pray allow me to assure you that I intend to offer for her. Post haste. I shall procure a special licence and meet with her guardian this very day. Will that satisfy you?'

'It will,' Tony replied with a stiff nod.

'Good.' Simon's entire body seemed to relax. He bared his teeth in a smile. 'I should hate to have to put a bullet through your chest.'

Tony was not amused. 'For God's sake, man, why did you wait for me to force your hand? Where is your sense of honor? It was your duty to make amends. You should have offered for her the minute you'd disgraced her.'

Simon stiffened at the rebuke. 'I suppose,' he said, clasping his hands behind his back, 'it was momentarily diminished by my hatred of the matrimonial state.'

Tony shook his head at him. 'Gad, you really are a rogue. Cheer up,' he remarked and slapped Simon on the back none too gently. 'There's still an outside chance she'll refuse you. All your worries may well be over.'

Hope dawned. Simon hadn't considered an avenue of escape from this unholy mess. But of course, she could refuse him. She was free to do so. She'd be saving them both from a fate guaranteed to be worse than death. After all, it was total ruin she sought, not marriage.

Half an hour later, Simon's valet returned. Despite his master's foul mood, he saw to his lordship's ministrations with admirable skill. Donning a pale blue silk waistcoat and soft grey velvet cutaway, Simon hoped he looked sufficiently contrite, although contrition was an emotion altogether alien to him.

He heaved an impatient sigh and tore the neckcloth loose. 'No. Not this one,' he muttered and tossed it on the floor. His valet stood patiently by while Simon fought with his third uncooperative neckcloth.

Simon was dreading this afternoon's interview. The discomfort irritated him. Of course, the fact that he'd slept badly was not helping matters. He was not, by nature, an insomniac. Images of a fiery redhead lying beneath him, her blue eyes languid with passion and her wild erotic hair scattered over the pillows, haunted his sleep.

What the devil would the chit say when he proposed? Would she dare refuse him? Lord, he hoped so. Even if she did not refuse him outright, she might cry off after a short betrothal, claiming he was too disgusting to be borne and beg to be released from her promise. He would happily comply.

God knows he'd make the world's worst husband. What did he know about marriage? Not a damned thing. Save for the impressions he'd received during his early boyhood. Vicious fights behind closed doors. Ugly words expressed at dinner. His mother, dear sweet mother, blatantly cavorting with countless men in front of his father until he could not abide the sight of her any longer. His father was glad when she took up with a Frenchman and left for the Continent, never to be seen or heard from again. It was rumoured she died shortly thereafter from the pox.

Not that his father's second marriage had fared much better. His wife's inability to bear his children came as a bitter disappointment, one he made no effort to hide.

Simon had always felt a modicum of sympathy for his dear departed stepmother. For her part, however, the sentiment was not returned. She was ever devoted to little Emily and displayed a grave dislike for Simon. Affection was rarely found in the Barclay household save for the two children who seemed eager to make up for their cold, distant and invariably absent parents.

No, Simon thought with firm conviction, he would not inflict such a state on his worst enemy. It was with a heavy heart that he realized he had no choice but to issue a marriage proposal, this very day, to the most unconventional woman of his acquaintance. It would be farcical were it not so damned infuriating.

Still, reflecting on his conduct, he had to admit that his actions had been dishonorable. She, being a complete innocent, was blameless. The truth was that he'd comported himself badly. Very badly indeed. Not that it bothered him much, until he'd been called to answer for it.

Tony was right, he was a rogue. His lack of remorse should have bothered him. Why did it not? It would bother an honorable man. Why not him?

Satisfied at last with his cravat, Simon glanced at the small porcelain clock on the table and wondered how time could move so slowly? He was suddenly anxious to see it through to its bitter or sweet end.

CHAPTER 8

Simon waited in what he presumed, from the pale yellow upholstered couch, matching chairs and shards of warm golden sunlight streaming in through the large casement windows, to be the morning room. The illustrious Grandfather Wentworth was scheduled to appear at any moment.

Simon couldn't help but wonder what tack the old fossil planned to take. Without a doubt, affiancing his wayward granddaughter to the Earl of Barclay was the best outcome for which the old curmudgeon could hope. Given that Simon was honor-bound to offer for the little hellion, everything should work very nicely – provided she showed the good sense to refuse him. Yes, everything should work out splendidly. She'd have achieved her coveted state of ruin and he would have done the noble thing.

His fingers clawed at his neckcloth. It seemed to be restricting his breathing. His forehead creased in a deep frown. Dash it all, he sincerely hoped the virago had the good sense to refuse him. Could prove a trifle disastrous for the both of them if she actually decided to go through with it. He rubbed his chin and contemplated the workings of Celeste's mercurial mind. No woman in her right mind would ever agree to wed a notorious rake like him. Besides, she'd expressed an aversion to marriage, had she not? He was certain she had.

He breathed a little easier. His bachelor way of life would remain entirely intact. He admonished himself for the sense of dread that had threatened to upset his normal calm.

He lifted one leg across his knee and drummed his fingers on his immaculate black Hessians. By nature, he was anything but a patient man. This deliberate attempt to make him stew in his immoral juices grated on his nerves excessively. He got to his feet and prowled the room. Stopping to take note of the time on his gold pocket watch, his jaw clenched.

Twenty minutes. He'd been waiting for a full twenty minutes. His lips thinned. Another five, and the damned chit could stew in scandal's juices before he'd offer for her. He replaced his watch in his waistcoat pocket and continued his restless pacing.

At the sound of the doorknob turning, Simon swung around, expecting to encounter the irate Viscount Wentworth. To his surprise, the butler stood in the doorway. 'Lord Wentworth will see you now. In the library, if you please.'

Simon's features turned to granite. It took all his self-control not to turn on his heel and storm from the house. Self-control. And the unhappy truth that he was responsible for the current débâcle. Stiff-backed, he strode from the room. He followed the butler across the carpeted hallway into the white-walled library.

The door shut behind him. He stood, feet slightly apart, and braced himself for the tirade he felt sure would ensue.

Old was not the word to describe the tall, willowy gentleman who occupied the seat behind the enormous walnut desk. It struck Simon that dear old Grandpapa looked to be in mourning, garbed as he was in black from head to toe. He wondered with a rueful grimace if the forbidding man dressed in the macabre color routinely, or if the demise of Celeste's honor was the reason.

'So, you have come,' the brittle old man said at last. He allowed his disapproving gaze to sweep over the Earl of Barclay. 'I must admit, I am surprised,' he remarked with obvious disdain and retrieved a small snuff box from his pocket. 'I did not believe wastrels capable of restitution.' He pinched a bit of snuff and half-shoved, half-snorted it up his nose.

Simon's silver gaze narrowed on the shriveled old man. Wastrel? The war waging between the desire to rein in his temper and the need to issue a roaring setdown was very nearly lost. Then Simon reminded himself that he'd come here to do his duty. Given half the chance, he fully intended to issue an offer.

'You see, my dear,' the old man remarked with a chilling smile to someone seated in the corner of the room, 'you were wrong, he has come.'

Simon's head whipped around. A scant distance away sat a young woman who he knew must be Celeste. Her identity, however, was scarcely ascertainable from her disconsolate countenance. Her normally straight, delicate shoulders were slumped. Her unruly curls adorned a head that was grievously bowed in submission. She did not resemble the feisty harridan he had come to know in the vaguest manner. She looked pale and drawn as if she'd aged ten years overnight.

The situation was indeed dire, for what else could eclipse her eternal flame of tempestuous energy? Simon had no idea she would be present for this humiliating interview. It was a cruel exercise that increased his dislike for the old man tenfold.

'Tony must have been more persuasive than I gave him credit for,' her grandfather averred, rudely disregarding Simon's presence. 'I assume that is why he has made an appearance. He certainly felt no compunction to do so before.'

Before? What the devil did he mean by that? The idea of this disagreeable man being privy to his private indiscretions made Simon decidedly uncomfortable. He did not take kindly to being referred to as the disparaged 'he'. His desire to get this blasted interview over flared anew. Clearing his throat, he clasped his clenched fists behind his back and launched into his well-rehearsed speech.

'I have come to ask for your granddaughter's hand in marriage. I fear, inadvertently, her honor has been –'

'Destroyed. Yes, I know.'

Simon winced inwardly and cast a furtive glance in Celeste's direction. She looked positively ill. Her fingers clutched at her knees hard enough to turn the knuckles white.

'But I highly doubt it was inadvertently done,' the Viscount added with a derisive grunt. 'It is impossible for me to assume otherwise. We must all lament your wickedness. Hopes of a decent match for my granddaughter are irrevocably dashed.'

Simon's spine straightened. Decent match? For a viscount's wayward granddaughter she was doing quite well by Simon's estimation.

'An alliance between my granddaughter and a rogue like yourself would heretofore have been insupportable. But now, what can I hope for?'

'Grandfather, *please*,' Celeste beseeched in a tiny miserable voice. 'Do not do this, I beg of you.'

'Be silent!,' he exploded, slamming his fist down on the desk.

Recoiling from his fury, she lowered her gaze to the floor.

'Now, young man,' he muttered, addressing Simon once more, 'you will explain yourself.'

Young man! No one dared call Simon young man. Even if Wentworth was older than Methuselah, he was still a viscount. Simon was the Earl of Dragonwood, not some nobody off the street. He deserved a measure of respect.

'Constrained as you obviously are to offer for my granddaughter, you should feel compelled to be honest.' His disparaging gaze swept over Simon. 'If nothing else, it will be a novel experience for a scoundrel like you.'

Scoundrel! Simon's clenched his jaw hard enough to crush his teeth. He had heard more than enough. Were it not for the promise he'd made Tony, Simon would have issued the verbal laceration the old man richly deserved.

'I've come,' he replied coldly, struggling to maintain the outward appearance of calm, '*that* should be enough.'

'It is not,' the old man said bluntly.

'If I were the scoundrel you suggest,' Simon gritted, 'I would scarcely offer your granddaughter the protection of my name.'

The Viscount waved his blue-veined hand in the air. 'Your name,' he scoffed. 'What consolation is that? You, sirrah, are a renowned rake.'

Every inch of Simon's body went rigid with anger. It took supreme self-discipline to squelch the powerful urge to throttle the disagreeable man.

'Given your granddaughter's outrageous conduct,' he said with icy precision, 'you would be fortunate to receive a single offer.'

Out of the corner of his eye, he heard Celeste's sharp intake of breath.

'As to the rest,' he continued in a voice that held a distinct edge, 'my family, to the best of my knowledge, is completely above reproach.'

'It is bandied about all over town that you fathered your own sister's child.'

'She was my stepsister,' Simon corrected through his teeth, 'and I am not the child's father. But we digress,' he imparted sharply. 'I have the means, and the desire, to care for your granddaughter in a

160

fashion, I dare say,' he remarked, casting his disdainful gaze around the modest room, 'that far exceeds the manner in which she was raised. That should satisfy you.'

The old man vaulted to his feet, shoving the leather chair against the wall with a loud thud. 'She was raised with the finest influences!,' he exploded in a white-hot fury.

'Indeed?' Simon queried with a dubious frown. 'Then what, pray, was she doing in the middle of the night with a man who was not her husband?'

A cry of abject misery tore from Celeste's throat.

'Enough! I have heard more than enough,' she interjected with surprising energy.

Both men stopped to stare at the petite woman who had spoken with such force.

Drawing a deep breath as if the words were difficult to express, she addressed Simon,

'I thank you for coming, my lord,' she said quietly, 'but it was not necessary. I shall be quite content to retire to the country. You've no need to worry that I shall capitalize on scandal.'

'Do you see what a headstrong, disobedient hoyden she is?,' the old man blustered angrily, wagging a bony finger in her direction. 'I am not a bit surprised she's disgraced the family.'

A look of pain crossed Celeste's face. 'Grandfather, *please.*'

Her plea went unanswered. He merely regarded her with a look of disgust. 'She is a severe disappointment to me. I knew she would bring nothing but heartache. She takes after her father. *He* was a commoner.' His voice rang with abhorrence. 'It does not do for the classes to mix. *That*,' he muttered, savagely motioning towards his granddaughter, 'is the vulgar, earthy result of such a union.'

Celeste sank into the chair in a crumpled mass of hurt humiliation.

Simon did not miss the grimace of pain that contorted her face. He was filled with compassion for the spirited young thing. How difficult it must have been for her to be raised by a brutal man who made no secret of the fact that he harboured nothing but contempt for his own flesh and blood. Simon well knew the humiliation of being the brunt of disdain. His need to rescue her from a life of utter misery mounted with a vengeance.

'Joy takes after her mother,' the disgruntled Viscount went on to say with pride. 'She is everything a woman should be, gentle, obedient and graceful. And beautiful. Not like *her*.' He eyed the girl, who was now weeping softly in the corner, with cold dislike. 'That hair –' he bristled in revulsion '– it is shocking. So wild and unruly. A perfectly hideous color.'

'It is very beautiful,' Simon heard someone say softly in a voice that sounded remarkably like his own.

Celeste's head lifted. Astonished, she blinked at him through glistening tears.

'It is vulgar in the extreme,' Wentworth countered firmly. 'Jezebel offspring,' he hissed under his breath. 'It comes as little surprise to me that she destroyed her reputation. Given her character, it was merely a matter of time. But to what extent has she been compromised? Have you taken her honor as well as her virtue?'

Simon's nostrils flared. 'I have nothing satisfactory to report to you. I've already offered the protection of my name.' His voice was taut with anger. 'All that is left is for *Celeste*,' he intoned with meaning, 'to decide if she will accept me as her husband.'

'Her wishes do not enter into it. She will do as she is told. Or be brought to heel. I am her guardian. *You* will deal with *me*,' Wentworth bellowed vehemently.

Simon's eyes glinted with blistering contempt. 'I have no intentions of gratifying your salacious tendencies with graphic details,' came his acrimonious reply. 'I am sure you can conjure up suitable images to satisfy your sordid curiosity.'

Accustomed to getting his own way, the domineering man thundered, 'You are not in a position to argue. You have brought ruin upon this house.' He pounded his fist on the desk. 'I demand a full explanation. By God, I shall have one!'

'I have no explanation,' Simon replied, cool and remote in the face of pure rage. 'I freely admit I behaved abominably. I have indicated that I am prepared to make restitution. More than that, I will not do.'

'You will!,' Wentworth blazed, his normally grey countenance inflamed with rage.

'No,' Simon retorted in a voice that brooked no disagreement. 'More than the protection of my name I *refuse* to give.'

'This is an outrage!' The aged Viscount raised his fist in the air. 'I have the right to know.'

'I am persuaded your granddaughter has already told you all you need know. Her confession is, after all, why I am here. Surely,' Simon imparted with a decided chill, 'it was sufficiently sensational to satisfy you.'

Casting a speculative glance at Celeste, Simon noted she'd dried her eyes and was beaming from ear to ear. Evidently, she thoroughly enjoyed the blistering setdown he'd just issued. It struck him as odd that her grandfather did not know already what had transpired. He frowned slightly. What had she told the churlish old goat?

'If by that you mean she behaved like a common trollop,' her grandfather's voice was bitter with loathing, 'then I quite agree with you.'

Simon's features hardened into a glowering mask of rage. 'You have said more than enough,' he snapped in a lethal tone. 'I fully comprehend your feelings. You need say nothing more. I warn you, have a care, you are speaking of the woman soon to be my wife.'

'You think *her* worthy of your esteem?,' Wentworth asked with heavy mockery.

Simon gave him a hostile glare. 'Eminently,' he imparted with conviction.

The old man sniggered viciously. 'You are gravely mistaken. Mark my words, she will make you miserable, wreak havoc on your ordinary existence and drive you to distraction.'

'She will no longer be your concern,' Simon bit out, his tone like ice.

His rejoinder took the wind out of Wentworth's sails; he sank into his chair. 'You are steeped in scandal. It is a wonder you dare show your face in polite society,' he muttered.

'None the less, your granddaughter will shortly be wed. A scandal will have been averted. And you may hold your head up once more in polite society.'

The old man's thin lips pursed. 'Very well, I give her to you with my compliments. I will not wish you happy. I know you will both be miserable. In my view,' he sneered, 'you deserve each other.'

'If nothing else,' came Simon's visceral retort, 'it will be my great pleasure to rescue her from your clutches. You've made two fine matches for your granddaughters. The second hasn't cost you a farthing,' he remarked with biting sarcasm.

'No.' The Viscount's watery blue eyes narrowed with contempt. 'You took what you wanted without the benefit of matrimony. I should insist on compensation for the misery you've wrought on this family.'

Simon's jaw might have been hewn of iron. 'I shouldn't worry overmuch. I am sure you'll survive what you clearly regard as a mere inconvenience. At present, it is my wish to speak to my betrothed. Alone. Surely,' he said, baring his teeth in a frigid smile, 'you can have no objections to such a minor request?'

'She is yours to do with as you please. Or should I say,' he averred crudely, 'continue to enjoy as you please.' Leaning heavily on his black cane, he managed to get to his feet and walk across the room. Opening the library door, he cast one final glare of censure at his mischievous granddaughter and quit the room.

Celeste released a weary breath and lowered her gaze to the floor. Well, she was duly ruined. And it felt dreadful. Had she truly wished for such a miserable state? She was certain today ranked as the worst day of her short life, for it very nearly felt like the end of her life – life as she'd known it. She felt as if she were in a dream state when one realized the disturbing direction their dream was taking and wanted to wake, but couldn't break free from the gripping nightmare.

When Grandfather summoned her to the library earlier this morning, she never imagined she'd encountered the last person on earth she wanted to see. Barclay's presence astounded her. And his impassioned declaration for her hand dumbfounded her. Despite the fact that she was certain his proposal was born from a strict sense of honor rather than genuine affection, she revelled in that fleeting moment of triumph. The Dragon had actually come, defended her honor, and gallantly offered for her hand in marriage. She truly had not believed he would come. Why would he? After all, she was scarcely worth any man's trouble, particularly not one as beautiful as the Dragon. He could have any woman his heart desired . . . so, why *had* he offered for her? Notorious rakes never suffered from moral dilemmas. He could not truly wish to wed her. He was merely being kind or perhaps, at the very most, dutiful. She would refuse him, of course, and thereby save herself from the embarrassing truth. He did not really want her.

She could feel the instrument of her once-coveted ruin staring at her. His dark gaze weighed heavily upon her bent head. Glancing up, she meet his eye. Colour flooded her cheeks and she quickly looked away.

Clearing her throat, she managed to say shyly, 'You should not have come, my lord. I did not expect it.'

He reached out his hands to her. Of their own volition, her palms slipped into his. Dark grey eyes gazed down at her. Unnerved by their intensity, her own gaze skidded away.

'I had to come,' he said, giving her hands a squeeze.

Of what? Affection? Encouragement? She wasn't quite sure. But she was thrilled by the gesture. It made her feel safe. She frowned at her strange train of thought. Safe with the Dragon? How utterly bizarre.

She shook her head. 'No. You did not. I am as much to blame as you. If I –'

He pressed his finger to her lips. 'It is all arranged,' he told her, his voice full of tenderness. 'I have purchased a special licence. We will be married this coming Saturday.'

She looked blank with surprise. Was he in earnest? No. He could not be. Besides, even if he were she would never make the Earl of Barclay a proper wife.

'Married,' she repeated softly, 'this Saturday. But . . . that is the day after tomorrow!'

He smiled down at her staggered expression and affectionately tucked a stray curl behind her ear.

'There are some advantages to being the Earl of Barclay,' he remarked dryly.

Retrieving her ice-cold hands from the warmth of his grasp, she wandered over to the window. He wasn't making this any easier. No girl in her right mind would refuse a man of his wealth and stature – except Celeste. 'My lord, you are kindness itself,' she managed with a hard swallow. 'I thank you for your offer. I know it was graciously meant. But there is no reason for us to wed.'

In three purposeful strides, he crossed the room to where she stood. She was acutely aware of him, a blatantly masculine presence at her side. She tried to step away, but he would have none of it. Grasping her by her shoulders, he turned her to face him. 'On the contrary, there is every reason,' he countered with a measure of force. 'You were alone with me, in the middle of the night. I took shocking liberties. Touched you, intimately. As only a husband has the right.'

Embarrassed color suffused her cheeks, she lowered her lashes.

'I have no choice but to offer you the protection of my name.' His fingers curled under her chin and tilted her face upward. His compelling silver gaze beseeched her. 'You must accept me as your husband.'

'Very well done, my lord –,' she tried to smile and failed, '– but completely unnecessary. I assure you, I have no intentions of accepting you.' She sighed woefully. 'I am entirely to blame. If I had not insisted on unearthing details about that recent murder, neither of us would be facing this pathetic state of affairs.'

Pathetic state of affairs? His jaw tightened. 'Your honor has been compromised,' he said stiffly. 'The blame lies with me. You are an innocent, a mere child. I took full advantage of the situation. The fault lies entirely at my feet. I am willing to make amends. I *insist* on making amends,' he added, his voice firm in its finality.

'To save me from ruin?,' she asked, fighting the absurd need to laugh.

'Yes. Preposterous, is it not? But that is the situation in which we find ourselves.'

'But it need not be,' she insisted in earnest appeal. 'You have done the noble thing. I have refused you. You are free.'

Simon scowled at his own conduct. What the devil was the matter with him? She'd given him his freedom precisely as he had hoped. But he knew he would not – could not – accept it. He would marry her. If only to deprive that walking fossil of the pleasure of gloating. After meeting the hateful man, Simon understood immediately Celeste's aversion to him. He was narrow-minded, judgmental and domineering to the point of suffocation. Simon felt an irrational need to rescue the fragile bird from the claws of a vicious cat.

He framed her face with his hands. 'Do you think I could walk out that door and never look back?' His eyes, tender and compassionate, searched hers. 'I am wholly responsible for your plight. Marry me,' he urged her softly.

She shook her head and pulled away from him. 'I cannot accept you. It is out of the question.'

His features hardened. 'The devil it is!,' he exploded hotly. 'I don't intend to give that curmudgeon the satisfaction of knowing you refused my offer.'

Pride! His damnable pride would be the death of him. He was galloping toward utter disaster without a thought to anything but his unswerving desire to shove his nuptials down the brittle old man's throat. That, and the notion of saving the pale, unhappy child he'd grown decidedly fond of from the depths of utter misery.

'It comes down to this,' he imparted roughly, 'marry me, or face a life of drudgery with that domineering old goat.'

Celeste gulped, clearly revolted by that horrid prospect.

'Imagine your life, your miserable future, enduring endless days and nights of solitude with your grandfather. He will be the ever-present vicious reminder of your grand *faux pas*.'

She looked simultaneously frightened and repulsed by the prospect. 'You make your point all too clearly, my lord.'

'Then accept me as your husband,' he urged thickly, 'and all will be well.'

She gave him a whimsical smile. 'How confident you are. You make it sound facile with your charming proposal and romantic words. But I know very well that I'll never be a proper wife to you.' She rested her head in her hands. 'I'd go mad living in the country, breeding endlessly. I want more out of life than that. Perhaps I don't deserve it, but I want excitement, intrigue, challenge. You can offer me none of those things.' She drew a deep sigh. 'Even if I were foolish enough to marry a notorious rake – which I am not – I would scarcely choose you.'

His hands fell to his sides. 'Obviously,' he uttered coolly, 'your aversion to me was not strong enough to ensure secrecy. Let's not forget, dear heart,' he averred bitingly, 'it was your unconventional behavior that brought this on both our heads.'

She turned a whiter shade of pale. 'You are entirely correct. I am truly sorry, I never thought it would come to this.' She looked utterly depressed. 'I must confess, total ruin is far worse than any imagining could have been. It is not at all what I had hoped.'

His lips twisted with rancour. 'Marriage to me is a fate worse than death, is that it?,' he asked her bitterly.

'You cannot possibly want this,' she cried, willing her voice to remain steady.

'What I want is irrelevant,' he snapped, his tone curt. 'It is what I must do. The honorable thing must and will be done.'

A look of disbelief crossed her face. 'You're a rake of dubious repute,' she spluttered in frustration. 'You are not supposed to be honorable.'

His mouth curved into a cold smile. 'Sorry to disappoint you.'

She shot him a rueful look. 'I would be a fool to trade one domineering master for another.' *Especially one who does not love me*, she added silently.

171

His sharp, gray gaze bore into her. 'You mistake me,' he told her, his voice like steel cloaked with velvet. 'I offer you no choice. Saturday, at St George's Church, you will become my wife.'

She gaped at the dark forbidding stranger before her. 'Are you saying you love me?,' she asked softly.

'Of course not,' he snapped impatiently. 'How could I?'

How, indeed? she thought with a pang of sadness. A man like him would never love a woman like her. Why was she forlorn? It was not as though she ever expected to find love. She wasn't a romantic fool like Joy. Why, then, was she behaving like such a sensitive flower? He'd merely stated the unvarnished truth. He did not love her now, nor would he ever.

That was all right. She was no frivolous female. It was just that she could not help remembering how wonderful it felt to hear his fervent expression of his intentions. To learn he was not sincere was a slight disappointment. But she would survive. Hadn't she always?

'Accept me now, and be done with it,' he urged her, his breath warm against her temple. 'Believe me when I say I have earned my reputation. Once decided, my mind is set. I will make you my wife.'

Her shoulders slumped. She expelled a deep sigh of resignation. Marriage did have one saving grace – freedom, if she could wangle it. 'Very well, my lord, you seem bound and determined to wreck havoc in both our lives. I will marry you . . . on one condition.'

172

His steely gray eyes threatened to impale her. 'Condition?' His brows snapped together. 'What damned condition?,' he growled at her.

She clasped her hands together demurely at her waist. 'It is quite simple. You have no real desire to gain a leg shackle. I have even less desire to be dominated. We will agree to allow each other to continue as before.'

His piercing gaze narrowed on her pale face. 'What precisely do you mean by that?,' he ground out.

Her tongue darted between her dry lips. 'I mean,' she said with a swallow, 'you may continue to – to . . .' Her cheeks turned a lovely shade of pink and her voice trailed off.

He cocked a brow. 'To?'

Her gaze skidded away. 'Well, do whatever it is you do with, um, your mistresses or whomever. I shall be permitted to pursue my work. Uninterrupted.' She stole a glance at his forbidding expression. 'Agreed?'

He crossed his arms over his chest and regarded her in taciturn silence. 'Allow me to paraphrase. You are giving me leave to bed countless other women, to enjoy my rakehell existence to the fullest, heedless of the fact that henceforth I shall be a married man, is that it?'

Her cheeks brightened. 'Yes.'

'All this you will graciously allow, provided, of course, that I overlook your bluestocking tendencies and do not interfere with your work. Is that the bargain you wish to strike?'

'Yes. I believe you have the gist of it, my lord,' she murmured, not meeting his eye.

'I suppose I should consider myself fortunate,' he said on a derisive chuckle. 'I imagined I would gain a soulmate, a confidant, a wife and a lover. A kind, caring mother for my children. In actuality, however, I am merely going through the motions of matrimony so that we may both continue to live as before.'

She bristled at his tone. 'I think it is a very sound solution to our problem. Besides, it is hardly the thing to be in each other's pockets, now is it?'

'Heaven forbid,' he mocked. 'But what of the Barclay heir?' he asked, arching one ebony brow in query. 'I will at some point have to fulfil my obligation to the title.'

She squirmed with discomfort. 'Yes . . . well. We will have to . . . to –'

'Renegotiate terms?,' he supplied.

'I should imagine so, yes.'

'Ah. How clever you are.'

Her eyes sparkled blue fire. 'I think it a sound solution to both our problems,' she declared defensively.

His slow seductive gaze slid over her with shocking thoroughness. 'You think that your cosy little arrangement would be mutually satisfactory, do you?' he murmured huskily.

Gulping, she stammered, 'I – I don't see why not.'

His lips curled into a wicked smile as his finger caressed her cheek. 'You don't think you'd mind my pleasuring other women while you devoted all your energies to intellectual pursuits?,' he asked, his voice like a satin caress.

'Why should I?,' she croaked and hastily cleared her throat. 'It goes without saying that you will be discreet,' she said, brushing past him, eager to escape his dangerous heat. 'No one need know about our private affairs.'

'Oh, yes, you are quite right on that point. Discretion is the better part of valour. Don't I know it,' he drawled out amusedly. 'Very well, my dear, I accept your condition. With one addendum.'

She whirled about to face him. 'What might that be?'

His lips twitched. 'That I may be free to make alterations to our agreement should I see fit.'

She gave him a startled look. 'Why should you wish to do that?'

One end of his mouth lifted slightly. 'I have my reasons. What say you?'

Frowning, she glanced at him dubiously. 'I cannot think why you should wish for such an arrangement.' She cocked her curly head to one side. 'I must say, my lord,' she remarked, studying his handsome countenance, 'I can never tell if you are serious or not.'

'I assure you,' he intoned gravely, 'I have never been more serious in my life.'

She sighed and shrugged her shoulders. 'Oh, well, I suppose, in time, we shall get to know each other's idiosyncrasies.' She stuck her hand out to seal their bargain. 'I will wed you, my lord. As you wish, Saturday at St George's Church.'

He squashed the urge to smile. His large masculine hand closed around her small delicate one.

'Don't be late,' he said, gazing deeply into her clear blue eyes. 'I don't like to be kept waiting.'

'I make it a habit always to be punctual, my lord,' she said softly.

'Capital notion,' he murmured, smiling down at her. 'You see, we are off to an excellent start. We shall leave for the country directly,' he assured her, his gaze tender and serene. 'You will like Lindhurst, my dear. Very much.' He caressed her pale cheek with the back of his hand. 'The color shall return to your cheeks and the sparkle to your eyes. I will see to it that you are happy.'

She returned his smile. In that moment, she felt that all would be well between them despite their differences and the manner in which they had been thrown together. At least, she'd be free of her grandfather's cruel yoke. How much worse could it be to marry a man who harboured no affection for her whatsoever?

CHAPTER 9

As it turned out, St George's was not available for Saturday. In fact, that fashionable site where most *tonnish* marriages were celebrated was not available for several months. Simon assured himself as he stood at the alter in the comparatively small Grosvenor Chapel that it was not an inauspicious beginning to their nuptials.

What was undeniably peculiar was the paucity of guests. Neither his family nor Celeste's grandfather were in attendance. Simon had not seriously expected any of his relatives to make an appearance. In a way, he was glad he'd been spared the usual disparaging looks and derisive remarks. A mere handful of men and women occupied the first two rows. Even at that, the small pitch-pine pews looked stark and empty.

He forced his gaze from the meagre surroundings and turned to face the altar. His forefinger slipped between the crisp cloth and his moist neck and tugged. In a matter of minutes, he would emerge from the dimly-lit brick edifice a married man. A condition that would undoubtedly feel . . . odd. A frown touched his lips. More than odd. Terrifying. Bizarre. Damned unnatural.

What the deuce was he going to do with a wife? What grated most was that he had brought this calamity on himself. His bride-to-be had been understanding itself. Why in heaven's name had he not bowed out gracefully when she'd given him the chance?

After meeting her oppressive, despicable grandfather, he knew why. Somewhere in the recesses of his cold heart he felt responsible for her. No matter how much she might deserve to suffer the ramifications of her foolish quest for ruin, Simon couldn't very well abandon her to wallow in abject despair. Not when he could save her with a measly – easier said than done – proposal. It wasn't as though he was sacrificing himself. He needed to marry at some point, it was expected. His obligations to the title had to be considered. He just had not envisioned the matrimonial noose tightening quite this soon around his neck. Particularly not to a headstrong, unpredictable girl of eighteen.

He blew the air out of his cheeks. Where the blazes was she? Everything seemed to be moving far too slow this morning. He wanted to get the ceremony over with. He longed to retire to the country for a few weeks. He clasped his hands behind his back and gazed aimlessly at the reredos and traceried windows looming above him. He hated to be made to wait. Hadn't he told her as much?

His lips thinned. Their marriage was definitely off to a bad start. Marriage to his mind offered paltry benefits. One thing was for certain, he intended to enjoy the marriage bed at every opportunity – regardless of that damned stupid agreement. She was his wife, his possession to do so with as he pleased.

He had never been stingy in the bedroom. He would see to it that she found a measure of enjoyment in his arms. Unless he was gravely mistaken, that should not prove too great a hardship for either one of them. She was a deeply passionate woman who would bloom nicely under his most excellent tutelage.

A slow smile of satisfaction spread across his lips. If their previous encounters were any indication, he would suffer through this deuced arrangement quite nicely. He had no reason to be nervous. None whatsoever. He felt the tension ease from his taut muscles. Yes, marriage would have definite advantages. His bride's lessons would commence this very night. He could scarcely wait to be done with the deuced formalities.

He scowled at his eagerness. His impatience to introduce his bride to the sensual world surpassed all comprehension. It was not as though he'd never made love to a woman before. But this was different. Tonight, it would be his wife he worshipped with his body. They might even make a baby together.

He loved dear little Annabelle with all his heart. But fatherhood was not a condition he'd ever fancied before in his life. He could not imagine the depth of feeling for a child of his own loins.

Certainly, the love one feels must be even more intense. He never realized how much he wanted a child. He chuckled softly. It was ironic, given that he'd spent most of his life trying to avoid that particular dilemma.

At long last, the soft strains of music drifted through the church and Simon's heart thudded against his ribs. The time had arrived. Tradition dictated that he face the altar while his bride walked up the aisle, but the insane desire to turn around and watch her walk towards him threatened to overpower him.

He quelled the urge. This whole thing was affecting him far too seriously. He needed to get a hold of himself. It wasn't as though theirs was a love match for heaven's sake. He was marrying her because he'd disgraced her and, more to the point, because Tony had threatened to call him out. Definitely not the stuff of which romantic dreams are made.

Feeling her presence at his side, he glanced down at the woman who would shortly grace his household and, more importantly, his bed. His heart gave a slight squeeze at the sight of her. She looked like an angel. He assumed the gown belonged to her sister, for no London dressmaker could have worked such a miracle in the allotted time. His gaze drifted over her bent head, bowed in uncharacteristic submission. He clasped her small, delicate hand in his. It felt like ice.

His brows sloped downward. His angel was pale and frightened. The discovery disturbed him.

Why, he wondered, as he recited the words the rector had spoken, did she look so utterly depressed? He was in the midst of swearing to worship her with his body and to endow her with all his worldly goods. And she looked ready to be ill. It did not sit at all well.

She was supposed to be glad. Happy. Grateful that he'd whisked her from the jaws of her vicious guardian. Pleased that he'd agreed to her outrageous premarital stipulations.

Instead, she looked like a scared little rabbit. It was bad enough that her left hand was stiff and reluctant as he'd slid the shining gold symbol of ownership on her third finger. But the fact that he was forced to lean down to hear her promise to cherish, honor and obey him, nettled him to the core.

He reminded himself that she was young and undoubtedly nervous. Lord knows what she'd heard about marriage. He gave her a small smile of encouragement, which was met with a cold, sombre expression.

His mouth thinned. So much for sympathy, he thought with a scowl. This was not the sort of day he had envisioned for his wedding day. Not that he had ever dreamt of living through such a day. But he did expect his bride to be blithe and gay. Weren't all brides joyful?

'You may kiss the bride,' the rector said with a beaming smile. He closed his leather-bound bible and crossed his hands reverently over his chest.

Simon turned to face the woman who was his wife before God. He clasped her by her shoulders and turned her to face him. Hell's teeth! She seemed to be fashioned out of wood. He drew her statue-still figure against him. Gazing down at her, he was intent on deciphering her unfathomable mood. But she kept her gaze averted from his assessing grey eyes. Worse yet, she made no move to accept his kiss. Lifting her bowed head, he angled her face to receive his kiss. And then his arm slid around her waist and he caught her hard against him. She grimaced and closed her eyes in revulsion.

Anger ignited deep within him. Repulsed, was she? Well, too bad. She was his wife now, his to do with as he pleased. She'd endure a kiss from her husband at the altar whether she welcomed it or not.

His head swooped down. His lips crushed hers in a bruising, punishing, angry kiss. Her hands curled into fists against his chest. She pushed against him. But his iron grip tightened around, imprisoning her against his hard, cruel, unyielding body. He heard her groan in protest. The passion drained out of him. He'd never forced himself on a woman and he'd be damned if he'd start with his wife.

Lifting his head, he loosed the blaze of his furious gaze on her. Her breathing was ragged, he noticed with a surge of male satisfaction. A look of staggering dismay was etched on her ghostly stricken face. But she uttered not a word.

So be it, he thought with cold fury, as he took her by the hand and roughly marched her down the aisle toward the back of the church.

He strode passed the small gathering of tearful well-wishers. She'd made her feelings patently clear.

No wonder she'd demanded he agree to those ludicrous conditions prior to their wedding. What a fool he was to imagine she was a blushing bride. Her insistence was born of contempt, not maidenly fear.

She truly did not wish to be his wife. His lips twisted into an angry snarl. The whole notion of marriage no doubt offended her delicate sensibilities. What had she said to him? *Even if I were foolish enough to marry a notorious rake – which I am not – I would scarcely choose you.*

Fine. He comprehended the situation all too well. Once he'd got her with child, he would leave her in the country. Good riddance. He only hoped she'd bear him a son. He did not wish to have to be involved with the little witch any more than courtesy demanded.

He'd find his comfort in the arms of a mature widow. Lady Estor struck his fancy. It would not take long to come a mutually beneficial arrangement with her. His little wife need not worry. She'd have her quiet country life. He fully intended to leave her there for the next twenty years. She could write her fill.

Simon managed to stand stoically at the back of the church and endure the saccharine well-wishers with cold indifference. He wanted to be done with the pomp and circumstance. His bride, he noticed with irritation, showed more warmth to virtual strangers than to her lawfully-wedded husband. It was only when Tony suggested they should depart for the wedding breakfast that she darted a glance in her husband's direction. Her gaze collided with his haughty, frigid expression and quickly skittered away. In far too bright a voice, she suggested to her sister, 'Why do you and Tony not travel to the wedding breakfast in our carriage?'

Tony gave her a look of surprise. 'You should be alone with your husband,' he reminded her gently.

Simon did not miss the look of horror that crossed his wife's face.

'That is not strictly necessary, Tony,' Joy remarked quickly, warming to the idea. She, at least, had the good grace to consult the groom. 'Have you any objections to our accompanying the bride and groom, my lord? Perhaps you would like time alone with your beautiful bride?'

Simon's icy gaze never left Celeste's ghostly face as he said, 'No, not at all. My bride and I owe you a debt of gratitude. Who else, under the circumstances, would have offered to host our wedding breakfast?'

Celeste bowed her head. Her nervous hands fidgeted with her small white bouquet of roses.

'The streets are crowded at this hour of day. It could take quite some time to arrive at Berkeley Square. I welcome Tony's company,' he said unkindly.

'Then it is settled,' Joy exclaimed with nauseating cheer.

The two girls descended the stone steps to the street. Their two heads were pressed together – chattering, no doubt, about some meaningless feminine trifle, Simon thought with annoyance.

Tony turned toward his friend and smiled broadly. 'I can scarcely believe it!'

'Believe what?' Simon asked, his gaze riveted to his reluctant bride.

'I never thought I'd see the day when you got caught in the parson's trap.' His hand came down on Simon's back in a hard slap. 'Congratulations, you are now a respectable married man. How does it feel?'

Simon looked away. It felt dreadful. He'd give anything to undo the last week of his life. What the devil had he been thinking? They'd never suit, much less find happiness. He must have been mad to offer for the chit.

Tony laughed. 'Matrimony has a way of insinuating itself into your life whether you like it or not.' His warm gaze drifted over his beloved wife chatting with her sister at the base of the church steps. 'They are quite a pair.'

'Indeed, they are,' Simon replied, his voice cool and reserved.

'Mind you, I doubt you stood a ghost of a chance once they'd set their sights on you.'

Simon's head turned sharply. 'What do you mean, set their sights?' he asked, his grey eyes narrowing into silver slits.

'Come along, old man,' Tony teased with a wry sideways glance at his friend, 'you know as well as I do, no man ever gets married because he wants to. We are all cajoled, pushed and finally seduced into it. Not that we regret it, mind you.'

Simon's face hardened to stone. 'No. I did not

know. How *precisely* was I cajoled into this marriage?,' he ground out.

Tony chuckled. 'I, myself, was surprised at the level of deceit involved in your particular case.'

'Were you?,' Simon mused, his irate gaze fixed on his bride. 'Why is that?'

'You should be flattered, old boy. You were selected from a long list of eligible bachelors.'

'Is that a fact?,' Simon bit out.

'Joy is convinced reformed rakes make the best husbands,' Tony explained. 'I am afraid I'm to blame for that misconception. You'll never believe it when I tell you,' he said, unable to conceal his jocularity, 'she actually felt sorry for you. Bachelors are never happy, don't you know?'

Simon's jaw clenched. 'Am I to understand,' he ground out, 'that your hopelessly romantic wife took it upon herself to pawn her wayward sister off on me?'

A look of astonishment crossed Tony's face. 'Never say you actually believed that Banbury tale about being ruined? If I know those two,' he remarked as he descended the church steps with Simon beside him, 'it was all a carefully orchestrated plan to snare the notorious Dragon.'

Simon's handsome face contorted with resentment. Oh, yes, it was all patently obvious to him now. The mercenary little cretin manipulated the situation with amazing finesse. The carefully-orchestrated escapades that drew him in to repeated scandalous circumstances. The teary-eyed stoic performance in front of the harsh grandfather. The coy refusal to

Simon's insistence they marry. It was all very well done indeed.

'I cannot tell you how ecstatic Joy was when you stumbled into that ridiculous, compromising situation all on your own. How *did* you two end up in Lady Declaire's bedroom?' Tony asked, his shoulders shaking with mirth.

Simon went rigid, contempt evident in his every feature. 'Why, your scheming sister-in-law contrived to meet me there, how else?' he replied, his temper near boiling point.

Tony laughed. 'I would not put anything past her.' He caught sight of his friend's countenance and frowned. 'I say, you aren't by any chance vexed, are you? Joy was concerned that you might not find their machinations as diverting as I. She swore me to secrecy. But I assured her that you had an excellent sense of humour.'

Simon watched the co-conspirators climb into his carriage. 'Did you?,' he murmured, contemplating murder.

'You don't really take exception to being led astray by feminine wiles?'

Turning towards his friend, Simon flashed a frigid smile. 'Of course not. As you say, all women are guilty of cunning and deceit.'

'I must say, it was deuced clever of our little Celeste to refuse you so adamantly at first. Nothing like a challenge to spur a man on, would you not agree? When poor Joy heard the news, she nearly swooned for fear that you might have retracted your offer.'

One end of Simon's mouth lifted in a sneer. 'Her little sister is a sound judge of character. She knew that, once issued, it was unlikely I would withdraw my offer.'

Oh, yes, the wily little charlatan made an excellent match for herself. He had twenty thousand a year and Lindhurst Manor. What a fool he was to believe in her. She'd played him like a fiddle. He couldn't credit his stupidity. At the ripe old age of two and thirty, how had he actually become tangled in such an obvious web of deceit? The mere idea infuriated him. No one forced his hand, least of all a hapless child. When he reflected on the guilt he'd suffered, believing himself responsible for her, he could explode.

As the conveyance wound its way through the bustling city streets, Joy and Tony engaged in forced idle chatter. Celeste managed to issue the occasional complaisant rejoinder. Simon, however, sat in brooding silence and wrestled with the unbecoming urge to throttle his bride. He could not credit the guileless woman he'd come to know as being capable of such heinous deceit. Tony had as much as admitted her female treachery without an ounce of shame. She was a practised little actress, just like every other woman he'd ever known. The only thing fresh and new about her was the packaging.

The wedding breakfast proceeded without incident. The gruelling three-hour affair consisted mostly of mindless chatter and romantic toasts. Teeth clenched, Simon sat at the head of the table, not once deigning to address his bride.

The guests grated on his nerves. They all seemed too animated. Their laughter sounded coarse to his ears. He could not abide another person wishing him happy.

'When do you leave for the country?,' Simon's good friend, Freddy Thompson, asked, munching on a slice of wedding cake. A piece of the very same confection lay conspicuously untouched on Simon's plate.

'I am in no hurry,' came Simon's terse reply.

Celeste's worried gaze flew to her husband's rigid face. She looked unnerved by his remark. 'I thought . . . we were to leave this very day?'

He fixed her with a hard look. 'No,' he uttered with decisive coolness. 'I have business to attend to in London.'

Given the state of his unholy marriage, he intended to continue his pursuit of the villain who had impregnated Emily and abandoned her, then they would travel to Kent for the dreaded interment. The sooner he suffered through the necessary period of time as man and wife and deposited the urchin at Lindhurst, the better.

'But surely you are as eager as I for the country?,' she asked in a futile attempt at civility.

'You mean,' he practically snarled, 'eager for my ebullient bride?'

Her gaze flittered away from his mordant expression.

'You should be pleased, my dear,' Freddy piped up.

Celeste essayed a bright smile. 'Why is that?'

'Your devoted husband must desire a long honeymoon if he chooses to finish his pressing business in London before undertaking the journey,' Freddy teased with a wink.

Simon offered no comment. He sat mutely at the head of the table, his countenance stark and forbidding.

Freddy's quip fell on an awkward silence. He cleared his throat and mumbled something about the delightful wedding cake.

A mantle of red spread over Celeste's cheeks. She ran a nervous finger over the gilded edge of her cake plate.

Simon's gaze weighed heavily on his bride. If the cunning little virago thought her feminine wiles would soften him, she was gravely mistaken. He was not a man who suffered deceit easily. If she was miserable, she had no one to blame but herself. He threw his napkin down on his uneaten piece of wedding cake and got to his feet.

'Come, let us away.'

Celeste was glad of the timely reprieve, however ill-meant. It had not taken her long to deduce, from her husband's terse demeanour, that she, alone, was the object of his displeasure. Why that should be so was beyond her reckoning.

It was, however, making her terribly nervous. His harsh countenance throughout their interminable wedding breakfast had her nerves in shreds. She could scarcely recall a more gruelling episode.

She felt perilously close to weeping, a self-indulgent pastime she'd given up years ago. And yet it took a supreme effort not to burst into copious tears. She couldn't understand her pathetic weakness. She dearly hoped she was not turning into a watering pot.

The only thing that saved her from sobbing was the sure and certain knowledge that her brutish husband would be pleased to see her break down under the strain. And she refused to give him the satisfaction. Besides, she knew from experience, self-pity was a useless waste of her time and energy.

The customary pleasantries finally endured, the wedding-day celebration drew to a close. The four family members gathered by Simon's carriage in a solitary circle.

'Celeste, you were the most lovely bride I have ever seen,' Tony remarked with a sunny smile.

'Indeed, you are,' Joy cried, and pressed a kiss to her sister's pale cheek. 'What a wonderful mistress of Lindhurst you will make, dearest.'

Sickened by the sight, Simon stated with abrupt rudeness, 'It is time we left.'

Heedless of the gawking onlookers, he caught his bride by the arm and gruffly steered her towards the open door of his carriage. Celeste glanced over her shoulder at her concerned sister and brother-in-law and tried to smile. They waved goodbye. Joy blew her several kisses and wished her happy.

'Get in,' Simon said curtly. Seeing his dark forbidding expression, her lashes fluttered downward and she climbed inside his private carriage.

The carriage lurched forward, carrying her from the people she loved most into a new and uncharted existence as the Dragon's wife. Try as she might, she was unable to loosen the painful knot in which her stomach was twisted. She shivered with trepidation. What had she got herself into with her foolish headstrong ways? Total ruin was eminently superior to marriage.

Celeste could feel her husband's dark, penetrating stare, but she remained glued to the conveyance wall. Keeping her gaze fixed on the mundane events transpiring beyond the window saved her from a confrontation with the ominous stranger she'd just sworn to honor and obey till death do them part.

She sensed, at long last, when his burning gaze drifted from her. Her breathing came a little easier. Stealing a covert glance at his chiseled profile, a dead weight settled on her chest. His jaw looked to be fashioned from granite.

The furious expression he wore was horribly familiar to her now that they were man and wife. Gone were his roguish eyes and teasing manner. Reluctantly, she admitted she preferred the playful rake to the ogre he'd transformed into seemingly overnight. What had she done to deserve his censure? As if sensing her scrutiny, he turned his cold grey eyes to hers.

'Happy, dearest?' His smile was a travesty.

She dropped his gaze. Her tongue darted nervously between her parched lips. 'My lord, I fear I have displeased you in some way,' she said, making a stab at cordial conversation. 'Pray, tell me what is troubling you so that I may remedy your displeasure?'

Your deceitful nature. 'Nothing is troubling me,' he replied, his tone like ice. 'Certainly nothing that my *devoted* wife could remedy.'

She stiffened at his sarcastic barb. 'I could hardly lay claim to devotion, my lord,' she replied in a voice that held a note of challenge, 'any more than you could swear your undying fidelity and expect me to believe it.'

He flashed a humourless smile. 'Ah, yes, our mutually beneficial agreement. How clever of you to insist upon it before the ceremony.'

Nonplussed, she stared at him and tried to fathom his strange mood. 'Neither one of us wished to marry,' she reminded him pointedly.

'Even so,' he said, his grey stormy eyes gleaming, 'you must be quite pleased with yourself.'

'What cause do I have to be joyous?,' she asked with a hint of bitterness.

'Why, you've married a man with twenty thousand a year and three enviable estates. I'd say you've done very well. Very well indeed.'

She disliked his insinuation heartily. 'I care little for such luxuries, I assure you, my lord,' she countered, her mien cool. 'It is evident, however, you are of a different mind altogether. Nothing I might say will invoke your good opinion.'

He uttered a derisive snort. 'A novel experience for you, to be sure.'

If he intended to continue in this implacable mood, their union promised to be intolerable. She drew a weary sigh and turned her attention once more to the bustling world out the window. She wondered wryly

193

whether the happy pedestrians had any inkling of how miserable the Dragon's bride was?

Celeste barely had time to admire the elegant, dark green marbled foyer of Simon's fashionable townhouse. The moment they arrived, he barked instructions at his stodgy butler to have his bride's possessions installed above stairs. A light supper was to be prepared for Lady Barclay in her boudoir. Simon would be going out directly.

'If you will follow me, Lady Barclay,' he said in a brusque tone that brooked no disobedience.

Without so much as a backward glance in her direction, he strode down the narrow hallway towards a small sitting room. She had no choice but to trail submissively behind him.

When they were alone, he addressed her, the strain of maintaining civility evident in his terse manner. 'The servants will be only too happy to accommodate you, you need only ask.'

'What of you, my lord?,' she dared to inquire, curiosity making her bold.

He hesitated for a moment before he told her in no uncertain terms, 'I have some personal matters to attend to and shall dine at my club this evening. For the present, it would be best if you tried to rest. We've a long night ahead of us,' he told her with a meaningful glint in his eye.

The color drained from her face. 'A long night?' Her voice sounded high-pitched even to her own ears.

He leaned his elbow against the mantle and stared at her for a long, charged moment. His steely grey eyes glittered with inexplicable anger and something else she could not quite discern. 'The arduous task of greeting all your servants awaits you, my dear. I know you wish to make an excellent impression as the new Lady Barclay,' he remarked with thinly veiled sarcasm.

'Yes, of course. How foolish of me. I quite forgot about my household duties. Rest assured, I shall not disappoint you, my lord.'

He fixed her with a sardonic look. 'A word to the wise, my dear,' he averred sharply. 'It is ill-advised to make promises you cannot keep.'

'Is that the voice of experience?,' she flung back at him before she could halt her tongue.

His withering and cold gaze stabbed at her. 'I am sure your eagerness to revel in the spoils of your excellent marriage will help you endure the strain of being married to me,' he said bitterly.

He strode across the room to gaze out the window as if he could not bear to gaze upon her.

What had she done to incur his wrath? Celeste could do little more than stare at the ominous man with his proud, angry back to her.

Spoils of marriage? What that cryptic remark was meant to convey she could not imagine. Nor did she wish to try. At the moment, she was tired and extremely uncomfortable.

'I am sure I shall weather the storm quite well,' she murmured on a miserable sigh and quietly left the room.

CHAPTER 10

It lacked the hour of ten that evening when his lordship strode into his wife's bedroom – unannounced and, for that matter, uninvited.

The bedroom door swung open. Celeste looked up. Her startled gaze collided with her husband's piercing grey orbs. He'd shed his wedding clothes and wore superfines that fit like a second skin, she observed with a hard swallow, and a linen shirt that bared a healthy portion of inviting bronze skin.

'I'll see to her ladyship's needs for the rest of the evening,' he said, his eyes dancing with devilment.

Celeste flushed crimson at his blatantly sexual insinuation. 'That will be all, Fanny,' she said softly.

'Yes, milady,' the maid replied with a quick curtsy. Darting a nervous glance at his lordship, Fanny scurried from the room like a frightened mouse.

Celeste willed the rampant butterflies in her stomach to settle down. No cause for concern – after all, they had an agreement. One thing nagged at her, however – what was he doing in her bedroom?

196

His slow seductive gaze roamed over her. Unnerved, she felt herself grow warm and quickly looked away. She shook off her trepidation. Even if her husband was behaving strangely, he would never go back on his word. A sinking feeling invaded her stomach. Or . . . would he?

'Would you care for something to drink?,' he asked, sauntering towards her, crystal decanter in one hand and balloon glass in the other.

Celeste's head snapped up. A drink? Did women of his acquaintance drink?

He chuckled softly at her look of surprise. 'A glass of brandy, perhaps?,' he offered amicably and took a swallow of the amber liquid. 'I am afraid I am all out of lemonade and ratafia at the moment.'

He was mocking her, of course. 'No, thank you,' she replied with prim curtness and resumed the braiding of her hair. She tried to project an outward calm. In reality, however, her heart galloped almost painfully in her chest. She couldn't quite believe she was married. And to the Dragon.

She was his. To do with as he pleased . . . whenever he pleased. A dizzying current of excitement ran through her. What would she say if he pressed her to perform her marriage duty this evening? She caught her lower lip between her teeth. Egad, what then?

The stack of novels she'd cast haphazardly on the end of the bed caught Simon's eye. He cocked his dark head to read the binding. *Ivanhoe*. He gave her a blank look of surprise.

'You've read *Ivanhoe*?,' he asked, amazed by the

197

discovery for he had scarcely managed to find time to crack the binder.

'Naturally, I've read it. I *can* read, my lord,' she muttered tersely. 'I've been given to understand my penmanship is more than merely passable. And I still have all my teeth.'

'I've noticed,' he remarked, rifling through the pile of novels. *Coelebs in Search of a Wife*, *Evelina* and *Glenarvon*. 'They are almost as sharp as your barbed tongue.'

He snatched Lady Caroline Lamb's *Glenarvon* from the pile. 'Where the deuce did you get this?'

Celeste frowned at his reflection in the mirror. 'I suppose,' she muttered on a bored sighed, 'you are shocked that I have read it.'

Shaking his head, he tossed the scandalous book on the bed. 'On the contrary, you never cease to amaze me. Tell me,' his dark drawly voice asked, as he dropped into the chair beside the crackling fireplace, 'is there no end to your eccentricities?'

Her chin came up. Hateful man! Wouldn't she *love* to wipe that arrogant smirk off his far-too-handsome face.

'Indeed not. I've read all of Byron. And most of Shelley too,' she told him with an imperious air.

One ebony brow elevated slightly. 'Have you, indeed? *Prometheus Unbound?*,' he queried with maddening condescension.

She scowled at him. That book had only recently been published. He knew full well she could not possibly have read it. 'No. But I have read Mary Shelley's *Frankenstein*,' she replied pointedly.

He flashed an indulgent smile. 'How'd you like it?'

'Not at all.' She wrinkled up her nose in disdain. 'What utter rubbish. Re-animating a dead person – it is preposterous to imagine a current running through each one of us.'

A satyr smile spread across his face. 'Oh, I don't know.' His hooded, deeply sensual gaze raked over her gossamer-thin nightgown. 'Looking at you right now, I don't have too much trouble believing that.'

My! He *was* wicked! The way he was looking at her would put a harlot to the blush. Never before had she been on the receiving end of a purely lustful gaze. Her cheeks flooded with color. She lowered her gaze. She felt like an inexperienced lamb in a hungry lion's den. And yet she found herself strangely excited by the dark, imposing man who was her husband. Mercifully, he changed the subject.

'I don't suppose your grandfather had any inkling of this unusual pastime of yours?'

She pulled a face. 'Heavens, no. Tony gets the books for me.'

'Ah.' Simon took another sip of brandy. 'Dear old helpful Tony. What would we do without him?' he mocked.

She set her brush down and turned to face her taunting spouse. 'I happened to be very fond of Tony.'

He gave her a frigid smile. 'A nice cosy little family circle,' he opined with scorn.

Her eyes flashed with temper. 'Nice is not a word that leaps to mind where you are concerned.'

The firelight glow cast his face in a saturnine light. 'Marriage not all you hoped it would be, *dearest*?'

'How could marriage to you be something any girl hoped for?'

His impressive male figure unfolded from the chair. In a heartbeat, he crossed the room to where she sat. Craning her neck back, she stared up at him. Dark and forbidding, he was a man who could easily bend a frail female to his will. But she was not frail, she reminded herself with a hard gulp.

Acutely conscious of his raw masculinity towering over her, she got to her feet. It was a futile attempt to deflect his intimidating power and size. And it failed. What had she got herself into? she wondered with a spine-tingling shiver. How on earth would she survive the kind of intimacy Joy described with an implacable, angry man like him?

'It doesn't hurt that your husband has twenty thousand a year,' he ground out with icy contempt.

'I dare say it does little to make you more agreeable to my way of thinking,' she replied, despising the breathless quality of her voice.

His angry gaze threatened to devour her whole. 'No?' he snarled. His hands closed over her arms, dragging her against his rock-hard chest. 'My zest for life poses a problem for your mercenary little heart?'

Anger flared in her breast, loosening her tongue. 'My heart is not in the least mercenary, my lord,' she told him brusquely. 'But even if it were, what possible difference could it make to you?'

His piercing silver gaze flickered her face. 'I assure you,' he told her bitterly, 'it makes no difference to me, one way or the other, provided that when I choose to bed you, you are warm and willing in my arms. And you please me to my satisfaction.'

She drew in a shocked breath. 'We had an agreement,' she insisted, her voice laced with trepidation. 'You said –'

He fixed her with a level stare. 'Your naïvety astounds me, dear heart.'

'But you gave me your word,' she insisted, her voice nearly shrill with panic.

As if dealing with a temperamental child, he offered her a benign smile. His tone, however, was curt and steel-edged. 'I am your husband. I'll decide what should be done with you. And when.'

She knew the direction this conversation was taking and swiftly decided to put an end to it. 'I have nothing further to say to you,' she said, willing herself to stop quivering. But it was no use. Her husband was far too alluring an opponent for her body to resist.

'No?' His derisive chuckle made her shiver. 'How odd. I have a whole host of questions to put to you.'

Her tongue nervously darted between her parched lips. 'L-like what?,' she croaked.

He bared his teeth in a lethal grin. 'Just wait and see, my little minx. Wait and see.'

The color drained from her face. 'You cannot mean to –'

'I intend to secure my heir by the new year. Your beautiful ripe body is the only advantage I am likely to enjoy from this blasted arrangement. I've no doubt I'll find some measure of comfort in your arms.'

His crudity served to heightened her trepidation no small degree. She swallowed. Her throat felt like flint. But her indomitable spirit would not allow her to back away from a confrontation.

Casting a defiant glare at him, she spat, 'You comport yourself like an offensive boor. I have no intention of submitting to you. It would be best were you to leave before you make an even bigger fool out of yourself.' Having thrown down her gauntlet, she held her breath and braced herself for his response.

For a scant moment, she thought he might heed her advice, but then he uttered a low growl of desire and crushed her to him.

Before she could protest, his open mouth came down on hers, hot, wet and demanding. His arms tightened around her, imprisoning her intimately against his strong, solid, masterful body. He smothered her lips in a bruising passionate kiss. Impatient hands tore at her nightgown, eager to feel her soft silky skin beneath his palms. His hand slid down her back, branding her with his searing touch, and smoothed over her hips, caressing her soft curves, grinding her hips against his, making her all too aware of the effect she was having on him.

At first, he thought her moans were from pleasure. It did not take him long to realize he repulsed her.

He pushed her away. 'What the devil is the matter with you?,' he panted, his face flushed with desire. 'Why do you recoil in disgust every time I touch you?'

She turned her back. 'Please . . . leave me,' she choked out, clutching the bedpost for much-needed support.

'Devil take it, madam, I am your husband,' he told her roughly.

Hurt and angered by her rejection, he reached for her, but she shied away from him. 'By God, I've the right to touch you,' he growled and caught her nightgown in his fists, partially baring her back. What he saw made him pause. 'Good Lord,' he breathed. Her back was covered with black and blue marks. 'What happened?'

She tugged her nightgown over her shoulder. 'It is nothing,' she said with a sniffle that told him she was crying. 'Pray, my lord, do not concern yourself.'

At seeing the cruel evidence of abuse, his resentment dissolved instantly. Whatever else she might be, she certainly did not deserve to be beaten like an animal.

He told himself he was not softening toward her. He was still livid with her deception. But that did not prevent him from feeling compassion.

He took her by the shoulders and turned her to face him. 'I do concern myself.' Cradling her face between his hands, he lifted her tearstained face to his. 'Who did this to you?' he asked softly, the pads of his thumbs brushing the tears from her cheeks.

Her lashes drifted downward. 'Can you not guess?'

He frowned with cold fury. 'That heartless brute,' he ground out. 'He did this to you?'

She nodded and hugged her waist. 'I believe the expression is caning, my lord. Ordinarily, I am put on bread and water and locked in my room. The very worst he'd ever done before was cut my hair. Apparently,' she said, mopping the tears with her sleeve, 'bringing disgrace on his good name was the final straw. Total ruin warranted something a trifle more drastic.'

'When?,' he demanded, his anger waxing by the minute. 'When did he do this to you?'

'Directly after your interview. I am afraid he took a rather strong dislike to you, my lord. He does not enjoy having his nose tweaked. And I am afraid you tweaked it rather hard.'

Simon swore under his breath.

'My wicked indiscretion deserved severe punishment. Goodness knows he has a formidable temper.' She winced at the memory. 'I wonder if it might not have been better for us both had you not come,' she said, gingerly inspecting the condition of her back. 'It would seem to be excessively poor form for a Wentworth to be compromised by a rake, but stooping to marriage is beyond the pale.'

His brows snapped together. 'Precisely how often has this sort of thing happened?' he asked, his tone grim.

'This is the first. And I hope the last time.' She tried to smile but sniffled instead. 'Unless, of course, you own a cane?'

He did not look amused. 'You must see a doctor.'

She shook her head and tried to put a bright face on an utterly mortifying circumstance. 'I'll feel all right in a few days. It is just a bit tender at the moment,' she remarked, wincing.

He thrust his fingers through his thick black hair. Hell's teeth. No wondered she was stiff and reserved in the church. The condition of her back certainly went a long way towards explaining her lacklustre attitude at the altar. That embrace he gave her must have hurt.

'Why the devil did you not tell me?,' he snapped, his anger directed at himself rather than at her.

She shrugged and grimaced for her effort. 'I was . . . humiliated.' Her eyes welled with tears. 'I – I did not want you to know.'

He caressed her red blotchy cheek with his palm. 'Did you think that likely, given that we are man and wife?,' he asked, his tone softening.

She blinked away her tears. 'I don't see why not.'

He dismissed her naïve assumption with a deep frown. 'No,' he said, dropping his hand, 'you wouldn't.'

'The embarrassing truth would have remained a secret had you honored our agreement,' she grumbled, dragging her sleeve along her running nose.

He fixed her with a sardonic look. She looked like a child. Corrupt blood must run in his veins. He was sorely tempted to pull her into his arms and smother her swollen rosebud lips with his own.

'Our so-called agreement allowed for a change of heart, if you will recall.'

'You never intended to honor our agreement, did you?' she asked, her voice nearly cracking with emotion.

He frowned slightly. 'Enough about that damned foolish agreement,' he replied irritably.

'You lied to me.'

'Not . . . exactly,' he said with a good deal of discomfort. What the devil was the matter with him? Tonight was his wedding night. By all rights, she should be apologizing to him.

'I am no more guilty of deception than you,' his voice was suddenly harsh, 'you are not the innocent you pretend to be.'

She fixed him with a frosty glare. 'I think you are despicable.'

His grey eyes turned cold and distant. 'Regardless of your fine opinion of me,' he told her brusquely, 'you will see a doctor first thing tomorrow morning.'

She nodded her head and issued a dutiful, 'If you insist, my lord.'

His jaw clenched. What he would not give to get his hands on her hateful grandfather. 'You will never see that vicious old man again. Do you understand me?'

She smiled at him. 'You've no need to worry, my lord. He has disowned me.'

'Good riddance. Nothing like this will ever happen to you while you are under my protection. I am not given to uncontrollable fits of rage.'

'That is immensely reassuring, my lord. What, pray, am I to do when you decide to break your word and pounce on me?,' she asked flippantly.

'I did not pounce,' he bit out. 'And if memory serves,' he said, letting his sultry gaze drift over her, 'you did not seem to mind overmuch. Until I touched your back, you seemed to enjoy being pounced on.'

'I did nothing of the sort,' she countered sharply. But the hot color suffusing her cheeks told him differently.

He massaged the back of his neck. 'It is getting late,' he said with a weary sigh. 'You need some rest. I'll send for the doctor first thing tomorrow.'

'Does this mean you intend to honor our agreement after all?'

He gave her a hard look. 'You have precious little to fear from me, dear heart.'

'Fiddle faddle!,' she cried. 'You are evading the issue, my lord.'

He refused to dignify her childish reaction with a response. His feet carried him across the threshold of his bedroom. He slammed the connecting door shut with a resounding thud. He shook his head and wondered what the devil *fiddle faddle* was meant to convey?

Having spent the better part of a sleepless night digesting the ramifications of her predicament, Celeste decided it was totally unpalatable. It was nearly three o'clock in the morning before she'd arrived at her brilliant conclusion. Just because she *was* married to Simon did not mean she had to *stay* married to him. She could easily get an annulment, or even a divorce.

She did not have a moment to lose, for she intended to announce her intentions to him this very morning. Honour had been served. He'd done the noble thing. He'd married her and saved her good name. What difference would it make to him if they annulled their farcical marriage?

Very soon now, she'd have her quiet country life and he could return to his rakish ways. Both of them would be blissfully happy. Or, at least, as happy as they'd ever been prior to meeting.

She heard footsteps shuffling across Simon's room. She stiffened. After last night's exchange, she dreaded their next encounter. Taking a deep fortifying breath, she decided it was now or never. A quick, nervous examination of her reflection in the mirror made her frown.

She bit her lip. Oh, dear. Her pale yellow muslin morning gown made her look like a spinster. Oh, bother! What did she care? It wasn't as if the Dragon found her attractive in the least. On the contrary, he despised her.

Grandfather was entirely correct, no man would ever admire her looks. She was too unconventional to be considered even remotely attractive. She tore her gaze away from the reflecting glass, for it never contained a satisfactory image.

Mustering her courage, she assured herself that this was for the best and decided to dive headlong into the fray.

Nevertheless, her hand shook as she clasped the door knob to the connecting door and tapped lightly. There was a momentary hesitation before she heard him utter a gruff, 'Come.'

She opened the door and froze. To her amazement, he was standing before her shirtless. Obviously fresh from a bath, his wet hair was slicked back from his handsome face.

Her heart galloped in her chest. Heavens. If possible, he looked twice as handsome as usual. Her fascinated gaze pored over his hard, lean body. She gulped. She'd never seen a man – half-naked or otherwise. The effect was rather . . . unsettling.

Living in a female-dominated house with her sister most of her life, she never dreamed anything quite like the Dragon existed. The difference between the masculine, well-muscled specimen standing before her and her wrinkled aged grandfather threatened to overwhelm her. His raw masculinity was oddly exciting.

She knew Simon's body was formidable. She'd felt his hard sinewy muscles beneath his shirt. But his bare chest was broader than she had imagined. And his shoulders were much wider than her mind could ever have conceived. He was quite magnificent, she thought on a dreamy sigh.

Heat crept into her face. Her greedy eyes devoured over his taut, firm stomach that rippled down to his nicely tapered waist. It looked not unlike the wash-board the servants used for scrubbing. Thick black hair covered his well-defined chest. She had to quell the urge to touch him, to weave her fingers in his coarse hair and savour the solid muscles hidden beneath.

Flustered, she tore her fascinated gaze away and forced herself to look anywhere but at her splendidly-made husband in all his semi-naked glory.

'I'm sorry . . . I – I didn't realize you were . . . were indisposed,' she stammered nervously. In an effort to shield her acute discomfort, she turned around aimlessly in search of her own room.

'I am not indisposed,' he replied with curt indifference and dismissed his valet who was lurking obediently in the background. When they were alone, he fixed her with a chilling glare. 'What is it you wanted?' he asked, his voice stiff with civility.

She could not bring herself to look at him. He was far too tempting. She would further embarrass herself by ogling the man. Lowering her lashes, she said in a voice that did not sound at all like her own, 'I have been thinking –'

He cocked a dubious brow. 'Have you, indeed? This is becoming a rather unfortunate habit.'

Pricked by his insult, she lifted her defiant gaze to his.

Regarding her with a cynical smile, he put his hand on his narrow hips emphasizing his powerful thighs and his tapered hips. 'What is it this time, my sweet?,' he asked in a voice that dripped condescension.

'I want a divorce,' she told him bluntly.

'You want *what*?,' he thundered, truly amazed by her audacity. After twenty-four hours of the marriage she'd manipulated him into, she had the impudence to demand release.

In two angry strides, he closed the distance between them. His powerful, hard, lean body moved with lithe grace. She took a step back from his towering wrath. Her back collided with the door.

'I – I want a divorce, or an annulment, if you prefer,' she repeated, trying to remain calm. 'It matters not to me.'

'There has never been a divorce in my family,' he ground out, pinning her against the door. 'I do not intend to break with tradition. In other words, madam,' he said icily, 'the answer is, unequivocally, no. No divorce. Ever.'

Incensed, she slapped her hands on her hips and glared up at him. 'Why not? After all, my lord, we are hardly in each other's pockets.'

His savage expression loomed perilously close to her face as he leaned down, trapping her between two powerful, well-toned arms. Her spine pressed against the wall.

'I have no intentions of disgracing my family with the scandal of divorce,' he said, fighting for control over his temper. 'Our marriage is steeped in sufficient controversy as it is, do you not agree?'

She flushed in unspoken accord. 'Fine.' She cleared her throat. 'If not a divorce, then an annulment.'

His gleaming eyes narrowed into dangerous silver pinpoints. 'Under the law, you are my chattel, my property, to do with as I please. And I say there will be no divorce. The only thing that is going to separate us, dear heart,' he said brutally, 'is death. I suggest you get used to being Lady Barclay.'

'Ooh!' she railed, stamping her foot. 'You are impossible! You did the noble task of marrying me. Your family will not suffer if we get an annulment.'

'There will be no annulment!' he roared.

'We clearly do not suit,' she protested with energy. 'There is no reason to remain in this mockery of a marriage –'

'My dear girl,' he said harshly, 'it is of little consequence to me whether we suit or not. If necessary, I will eliminate any possibility of an annulment, bruises or not.'

She recoiled in dismay. 'Pray, my lord, do not be vulgar. You make your point with brutal clarity.'

'Good,' he said in a lethal tone and moved away from her to prowl the room like a caged panther. 'I cannot credit your insolence. You got what you wanted,' he lashed out cruelly. 'You thought to escape the consequences of your scheming *and* to garner a yearly income from your gullible husband, is that it? Well, unpalatable or not, you asked to be Lady Barclay. And I come with the title, madam.'

Outraged, she cried with energy, 'How precisely did I ask for this? I had no wish to marry you.' Tossing her curly mane over her shoulder, she crossed her arms over her heaving chest. 'I dislike you heartily. You have nothing to recommend yourself. Your character is churlish and argumentative. Furthermore, my lord husband,' she panted with fury, 'your main inclination is to be unkind and selfish.'

The pulse in his cheek throbbed with a vengeance. 'Are you quite finished assassinating my character?,' he asked through his teeth.

She arched her chin defiantly. 'For the moment,' she replied tersely, 'yes.'

His chiseled features set in a furious scowl. 'Since you are such an excellent judge of character, pray tell me your opinion of a young woman who, in collusion with her dear sister, contrives to entrap a man, a very affluent man, mind you, by spinning tall tales and waxing deceit. Have I etched an accurate portrait of your character, do you think?'

Her eyes widened owlishly. 'I never did any such thing,' she gasped. 'You conceited, arrogant, bombastic man! How dare you flatter yourself into thinking I set my cap for you. I would have to be stark raving mad to desire you for a husband.'

His disdainful gaze swept the length of her. 'Perhaps you are stark raving mad,' he taunted, for he obviously disbelieved her heated rebuttal. 'It would be consistent with my lack of fortune.'

She fixed him with a frosty gaze. 'My lord,' she blustered with contempt, 'understand me when I say *you* are hardly the quintessential husband and are the very last man I should ever wish to marry.'

His silver gaze sharpened. 'Is that so? Why, then, did your beloved brother-in-law confess your wretched scheme to me not five minutes after you'd secured your position as my wife?'

Her brow furrowed in confusion. '*Tony* told you this fantasy?' She was all astonishment.

'Fantasy?,' he muttered with scorn. 'I wish it were. Your jubilant sister confessed your contrivance with relish.'

Celeste looked more confused than ever. 'Joy?' she echoed dumbfounded. 'What does she have to do with this?'

Slowly, the truth dawned. A sense of dread enveloped her. She slumped down on the edge of the bed. No wonder Joy had plied her with enticing details of the infamous Dragon.

'I'll strangle her,' she hissed under her breath. 'The meddling, foolish, henwitted romantic. How could she do this to me?,' she groaned, her head in her hands.

He uttered a derisive grunt. 'You don't figure largely as the victim, dear heart.'

'My lord,' she moaned as her fingers washed over her miserable face, 'I fear we have both been the pawns of a most heinous cupid.'

He gave her a dark sceptical look. 'If you expect me to believe you are innocent –'

'Oh, do come along. If I had wanted to trap you, I could have easily done so at Holmes's garden party.'

'If memory serves, you did try,' he countered coolly.

'To achieve ruin, *not* marriage. A simple confession from me relating the salient points of your scandalous kiss in the library would have elicited a harsh demand for a marriage proposal from dear old Grandpapa. Of that, you must have no doubt.'

He did not look convinced.

'How can you be so dimwitted as to believe I play a part in securing for myself a fate that promises to be worse than death?'

He fixed her with a crushing gaze. 'It is you who are dimwitted, if you think for one moment this performance will sway my opinion.'

She was utterly nonplussed. 'I scarcely would demand release if I'd invested time and energy to lure you to the altar. Even your colossal ego will allow that much.'

He shrugged. 'Marriage to me is not all you had hoped.'

'I commend you, my lord,' she sniped with sarcasm. 'You have, at last, arrived upon the truth.'

'Indeed I have. You, my dear, are a grasping, cunning young woman who'll go to any lengths to get what she wants.'

Her temper rose. 'Oh! You are beyond the pale,' she cried, her frustration growing by leaps and bounds. 'Would I have insisted on our nuptial agreement if I were eager to wed you? I care not one farthing for your money, your title or your splendid home,' she told him bitterly. 'It is my heart's desire to be free to pursue my intellectual interests, not marry an egotistical puffed-up man who is conceited enough to believe I trapped him into an unwanted marriage.'

Simon gave her a dark look.

'If you do not believe I have provided a faithful description,' she imparted on a huff, 'you may ask Joy for the true narrative of events.'

'Your sister will produce a similar fabrication, of that I've little doubt.'

Flabbergasted, she stared at him. 'You think I intended to be caught in Lady Declaire's bedroom?'

His mouth was a grim line of reproach. 'I doubt the circumstances were of great import.'

Her mouth fell open. 'Is your conceit boundless? In your infinite arrogance, you actually imagine I purposefully trapped you?'

'I do not imagine it,' he told her, his expression like ice. 'I know it.'

She was at her wit's end with the maddening man. 'In that case, why did I refuse you? If I were eager to snare a wealthy mate, I scarcely would have dared spurn your offer for fear that you would have retracted it,' she threw the words at him.

He offered her a twisted smile. 'Ah, but you are a clever little minx, are you not? As an avid student of human nature, you knew all too well that what seems unattainable to a man becomes a burning necessity.'

She blinked at him in complete astonishment. 'You think . . . you truly believe I purposefully refused your offer in order to arouse your interest?'

A wicked gleam lit his gaze as it drifted, with excruciating thoroughness, over her flushed face and heaving bosom. One end of his enticing mouth lifted slightly. 'Among other things,' he imparted with hateful mockery, 'yes. Now, if this charming little interview is at an end, you may do me the honor of getting out of my sight.'

She gaped at him, incredulous. The arrogance of the man was untenable. How dare he insinuate she was a liar? She, set a trap to snare him? It was unconscionable. The very last thing she wanted was to be the wife of a boorish, conceited buffoon like him. Her blood boiled.

'Nothing,' she flung back at him, 'would give me greater pleasure. Your insufferable attitude is too much to be borne.' Turning on her heel, she fled the room in a swirl of yellow muslin.

A scant hour later, the elderly Doctor Ennis was summoned. Simon chose, to Celeste's acute dismay, to remain present during the humiliating examination. Silent and brooding, he stood with his arms clasped behind his back, watching her with those piercing grey eyes.

It was mortifying. The single pleasurable moment was derived when the doctor made the assumption that Simon was responsible for his wife's condition. Affronted, Simon swiftly assured him to the contrary.

Doctor Ennis pronounced Celeste's back 'bruised' and offered some salts for daily use in a warm bath. She was not at all certain they'd promote healing, but she intended to use them for fear her husband insisted on their use – personally. Of course, that would require he acknowledge her presence, which he showed little inclination to do.

It was unsettling the way Simon watched with keen interest as she fumbled with her nightgown in an effort to shield her nudity from his penetrating dark eyes. She could not fathom why her husband stood mutely at the side of the bed. The doctor had taken his leave.

She chafed beneath his smouldering gaze and asked him pointedly, 'Was there something you wished, my lord?'

Slowly, he tore his scorching gaze from her round firm breasts shielded only slightly by her thin cotton nightgown and raised his eyes to hers. 'As soon as you are able to travel,' he told her curtly, 'we shall leave for Lindhurst.'

One eyebrow arched slightly. 'We?,' she queried brazenly. 'I thought we meant to lead separate lives.'

The muscle leapt in his cheek. 'I intend to accompany you only for the sake of appearances,' he said tightly.

'Yes, of course. Appearances. Pray remember, my lord,' she said, toying with the lace cuff of her nightgown, 'I have no illusions of a romantic

217

honeymoon. Nor do I wish for one with you. You are free to return to London with all possible haste.'

His eyes flickered with rage. 'In that case, we both have reason to celebrate.'

She gave him a startled look. 'I cannot think of a reason. You and I are still man and wife,' she quipped with sarcasm.

He placed his hand on the headboard and leaned down. His dark, finely-carved features sharpened. Her instinct was to lean away from him, to slink back into the pillows. She quelled it.

'Never fear. You will realize your ambition, my sweet,' he told her in a deadly voice.

Her heart lodged in her throat. 'What ambition is that?' she dared to ask, despising her quivering voice.

'I fully intend to leave you in the country, pursuing your intellectual interests, till you are old and gray.'

CHAPTER 11

Several days later, as Simon descended the steps of his townhouse, his mood was not further improved by the torrential downpour that pounded without mercy upon his back. The thunderous crack that traversed the darkened sky came as little surprise to his jaded ears. Foul weather suited his disposition and his fortune of late, he thought as he climbed into his waiting carriage.

As the conveyance lurched forward, he scowled at his own lack of foresight. Had he actually been foolish enough to envision a romantic honeymoon in the country with his child bride? The little chit's duplicity nettled him even now. How dare she act the wronged innocent when all along she'd connived and weasled her way into his home and his deep pockets? After more than a decade of blissful freedom and sexual foraging, he'd done the one thing he'd sworn never to do: let a coquette dupe him.

Gad, he thought, throwing his endless legs on to the opposite seat, the past few days had been a living hell. He was eager to quit the lavish townhouse that had once been his bachelor refuge. Every room seemed to smell like his wife. He could practically *feel* her presence permeating the entire household. Only this afternoon, he had come across a lacy scented handkerchief with the initials CW crookedly embroidered across the top lying on his favourite reading chair. How dare she invade his private sanctuary with her soft, enticing femininity?

The woman was obviously useless with the needle. In fact, he could not think of any ordinary female pastime at which she excelled. Still, he had never noticed before how luxurious and shiny her coppery hair was. He longed to reach out and touch it. It would feel so damned good to run his fingers through her soft tresses and inhale the sweet scent.

He had never taken notice of the endearing habit she had of running her tongue over her lips when she was nervous or deeply engrossed in thought. He'd been tempted on those occasions to cover her delectable mouth with his own.

The chit was deuced inviting. Not at all what he wished to be confronted with at the breakfast table each morning. She was far too desirable for his liking. He could not believe how incredibly appealing she looked garbed in the modest, schoolgirl gowns that fit all too snugly over her soft, round bosom. They were not meant to be the least bit provocative. But the deuced gowns were driving him wild. He was becoming aroused just thinking about her!

It simply would not do. He must keep his mind on more grievous matters, like finding the scoundrel who impregnated Emily and abandoned her in her hour of need. He despised having Celeste under the same roof. Her very existence grated on him as a constant reminder of his gullibility. His fingers massaged his temples. He concentrated on banishing the silly wench from his mind, and met with his customary lack of success.

The carriage turned down Mount Street and ground to a halt outside Paine's modest townhouse, the contents of which, Simon had on good authority, were being auctioned to settle his mounting debts.

The sky had graciously ceased its wet deluge, allowing Simon to mount the stone steps in relative comfort. Interrogating a man of dubious character was not how Simon had envisioned spending his honeymoon. Perhaps it was fitting. He should have kept his mind fixed on his goal, to discover the man responsible for Emily's downfall, and not been led astray by a redheaded wild urchin.

After what seemed an eternity, a butler of advanced years opened the door. Reluctantly, he led Simon through the conspicuously unfurnished foyer, down the bare-walled hallway, into a drab-looking drawing room which appeared, for the time being, to have retained its original furnishings, however modest.

Simon glanced around the dimly-lit room. It smelled musty from stale tobacco and cheap liquor. Dust clung to the drooping curtains, diminishing their original brilliance.

A presumably inebriated Paine reclined, his clothes and hair in complete disarray, across a once-stylish striped chaise that presently showed signs of excessive wear. At recognizing an intruder in his private hell, Paine struggled to pull himself up and focus his bloodshot eyes.

Simon frowned at the image before him. Tales of Paine's demise were greatly underestimated. His pockets had obviously been to let for quite some time. Simon's disgusted gaze crept over the dingy cravat that looked as though it hadn't been pressed in days. The soiled, once-green velvet coat was frayed around the edges.

He would not allow himself to pity the desperate fool who had destroyed himself over the turn of a card. He was involved in something nefarious. Simon was bound to determine what.

Paine's hooded eyes narrowed on Simon's face. 'Who the devil are you?'

'Simon Barclay, Earl of Dragonwood. *Emily Barclay*,' he said pointedly, 'was my stepsister.'

Paine sat bolt upright. 'You! You're the one who got that deuced Runner on my tail. What the hell do you want?'

'Some information. I should very much like to know why a group of men would choose to wear a certain gold emblem.'

Paine sneered and reached one arm down to grope the floor. 'None of your damned business,' he retorted viciously and lunged suddenly towards Simon.

A flash of metal glinted before Simon's eyes. Instinctively, he kicked the dagger from Paine's hand. Paine lunged toward him with murder in his eyes. Simon sidestepped the punch and countered with a hard right to the whelp's jaw, which sent him stumbling backward.

Shaking his head to clear it, Paine growled with rage and leapt forward, taking a swing at Simon's jaw. Simon ducked and landed a hard swing in the cad's stomach, followed by a powerful blow to his opponent's chin, which sent him to the floor in a dishevelled heap.

Simon stooped down and picked the knife off the floor. Examining the object with a critical eye he asked gruffly, 'Who are you protecting?'

'Go to the devil,' Paine snarled.

Simon tapped the jewelled dagger against his palm. 'I need a name,' he said with brisk impatience. 'I suggest you tell me what it is I wish to know before I lose my temper and put this dagger of yours to good use.'

Paine wiped the blood dripping from his mouth with the back of his hand. Staggering to his feet, he tested the condition of his split lip. 'What have I got that you'd want to know about?' he asked, taking a swig from a half-empty bottle of cheap brandy.

'I want to know the significance of the snake and the maiden.'

He chuckled with derision. 'I haven't got the ring any more.'

'I know. It was taken from you not so long ago.'

He shrugged. 'Was it? I don't recall.'

'Perhaps five pounds will jar your memory?' Simon inquired, dangling the money like a carrot before a desperate rabbit.

Paine grunted and took another gulp of liquor. 'It would take more than that.'

'How much more?'

Paine belched. 'How much have you got?' he asked, his greedy eyes alight at the prospect.

Simon smirked. 'First, tell me what you know. If your information is worth my while, I'll consider compensating you.'

Paine snorted and shook his head. 'How do I know you'll pay?'

'You don't. But judging from the current state of your affairs,' Simon drawled, casting a critical glance around the room, 'you can scarcely afford to be particular. Now, why would a group of men all wish to don identical rings?'

Paine raked his hands through his greasy brown hair. 'If you want to know about the club you've come to the wrong man. I've been excommunicated.'

'How sad for you,' Simon muttered with scorn. 'Who founded the disgusting club?'

Paine shook his head. 'I've already told you, I'm out.'

'Mmm. But you know about the others.' Simon yanked Paine to his feet by his shirt collar. 'I want to know which one of you destroyed Emily.'

'Why should you care?' Paine asked with a sneer. 'It's got nothing to do with you.'

'On the contrary, it has a great deal to do with me,' he said in a low, ominous voice. 'One of you ruined my stepsister.'

Paine wrenched himself free. 'It wasn't me,' he said, slumping down on the chaise once more. 'I don't go for the respectable types,' he sneered.

'No?,' Simon bit out, his savage expression perilously close to his adversary. 'Then which one of your charming cohorts does?'

Paine nervously ran his shaky fingers over his chin. 'He'd kill me if I told.'

'I might just kill you myself, if you don't,' Simon snarled.

'Go ahead,' Paine jeered.

Simon stood straight, a look of loathing on his face. 'I know about your charming pastime. You, Hobson and Everly.'

'So what?' Paine laughed. 'It is no crime to seduce a woman, even if she is untried.' He grinned at Simon with salacious pleasure. 'It is just more of a challenge, especially when she puts up a fight.'

Simon took Paine by the shoulders and shook him hard enough to rattle his teeth. 'Give me the other two names,' he ordered in a ferocious growl, 'or you won't get a farthing from me.'

'Shelton. James Shelton,' Paine burst out. 'He was one of us.'

Simon's eyes narrowed. 'He knew Emily?' he asked roughly. 'Is he the one? Who put her name in that revolting book?'

Paine shook his head. 'I won't give you *his* name. Not for a thousand guineas.'

Sickened by the scenario, Simon shoved Paine from him.

'I suggest you contact your friends at the club. I am sure you could blackmail the man I am looking for quite effectively now that you've proven yourself such a loyal follower. Oh, and when you see him,' he advised in a tight, rigid tone, 'tell him I want him. I intend to kill him. Has that permeated into your liquor-soaked brain?'

225

Paine swallowed audibly and nodded his head.

Simon threw the dagger at the dust-covered mahogany table at Paine's side. The blade sliced into the top and gyrated for a few seconds from the force of the throw.

Utterly repulsed by the scene he'd just witnessed, Simon made his way from the dingy townhouse. God, he thought. Lord God. Had Emily been raped by one of those men? The mere thought made his stomach churn.

Distracted by the disturbing revelation, he hurried down the stone steps. Not taking notice of the other occupant on the pavement, he careened into a rather tall, slender gentleman.

'I say, I am sorry, old man,' Simon heard a male voice cry out.

Not focused on the present, Simon managed to issue a curt apology and continued on his way.

'Simon Barclay, is it not?'

Simon stopped and turned around to confront the faceless body he'd bumped into. 'Yes?,' he replied, his tone abrupt.

The tall, impeccably dressed blond man smiled amicably and extended his hand. 'George Wilkinson. We met some years ago. My property in Kent borders on your family's estate.'

'Oh, yes, of course,' Simon replied, shaking the man's hand. The Wilkinsons were one of the most prestigious families in England. Simon had a vague recollection of meeting George's father some years past. He was renowned as an honorable gentleman with a pristine reputation. Simon knew very little about the son. 'Good to see you,' he murmured politely.

Wilkinson smiled with warmth. 'I do believe congratulations are in order.'

Simon's brows snapped together. 'Congratulations?' he echoed testily.

'On your recent nuptials,' Wilkinson supplied. 'I hear tell your bride is as radiant as she is youthful,' he said with a feline smile. 'You are indeed a fortunate man.'

Simon grimaced inwardly. Fortunate? He was anything but fortunate. 'We must all consider our obligations to the peerage,' came his non-committal retort.

Wilkinson emitted a sigh. 'True, true,' he muttered. 'I can scarcely conceive of a woman of my acquaintance capable of diverting conversation, let alone worthy of my good name,' he intoned airily.

Eager to disengage himself from the innocuous conversation, Simon imparted with curt civility, 'Perhaps some day you will share my good fortune.'

'Perhaps,' Wilkinson allowed. 'It may be too much to hope for. But you must also allow me to extend my most sincere condolences on the loss of your stepsister. I met her only briefly while on holiday in Bath some time ago. The waters can work wonders on people of all ages.'

He released a sigh. 'I cannot recall a more agreeable nature than your sweet stepsister possessed. I do believe I heard that she married an Italian count some time ago? There was a child, a little boy, was there not?'

'No.' Simon shook his head. 'A girl.'

A pause hung in the air. 'Ah,' was all the man said.

'She is my ward,' Simon explained.

'How delightful for you both. Still,' Lord Wilkinson said with a doleful smile, 'it must be devastating to lose someone so young and extraordinary as little Emily.'

'Yes,' Simon replied sadly, 'it was a tremendous loss.'

'How tragic.' Wilkinson glanced up at the townhouse from which Simon had recently taken his leave. 'I must away before the next downpour.'

Simon's ebony brows knitted. 'Never say *you* are associated with the likes of Paine?'

'Sad, but true,' the tall man remarked, plucking a frilly handkerchief from his breast pocket. 'The devil owes me an absolute fortune,' he lamented with a sniffle.

Simon snorted. 'Don't expect him to make good on his losses.'

'Alas, I fear,' Wilkinson remarked, stuffing his handkerchief into his pocket, 'he is perilously close to Fleet Prison. I've learned my lesson. Never take pity on a friend in need.'

Simon smiled at the dandified man. 'Generosity of heart is best reserved for charitable institutions.'

Wilkinson bared his pearly white teeth in a smile. 'Ain't it true? Good day to you, sir,' he replied with an exaggerated low bow.

Simon lifted his beaver hat. As he watched the willowy man trot up the stairs to Paine's townhouse, Simon shook his head. He had no clear recollection of ever meeting George Wilkinson. Or for that matter, Emily mentioning their acquaintance. It was of little importance. Simon had a multitude of concerns at the moment, not the least of which was what the devil to do with his wayward wife? One thing was for certain, he could not trust himself to pass another night with that temptress near at hand. He was eager to leave her in the country and rid himself of that enticement for good.

Rays of bright yellow sunlight streamed through the casement windows of the Upper Brook Street town-house dining-room. Garbed in a pale blue coat, navy brocade vest and grey pantaloons, Simon sat at the head of the enormous table awaiting the arrival of his breakfast. He hoped, by rising early, to avoid any contact with his bride.

It was bad enough that he was married to the little hellion. The constant temptation of a young, wildly-attractive female at his fingertips made him cantankerous. He should, by all rights, give in to his base instincts and bed the chit. At least then he'd get her out of his system. One thought prevented him from pleasuring himself with her beautiful, vibrant, highly-responsive body – she'd tricked him. He refused, regardless of how great the enticement, to act the part of a prize bull.

He heard the door open and swivelled around in his chair. He swore under his breath. The devil worked overtime of late. No sooner had he sworn to himself that he would not be lured by his bride than she appeared.

She took her seat at his side. Despite his stony expression, she offered him a bright smile. 'Good morning, my lord. Mmm,' she said running her tongue over her lips in an enticing fashion that drove him wild. 'I am starving this morning. What is for breakfast?' she asked, wriggling on the seat of the chair.

Confound it, Simon thought as he dragged his gaze from her cheerful expression, he'd like nothing better than to run his hands over her round, soft bottom. He watched her shake out her linen napkin and drape the enviable item across her silken thighs hidden beneath her soft white muslin dress. He found the tiny pink roses that dotted the fabric oddly alluring.

Forcing his gaze away, he took a gulp of coffee. Mercifully, Evans arrived, providing a diversion for Simon's lustful thoughts. The butler presented her ladyship with a crisp copy of *The London Chronicle*. Unfortunately, a second later, he disappeared, leaving the newlyweds alone once more.

'I hope you do not mind, my lord,' she said as she scanned the paper in search of a particular page, 'but I simply could not wait to see my article on Thomas Brown.'

Placing the article before him, she got to her feet. She placed her arm around his shoulder and leaned over to point out salient features of interest.

He could feel her breath soft and warm against his cheek. A smidgen more, and their faces would be touching. Feeling suddenly overly warm, he tugged at his collar and felt the uncontrollable urge to clear his throat.

The heat from her delicate body gently pressed against him threatened to send him over the edge. It took all his self-control to resist the urge to drag her across his lap and kiss her sensuous, rosebud mouth till she was breathless and weak and begging for more.

Simon was vaguely aware she was gabbling about something, but did not hear a word she was saying. His gaze was riveted to her lovely profile. Her peaches and cream complexion begged for his touch. He had to ball his hand into a fist so as not to touch her.

He drew a deep breath. Her heavenly scent invaded his nostrils. Lord, she smelled good, just like fresh lavender.

'I am forever in your debt, my lord, for suggesting the topic. Mr Hammersmith was quite impressed by my conclusions. What do you think?' she asked, turning her eager expression towards him.

'What?,' he repeated stupidly, utterly lost in her incredibly deep blue eyes.

'About my article? Do you think I gave the topic a fair assessment?' she asked with barely concealed eagerness.

He swallowed audibly. He felt like a schoolboy with his first crush. This would never do! By God, the chit got under his skin. He did not like the effect she was having on him. Not one bit.

'I don't give a damn about the deuced article,' he barked at her.

She inhaled sharply at his tone. Stunned and visibly shaken by his surge of temper, she recoiled from him. Her startled blue gaze searched his stark, forbidding features.

By Jove, she had a nerve to stand there looking hurt and confused while he was waging a war with rampant desire and losing the battle! Those damn juvenile schoolgirl dresses were provocative as hell. She was driving him insane. Throwing his napkin down on the table, he got to his feet.

'Why the deuce don't you buy some decent dresses instead of wearing those old rags?' he asked her sharply.

She blinked at him in dismay. 'I –'

'I expect my wife to dress better than a pauper's child.'

Embarrassed heat flooded her cheeks, her lashes fluttered downward. 'Yes, of course,' she said quietly.

'I suggest you pay a call to Bond Street this morning.' His gaze swept over her. 'And for God's sake,' he growled, his voice harsh with censure, 'get rid of those skimpy childish dresses. Burn them if you have to, but don't let me ever see you in them again. Is that perfectly clear?'

'But –'

'But what?,' he snapped at her.

'I . . . have no money, my lord,' she replied with a good deal of discomfort.

'Put it on account. I should think Madame Desjardin knows my tastes well enough by now to outfit *you* appropriately,' he muttered with curt irritation.

She glanced at him in surprise. 'Are you not coming?,' she asked him, her voice anxious.

'I've more important matters that require my attention. We will shortly leave for Lindhurst. Prepare yourself for a solitary life in the country, madam.'

She looked crestfallen. 'But what – what about my work?' she sputtered, extending the paper to him. 'Will you not give me your impressions?'

His derisive gaze swept over her paltry offering. 'Why don't you pen an article on animal husbandry?' he asked with biting sarcasm. 'You might learn something useful.'

With that he stormed from the room, leaving his breakfast untouched and his dumbfounded bride deeply hurt.

Biting her lip, Celeste expelled a doleful sigh. The workings of her husband's mind were beyond her. His mood swings were indeed baffling. From time to time since their marriage, she'd caught him staring at her, a burning, hungry look in his eye. Usually, a gruff remark summarily ensued and he would take himself off.

But what had she done to warrant his censure this morning? The man certainly had a formidable temper. She could not understand his violent reaction. And she wasn't at all sure an article on animal husbandry would be of interest to Mr Hammersmith.

The first leg of the arduous journey to Lindhurst commenced in taciturn silence. Celeste pretended to be interested in the countryside. It was not particularly appealing. Green fields punctuated by scattered cows chewing their cud and heavy thickets here and there made for a dull ride.

When at last she could no longer endure the tense

silence, she asked her disgruntled husband, 'My lord, could we not stop for a moment?'

'It is only a little further to Lindhurst,' he said without so much as a glance in her direction.

Anger flared in her breast. 'We have been travelling for what seems like hours.'

He did not even bother to dignify her remark with a reply.

She drew an irritated breath. 'My lord, I am tired and uncomfortable,' she said, barely concealing her frustration. 'We must stop.'

He turned from the window to look at her. 'It grieves me to hear it.' His manner was cold and distant. She knew he was not grieved in the least. 'We drive straight through.'

She fixed him with a chilling glare. 'Surely even the horses must rest, my lord?'

He tsked with mockery. 'Feigning concern for the horses is far too obvious. It does not do you justice, my dear.'

'Ooh,' she muttered and clenched her gloved hands in her lap, 'I am closer than I ever thought I'd be to despising you.'

He threw back his head and roared with laughter. 'Then you are in good company. Our marriage is not unlike those of the rest of the *ton*.'

She gave him a look of blazing contempt. It was one thing to be stuck travelling with him but quite another to endure his insufferable conversation.

Celeste must have drifted off, for she awakened to a gruff voice in her ear, 'Wake up.' Her eyelashes

234

fluttered open for her to find her husband leaning over her. 'We've arrived, Lady Barclay.'

'What time is it?,' she asked, still groggy from her nap.

'Time to see your new home. This is your first glimpse of Lindhurst. I hope you find it worth your trouble.'

Turning away from the hateful man, she came face to face with Lindhurst from the carriage window. Her breath caught in her throat. It was magnificent. An enormous square stone façade that, on one side, faced what appeared to be a lake and, on the other, sprawling woods. The famous Lindhurst gardens were doubtless at the back, for the front was adorned with a curved drive and a solitary fountain in the middle of the plush green lawn.

'It quite takes my breath away,' she remarked in soft admiring tones. 'I have never seen such grandeur.'

'Then you must regard your circumstances as happy indeed,' came his cool reply.

She glanced over her shoulder at him as a hint of anger flared in her tempestuous blue gaze. 'I cannot comment on my circumstances, only the majesty of your home, my lord.'

'I am glad you like it,' he muttered cruelly as the carriage rounded the drive, 'you will be spending a great deal of time here.'

The carriage came to a stop and the footman lowered the steps for Simon to disembark from the carriage. Celeste placed her foot on the top step and lost her balance. She fell against her husband's chest. For a tense moment, she worried he might let her topple to the muddy ground. Then, all at once, she heard a derisive grunt, and felt strong, capable arms encircling her waist to stop her fall.

She clutched his broad shoulders for support. His dark penetrating gaze roamed her hectic face. His mouth was close enough to press a kiss to her softly-parted lips. She flushed warm at the prospect.

She reminded herself that he believed her capable of treachery and was scarcely likely to show her any measure of affection. Regardless of the longing she thought she saw lurking in his silvery depths, he detested her.

Flustered at being pressed intimately against her husband who harboured a disgust of her, she averted her gaze. 'Thank you, my lord.'

Frowning, he set her down as if she were a tainted thing he could not stand to be near. Without further ado, he turned on his heel and marched into the house, leaving his wife to trail behind, flanked by two skinny footman and hordes of baggage.

Celeste was overawed by the regal household. The mahogany furnishings and plush carpets were indeed superb. Several large gold-framed portraits, boasting past generations of Barclays, gazed down at her with stern disapproval. The expansive stairway cloaked in dark green velvet wound its way up to the first landing. It split in two different directions and vanished into the dark shadows that led to the east and west wings of the house.

Celeste sighed with appreciation. Every inch of Lindhurst was elegant, but not in the least overstated.

As she glanced around her at the magnificent home, she had to admit that the Dragon's liar was quite exceptional. Masculine in every detail, but that went without saying. She could scarcely imagine pastels in such a place.

An enormous portrait flanked by two crossed shiny sabres mounted on the opposite wall caught her eye. She approached the portrait to better admire it. It was obviously commissioned during the war. The handsome young man depicted in the life-size painting was garbed in a crisp red uniform. He looked vaguely familiar.

She cast a speculative glance in her husband's direction. He was conversing with a slim woman of advanced years who possessed a friendly face. This Celeste took to be the housekeeper. Their exchange appeared to be complaisant.

How old *was* her husband? she wondered with a furrowed brow, as she gazed up at the painting. He couldn't be *that* old, could he? My, she thought, looking his broad-shouldered, sinewed physique over with rapt interest, he was in marvellous physical condition for any age.

Simon turned to his wife and issued a curt introduction. 'Mrs Putnam, I present my wife, Lady Barclay.'

The elderly woman smiled kindly at Celeste. 'We are indeed pleased to welcome her ladyship.' She turned to address Simon. 'We were expecting you to arrive quite some time ago, my lord.'

'My bride was not well enough to travel. But upon her recovery, she was eager to commerce her honeymoon in the country. I was only too happy to accede to her wishes.'

Celeste shot Simon a startled look which he ignored.

'All is in readiness,' Mrs Putnam boasted. 'I aired the master bedroom as you instructed, my lord.'

Simon stiffened. 'Have Lady Barclay's things placed in the adjoining room.'

A look of confusion touched Mrs Putnam's round face. 'But, my lord your instructions were very specific –'

'The adjoining room will suffice,' Simon told her curtly.

'Very well, my lord. I shall have a fire lit immediately to take the chill off. I hope you will be comfortable, my lady.'

Celeste smiled at the conscientious woman. 'You needn't worry on my account. I am weary from the journey and wish nothing more than to recline with a warm pot of tea.'

Simon's mouth pinched. How well she played the demure, unassuming bride in front of Mrs Putnam.

'I am sure everything will suit your humble needs, my dear,' he assured her coolly.

'I am sure it shall, my lord,' she replied with equally forced civility.

Having recovered from her arduous journey, Celeste decided to take an afternoon stroll rather than face her scowling husband. As she headed towards the stairs, she heard a strange sound and hesitated. Either her ears were deceiving her or someone was crying. She strained to ascertain from where the sound was coming. It was definitely the west wing. As she moved down the long corridor towards the ecru marble steps, the sobs grew louder. It was a child crying. Hastening her gait, she thought she heard the soothing sounds of a woman's voice. It was coming from the room on her right. Curiosity got the best of her.

Without thinking to knock, she threw open the door and crossed the threshold. A few yards away an elderly woman, who could only be the child's nanny, shushed a blond-haired baby in a large rocking chair.

Celeste opened her mouth to speak. But the grey-haired woman pressed her finger to her lips. The chubby little baby uttered a mewing sound. Slowly, the child's eyelashes drifted shut. Its mouth slightly ajar, the small bundle fell fast asleep. Little hands clung to the nanny's shoulders. Gently, the old woman placed the blond-haired cherub in the crib and lovingly tucked the soft blanket around the sleeping child.

'I – I'm sorry,' Celeste whispered to the kindly-faced nanny. 'I heard a child crying. I was curious,' she admitted with some embarrassment.

The woman's face wrinkled into a smile. 'Little Annabelle is teething,' she said and led Celeste into the next room.

Celeste's brow furrowed in confusion. '*Who* is

little Annabelle?,' she blurted out before she had time to stop herself.

'*She* is my niece,' a deep caustic male voice remarked from behind her.

Celeste whirled about and came face to face with a wall of pure masculine flesh and bone that could only belong to her husband. He looked exceedingly displeased.

'Good afternoon, my lord,' the nanny said dutifully.

Simon inclined his dark head in tactic greeting. 'Mrs Edwards. I see you have met my bride,' he intoned with a glare in Celeste's direction. 'How is your charge this afternoon?'

'Oh, well, my lord. Teething makes her a little grizzly. She's cutting another tooth. Poor little girl. It won't be long before she has a mouthful. She'll be right happy to see you, my lord.'

He smiled amicably. 'I shall see her before dinner in the playroom.' Without further ado, his fingers closed over Celeste's arm. Bidding Mrs Edwards good day, he propelled his bride from the room.

'In future, madam,' he growled against her ear, 'if you wish to know if I have any byblows, I suggest you ask me, not the servants.'

She opened her mouth to rebut his vile accusations, but could not. Truth be told, she had been wondering whether Annabelle was his daughter. It was dreadfully improper to ask who the child was, but he should have told her.

'Had you bothered to inform your bride of the child's existence, I would not have been reduced to asking the servants,' she countered sharply.

He came to a standstill in the hallway and gruffly released her. 'Very well, if you must know, she is my stepsister's child. She is my ward. *Not* my daughter. Which I suppose,' he intoned with contempt, 'makes you her aunt.'

Celeste glared up at him. 'Precisely when did you intend to inform me of her existence?'

He shrugged. 'I saw no reason to involve you in a private family affair.'

Dumbfounded, she gaped at him. 'Private family affair!' she spluttered at last. 'I am your wife. I have the right to know.'

'Perhaps,' he allowed at his most arrogant, 'though I do not ask that you spend time with the child. But I do insist that you be kind to her. I will not have her origins bandied about by you, or the servants.'

Celeste struggled to control her temper. Between his infuriating conviction that she'd lured him into marriage and his heartless belief that she would ever hurt an innocent child with a blunder of the tongue, she was perilously close to her breaking point.

'Do not concern yourself, my lord –,' her voice was rigid with control, '–I do not bandy gossip.'

She turned on her heel and disappeared down the steps to seek refuge in the privacy of her bedroom. Why did he not return to London and leave her in peace?

Another week of connubial co-existence passed, surprisingly, without further incident. In fact, it proceeded with gruelling, uneventful civility. Aside from the hours she spent playing with little Annabelle, Celeste was decidedly bored. She'd completed her interviews with the land steward and forwarded her article on animal husbandry to *The Chronicle*, although she had serious doubts whether it would be accepted. At present, she found that she had more time on her hands than she knew what to do with. This would never do!

She saw very little of her husband; save for meal times, they were constantly apart. When they were forced by convention to be in the same room, he uttered little more than a begrudged yes or no to the questions she thought to ask him. He was, it seemed, ignoring his wayward wife, a condition that grated on her, that is until the day she dared to enter his private sanctuary, the library.

She tapped lightly at the mahogany door and waited for his deep voice to resonant from within. 'Come in.'

He glanced up from his paperwork and did a double take. Evidently, her spontaneous interruption was not welcomed. Tossing his quill pen down, he sat back and regarded her in stony silence.

'I thought we might picnic,' she said brightly.

'Picnic?,' he echoed with blatant contempt for the pastime most people considered enjoyable.

'Yes. Come along, my lord, you must be vaguely familiar with the notion. Wicker basket. Wine. Delicious food. Soft warm, inviting blankets. Glorious sunshine. Rest and relaxation. You have been on a picnic before, have you not?'

'Not since I was a young child,' he snorted and resumed his examination of what appeared to be the estate books.

She rested her slender hip on the edge of his desk. 'Well, then,' she said, smiling down at his cross expression, 'it should be a delightful pleasure for you to indulge in a childhood fancy.'

His eyes met hers. 'I do not wish to picnic,' he muttered with thinly-veiled hostility.

She drew a deep breath and held her ground. He was not making this any easier, but she was determined to establish some level of cordiality between husband and wife.

'You have to eat some time,' she offered cheerfully.

He sat back and crossed his arms over his chest. 'Now why would my wife wish to picnic with the likes of me?,' he asked nastily.

She ignored his jibe. She wanted peace, not war, she reminded herself. 'I thought that since we are going to be irrevocably stuck together for possibly the next ten to fifteen years, depending on how long you live, we might decide to get better acquainted.'

His dark gray eyes sharpened. 'Are you suggesting I'm old?' he asked through gritted teeth.

'Well,' she said on a blithe sigh, 'you are hardly spritely, my lord.'

'The devil I am not!,' he growled and slapped the leather-bound book shut.

She leaned forward, draping her body across his

desktop. 'Care to see if you can best me on horse-back?,' she asked, a mischievous glint in her eye.

He chuckled with derision. 'You could never best me, madam.'

A scampish grin spread across her lips. 'We shall see, my lord, we shall see.'

CHAPTER 12

The pounding of the hoofs beneath her mingled with the sound of her mount straining for breath. As the wind whipped at her face, tangling her hair beyond recognition, a thrill of exhilaration ran through her. She looked down at the green meadow whisking by beneath the horse's long strides. Glancing over her shoulder at her husband edging closer, she shrieked with delight and urged her mount forward with a tap of her crop on the dapple grey's rump. If she landed on her posterior because she'd foolishly urged her mount too fast, she'd be mortified.

It was not, of course, a fair race. She was riding side saddle and lacked the advantage of clinging to the powerful beast with her thighs, which would have enabled her to fly like the wind as she had done countless times before when her grandfather was not looking.

She doubted the ferocious Dragon would take kindly to being bested by his wife. Unwilling to give free rein to the great speed the animal was capable of, she eased back on the bit and let her husband take the lead.

She reached the designated elm in time to find Simon waiting for her, his hands slung on his narrow hips. She jumped down from the saddle and twisted the reins around the tree branch. She turned to face her husband. Her heart tripped over itself.

His breathing was ragged from the strenuous ride. A fine sheen of perspiration covered his bronzed skin. He was staring at her. A blind woman could read the passion in his silver gaze. She was not green enough to misconstrue his thoughts.

'You have won, my lord,' she said with nervous smile. 'I shall have to demand a rematch.' Her eyes darted away from the fetching sight of her husband flushed with heat and sweat.

'We did not discuss my prize,' he murmured, his voice like velvet.

'Prize?' She fidgeted beneath his smouldering stare. 'I do not recollect mentioning any prize, my lord,' she replied and brushed past him.

'I doubt it will be worth much, given that my opponent let me win,' he said, catching her by the arm.

She looked up at him in surprise. 'I did no such thing. You bested me fairly.'

He eased her closer to him. 'Why did you pull back?,' he taunted. His dark sultry gaze ran over her face. 'Afraid of what might happen if you give the beast free rein?'

She colored fiercely. 'On the contrary,' she tossed back tartly, 'I know what will happen.'

Wrenching her arm free, she walked a safe distance away. She heard his low husky chuckle and despised him for it. Gazing idly about the plush green landscape, she pretended to be unaffected. In reality, however, the heady, overwhelmingly masculine scent of leather, sweat and horse invaded her senses and threatened to turn her knees to jelly.

'I must look frightful after that wild ride,' she remarked self-consciously. Her fingers fiddled with her hair, trying to repair the wind-blown mess, but achieved little success.

'Allow me,' Simon said from behind.

Reluctantly, she accepted his assistance. Swallowing hard, she tried to not to think how very much she liked his touch. Just having her near him, feeling his magnetism, was pure torture.

Simon watched her struggle with her unruly hair and smiled. His wild, carefree wife was in constant disarray, he mused, surprised by how appealing he found her. His fingers removed the last remaining precariously scattered hairpins and let her hair fall down her back. It was just as thick and soft and luxurious as he'd imagined. He had a difficult time resisting the urge to run his hands through her silken tresses. He watched her as she basked in his touch. Wrapping his hand in her hair, he grasped the back of her head and turned her to face him.

Her heart slammed against her ribs. She stared into his stormy grey eyes overflowing with his desire and she knew he wanted to kiss her. Her breath quickened with yearning. Try as she might, she could not look away. Of its own volition, her body seemed to close the distance between them.

And then his arms enveloped her small frame, cradling her in the warmth of his strong embrace. His warm lips captured hers. His kiss was tentative and surprisingly gentle.

Despite her insistence on a prenuptial agreement, she knew she could not stop this from happening. She yearned for him to touch her, to kiss, to hold her. Yes. Oh, yes, she thought, swept away by the moment. She wanted him. And everything that went with him.

Instinctively, she parted her lips and clung to his sinewed arms. His kiss became demanding. His mouth moved passionately over hers, bruising her soft pliant lips with burning desire. His fingers locked in her hair, holding her captive. Sliding her arms around his back, she leaned into him and returned his kiss with equal craving.

He scooped her up, cradling her in his arms, and walked towards the lake. Laying her down on the carpet of soft grass beneath the enormous shady elm, he held her close, his mouth clinging to hers, devouring her sweet taste. He kissed her passionately, violently, as if he could not get enough of her. His tongue intimately entwined with hers. With a soft moan of pleasure, she joined the love play.

They lay together in the plush green grass, his body partially on top of hers. Helplessly adrift on a sea of desire, she'd lost all sense of reality. She did not want the exhilarating sensations to stop. His palm slid over her breast and boldly caressed her. The pad

248

of his thumb rubbed against her sensitive nipple. It peaked beneath his touch. He deepened the kiss. His hands moved lower to caressing her hips, her waist and beyond.

Alarmed at where this might lead, she realized their passionate interlude had gone far enough. She tried to pull away. But mindless with passion, he moved on top of her, pinning her body beneath him. When she felt him tug at the buttons of her velvet riding habit, she reached up to stop his hand. He placed the offending member around his neck. She felt him reach inside her chemise, his large warm hand covered her bare aching breast. Rubbing his thumb against her already taut nipple, he squeezed it gently between his fingers.

Arching against him, she moaned against his mouth. She knew she was incapable of making him stop. Her body betrayed her. She craved the feel of his rough, calloused hands against her sensitive breasts. Then his mouth was at her breasts, showering them with kisses. Hot, wet and demanding, his mouth closed around each nipple and sucked hard. She gasped with pleasure. Threading her fingers through his thick raven hair, she clutched at him, never wanting the spiralling pleasure to stop. He trailed kisses along her shoulder and her neck. His teeth nibbled at her ear lobe.

'*Celeste*,' he breathed. 'I've waited longer for you than for any other woman. I thought I might go mad. I had to touch you,' he told her huskily.

She was too dazed to comprehend his meaning. Delirious from the new-found tempest of emotions raging inside her, she took his face in her hands and kissed his mouth. Grunting with pleasure, he kissed her back with fierce hunger.

'It will not do,' he grated hoarsely, against her lips, 'I must have you.' Fumbling for her skirt hem, his hand slipped beneath her skirt, and slid up her leg to caress the inside of her thighs and in between.

She panicked. Passion dissolved into fear. Instantly, her mind began to function properly.

Did he mean here? Right now? In the middle of the day? On the grass? This kissing was delightful, quite nice in fact, but she was not overly eager to endure the other, especially not here, in the middle of a field like some doxy. It was indecent.

She was not ready for this. She'd barely survived marriage to the cantankerous man – she'd never survive an afternoon of passionate lovemaking.

'Simon,' she gasped, pushing against him.

He did not budge. Not one inch. Instead, he kissed her while his fingers stroked her soft apex creating the most exciting, mindless response deep inside her. She felt hot and breathless and weak.

'*Simon*,' she whimpered, uncertainty mingling with fear. 'What . . . are you . . . doing?' She panted with excitement caused by the tormenting pulse of his fingers. 'You cannot think to . . . oh.' She bit her lip against the aching pleasure.

He smiled down at her with a wicked glint in his eye. All the while, he teased her soft feminine core with his probing fingers. 'You'll see,' he promised thickly and kissed the sensitive spot behind her ear. The situation was getting out of control. She moved her head away, but to no avail. He kissed her neck.

'Stop, you must stop!' She slammed her fist against his chest. 'I – I don't want to see. I've a very good idea what you are about. I am not . . . not ready for this.'

Lifting his head, he stared down at her, his breathing laboured, his face flushed with unrequited passion.

She was about to explain that someone might come along and that they should wait for privacy and more appropriate time and surroundings. She did not want to be initiated into lovemaking with her skirt hiked up like some cheap tart taking a tumble in the grass. The hard expression on his face gave her pause.

He stared down at the beguiling woman lying beneath him. She was driving him insane. Those blue eyes of hers bewitched him.

If their previous encounter was any barometer, he knew she wanted him as badly as he desired her. Most women found him utterly charming. Why, then, were his actions boorish when it came to his own wife? Many marriages were forced and they did not end up like this.

It injured his pride that his wife shrank from his advances. It further bedeviled him that she was able to hold herself from him when he coveted her with mindless desperation. If possible, Madame Desjardin's creations were even more provocative than the childish skimpy muslin gowns she used to wear.

He prided himself on his self-discipline. He was, after all, no young buck ruled by his emotions. He was in complete control at all times – except, it would appear, when it came to his young, extremely desirable bride.

His face was rigid with anger as he snapped, 'It seems I've married a coquette. I should have known,' he sneered cruelly. 'You tempt a man beyond reason and then cry off. I know your sort.'

'I suppose you are well acquainted with every sort of woman,' she spat out, her chest heaving with rancour and hurt.

'Oh, I don't know,' he murmured, letting his gaze slide over her face and partially-revealed bosom with insulting thoroughness, 'I've never tried your sort before.'

'You devil!,' she hissed and tried to slap his face. He caught her arm and held it firmly to the ground.

'Don't,' he snapped, pinning her to the ground with his weight. 'That is a nasty habit, one of which you'll find I am not very fond.'

Her anger was only marginally outdone by her shame. Her wild, enthusiastic response to him disturbed her. She had to develop some restraint where her husband was concerned. She could ill-afford such foolish sexual abandon with the Dragon.

'Let me go,' she cried squirming beneath him, 'you . . . you . . . misbegotten pig!'

'It seems I am to suffer every kind of insult in this dreadful arrangement,' he drawled with icy mockery and abruptly released her.

'If you find yourself trapped in a miserable marriage, you've no one to blame but your jealous paramour,' she flung at him bitterly.

252

His eyes narrowed on her flushed face. 'Jealous paramour?' he bit out. 'What the devil is that supposed to mean?'

'Your most excellent Lady Declaire, that is what. Or should I say whom.'

'She was never that,' he barked with irritation.

Celeste gave him a crushing look. 'Is that a fact? Pray, why then did she waste no time in spreading details of our scandalous encounter?'

He brow darkened. 'Harriet Declaire?' he echoed on a furious growl. 'I don't believe it,' he derided. 'What could she possibly hope to gain by doing such a thing?'

'I am at a complete loss, my lord. I thought *you* could tell *me*,' she muttered with heavy sarcasm. 'Whatever the reason, your charming paramour saw fit to divulge a rather sensitive scenario which reached the ears of a certain elderly gentleman who did not take kindly to learning his granddaughter was caught in Hobson's guest bedchamber with a notorious rake.'

His sceptical gaze searched her face. 'Do you expect me to credit this ludicrous story?'

'Quite frankly, I do not care what you believe, my lord.'

He caught her chin and turned her face to his. 'Are you claiming you never confessed to your grandfather?'

'Of course not.' She jerked her head back. 'Have you taken complete leave of your senses? Why would I confess? The very last thing I ever wanted was to marry you. It was only after the scandalous report was swarming all over London that Joy insisted I confess all to Tony. I cannot believe he failed to mention the instrument of my downfall, given how generously he imparted Joy's treachery,' she muttered crossly. 'Surely he must have told you all that passed before?' she asked, looking Simon straight in the eye. 'Didn't he?'

'I naturally assumed it was you who'd divulged the unhappy truth.'

She gave him a rueful look. 'My lord, I scarcely would have told that disagreeable old man anything as shocking as what took place in your carriage.'

He stretched out beside her, resting his weight on one elbow. A slow smile spread across his face. 'Shocking, eh?'

She was in no mood for jocularity. 'If you think I delight in our current predicament, you have lost your wits altogether. We are stuck in a most disagreeable arrangement with little hope for relief. I swear to you, I played no part in procuring our dreadful union. Indeed, my lord, it is my fervent desire that you return to London and never come back. Is that the portrait of a clinging smitten woman?'

His jaw tensed angrily. 'I understand your feelings towards me perfectly,' he averred curtly.

'I am vastly relieved to hear it.' Her voice was laced with asperity. 'At long last the truth has finally penetrated. We obviously do not suit.'

He winced. By Jove, he'd muddled it rather badly. He would like to murder Harriet Declaire, ring Tony's neck and spank her meddling sister. All three of them had a hand in manipulating him into marriage.

'Oh, I don't know,' he murmured, his tone warm and seductive. 'We might suit.'

'I don't know how you can bring yourself to touch me,' she spat at him, 'given what a manipulative, hateful creature you believe me to be.'

His lips twitched slightly. 'It's not too difficult,' he assured her dryly. He caressed the taut line of her jaw with his finger. 'You'd be surprised how easy it is.'

'Don't,' she snapped and swatted his hand away. 'I am not some plaything you may seduce on a whim.'

He expelled a deep sigh and got to his feet. Booted feet slightly apart, he stood with his back to her.

She glanced down at her once neat, elegant riding habit now thoroughly disheveled and halfway unbuttoned. 'Brute,' she grumbled at his back and hurried to set herself to rights.

He glanced at her over his shoulder, his greedy eyes raking over her. 'My dear,' he replied, a hint of a smile hovering around his lips. He reached out a hand to help her up. She eyed the appendage with trepidation.

'I don't bite, Celeste,' he muttered and snatched her hand, pulling her to her feet.

She smoothed the mass of wrinkles and brushed the bits of grass from her blue velvet riding habit. 'I would not be surprised if you did.'

He threw back his head and laughed. 'No. I don't expect you would be.'

She fixed him with a crushing glare. 'This was a poor suggestion,' she lamented. 'I am sure you'd rather pass the afternoon in your library. I've plenty of reading to do.'

He shook his head. 'No,' he countered fiercely. 'I've spent more time looking over those damned ledgers than I ever intended. It was the best place to avoid having to deal with you.'

She glanced up at him in surprise.

He laughed softly. 'Childish, I know, but none the less true.'

Smiling tentatively, she asked him, 'Shall we eat then, my lord?'

'Mmm,' he said, his scorching gaze threatening to devour her whole, 'I am ravenous.'

Rosy color crept over her cheeks. She turned away and walked towards the lake.

Simon fell into step at her side. They walked in awkward silence towards the willow tree by the side of the lake where the delectable feast awaited them.

Amazed, Simon surveyed the soft inviting plaid blanket adorned with every sort of food imaginable. 'You arranged all this?'

Shyly, she nodded her head and fell to her knees to prepare a plate of cold meats and chutney for him.

He dropped down beside her. 'Why?' he asked, his penetrating gaze fixed on her bent head.

She lowered her lashes, shielding her eyes from his searching gaze. Wordlessly, she shrugged her shoulders. She was not inclined to offer an explanation for fear that he would mock her. She was definitely not prepared to bear her soul to this taciturn stranger.

He lifted her chin with his index finger. 'I approve wholeheartedly, Lady Barclay,' he told her softly. His slumberous grey gaze held her captive. 'Thank

256

you,' he murmured against her mouth and pressed a tender kiss to her lips.

'You are entirely welcome, my lord.'

'My name is Simon,' he averred with meaning.

'Simon,' she corrected and busied herself with serving.

He grinned at her. 'As I recall, you were a decidedly bolder lass before we were married. Where is the girl who demanded I ruin her reputation before dawn?' he asked teasingly.

She laughed and cocked her curly head to one side. 'I was rather, was I not?' She gave him a small smile and met his gaze with an scampish glint in her eye. 'That girl is still here, I'm afraid,' she said unhappily.

He raised a questioning brow.

'She is the respectable Lady Barclay now with an image to uphold and proprieties to observe.'

His hand slid around her neck, his thumb caressed her cheek. 'Not with me, surely?' he insisted, a roguish smile tugging at his lips.

'Open the wine,' she told him, pushing him away with a playful shove.

'I am glad you made me come. It has indeed been too long since I was on a picnic,' he remarked as he filled their glasses. He took a sip and laid down on his back with a heavy sigh, one arm folded under his head. 'It was never like this when I was a boy.'

'No?' she asked and placed a plate of food beside him. 'What was it like?'

He set his gaze on the tree branches above his head. 'Not like this,' he replied, a sardonic lilt to his voice.

She wrinkled up her nose. 'Is that good or bad?'

He turned to look at her. 'This day,' he said in an achingly soft voice,' is far superior to anything in my childhood.'

Her face fell. 'You cannot be serious? Was it really such a trial for you then?'

He drew a deep breath and turned on his side to face her. 'My childhood,' he told her dryly, 'consisted mainly of solitude and tutors.'

She looked confused. 'But what about your stepsister?' she asked, biting into a slice of cold roast pheasant. 'Joy told me you were devoted to one another.'

'We were. I was sixteen when my father re-married. My stepmother, Charlotte, brought little Emily to live with us. Emily was barely two at the time. Not that Charlotte cared a whit for me,' he said bitterly. 'She was only slightly preferable to my maternal mother.'

Celeste swallowed her food audibly. 'Have you no fond memories at all?' she asked, appalled.

'I suppose I must. When I was very young, my parents were, well –,' he flashed a rueful smile, '– let's just say they were never devoted to one another. My mother was like me. Father did not approve.'

Celeste's eyebrows knitted. 'Like you?,' she echoed, taking a sip of wine.

He turned the full force of his roguish gaze on her. 'Wild. Immoral. Wickedly sinful. It is my blood, don't you know? Father detested us both.'

'How awful that must have been for you.'

He shrugged and downed the remainder of his wine in one gulp. 'I survived,' he muttered and sat up to eat.

'Tell me what happened to Emily,' Celeste asked quietly.

He looked her in the eye. 'I thought you knew,' he said tersely.

Colour flooded her face. Apparently, he had not forgotten her grand *faux pas* the night they'd met.

She shook her head. 'Joy filled my head with wicked stories. Her intention is now patently obvious,' she grumbled with irritation.

'I cannot credit her foolishness,' came his sharp reply. 'Surely she must have realized that her scheming would wreak nothing but havoc?'

'I sincerely doubt she ever envisioned that débâcle at Hobson's party. But, I dare say she was not beyond using it to her advantage. If I know Joy,' Celeste said with a tired sigh, 'she probably imagined you'd be overcome by love for me, and thought you'd give up your roguish ways,' she intoned theatrically, 'in favor of my hand in marriage.'

'Is that what she hoped?' His voice was like a satin caress. And his gaze, heaven help her, was hot enough to melt even the coldest heart. She cleared her throat and bowed her head. 'Silly, is it not?' she mumbled softly.

He offered no reply. But she could feel the weight of his stare. It made her uncomfortable.

'What was she like?,' she asked in an effort to shift the topic of conversation to safer ground.

'Who?,' he asked, his sensual gaze drifting over her with unnerving slowness.

She took another sip of her wine. 'Emily.'

259

'Emily was . . .,' he drew a deep sigh. 'She was wonderful. Sweet. Trusting. Kind. Very beautiful. Everyone loved her.'

'What happened?,' Celeste asked offering him a slice of pear. 'How did she –?'

'Die?,' he asked bluntly.

Celeste nodded.

'She died in childbirth.'

'Was she . . . I mean . . .' She dipped her head. 'Who was she –?'

'She was never married,' he interjected curtly.

'I see,' Celeste said quietly. She raised her eyes to his. 'Then who is Annabelle's father?'

He shrugged. 'I've not the slightest idea.'

She blinked at him. 'But Joy told me Emily died a Contessa.'

He gave her a sardonic look. 'Your devoted Joy is a wellspring of knowledge.'

'It was not viciously meant. To be fair, she never thought ill of you. I expect you were not unlike forbidden fruit. It was her intention to make you seem dark and dangerous and wildly exciting.'

He chuckled a little ruefully. 'I am scarcely that.'

Oh, yes you are, Celeste thought, but held her tongue.

'Little Annabelle is indeed a Contessa. It is not very difficult to acquire titles or feign marriages in Italy. I arranged it.'

'Oh,' she said after an awkward silence. 'That was good of you.'

He looked away. 'It was nothing. It was a lot less than Emily deserved.'

'What could you have done?'

260

'More. I managed it badly.' He got to his feet and drove his fingers through his hair. 'Do you know what they said after I buried Emily and news of Annabelle's birth reached the *tonnish* elite?,' he asked her roughly.

Pain etched on Celeste's features. 'I'd rather not hear,' she murmured quietly.

'It doesn't matter to them that a blackguard took her under his spell and got her with child and then deserted her,' he said bitterly. 'All they care about is whether the child is mine.'

'Don't, Simon,' Celeste implored him, 'don't do this to yourself. Annabelle is yours now. She is an innocent child. What can it matter who her father is? She knows how much you love her. I hope, in time, she will come to have regard for me as well.'

He gazed at her, admiration shining in his slate grey eyes. 'What a rarity you are, my dear,' he said softly and dropped to his knees before her.

She glanced at him askance. 'I suppose I must plead guilty to that trait,' she allowed ruefully.

He reached out and brushed a stray curl from her cheek. 'I know about your daily visits to the nursery.' He smiled at her startled expression. 'Mrs Edwards tells me everything about little Annabelle. You are fast becoming her favorite playmate. I am more appreciative than I can say.' He sighed wearily and dropped his hand. 'Heaven knows, she needs more than I can ever give her.'

'That is not true,' Celeste countered with energy. 'She needs you. Mrs Edwards cannot stop talking of the child's devotion to you.'

'Still, I am grateful for your kindness.'

Self-conscious, she scoffed at his remark. 'It is little enough for me to try to bring her some measure of happiness,' she said with modesty.

'What of your husband's happiness?' He gave her a sensual smile that was designed to make her grow weak with longing. And did. 'Have you no pledges for him?'

She lowered her gaze to her lap. 'What would you have me say?'

He tilted her chin up. His eyes held her gaze with a burning intensity that fairly singed her. 'Tell me you want me as much as I want you,' he said his voice hoarse with desire.

Her eyes widened. 'My, you are quite direct, my lord. I scarcely know how to take you.'

He chuckled softly. 'Do not worry overmuch, my sweet.' He caressed her cheek with his palm. 'I'll be only too happy to show you how I like to be taken.'

She flushed to her roots. 'I shall bear that in mind, my lord,' she murmured dryly.

He threw back his head and laughed. 'You do that, my sweet. I own,' he said, gazing at her with a quizzical expression of his face, 'you are not at all what I expected my wife to be.'

Celeste's heart turned to lead in her chest. She quickly averted her gaze. Of course, she wasn't. She was scarcely what anyone would expect a lady of consequence to be.

'It's getting late,' she said a bit too quickly. 'We'd best be getting back.'

'If you like,' he replied with stiff civility. He got to his feet and extended a helping hand to her.

Sated and replete, husband and wife rode across the plush green meadow towards the house in silence. Celeste tried to shake off her feelings of inadequacy. Why should she care what this man thought of her?

Oh, but she did care. Terribly. She wanted Simon to be proud of her. She realized with a jolt that she wanted to please him. Her forehead wrinkled in confusion, for she couldn't imagine why. After all, aside from a few wonderfully exciting sensual encounters, she barely knew him.

This afternoon was the first enjoyable occasion they'd actually spent together since their marriage. But it was a pleasant day. More than pleasant. She'd been sorely tempted to let him have his way with her in the grass.

She darted a glance at her husband's stark darkly handsome profile. Oh, yes, she thought, biting her lower lip, she enjoyed his company far more than she cared to admit.

CHAPTER 13

That night, after sharing the first agreeable dinner with her husband since her wedding, Celeste found herself unable to sleep. After what seemed like hours of tossing and turning, she abandoned all hopes of peaceful slumber.

She sat up in the enormous canopied feather bed that threatened to dwarf her small figure and lit the taper on the bedside table. Several of her most coveted novels lay haphazardly piled on the table. Tempted to lift the cover and lose herself in the enviable prose, she reached out her hand for Jane Austen's *Emma*. Her hand fell shy of its mark. If only it were possible to find comfort in a book.

She sighed and leaned back against the mountain of snowy white pillows behind her head. The events of the past afternoon whirled about in her brain, tormenting her with possibilities.

What if she had let nature take its course? What if she'd made love to Simon? What then? How would she feel afterwards? She wrapped her arms around her knees and sighed. She wasn't sure she was capable of giving her body to him without her heart. He'd proved he could be cruel and rather difficult when the mood took him. Why should she make herself more defenceless than she already felt?

Two arguments waged war in her brain, the first being that it was her wifely duty. Her nose crinkled. Duty and conventionality never ranked highly on her list of concerns. On the contrary, she thrived on nonconformity. The second argument was far more compelling and rather disturbing. She wanted him.

Oh dear, she did, didn't she? She wanted to feel his body pressed against hers, run her fingers over his taut hard muscles, feel the warmth of his skin, bask in his manly scent, and taste his hard, passionate mouth.

Heaven help her, she wanted to enjoy every measure of what a man had to offer a woman. She felt herself grow warm at the thought. What would it be like to touch his glorious naked body, welcome him into her bed and her body, in the manner Joy had described with such vivid and tantalizing detail?

Celeste pressed her palms to her burning cheeks. She felt mildly ashamed of herself. She couldn't think why. It was scarcely sinful to lust after one's husband. Or was it? She did not know. Quite frankly, she did not care. At the moment, it seemed the most natural thing in the world to her.

No wonder he'd been mildly amused by her prenuptial agreement. Given his wealth of experience with the fairer sex, he must have known that sooner or later, one, if not both of them would give into temptation. She just had not considered it would be sooner, at least, not quite this soon. And she never dreamed it would be her!

She glanced longingly at the connecting door that lead to her husband's bedroom. She bit her lip. Oh, crumbs! She could never bring herself to fling open that door, and beg him to take her to bed and make passionate love to her. A frown marred her forehead. A yellow hue shone beneath the door. Every once in a while, it was eclipsed by a dark form that was undoubtedly her husband. He was pacing the floor. Why?

Perhaps this afternoon's outing had shaken him as well. Was he, too, searching for a way to persuade her into his bed? She scoffed at her ridiculous conclusion. The man was a renowned rake. He needed no assistance when it came to bedding women. She flung herself on to her side and hugged the blankets to her chest and prayed for sleep.

Sleep refused to come.

This was utterly stupid. She wriggled on to her back. She would never get to sleep at this rate. She sat up in bed and cast a furtive glance in the direction of her husband's bedroom. Visions of the virile, handsome man clad in a dark brocade robe filled her mind. Did he have a satin robe? she wondered. If he did, she was certain it clung to his broad shoulders and sinewed chest with enviable closeness.

What on earth was he doing tramping to and fro in the middle of the night? Curiosity got the better of her. She racked her brains for a reason to intrude on his insomnia.

He had brandy. She'd seen the crystal decanter and glasses on the small mahogany table the day she'd asked him to release her from their vows. Brandy. What an excellent notion. If nothing else, it might help her sleep. She threw back the covers and hopped out of bed.

But, of course, there was always conversation, she told herself as she scurried across the chilly floor in bare feet and a modest cotton nightgown. They could converse about . . . she hesitated for a moment. Her forehead creased. What would they find to talk about? Whatever topic they chose would occupy their minds until they were ready to go to bed.

Separately. Of course.

A rush of tingling heat poured over her. She shook her head. No. She was not prepared to share his bed. She caught her lower lip with her teeth. At least, she didn't think she was. In fact, she was almost positive it would be disastrous, no matter how exciting the Dragon's passion promised to be. She held her breath and turned the door knob.

At seeing her head peer around the door, Simon's pacing came to an abrupt halt.

'Celeste,' he breathed, his face a portrait of complete surprise. 'What are you doing awake?,' he asked as if she were a disobedient child who should have been to bed hours ago.

Gracious heavens! Her heart flopped around in her chest. He does have a satin brocade robe. And it was clinging to his bare chest, just as she knew it would. She gulped. He was naked beneath the heavy plush robe, she realized with a flush of delicious warmth. She forced her hungry gaze to his face.

'I . . . um . . . could not sleep.' Her cheeks burned apple red. 'I saw your light . . . I am sorry. I should not have intruded,' she murmured and turned to take her leave.

In the blink of an eye, he closed the distance between them. 'No.' His hand closed gently over her arm. 'It is all right.' He smiled slightly. 'I am glad you are here.'

Her startled gaze flew to his. 'You are?'

'Mmm. Hmm,' he murmured drawing her close. 'I could not sleep either.'

She wet her lips. 'Why not?' she asked, her voice sounding breathless and weak even to her own ears.

His gaze flickered over her face. 'I fear my thoughts are preoccupied tonight.'

'Mine too,' she admitted with a yearning smile.

He cocked an ebony brow. 'I thought you were too young to suffer from such ailments?,' he teased lightly. His breath was warm and soft and tickled her cheek.

'I am not so very young,' she countered, mildly affronted. He was supposed to be swept away by passion at the sight of her, not remarking on her age.

'Yes,' he said, pressing a kiss to her forehead, 'you are.' He drew a pensive sigh and dug his hands into the pockets of his plush robe. 'Very young indeed. Completely innocent of the ways of the world.' He crossed the room and leaned his weary elbow on the fireplace mantel. 'You've no idea what evil lurks in men's hearts.'

She frowned in frustration. Splendid. He was in his patronizing mood again. She despised being treated like a child. The very last thing she wanted at the moment was a benevolent brotherly chat.

She slapped her hands on her hips. 'I am all astonishment, my lord,' she muttered with heavy sarcasm. 'I had thought you were merely heartless. Alas,' she said on an exaggerated sigh, 'evil lurks mordantly where your heart should beat.'

He looked up at her sharply. 'Pray,' he mocked coolly, 'don't sound overly disappointed on my behalf.'

'How could a mere child like myself hope to do otherwise?' She imbued her voice with an acerbic edge. 'I warrant it is all part of the trial you face with a child bride.'

He chuckled softly, his smouldering gaze drifting over her like a sensual caress. 'Is that what you are?' His voice sounded oddly husky. 'My child bride?,' he asked, closing in on her like a stealthy dark predator.

Her stomach somersaulted. She backed away from his overwhelming masculinity. Her legs bumped into the enormous canopied bed that loomed behind her like a blatant sexual reminder.

Pressing her palms on the soft downy coverlet for much needed support, she forced herself to look anywhere but at the alluring wedge of bronzed skin. It was rather difficult, for his well-defined chest was directly at eye level.

'When you patronize me, how else should I feel?,' she asked in a horribly small voice.

'If I condescend to you,' he countered leaning down, his handsome face perilously close to hers, 'it is because I have the benefit of fourteen years more of life's experience.'

She swallowed. 'Yes, well,' she rushed out, breathlessly, 'I dare say you have made several more blunders than I.' Her fingers nervously toyed with the satin ribbon at the neck of her ruffled nightgown. His dark sensual gaze followed the direction of her fingers. She dropped her hand and cleared her throat. 'As for the remainder of your case, I see no evidence to support it.'

He grunted and gave her with a hard, withering look. 'It's late, Celeste.' His breath was warm against her face. She shivered. 'I am no mood to argue with you.'

Truth be told, in her current situation, her desire ran in a much more amicable direction as well. The conversation had taken a decidedly sensual turn. She found to her dismay that her brain had ceased to function properly, at approximately the same time as her pulse started to soar, which, as a matter of course, was always when her husband was near. Snatching a fistful of coverlet in each hand, she hung on for dear life. She wet her parched lips.

'W-why could you not sleep?,' she asked in an effort to change the direction of their disturbing cosy little chat and to quell her raging pulse.

He drew away from her. 'I've been thinking about the instrument of Emily's disgrace,' he said with a heavy sigh and massaged the back of his neck.

Celeste's brows snapped together. 'I was given to understand you did not know his name?'

Simon's jaw tightened. 'I don't.' He retrieved a large gold ring from his pocket and examined it with a dark brow. 'But I will. In time.'

'How?'

'I've hired a Runner to do some poking about.'

Her eyes sparkled with intrigue. 'Have you, indeed?' She plumped down on the end of his bed. Leaning back on her palms, she dangled her bare ankles like the child she swore she was not. 'What unsavoury clues has he unearthed?,' she asked, barely containing her excitement.

He etched a crooked smile. 'Not nearly what I had hoped,' he remarked, gazing down at the gold object in his hand as though it held the key to the questions burning in his mind.

'That ring is like the one we found at Hobson's.'

He glanced up at her. 'What makes you think so?'

'I am not a fool, my lord. I knew the moment you saw it at Hobson's it had significance. Where did you get it?'

'Amongst Emily's belongings. It was tucked away in a locked drawer along with a love letter.' He looked pained by the memory.

'Love letter?'

He crossed the room to the bedside table, retrieved a folded piece of paper from a wooden box and handed it to Celeste.

She glanced quizzically at her husband and unfolded the worn parchment paper. It was heavy stock, obviously good quality, she observed, as her eyes scanned the flowery black writing strewn across the white page.

My own true love, how I miss you! It will not belong before we are together again, reunited in our love. I have missed you, my pet. What a treasure you are to me. So young and vibrant and innocent. I have never experienced such mindless devotion as what you give unselfishly to me. Do you truly love me, little one? Dare I hope to hear your soft profession whispered in my ear soon? You are never from my thoughts and always near my heart. Come back to me soon, my beloved, for I cannot exist without your love to guide me. I long to take you in my arms and make you mine for all eternity.

I am as ever, your most gallant knight

Celeste frowned slightly. She folded the missive and handed it back to her husband. ' "Gallant knight" is not a terribly helpful clue to his true identity. It was a man with whom she was obviously very well acquainted.' She bit her thumbnail. 'How many could there be?'

'Evidently quite a number,' Simon snorted with derision, 'but none of wicked persuasion.'

'Save for one,' she said on a sigh.

'Yes, save for one,' Simon muttered pensively as he shoved the note in his pocket. 'But I'll be damned if I can find him.'

'Have you consider the possibility that the knight reference is genuine?'

He cast a dubious look over his shoulder.

'Perhaps they met in a chivalrous context, or often rode together. Is that not possible?'

His tormented strides commenced once more before the burning embers in the fireplace. 'How could I hope to ascertain such details of a relationship? To the best of my knowledge, she kept him a secret from the world.'

'Not the world, surely?'

'She never made mention of any knight, gallant or otherwise, to me. We shared everything, she and I.'

Celeste planted her chin on her palm. 'Obviously, he swore her to secrecy. Either that or she was ashamed of her own conduct. Still,' she thought aloud, furrowing her brow, 'someone must know of this gallant knight.'

'No one knows,' Simon fired back. 'I've left no stone unturned. I've considered every possible avenue. I can find nothing.'

Celeste hesitated for a moment. 'A girl usually confides in her mother. If she has no mother, a sister. Had she a close friend? A confidant?'

He stopped short. 'To the best of my knowledge, *I* was her confidant,' he intoned sharply, drumming his index finger against his chest.

Celeste frowned at him. 'Oh, do come along, my lord. Don't be over-sensitive. If she were involved with a man without the benefit of wedlock, she would doubtless *not* share the burden with her overprotective stepbrother. It would have to be someone less –'

'Punitive?' he suggested with a hard glint in his eye.

She shifted uncomfortably on the gold satin coverlet. 'That was not the word I was searching for, but, yes, someone she felt would not deter her from what might prove to be a disastrous relationship. Can you think of someone to whom she might have felt safe to bare her soul? Under the circumstances, it would most definitely have to be a woman. It is decidedly awkward to share such matters of the heart with a man.'

One eyebrow elevated slightly. 'You, I take it, are an authority on the subject?' he asked, his voice dripping with mockery.

She gave him a frosty glare. Was it strictly necessary that he behave like a pigheaded idiot all of the time? she wondered with mounting ire.

'Certainly not,' she snapped. 'But I do know she'd have to be stark raving mad to risk being caught doing anything scandalous.' She folded her arms over her chest. 'I should think the disastrous consequences of discovery would be ever fresh in your mind, my lord,' she added with a meaningful glint in her fiery blue orbs.

His dark, crushing look told her precisely how much he enjoyed her terse reminder of their forced nuptials. 'You may be right.' He rubbed his chin thoughtfully. 'I had thought not to involve anyone else for fear the gossipmongers would get wind of it.'

'Oh, but my lord, the person of whom I speak would be a trusted confidant. If Emily felt safe to bare her soul, we need not fear indiscretion.'

'It is possible . . .,' he allowed. 'You may have a point.'

'Why, thank you, my lord,' she intoned with biting sarcasm.

He dismissed her remark by ignoring it. 'But I can think of no one in particular in whom she would entrust such a secret. What is more, I cannot very well broach such a scandalous topic in the hopes of finding her supposed confessor. I must think of Annabelle.'

'Of course you must. Whoever Emily's soul mate was, she would most definitely have kept in touch while you were abroad. Have you any recollection of a particular person Emily wrote to whilst in Italy?'

He shot her a dubious frown. 'Our excursion was rather hasty. I assure you, I did not publicize the fact that my stepsister was increasing. I cannot think of anyone who knew our whereabouts. These things are best handled with the utmost discretion.'

'Even so,' Celeste replied, 'I cannot believe she contacted no one during her confinement.'

'I recall receiving only one missive from a relative that seemed to upset her. I never understood why.'

Celeste's ears pricked. 'Do you recollect any of the pertinent details?'

He shrugged. 'A few. There was something about Lady Caroline Martin. Emily and she had been friends since childhood.' He gave her a small smile that made her heart thump wildly in her chest. 'I remember that much. It seemed to upset Emily when Caroline married. I've not the slightest idea why.'

'First thing tomorrow morning, we will pay Lady Caroline a call.'

A sceptical brow drifted upward. '*We?*'

'These things often require a woman's touch, my lord. You cannot expect Lady Caroline to divulge all to you.'

A dark frown marred his otherwise perfect features. 'You are not to get involved in this. This is my

275

affair, I will handle it in the manner I see fit. I've known Caroline most of her life. She has no reason to be uncomfortable in my presence.'

'If she knows our gallant knight, she will have every reason,' Celeste countered evenly.

One eyebrow elevated slightly. '*Our* gallant knight?,' he echoed.

'I am your wife, my lord.'

His gaze flickered over her like a satin caress. 'Mmm,' he said huskily, a slow smile creeping across his face, 'I had noticed. I should recognize that gleam in your mischievous eyes by now. You are bent on interrogating poor Caroline, regardless of what I say.'

Celeste wrinkled up nose. 'Interrogate is such an unpleasant word. I had something more civilized in mind, say, an afternoon visit from Lord and Lady Barclay. She does, I assume, reside somewhere nearby.'

He gave her a sideways glance. 'Caroline married the old and very well-respected Lord Geoffrey Eastmore who has a formidable estate in Surrey.'

She looked up at him in surprise. 'Eastmore? I thought certain he was too old to be interested in marriage.'

Simon smiled at her choice of words. 'On the contrary, I believe he is very interested in the marriage bed. That is the prerequisite for producing the Eastmore heir.'

The heat of embarrassment scorched her cheeks. She quickly darted her gaze away from Simon's amused silver orbs.

'Eastmore was looking for a young healthy bride from a respected family. Evidently, Caroline was it. She must have come with an enormous dowry.'

'I see. Very well then, my lord.' Celeste released a determined sigh. 'We shall have to travel to Surrey.'

He shook his head at her. 'Without the benefit of an invitation? Permit me to remind you, your last impetuous jaunt resulted in our hasty marriage.'

'In that case, you have little to fear from scandal. More important, my lord, have you the time, or the inclination, to await an invitation?'

His lips curled into a wicked grin. 'I've known midshipmen during the war with better manners than you.'

'Have you, indeed? I thought I recognized you in the portrait downstairs. I must say, you cut a rather dashing figure, my lord.'

'You put me to the blush, madam. But you are quite correct, I am impatient to learn all that I can. I don't suppose it would do me any good to forbid you to come to Surrey?,' he inquired silkily.

She smiled up at him sweetly. 'I am afraid not,' she said, shaking her disheveled curly red head. 'I am bound and determined to find out who is perpetrating these vicious crimes.'

He knitted his brow in poorly-feigned ignorance. 'Vicious crimes? Whatever can you mean?'

'You think Emily's misfortune is related to Jane Greenly's death as well as I do. That hideous ring is too much of a coincidence not to be a valuable link. No use pretending, I am on to you.'

His smile turned roguish. 'You are, are you? Well, in that case,' he murmured in what can only be described as a bedroom voice, 'I'd best cooperate. Fully.'

Celeste's pulse skittered unbearably. 'I think that would be best,' she replied in a soft throaty voice that sounded nothing like her own.

'I am fairly certain there is a group of men who belong to a so-called secret society; at least nobody seems inclined to discuss it. The snake and the maiden insignia is the only link among them, thus far. It is possible Jane Greenly was their unwilling victim.' He fell silent. A brooding expression overtook his face.

Celeste slid her small hand over his much larger one. 'I know what you thinking.'

He stared down at her, his silver eyes serene and darkly compelling. 'Do you?' he asked thickly.

She framed his face between her hands. 'You must not think of poor Emily as a victim. It cannot be. The letter from her malefactor is, I believe, genuine. He must have loved her.'

For a long moment, he stared deeply into her guileless blue eyes. Then he pulled her hands from his face and withdrew. He stood before for the fireplace with his back to her. He put his hand on the mantel and stared down at the dying flames.

'You are supposed to believe in him,' he said after a while. 'That is why men like him are successful at destroying unsuspecting innocents. You believe his honeyed lies.'

'How could someone purposefully lie like that?'

'It happens all the time.' His tone was cold and distant. 'Men manipulate women with false declarations of their feelings every day.'

'But why? What would be the object of such a heinous deed?'

He turned to face her. 'Can you not guess?'

Yes, she thought with an unhappy sigh, she could. 'Even so, such an arrangement could, at best, be short lived.'

He uttered a growl of frustration. 'Is it possible that you are that naíve? It suits the man's purposes. He wants nothing more than a romp between the sheets. He cares not how he connives, or whom he hurts.'

'I see,' she said quietly and occupied herself with the examination of the floor.

Simon was instantly contrite. He glanced over at her head, bent in what he guessed was embarrassed discomfort. He eclipsed the space between them and cupped her chin with his palm, lifting her face to his. 'Forgive me, it was not my intention to speak harshly,' he said in an achingly soft voice that made her weak with longing. 'It is just that you are so like Emily at times. Young and inexperienced. You know nothing of the world.'

She bristled. 'I am not Emily. I am Lady Barclay, your wife. I know more of the world than you think,' she flung at his head.

He scoffed at her. 'You know precious little, my sweet. Of that, I am glad,' he said, gently caressing her cheek with his thumb. 'It is not a particularly nice place to be. Don't be in too much of a hurry to grow up.'

279

She jerked her head back. 'Stop treating me like a child of twelve! I am a full-grown woman, a fact you seem to remember quite clearly when it suits your purposes.'

His gaze turned sinfully seductive. Her stomach quivered. Before she could stop him, his hands slid around her waist. He dragged her to the end of the bed and pulled her close.

'You are quite right,' he murmured as he let his eyes drink their fill of her gauzy white nightgown that thinly veiled her naked body. 'You are a woman.' His voice was smoother than velvet. His softly seductive tone seemed to underscore the provocative, slow, strokes of his thumbs against her abdomen. She felt her stomach muscles contract and drew in a sharp, startled breath. 'Or had *you* forgotten?'

'No,' she managed to reply, captivated by his smouldering silver gaze, 'I . . . have not forgotten.'

He smiled like a wolf about to devour a helpless lamb. 'Good,' he murmured against her mouth, 'neither have I.'

Warmest blue gazed into smouldering grey. Slowly, he pressed her down on the bed, intimately blanketing her body with his own. His mouth moved against hers in a gentle kiss. Her silky arms wrapped tightly around his back. With a tortured groan, he kissed her, crushing her mouth beneath his.

Her eager body responded, burning with excitement from head to toe. She felt warm all over and her heart was pounding wildly in her chest. It was as if she'd run a very long distance. All these riotous reactions, and he had only kissed her. How would she survive the night? She had to gain some ground here or she would be lost.

'Simon . . . I need –'

'I know what you need,' he mumbled breathlessly as his hot, wet lips caressed the ivory column of her neck.

His hands were all over her; caressing her breasts, her waist and her hips, creating a powerful burgeoning desire deep inside her. He slipped her nightgown from her shoulder and trailed tiny kisses along her collar bone. One hand settled on her breast while the other was buried in her soft red curls, cupping her head in a soft caress as his mouth moved against hers, tasting her intoxicating sweetness. He gently squeezed the round mound in his palm and his thumb grazed the hidden nipple. Tension coiled deep inside her. Her breast ached. She leaned into his caress, desperate for more of what she knew not, only that her husband held the key. His kisses ignited a fire within her.

His mouth found hers once more and he whispered against her lips, 'I never wanted a woman as much as I want you,' and covered her mouth with his in a deeply erotic passionate kiss. His hand slid down her back, pressing her slender form intimately against his. She felt the heat of his desire and, with a tiny moan, moved against him devouring his lips with an ardour equal to his own. His hands tugged at her disheveled nightgown until her soft luscious breasts were bared to perfection.

'You are beautiful,' he breathed as his mouth closed over her taut peaks and gently sucked. 'Perfectly beautiful.'

She arched her back and her hands delved into his raven hair as his tongue worked its magic. He lifted his head, his passion-filled orbs burned into hers. Gently, she cupped his face in her hands, marvelling at his beauty. Her thumb lightly traced his moist lips. He uttered a groan of desire and kissed her. Impatient hands rid her of her nightgown and tossed it on the floor. His eyes greedily travelled the length of her, scorching her creamy flesh. She tried to shield herself, but he would have none of it. She felt a rush of heat surge through her body, excited by his frank, sensual perusal. She longed to boldly caress his rippled muscles that she knew lurked beneath his satin robe. His eyes smiled into hers in appreciation of her wanton admiration. He shrugged off his robe with a haste born from his intense burning need. As he leaned down to kiss the valley between her breasts, the softness of her belly, the roundness of her hip and the inner flesh of her thigh, she realized she was breathless with longing. She could stand it no more. His intimate kisses fuelled the fire of her already intense longing. Cupping his handsome passion-flushed face between her hands, she pulled him to her and took his mouth in a torrid kiss that reflected the passion ebbing inside her. He spread himself over her. She felt the heat of his skin against her own, the tickle of his coarse chest hair against her aching breasts.

'*Celeste,*' he breathed with aching softness as he kissed her neck and nibbled at her ear. He rained kisses all over her face and mouth. 'I am not sure I can wait much longer. I've got to be inside you.' He groaned, leaving her swollen, wet, ruby lips to cover her naked body in kisses.

He savoured every inch of her with his hands, his mouth and his tongue. His touch excited her beyond all imagining. She was awed by the reaction he created deep within her.

She quivered and ached simultaneously. His name escaped from her lips on a tide of longing. She could endure such sweet torture no longer.

He pressed hot, searing kisses along her stomach. His hands caressed her narrow hips, the flat of her abdomen, and slowly moved to cup her breasts. She thought she would die if he continued this a moment longer. His lips captured hers. Her hands rippled over his hard, muscled shoulders, basking in the wonderful feel of him. He was magnificent. She caressed his neck, threading her fingers through his ebony mane. She uttered his name with a ragged breath. His lips moved to take her mouth in a savage kiss. As their tongues began their love play, each was hungry for a deeper sampling of the other. He nudged her legs open with his muscular thigh and settled against her. She could feel the heat and breadth of him against her warm, moist womanly flesh. Slowly, ever so gently, he eased into her. She felt her body open to him. Another wave of delicious warmth cascaded through her. She felt the fullness of him invade her completely and gasped in surprise at the raw burst of sharp pain. He cradled her head between his hands and kissed her face. She could feel the warmth of his breath on her face and hear the urgency in his voice, as he whispered, 'Celeste . . . Celeste. My beautiful wonderful wife.'

She caressed his cheek and traced his lips tentatively with her fingertips. 'Show me . . . I want to please you, but I don't know what you want.'

He stared down at her, his face flushed with passion, his breathing ragged and his eyes brimming with emotion. His lips lingered above her mouth. He released a half-groan, half-laugh. 'I have what I want.' His mouth claimed hers in a torrid kiss.

Her arms went around him. Her mouth slanted hungrily over his. The initial ache of his intrusion faded as he moved inside her, withdrawing almost completely and then driving into her soft wet sheath once more. His rhythmic movement rekindled her intense pleasure. Each quickened thrust created waves of ecstasy deep within her. She could hear his hoarse, ragged breathing, and feel the pounding of his heart against hers as he drove onward to new heights of pleasure. She had never known such bliss, such complete fulfillment, and all-consuming joy. The two had become one and it was beautiful. Two hearts, minds and bodies had come together, driven by their passion for one another, they soared to untold heights of pleasure. Their souls united in this one moment as man and wife.

'*Celeste . . . oh God, Celeste,*' he murmured breathlessly against her neck, his thrust hard and deep.

So filled with emotion was she that she could utter no reply. She did not need to, she knew what he was feeling for she was feeling it too. She turned her head in search of his mouth.

'I . . .' She was about to say she loved him, but his movements increased to such a frenzied pitch that the words were lost on the tide of her fulfillment. Completely swept away by the moment, she uttered a moan of exquisite pleasure and clutched him to her. A glorious sensation of pure ecstasy blossomed deep inside her. The feeling was so potent and so overwhelming, she wondered if she could endure another moment without going mad with pleasure. It did not seem possible to reach an even higher plateau of delirious ecstasy.

'Don't fight it,' he breathed, his mouth inches from her own, loving her with hard, deep, fast strokes. 'Let it happen.'

As the waves of sublime culmination washed over her, she cried out his name. With a groan of supreme pleasure, he climaxed deep inside her.

CHAPTER 14

Their passion finally spent, Simon collapsed onto his back beside Celeste. His breathing was coming hard and fast and his body was covered in a fine dew of perspiration. He looked over at her. She gazed back at him with an expression akin to wonderment. He smiled slightly and gently brushed her flushed cheek with the back of his hand. Then, all at once, he pulled her into his arms. She felt him press a kiss to the top of her head and brush her damp hair away from her face. Snuggling against his chest, she listened to the comforting sound of his heart pounding beneath her ear, and luxuriated in the feel of his strong, loving arms around her.

The sounds of the crackling fire, combined with the gentle stroke of his hand along her spine, lulled her towards sleep. His hand slowed and finally went limp against her. His breathing became slow and deep. She knew he slept. Thinking she ought to return to her own bed, she tried to move away from him, but his arms tightened around her.

'No. Don't go,' he mumbled, stirring partially

from his much-needed slumber, 'stay with me.' His arms tightened around her. 'I want you near.'

She relaxed against his hard muscular chest and smiled a secret little smile. Closing her eyes, she hugged the special moment to her heart and drifted off to sleep, content with the knowledge that her rakehell husband needed her.

Celeste slowly emerged from her deep slumber and felt Simon's hands on her body; caressing her, awakening her desire once more.

'Celeste,' he breathed, kissing her cheek and her eyelids, 'I want you,' he murmured, as his mouth moved to kiss her temple. 'I need you,' he rasped, kissing her eyelids. 'Make love to me, my precious little one,' he whispered into her mouth before he kissed her, smothering her lips with his own.

As his mouth slanted voraciously over hers, her arms slipped around his back, drawing him against her aroused body.

His lips moved along her soft skin. He nibbled at her shoulder and kissed her collar bone, her throat, her neck and then finally the back of her ear. Desperate to be kissed, to feel his lips upon hers, to taste him fully, she whimpered and turned her face toward his in search of his mouth. His lips captured hers once more. Their tongues danced erotically together. His hands roamed over her body. She could barely contain herself, she wanted him with such wild desperation.

His palm slid over her abdomen and pulsed against the apex of her thighs. 'Are you ready for me, little one?,' he murmured huskily against her cheek. His finger slid inside her snug channel. He smiled down at her. She was dripping with sweet honeyed wetness, and was more than ready for him.

'*Yes, Simon, yes,*' she gasped breathlessly, her blood pulsating like a tempest storm through her body.

His arms slid around her, his body blanketed her with his warmth. She opened for him, her body craving for an end to this sweet torment in their blissful fulfillment. He entered her, filling her completely with one powerful thrust. She sighed, catapulted to a world of complete rapture; a host of wonderful spiralling sensations assailed her. His every movement heightened her senses. When she thought she could experience no greater bliss, he took her higher, and higher still, to a new undiscovered plateau of pure ecstasy. Their lovemaking was all-encompassing. Nothing else mattered. They gave freely to each other in this exquisite cleaving of man and woman. She never wanted these feelings to end.

In the afterglow of their lovemaking, she lay against his chest, softly tracing the hard contours of his muscular chest.

'Simon?,' she whispered.

'Mmm,' Simon mumbled, his voice heavy with sleep.

'The night before our wedding, Joy told me what to expect from the, um, the marriage bed. She mentioned there were ways to ah, prevent . . . well, to avoid making, um, a baby.'

That woke him! Good Lord! 'What?,' he burst out, shaking the cobwebs of slumber from his brain. His wife had a penchant for talking at all the wrong times. This was by far the most bizarre conversation he'd ever had – especially in bed. He did not wish to discuss the prevention of babies with his wife. It made him uncomfortable.

'I was wondering . . . did you –?'

He stiffened. 'No,' he told her curtly. 'You must know I did not.'

'Oh. I did not think you had.'

Devil take it! She sounded disappointed. He tilted her chin upward. 'Celeste,' he imparted in a tone that brooked no disagreement, 'I don't intend to either.'

She looked dumbstruck. 'Why ever not?'

His jaw clenched. 'You are my wife, that's why not,' he practically snapped at her.

She blinked at him. 'What difference should that make?' Draped across his chest, she was a lovely naked invitation to the pleasure from which she was suggesting they abstain.

He sat up and dragged his hand through his tussled raven hair. 'All the difference in the world.'

She sat up beside him. Tugging the sheets over her bare breasts, she gazed at him. Her wild red locks, damp from their lovemaking, cascaded down her back and over her shoulders like those of a siren temptress. 'I do not see why,' she said, looking more desirable by the minute.

Simon grimaced. 'The natural result from our union is children,' he muttered uncomfortably. 'Surely you must be aware of that.'

'That may be the natural course,' she retorted, 'but I am too young to become a mother.'

He burst out laughing. 'Is that what is worrying you?,' he asked, caressing her soft, rosy cheek with his knuckles. 'Your age?'

'I think it's a valid concern,' she countered, her mien cool.

'You will be a wonderful mother,' he assured her, kissing her softly on the mouth.

'Stuff and nonsense,' she replied, shoving her palms against his chest.

He blinked down at her in surprise. Well, at least she had not shouted *poppycock* at him. Things were looking up. Now she sounded like a stodgy old man. But she did not look like one, he noted with a surge of white-hot desire.

'You mistake my meaning. I do not want a baby,' she told him, enunciating each word quite clearly. 'I've no desire to be breeding endlessly whilst you enjoy yourself in London.'

'Fine,' he agreed and busied himself with kissing the curve of her delectable neck. 'I promise to remain with you during your confinement and afterwards, if you like,' he breathed against her skin.

She gawked at him. Incredulity mingled with anger. 'You are kindness itself, my lord. I should consider myself fortunate indeed to have such a generous husband.'

He did not miss her acid tone. 'A child would be good for you, Celeste,' he told her huskily as his forefingers caressed the valley between her breasts.

She swatted his hand away. 'No, my lord, a child would be good for you.'

He framed her face between his hands. 'Think of how devoted you are to little Annabelle. Do you not wish for a child of your own body? A child of our making, yours and mine?,' he asked her softly. She seemed to waver slightly. Good, he thought, her maternal instincts were his ally. 'We would make a beautiful baby together, you and I,' he coaxed, kissing her on the mouth.

'Simon,' she murmured, sliding her hands over the top of his, 'pray, listen to me. We must discuss the matter fully.'

He chuckled deep in his throat. 'I agree whole-heartedly,' he whispered and trailed hot, wet kisses along her shoulder. 'Fully.'

She drew in a sharp breath. 'Unless you agree to – to use the, um, proper, er, method,' she declared boldly. 'I – I refuse to share your bed.'

He shook his head as if to clear it. 'What?,' he asked, looking dazed and confused by her declaration. 'What are you saying?'

She lowered her lashes from the hurt look on his face and toyed with the bed linen under her fingers. 'Well, you would keep touching me.'

He tipped her chin upward with his forefinger. 'Are you refusing me your bed?,' he asked, his piercing grey gaze locked with hers.

She swallowed. Her gaze darted away from his penetrating stare. 'Not exactly . . .'

He flashed a smile of pure male satisfaction. 'I thought not. Let us not have any more talk of it.'

'Very well, my lord,' she mumbled and pulled back the bed linen.

He scowled at her. 'Where the devil do you think you are going?'

'To my bed.'

He utter a growl of frustration and hauled her down on the bed. 'The devil you are!,' he grumbled, kissing her hard on the mouth.

Wrapping his arms around her, he cradled the soft voluptuous woman against his hard, lean body and told her gruffly, 'I am in no mood for your childish games, Celeste. Go to sleep.'

'Yes, Simon,' she said on a lusty yawn and settled comfortably in the succor of his embrace.

Almost before Celeste's eyes flickered open, she reached for her husband. The bed was empty. She moved her legs beneath the blankets and felt the soreness from their strenuous lovemaking. She pushed up on her elbow to survey the room. Judging from the bright sunshine peeking around the heavy brocade drapes, it was a glorious day outside. She lay back on the pillow with a delicious sigh. It was a glorious day inside too. She lay quietly reliving the wonder of last night.

She wished Simon had not abandoned her this morning. It made her feel slightly despondent, almost as if last night's passion had been an aberration or a wonderful fantasy she alone had experienced. She hugged the blankets to her and let out a doleful sigh. Given his chequered character, it might have been little more to him than a moment's pleasure. What could she ever mean to a man like him?

'Thinking of me?,' a dark drawly voice asked from the doorway.

Startled, Celeste's head shot up. One look at his coal black hair, piercing grey eyes and perfectly chiseled features – she melted. Her heart thudded at the sight of him handsomely clad in tight fawn-colored breeches and a navy velvet coat. His lips curved into a slow sensual smile. She felt the color rise in her cheeks as she recalled his hot, wet mouth all over her.

'Yes,' she said with a swallow, 'as a matter of fact, I was.'

'Capital notion, my sweet,' he murmured, his gaze drinking her in as he crossed the room to the side of the bed, 'my thoughts are always of you. Only you.' He pressed a kiss to her cheek. 'Did you sleep well?,' he queried, his tone sinfully suggestive.

'Yes, thank you.' She gave him a small smile. 'I . . . missed you this morning,' she admitted shyly.

'Did you?' His lips curled into a wolfish grin and he sat down on the bed beside her. 'I am glad,' he whispered, kissing her on the mouth, 'I missed you too.'

She was immediately uneasy with his tender mood and the gentle caress of his thumb along her jaw. She knew where this situation could lead and she was ill-prepared to deal with it. If last night was any indication, she was helpless to resist him. At this rate, she'd be increasing by the end of the month!

The passion lurking in his smouldering gaze fairly singed her. A rush of heat swept over her. Good gracious, he was wicked. It was broad daylight.

His lips captured hers in a searing persuasive kiss that banished all rational thought from her mind with amazing finesse. His arms tightened around her, pressing her snugly against the hard length of him.

'*Simon*, it is light out,' she murmured against his far too persuasive lips.

He lifted his head and glanced over his shoulder. 'So it is,' he replied and began to kiss her delectable rosy mouth once more. She moved her head. His hot, searing lips found the quickening pulse at her throat. 'Simon . . . you are dressed.'

Her complaint was acknowledged with a deep throaty chuckle and several more heated kisses which threatened to drive her to the brink of total abandon. 'You're not,' he chuckled.

'Should we not at least have breakfast?,' she ventured, feeling awkward and unsure of how to extricate herself from her current position.

His lazy, sultry regard made her pulse skitter unbearably. He frowned at her with playful admonishment. 'It is nearly noon,' his deep drawl swirled around her like a sensual caress. 'You slept most of the day away,' he murmured, watching as his hand cupped her breast and grazed her nipple. He smiled as her nipple hardened beneath his touch.

She pushed his hand away. 'Why did you not wake me?,' she asked, embarrassed by the news.

He shrugged an indolent shoulder. She could not help but notice how well the velvet fabric clung to his broad shoulders, any more than she could squelch the memory of how she'd clutched those same shoulders while he drove into her with deep, long strokes that took her to unimaginable peaks of ecstasy.

He flashed a crooked grin. 'I assumed you needed your rest,' he said in a husky voice and pressed a kiss to the soft enticing valley between her bare breasts. 'It is customary for the bride to sleep in on her honeymoon.'

Her cheeks pinkened. 'Oh, is that all?' She lowered her gaze to the coverlet. 'I thought perhaps you might be . . . angry.'

'Angry?,' he chuckled softly and, lifting her face to his, kissed her on the mouth. 'Now, what would I have to be angry about?,' he drawled out, tucking a stray curl behind her ear.

She reached out and caressed his handsome face with her finger tips. 'Then you are not upset about what we discussed last night?,' she asked, her voice wavering with uncertainty.

'We discussed a great many things last night. To what, precisely, do you refer?,' he asked, trailing kisses along her neck and bare shoulder.

She lowered her lashes to shield her discomfort. 'You know what,' she said softly.

'Ah.' He sat back. 'You mean your ridiculous refusal to bear me a son?'

Her eyes flashed wide. 'Is that how you see it?,' she gasped in dismay.

His hand gently brushed her tussled hair back from her face. 'How else should I?,' he asked with maddening nonchalance.

Astonished, she stared at him. 'You might consider my feelings,' she said tartly.

'As you might mine,' he replied with a cool smile.

'Please, Simon,' she entreated him, 'we are not enemies. Why must we remain on opposite sides of the issue? Can you not understand my feelings on the matter in the slightest?'

A look of utter incredulity touched his handsome face. Gawking at her, he uttered a short laughing sound. 'You are serious about this?'

He hadn't taken her objections last night to heart. All women wanted children. She was merely frightened. And justifiably overwhelmed. After all, her body had recently been introduced to the sensual world. Lovemaking was naturally alarming for an inexperienced girl of eighteen.

'I am in earnest, my lord,' she said, her soft blue gaze locked on his staggered expression.

He lifted his gaze heavenward. 'Lord, save me from feckless females,' he muttered with a sardonic edge to his voice.

'I am not feckless,' she flung back at him. 'You yourself said I am young. I have so much of life to live, so many things yet to experience. We have time to make a baby. All the time in the world.'

'No,' he snapped in a curt tone, 'I do not see. You are my wife. I expect an heir, Celeste.'

Taking his hand in hers, she pressed a kiss to his palm and rubbed her cheek against it. 'I know you do. And, in time, I will give you as many children as I can. But for now,' she pleaded, 'can we not get better acquainted with one another?'

He pulled away from her and stalked across the room to gaze stoically out the window. 'We are well enough acquainted,' he muttered with ill-concealed irritation.

She drew a deep sigh. 'Simon, please, do not be cross with me.'

He turned on her, his silver gaze glittering with resentment. 'How do you expect me to feel?,' he burst out, furious. 'You are my wife. I desire your body. You have forbidden me to touch you,' he gritted. 'Is that not a faithful depiction of our future life together?'

'Please try to understand. I simply do not wish to – to –'

'Bear my children,' he supplied in a tone that was decidedly cold and abrupt given his recent warmth.

She paled slightly. 'Please . . . Simon . . . don't,' she begged and wished the animosity between them would vanish. This was not at all what she wanted. Why could he not show her some small measure of kindness and understanding?

'What else am I *not* supposed to do?,' he lashed out angrily.

She released a weary sigh. 'You are being impossible.'

He sent her a hard look. 'I fully comprehend your feelings, madam,' he told her, his slate grey eyes gleaming dangerously. 'We shall see who is the intractable one.'

She turned her face away. 'You cannot make me bear you children,' she averred with the characteristic defiance he found deuced annoying.

He laughed unkindly. 'I could. If I so chose.'

Her head turned sharply. She stared at him with a mixture of indignation and fear.

He shook his head at her stricken expression. 'I won't,' he muttered with barely-concealed contempt.

'Then . . .,' she asked tentatively, 'you will respect my wishes?'

He hesitated before he spoke. 'I give you my word. I will never force you. More than that, I cannot give.'

Distress filled her gaze. 'Then we are at cross purposes, my lord.'

A wicked smile softened his otherwise harsh features. 'Not necessarily,' he said, his tone treacherously soft. 'You may change your mind and find you want what pleasure I can afford you. I believe I am not wrong, nor am I egotistical, when I claim you welcomed me inside you as much as I enjoyed being there.'

Hot color scalded her cheeks. She lowered her lashes. Wordlessly, she nodded her curly head.

A satisfied smile edge his mouth. 'I thought as much.' He knew it was true. Oddly, he wanted to hear her say it. His little vixen wife had come alive in his arms in a way no other woman had ever done. He was mildly disappointed that she had not verbalized her feelings, for he had little doubt as to his own. He wanted her right now. But he would wait.

'I don't think we need concern ourselves on such a minor point. As an avid student of life, I am certain you will soon be eager to further your –,' his lips twitched '– experimentation, shall we say.'

Her face brightened. 'Then you will –'

His gaze frosted over. 'No,' he told her sharply, 'I will not.'

She folded her arms beneath her bosom. 'In that case, my lord,' she imparted crisply, 'there will be no experimentation, sensual or otherwise.'

A sharp intensity blazed in his silvery depths. His mouth slashed in a grim, tight line of fury. By God, she had gall. No one dared dictate to him. How dare she draw up such a ridiculous marital accord and expect him to abide by it? It was too much to be borne. He clenched his jaw, grinding his teeth. She was a hellion from the netherworld, come to wreak havoc in his well-ordered life.

Planting a hand on either side of her hips, he leaned perilously close to her. His savage expression battled with her stubborn upturned face.

'You have thrown down the gauntlet, madam.' His voice was rough and deeply masculine. 'I shall prove your worthy adversary, depend upon it.'

He stood straight and gazed down at her with cold, bleak grey eyes.

'Get dressed,' he commanded, his manner brisk. 'We must away. We've a social call to pay in Surrey. In this matter, at least,' he said unkindly as he let his chilling gaze drift over her, 'you may prove useful to me.'

The color drained from her face. His tone was hateful. She could not believe after the intimacy they'd shared that he had transformed into a cold stranger once more. Disbelieving blue eyes searched his dark features for signs of emotion and came away wanting. Where was the man she'd made love to last night? No one would guess he'd spent the night locked in the throes of passion, worshipping her body.

'Very well, my lord,' she mumbled, pushing back the bed linen to get out of bed. She glanced down and saw the telltale signs of her lost innocence.

His gaze flickered over the splattering of blood. Her face burned with humiliation. How proud he must feel. His lordship had bedded his wife at long last. His only regret was that she refused to act like a prize cow and bear him a son. What a fool she was to believe his romantic declarations and hungry kisses. She was a convenient vessel for his heir. Nothing more. Swallowing the painful lump in her throat, she draped the sheet over her body and tramped across the room in desperate need of a bath. No amount of soap and water would wash away the burning memory of their passionate union, or cleanse the deep ache from her breast.

Garbed in her prettiest lavender morning gown and deep purple velvet spencer, Celeste gazed out the window at the geese preening themselves by the side of the pond on Lord Eastmore's estate. Neither she nor Simon had exchanged a single word the entire way from Kent. He was cool, reserved and darkly handsome in his black great coat and beaver hat. Even in the face of total acrimony, her heart raced in his presence. One look at his stern, forbidding face and she sincerely wished she had not made the effort. His mood had not improved any. If possible, the detestable wall of polite coolness that separated them was fortified by anger.

He stood, a towering dark figure beside the fireplace, and waited for Lady Caroline to appear. A look of fierce determination was etched on his handsome face. Celeste could well imagine the depth of his feelings at this moment. She longed to go to him and ease his worry, but she stifled the urge. No matter how much she wanted to throw her arms around his neck and beg for his forgiveness, she would not. He was behaving like a domineering, uncompromising boor.

Still, she could not endure this wretched awkwardness between them. 'Good gracious,' she said, endeavoring to forge a cordial feeling as she gazed at the portrait above her husband's left shoulder, 'Eastmore looks old enough to be Lady Caroline's father'.

Simon glanced at the painting. 'He isn't *that* old,' he replied, imbuing his voice with perfect indifference. 'It is rumored he is in remarkably good physical condition. In some circles, he was considered a fine catch, despite the fact that he walks with a cane, has a mop of snowy white hair and is twice a widower.'

She wrinkled up her nose in disdain. 'My lord, Eastmore is easily twice her age.'

'Verily, my dear.' Sarcasm swirled through his low, velvet voice. 'You have hit upon it. He cannot last very much longer. In due course, I expect Caroline shall be a wealthy widow.'

Celeste drew in her breath, shocked by his ugly suggestion.

He smiled at her unkindly. 'I dare say even a bluestocking like you surely must know how these things work. She was undoubtedly hand-selected by Eastmore during her first Season. I doubt she had much say in the matter. It was all arranged.'

It was then that Lady Caroline appeared. She blended remarkably well into the stark sitting room decorated predominantly in olive tones and puce. She was older than Simon recollected. And, he acknowledged, with a modicum of distress, thin and pale and sad. He would scarcely have recognized her as the same girl who played with his sister except for the fact that she knew him at once.

Simon could not credit how the young carefree girl he'd once known could have aged so excessively. Her brown hair lacked its original shine. Her once-bright brown eyes looked flat and devoid of all emotion. Perhaps that is what comes of marrying a man old enough to be your father.

Recently widowed for the second time, Lord Geoffrey Eastmore had been in the market for a young, fertile wife. An Eastmore heir had continually eluded him through two marriages. He had a younger brother who had produced a veritable litter of children. Obviously, Geoffrey still held out hope of planting his seed in a fresh field. But Caroline, marry a man like Eastmore? It was outlandish. Hell's teeth. It was bizarre. A once-youthful, vibrant young woman married to that old, prunish curmudgeon? His lips curled with disgust. He couldn't get passed the injustice of it, nor what had happened to her since her wedding day.

What Caroline said next took Simon completely unawares.

'I knew you would come,' she said, quietly folding her hands at her waist. 'I knew. I have dreaded this moment, but I knew.'

Celeste glanced covertly at her husband as if to say, 'I told you so.' He slanted her a dark look of irritation. 'I must speak to you –' he rushed out.

Lady Caroline kept her voice low as she said, 'You will want to know about Emily, I expect.'

'You must tell me everything you can recall about the man who wronged her brutally,' Simon imparted in a blunt tone that won him an admonishing sideways glance from his bride.

The drawing-room door creaked open. Out of the corner of her eye, Celeste caught sight of the aged, white-haired, bushy-browed Eastmore making his way across the room. She clutched Simon's navy velvet sleeve and shook her head at him.

Good Heavens, Celeste thought, Eastmore was even worse than the portrait depicted. The man looked like a shriveled skeleton. He watched his wife with pale blue watery eyes. Pinning a smile on her face, Caroline nodded her head in his direction.

'We have visitors, my lord.'

'So I see,' he grunted.

'Perhaps you would care to offer Lord Barclay a glass of port in the library?'

The old man snorted. Leaning heavily on his cane, he muttered a beleaguered invitation to Simon to follow him, noisily lamenting the state of affairs when a man was not master in his own house. Simon observed the stilted exchange between husband and wife with keen interest. He gave a silent nod to Celeste, granting her licence to interrogate Lady Caroline.

CHAPTER 15

The men had taken their leave and not a moment too soon. Celeste had the uncanny feeling Lady Caroline wanted to be alone.

'I had no idea Lord Eastmore was so–so . . .,' she hesitated, grappling with the appropriate polite phrase to describe such a mismatch.

'Old?,' Lady Caroline queried with a slight smile.

Abashed, Celeste nodded her head.

'Indeed. We rarely, if ever, make social appearances,' Lady Caroline remarked. 'Which pleases me as well. I have little desire to visit London.'

Celeste's forehead wrinkled in consternation. Lady Caroline seemed more than melancholy. She was depressed.

Lady Caroline forced a wan smile. 'You mustn't feel sorry for me. My future is not that dreary,' she explained, making a stab at optimism. 'We lead a quiet, undisturbed life which suits my needs perfectly.'

Celeste thought of her own bizarre marital circumstance and smiled. Apparently, not all marriages were made in heaven.

'Then I am happy for you. It is seldom possible to find a suitable companion.' Something she knew all too well. Was she not the woman who swore she wanted nothing more than to pursue her intellectual inquiries in peace and solitude? Wasn't that what she wanted? Of course it was, at the time. But now, after spending last night in her husband's arms, her conviction waned.

Lady Caroline lowered her gaze to the floor. 'Only consider poor Emily.'

Celeste reached out and squeezed Lady Caroline's hand. 'You know the identity of the gallant knight.' Her assertion was not a question.

Lady Caroline nodded.

'I suspected as much. Can we not sit and talk a while?,' Celeste offered at seeing Lady Caroline's shoulders slump.

When they were seated on the dark brown velvet settee, Lady Caroline clutched her hands. Her grip was tight enough to cut off circulation. 'She met him the second time at the beginning of the Season, at Almack's. I became . . . acquainted, through a serious misfortunes, with a friend of his.' She glanced at Celeste and smiled sadly. 'When I have offered an account of what tragedy I experienced, you will have little doubt why I am today Lady Eastmore. You must never think of dear Emily in the same light as me,' she hastened to add nervously, wetting her parched lips. 'I will always believe, regardless of how it ended, that hers was a love match. That he led her astray, I can easily attest to, but I know he did not misuse her.'

Lady Caroline gripped her knees with her hands. 'I have never spoken of what happened to anyone, out of fear that they would betray me to my family or to my husband. Only Emily knew the truth. It was not until after she had been so horribly wronged that I confided the vicious account to her.'

Celeste leaned closer and covered Lady Caroline's white-knuckled hand with her own. 'You must not tax yourself. If it is too painful to relate all to me, then I beg you, reconsider. Lord Barclay need only hear of Emily's circumstance, not yours.'

Lady Caroline dabbed the tears that welled at the corner of her sad brown eyes. 'I should like to impart the abominable act to . . . someone. It has been difficult for me to keep it locked away.'

'In that case,' Celeste said with a sympathetic smile, 'I am honored that you have paid me the great compliment of your confidence.'

'Emily was seduced by a handsome, suave villain who swept her off her feet with honeyed words and romantic ideals. I was . . . not. He came upon me in the darkened bushes at Vauxhall Gardens. I could do nothing.'

Lady Caroline was too engrossed in her own grief to notice Celeste's sharp intake of breath.

'I was stunned. Shocked. He overpowered me with little difficulty. I was utterly helpless. The fireworks, you see, the cheers from the crowd, eclipsed my cries for help.'

Celeste cringed in abject horror. The thought of such a violent, forceful experience made her shudder with revulsion. She could not envision the beautiful

307

expression of love that she'd shared with Simon turned into something heinous and violent. Unsure of what to say, or how to lend comfort, she waited in silence for Lady Caroline to recover.

Her shoulders shook from the force of her tears. Celeste hugged Lady Caroline, unable to think of any other way to lend comfort to the poor woman who had suffered brutally at the hands of a man. Pulling away at last, Lady Caroline wiped the tears from her cheeks with the back of her hand.

Drawing a deep breath, she forged ahead. 'A-after that, I knew I must marry. Immediately. I was terrified that my family, my father, would discover my hideous secret. So, I married. I married someone who would not know . . . would never learn of what happened to me.' She lifted her red-rimmed, teary eyes to Celeste's concerned face. 'You see, Geoffrey and I live separate lives. We scarcely see each other. He has never touched me, or even tried to kiss me, for which I am eternally grateful.' She squeezed her eyes shut against the devastating memory. 'I could not . . . bear to . . . to be touched by a man ever again.'

Apparently, Simon's assessment of Eastmore and the old man's motivations for marriage were incorrect. Celeste cleared her throat. 'Were you . . . acquainted this sinister man who attacked you?'

'Oh, yes,' she said with staggering venom, 'I knew him. James Shelton. He was handsome, debonair, the picture of charm itself. He pretended to love me. And then . . .' She bowed her head and emitted a tortured sob.

Celeste's brow drew together in an agonized expression. 'But his actions were those of a criminal. Why did you not tell the world of his villainous deed and bring him to justice?'

'How could I confess the horrible truth? Who would have believed me? Shelton is a well-respected gentleman. It would have meant total ruin and disgrace for me and my family. I had to consider my father and my younger sisters.'

Celeste rubbed her back while she wept. 'And his friend? Emily's lover, were you acquainted with him?' she urged gently.

She shook her head and pulled away. 'She met him in Bath a few years ago. He quite swept her off her feet.' She sniffled. 'Of course, they were always together in Kent. His estate borders on the Barclay estate. It was there that he seduced her into his bed,' she hissed with disgust.

Celeste hesitated before she spoke. 'This man who attacked you, did he wear a ring that you can recall or, perhaps, a medallion?'

Lady Caroline blinked. 'A ring?'

'Yes, a gold signet ring.' Celeste drew a revolted sigh. 'I fear you would not forget such a piece. It is singularly ugly.'

Lady Caroline hesitated for a moment, struggling to remember. 'I recollect when I first knew him that he had a ring. Yes, I am sure he did. I remember, I inquired about it. He said it was a sign of prowess and laughed it off. He must have removed it after that. I don't recall seeing it ever again.'

Celeste hugged Lady Caroline tightly. 'Thank you. I can imagine how difficult that confession must have been for you. I am sure my husband will be eternally grateful for your candour. You must come to visit us at Lindhurst as soon as you are able. I should be pleased to consider you one of our dearest friends.'

Lady Caroline dabbed her moist cheeks with the edge of her handkerchief. 'Thank you,' she sniffled, 'I shall be pleased to accept.'

Celeste desperately needed to speak to Simon. He must know the identity of poor Emily's seducer and not realize it. Whoever the ungallant knight was, he was obviously a master of pretence.

Anxious to hear what Lady Caroline had confided in his wife, Simon hurried through their goodbyes and hastily handed her into their carriage.

Throwing herself against his chest, Celeste clung to him for comfort. 'Oh, Simon, it is the most despicable thing I've ever heard,' she cried in disgust.

Gently, he stroked her back soothing her. 'Tell me. What happened?'

'You cannot imagine how that poor woman has suffered at the hands of Lord Shelton,' she choked out.

He stiffened. Shelton? James Shelton? Of course, he was one of them! 'Yes, my love, I am very much afraid I can.'

'He deserves to be locked up in Newgate, rotting for what he's done to Lady Caroline and who knows how many others,' she said with venom.

His arms tightened around her. 'Not . . . Lady Caroline too?'

Celeste nodded her head. 'Oh, Simon, it was horrible.'

'And what of Emily?,' he asked in a taut cold undertone that masked his deeper emotions.

She pulled away from him and managed to compose herself, but not without the help of his well-placed handkerchief on her tear-stained cheeks. 'You must understand, she believed herself in love.' She sniffled. 'Simon, if it is any consolation, I do believe he must have loved her.

'Huh,' he grunted in disgust. 'Whatever that means.'

Celeste chose to ignore his disparaging attitude towards love. He was merely upset, and rightfully so. He was capable of love and he did believe in it. He must.

He looked positively grim, however, as he demanded, his tone harsh, 'What, precisely, happened to Emily?'

Celeste swallowed audibly. 'She was . . . seduced, but not . . . defiled.'

His steel-grey eyes ignited with a fiery intensity. 'I suspected as much. Who?' he bit out.

'Lady Caroline knew only where they met and when he . . .' She lowered her gaze to her lap.

'Go on.'

'They were . . . together in Kent.'

'Kent?,' he blazed with raw hostility.

Celeste nodded her head. 'His estate is near your family's. Evidently, they met a few years back in Bath on holiday,' she said on a sniffle. 'At least, that is where he took her under his spell, according to Lady Caroline.'

Alarm darkened Simon's eyes. 'Bath, did you say? They met in Bath?' He slammed his fisted hand into the velvet squabs. 'By God, what a fool I've been.'

'Do you know the identity of the gallant knight, Simon?'

He uttered a low growl of rage. 'How could I have been such a dense fool?' He thrust his hand through his raven hair. 'Of course, Annabelle is blonde and she has brown eyes.'

Celeste's brows drew together. 'What has that to do with Bath?,' she demanded, her tone curt with impatience.

'Evidently,' he said bitterly, 'a great deal more than I realized.'

'I am at a complete loss, my lord.' Confusion meddled with her mounting impatience to learn the blackguard's true identity. 'Dare I hope you have fallen upon a useful clue?,' she asked in frustration.

Simon's jaw set. 'Indeed, I have. Wilkinson. George Wilkinson. He destroyed Emily. I am sure of it.'

'Are you certain?'

'Oh, yes, I am absolutely certain. I paid a visit to the ignoble Lord Paine, who is teetering on the brink of Fleet Prison. Whom did I run into outside Paine's townhouse but George Wilkinson. I thought it odd at the time that he should inquire after Emily.' He snorted derisively. 'I had no idea they were *inti-*

mately acquainted. He was interested in the child as well. He seemed to think it was a boy. That must have appealed to his vanity.' Elbows on his knees, Simon clutched his skull between his hands. 'How could I have been so deucedly blind?'

'Simon,' Celeste said, touching his arm, 'do not blame yourself. These recent events are too horrific to imagine.'

'He told me they'd met at Bath some time ago. He admitted he was always fond of little Emily. He even had the audacity to mention his estate bordered on the Barclay grounds. I cannot conceive of such a man.'

She shivered. 'Nor can I,' she said softly.

'There is more. I have hesitated to disclose the sordid details for fear of offending your delicate sensibilities.'

She offered him a lopsided smile. 'You need have no fear of that, my lord. I've survived the worst, I suspect. Nothing you tell me at this junction would come as a surprise to me.'

'This group of nefarious men cavorts around London, preying on innocent young women. I am presently convinced that Wilkinson founded this disgusting male society. And I am very much afraid the secret society's charter is to prey on virgins for sport. These men enter various names of debutantes into a book and place wagers. Winner takes all, so to speak.'

The color drained from Celeste's face. 'I suspected something untoward, but I never imagined this. What will you do?' Her gaze was heavy with anxiety.

Simon's hand fisted. 'Bring him to justice. We head for London with all possible haste.'

Celeste drew in a shocked breath. 'London?'

'I've not a moment to lose.'

She blinked at him, a look of complete surprise etched on her face. 'B-but what of Annabelle?' she stammered, greatly dismayed. 'I never said goodbye.'

He smiled slightly at her forlorn expression. This, from the woman who swore she would not bear him a child. He reached out his hand and rubbed his knuckles along her cheek. 'I am sorry, my dear,' he said, his voice thick with emotion, 'I know this must be hard for you to understand. I've waited too long and wasted too much time already. I must confront this blackguard with the truth.'

A compassionate smile softened her lips. 'I understand how you must feel. To think,' she murmured feeling utterly desolate, 'Emily loved him. Or thought she did. She gave herself to him. Willingly.'

A resentful iciness cloaked Simon's dark features. 'He played on her emotions, you can be sure,' he imparted coldly.

'Seduction is not a crime, Simon,' Celeste reminded him softly, her thoughts suddenly turning to her own marriage. Had Simon played on her emotions? Without a doubt, her husband was an expert at seduction. Her brow creased with pain. When he learned of her need to kindle a relationship rather than give in to his demands to bear him a son, he'd been ruthlessly unkind. Did he harbor no real affection for her, then? Was he merely using her as a means to an end?

314

He turned the full force of his ominous gaze upon her. 'Rape is,' he countered fiercely.

Confronted with the reality of Lady Caroline's predicament, Celeste mentally chastised herself for wallowing in self-pity. Whatever the state of her marriage, she was not a helpless victim subjected to her husband's violent whims.

'Yes,' she said, fighting the revulsion that welled up inside. 'It is. But it will be terribly difficult to prove. How will you manage it?'

'Leave it to me. I will see that they pay. Every last one of them. Particularly Wilkinson. Emily could not have been his only victim, of that I've little doubt. She fared only slightly better than the rest.'

'Oh, Simon,' Celeste moaned deeply distressed, 'it makes me shudder to think of Jane Greenly viciously murdered by one of these horrid men, Emily seduced by a conniving scoundrel and, now, Lady Caroline brutally —'

He crushed her to him. Covering her mouth with his own, he kissed her deeply, his passion banishing all worry from her mind.

Expelling a huge yawn, Celeste pulled the soft cotton nightgown over her head and tied the pink satin bow at the neck. She was glad, she admitted as she wrestled with her unruly hair hoping to gain some semblance of order, to be back in London. After the arduous journey from Surrey and Lady Caroline's disturbing news, Celeste was eager to lose herself in some much-needed peaceful slumber. Satisfied that nothing short of a pair of scissors could bring her mane to heel, she gave up the fight and set the brush down on the dressing-table.

'You look ready for bed,' a deep husky voice remarked from behind.

Celeste looked up from where she sat to find her husband lounging in the doorway. His muscular shoulder was propped against the door jamb. Her stomach flip-flopped. His dark smouldering gaze held a warm, sensual gleam. She quivered.

He shoved away from the door jamb and strolled toward her. 'Aren't you going to invite me in?,' he drawled in a silky tone.

Her back straightened. 'I was about to go to bed.'

His palm cupped her cheek in a soft caress. He leaned down and kissed her lips. 'Don't let me stop you,' he murmured against her mouth. She colored fiercely. He smiled. 'You are more beautiful every time I look at you,' he whispered in a velvet caress.

Riveted to her seat, she stared into his mesmerizing silvery depths of passion. Slowly he leaned down, then his fingers caught the ribbon of her gown.

'I want to commit every inch of your soft, beautiful body to memory,' he murmured tenderly as his fingers tugged at the bow. 'So I will never forget this moment.' He covered her lips in a lingering gentle kiss.

Her hand stilled his movements. 'Simon,' she managed to say, breathlessly, 'it is late.' Quickly getting to her feet, she slipped past him. 'I am frightfully tired. You – you must be exhausted.'

A low chuckle rumbled in his bare chest. He walked towards her, a faint look of amusement on his handsome face. She backed away from the approaching male heat.

He paused and leaned one arm against the bedpost. His dark, sensual, hooded gaze watching her as she nervously ran her fingers through her hair.

'Come here,' he urged with a smile that fairly singed her.

She shook her head. Chuckling softly, he closed the distance between them. Her pulse did not fail to observe that his brocade robe was parted to reveal a tantalizing portion of his broad chest and thick black hair. Her heart skipped a beat. She cursed herself for trembling. 'Y-you're breaking your word.'

'No,' he said, his voice achingly soft, and pulled her into his arms. 'I am not.' His mouth covered hers in a ravishing kiss. She felt his intense hunger, the desire to possess her completely, and she braced her arms against his chest. He tightened his hold on her pressing her even closer against the hard length of him. His mouth moved to kiss her cheek, her face and throat.

'You taste so damned good, like honeyed nectar,' he whispered against her skin, 'and you smell delicious. I could devour you whole.'

She closed her eyes. A thousand titillating sensations rushed through her. She was weakening by the moment. She tried to lean away from him, but he crushed her small frame against him. 'You are trying to seduce me,' she moaned against his lips.

Smiling down at her, he arched a sooty brow. 'Is that what I am doing?,' he murmured softly as his mouth descended to kiss hers again.

She turned her face. His burning lips kissed her neck. This was not going according to plan. She was perilously close to giving into him. His teeth nibbled at her earlobe sending shivers down her back.

She gulped. 'Simon . . . you promised.'

He lifted his head. The firelight flickered on the ceiling, casting shadows across the room, making it difficult for her to see the expression in his eyes. His mouth lingered over hers. 'So I did,' he concurred thickly and pressed a kiss to the side of her mouth.

'A man's honor is his word,' she croaked.

He chuckled softly. 'I never said anything about kissing you.' His breath was warm against her neck. He trailed his tongue along her collar bone and behind her ear. 'Or touching you,' he murmured, cupping her full breast in her palm. He teased the rosy tip into a hard pebble of desire.

His hands seemed to have a mind of their own. Touching her, teasing her, urging her body to respond. She felt the warmth of his breath on her neck and tingled down to her toes.

She turned her head to find his lips. 'No . . . you . . . did . . . not,' she managed between searing kisses. 'But I know,' she panted against his mouth, 'where this will lead –'

He covered her moist, softly-parted mouth with his own. 'It will lead where you want it to lead,' he said, his voice ragged with desire.

He kissed her temple. His breath tickled her cheek. Gulping, she whimpered, 'I don't think this is such a good idea.'

'No? I think it is,' he growled, his mouth capturing hers once more.

She could feel her treacherous body slipping into sensual abyss. Another searing kiss and she knew she would be unable to resist his ardent promise of passion. She suppressed the urge to wrap her arms around him and pull his hard, sinewed body closer.

Gracious, she was tingling all over as it was. Oh dear, she thought with a soft moan, she was utterly helpless to resist him.

'You are wonderfully soft and yet hard,' he murmured, burying his face against her breasts. He kissed her bare skin above the dangling satin ribbon and slowly slid her nightgown off her shoulders. It slid to the floor, forming a white cloud at her feet. His scorching gaze raked over her naked body. He cupped her soft mounds of creamy flesh in his hands and traced the rosy peaks with his thumbs. He took one pink jewel into his mouth.

Succumbing to the fire of his touch, she arched her back, filling his mouth with full ripe breast.

'Oh, Simon,' she whispered on a cry of pleasure.

As his hand caressed the flat of her stomach sending tiny little shivers all through her, she writhed against him. When his hand moved lower, she opened her eyes to look at him.

'I've a feeling we are . . . oh,' she breathed as his finger found her soft sensitive moist core, 'playing with . . . fire. We –' She bit her lip to fight against the tumult of pleasure his rhythmic strokes evoked. 'Should . . . not,' she uttered breathlessly. His finger eased deeper into her slick wet passage. His treacherous thumb teased the soft, sensitive, feminine nub of flesh.

'Ah, but we should, my beauty . . . and we shall,' he vowed with fierce determination as his mouth covered hers. Moaning into his mouth, she gave herself up to his savage kiss.

He fell to his knees before her.

'What are you doing?' she whimpered, feeling hot, breathless and weak.

He kissed her stomach, her abdomen, her hips. 'Kissing you,' he told her huskily.

'Yes . . . well . . .' He kissed her searing flesh and ran his tongue over her sensitive skin. Her stomach muscles contracted. 'I don't think . . . that is to say . . . I should very much like it if you . . .' Her lashes fluttered shut. As his tongue trailed lower to sample her sweet nectar, a moan of pleasure emanated from her throat. 'Oh . . . *Simon*,' she cried, clutching at his shoulders. She rocked her hips, desperate to reach the peak of ecstasy she knew lay just on the other side of this sweet heaven.

Swept away by her burning desire, she was vaguely aware when two strong arms went around her and dragged her beneath him on the floor. She opened her mouth to speak, but he deprived her of the power of speech. His mouth came down on hers in a hard, passionate kiss that stole her breath and her reason.

She put her hands against his chest. 'Simon . . .,' she panted.

He leaned over and took her hand in his. He kissed her palm and then her wrist. His grey eyes shone with unquenchable desire. He smiled down at her and slid her reluctant hands around his neck. 'Kiss me, Celeste. I need to feel your body close to mine.'

She ached for his possession. At his passionate declaration her body shivered. He leaned forward to sample her enticing mouth.

'*Simon, oh, Simon,*' she moaned softly against his slanting hard mouth.

'I know, little one,' he murmured thickly, burying his face in her neck. 'I am on fire as well. Do you want me to stop touching you?,' he asked, kissing her temple, her cheek, the side of her mouth.

Uttering a moan of bittersweet surrender, she felt desire swell within her at the touch of his lips. She melted in his arms like quicksilver, kissing him until she felt dizzy and breathless with anticipation.

When she made no intelligible reply, Simon rolled on to his side and drew her against him.

'I want you. I need you,' he admitted on a groan. 'Tonight, I need to know you need me.'

Her eyes fluttered open and she gazed into his steely languid orbs.

'Make love to me, *please.*'

'Oh, Simon,' she whispered as her eyes glistened with unshed tears of joy.

He lifted her thigh over his hip, angling her body to receive him. 'You have only to the say the word and I'll stop,' he told her huskily, his hips moving against hers. 'But please . . .,' he gasped, straining against the tumultuous storm of passion raging inside him, 'don't say no.'

She caressed his passion-flushed cheek with her fingertips. 'How could I? Oh, Simon, my wonderful

Simon, don't ever stop loving me.' As the two became one, her lips parted in a soft whimper of exultation.

He cast a tumultuous smile down at her. 'No regrets?,' he asked softly, his voice ragged with passion. 'Please, Celeste. Say you want me as much as I need you,' he muttered thickly.

She place her hand on his cheek. 'I could never regret anything we do together. I want to be with you, Simon. I need you. Desperately. More than you know.' She pulled his head down to hers. '*Love me*,' she whispered against his mouth. 'Oh, *please*, love me.' She covered his mouth with hers, kissing him with all the emotion pent up inside her. Strong and sure, his arms tightened around her. He drove into her, loving her with deep, hard strokes that took them both to nirvana.

His lovemaking was passionate beyond her expectation. She cried out his name on a blissful sigh of release. As he strained against her, a heart-wrenching groan of surrender was torn from his throat and his seed poured into her. Then, slowly, ever so slowly, the world came back into focus.

Throwing himself on to his back, he tried to catch his breath. He was oddly shaken by the experience of making love to his wife. He told himself it was the idea of his seed taking root in her womb that pleased him excessively. Despite her childish protestations, he hoped they'd made a baby together. He wanted that bond. He longed to see her body swell with the fruit of his loins. She need not fear, he would see to it that she received the finest care. No harm would come to her.

So entirely engrossed in his own thoughts was he that he failed to notice he'd made love to his wife on the cold hard floor.

'Good Lord, how did we end up here?,' he mumbled and pressed a kiss to her temple, before he scooped her up into his arms and carried her to the soft inviting feather bed. Laying her down, he pulled the covers around her. He smiled a bit sheepishly at her. He caressed her face with his palm.

'I am sorry,' he said, his dark grey orbs brimming with tenderness, 'that must have been uncomfortable for you.'

A mantle of red spread over her cheeks. 'I didn't notice,' came her shy admission.

He got into bed beside her and leaned over to kiss her tenderly on the mouth, slowly savoring her sweetness. 'I am glad,' he said, brushing her tangled hair back from her face. 'Are you tired?'

She nodded her head and turned her face away. 'Yes,' she said on a hard swallow. Wriggling away from him, she curled into a ball on the far side of the bed. 'Good night, Simon.'

His brow furrowed. 'Celeste?' He placed his hand on her slender bare shoulder. 'What is it? What is wrong?'

She shook her head, but he guessed from the tremor of her slight body that she was crying.

He leaned over her. 'Never say I hurt you?'

A cry of abject misery escaped her throat; she bawled in earnest. He pulled her on to her back.

Gazing down at her, he looked darkly handsome and deeply worried. 'Did I?,' he insisted, his brow deeply furrowed with concern.

'It is not that,' she snapped, avoiding his dark penetrating stare.

'Then what?' he coaxed, brushing the tears from her cheeks. 'Tell me,' he urged thickly. 'Why are you crying?'

'I think . . . I'm falling in love with you,' she replied on a heartwrenching sob.

He became deadly still. In love? With him? He almost said 'don't' but bit back the words. This he had not anticipated. He raked his hand through his hair. No one had ever loved him. Ever. Struck dumb, he rubbed her back while she wept.

'This startling revelation makes you cry?,' he asked with a levity he did not feel.

She nodded her head and gushed fresh tears.

'Why?' he asked, his own voice on the verge of cracking.

'B-because,' she sobbed, 'you're a heartless rake who can never harbor any real emotions for any one person, least of all me.'

Choosing to ignore her assassination of his character, he cupped her cheek with his hand and lifted her tearstained face to his. 'Why least of all you?,' he asked in a gentle soothing tone.

She blinked up at him and sniffled. 'Well . . . I am me. And you are – you are . . . you.'

He bit back the urge to laugh. 'Yes. We are. But what does that have to do with anything?'

'You could never come to love me.'

324

'And why is that?,' he asked, gently brushing her hair back from her blotchy face.

'I am so horribly uncouth, awkward and ugly,' she spat out in disgust.

His brow darkened. 'You are not ugly, awkward, or uncouth,' he countered sharply. He framed her face between his hands. 'My God,' he breathed, his gaze searching her unhappy face, 'you are the most precious, rare creature I have ever beheld. Beauty like yours is not merely superficial, it is inside you,' he told her, his voice deeply compelling, 'in your heart. And your beautiful, wonderful soul. That is what I cherish about you the most. Your uniqueness.' Tears cascaded down her cheeks. He kissed them away. 'I've never met a woman like you,' he murmured softly, 'and I've never felt more fortunate in my life to claim you as my own.'

'Oh, Simon,' she cried, throwing herself against his chest, 'I do love you. More than I ever wanted to. I cannot help myself.'

He chuckled softy and hugged her to him. 'Go to sleep, Celeste,' he commanded, his voice oddly low and uneven. He found himself having to stifle the peculiar urge to clear his throat.

She pressed a small kiss to his chest and laid her cheek against his beating heart. 'Thank you.'

'What for?', he asked, rubbing the small of her back with his palm.

'For saying all those wonderful things. I know you do not love me, but I am thankful for your kindness towards me.' Feeling all warm and cosy inside, she slept.

325

Simon remained awake, contemplating the soft bundle laying in his arms. He'd never even come close to being snared by cupid's arrow. Oh, he'd admire a woman's beauty often enough and applauded her talents between the sheets, but fall in love with a woman? Never. His emotions had never been kindled. Until . . .

He glanced down at the naked woman sleeping in his arms. He smiled at the top of her untamed, curly head burrowed against his chest. She looked like a little elf. This small slip of a girl was *his* wife. She was the most precious thing in his life, too, he reluctantly admitted. No one had ever issued a pledge of love to him and meant it. He was not inclined to believe this one either. It was simply the way she responded to passion. She mistakenly connected mindless, overwhelming desire with love. He knew better.

Yet, he acknowledged as she stirred, shifting her small weight on to a more comfortable spot on his chest, that her artless declaration had made his heart swell with emotion he thought long dead. He drew a deep breath.

Lord, he wasn't actually falling for the oldest ploy known to man – or, it seemed, woman – was he? No. Of course not. Let her think she was in love with him if it made her happy. The concept was not entirely unappealing to him either, he realized with a jolt. In fact, he liked the idea very well indeed.

CHAPTER 16

The following morning Celeste descended the stairs to find her husband speaking to a rather dingy-looking man standing in the marbled foyer. Simon glanced up and caught sight of her. His lazy, hooded gaze moved over her pink silk gown with blatant sexual appraisal that told her he found her appearance more than merely pleasing. A surge of happiness overtook her.

His sultry grey gaze locked with hers. Her heart fluttered. His lips curled into a slow sensual smile. And she knew he was recalling their passionate night of lovemaking. Colour washed over her cheeks. She gave him a small, shy smile. His grin broadened.

'Ah, my dear, you are awake. Come,' he said, extending his hand to her, 'I want you to meet our Runner, Mr Crawford. He's been helping us in our search for the villainous group. I sent him word last night that we had returned. He has some developments to relate.'

Our Runner? Celeste's heart soared. Her husband accepted her as his equal. She was deeply touched that he was willing to share his most private concerns with her. He must have some feelings for her. At the very least, he felt gratitude. Wasn't gratitude as good a place as any to start?

The Runner looked slightly taken aback.

Smiling at the scruffy man's reaction, Simon drew his wife to his side. Gazing down at her, warm admiration shining in his eyes, he told Mr Crawford,

'My wife has been an immeasurable help to me. It was she who discovered Hobson's involvement. I would never have considered questioning Lady Caroline were it not for my clever resourceful bride.' He raised her hands to his lips and kissed her hand. Celeste beamed up at him, her heart in her eyes.

Expelling an impatient breath, Mr Crawford cleared his throat. 'Milord, should we not get down business?'

'Hmm?' Simon murmured, lost in his wife's eyes. 'Yes, by all means.' His arm went around Celeste's waist. Drawing her against his side, he clasped her hand in his own and escorted her to the library.

The Runner rolled his eyes heavenward and trailed behind the two lovebirds with their heads bent together.

'I done some pokin' 'bout,' Mr Crawford remarked when all three were comfortably seated in the library. 'The Greenly chit was raped 'fore she died. What a mess he made o' her,' he muttered in disgust. 'She must 'ave fought 'im pretty 'ard. Caw, what a sight, poor lass. The way we figure it, he must 'ave strangled her while he was –' he darted a glance at Lady Barclay and cleared his throat '– durin' the attack. He tossed her body in the river when he was through usin' her.'

Simon's glance slid across the room to his wife. Sitting by the sun-streaked window, she looked several shades paler than usual, but she offered him a wan smile. He dragged his gaze from her ghostly complexion and addressed the Runner.

'Who did it?'

''T'weren't Hobson, he's got an alibi. Far as I can tell, Hobson ain't that deeply involved anyway. Must 'ave been Everly who done it, like y'suspected, milord.'

'He, I take it, is nowhere to be found?'

Crawford flashed a toothless grin. 'Right y'are, milord. Last we 'eard, he'd left for India.'

Simon uttered a disgusted sound. 'How convenient. What else have you to report?'

'Paine is dead.'

Simon sat forward. 'What?' His face darkened. 'When?'

Mr Crawford scratched his balding head. 'Near as we can tell, t'was roughly a fortnight ago. Y'must 'ave been the last one t'see 'im alive.'

'Not quite the last. George Wilkinson arrived as I was leaving.'

The Runner cocked a bushy brow. 'Aye, is that a fact? Well then, I guess lil' Georgie is guilty o' murder.'

'How did Paine die?'

' 'Anged 'imself.'

Simon shook his head. 'I doubt Paine's death was a suicide. He was terrified to name the blackguard who founded the club. If my suspicious are correct, Wilkinson is behind Paine's death and the nefarious club.'

'I agree but –,' the Runner twisted his lips '– t'is awfully 'ard to prove, milord.'

'Mmm, quite,' Simon muttered pensively. 'I assume all this came to light whilst I was in the country?'

'Aye, that it did. One o'them nobs came by t'see what Paine had t'sell. Found 'im swingin' from a rope. Been dead for days. Right stiff 'e was. 'E didna smell too pretty, I can tell you,' the Runner said with a laugh. 'His tongue was 'angin' down to his waist, eyes bulgin' from 'his 'ead. An' a right lovely shade o' –'

'E-excuse me,' Celeste interjected and fled the room, her hand clenched to her mouth.

Simon got to his feet, issuing a gruff apology, then fled the room in search of his pallid wife.

A few minutes later, Simon found her. She was in the kitchen, leaning over the scullery bucket. Mary, the cook, was pressing a cool cloth to his wife's neck.

He gave Mary a silent nod to leave them. 'I'll look after her now.'

He crouched down on his hunches beside his wife. Turning her pale face to his, he asked, 'Not feeling quite the thing, are you?'

She shook her head and wiped her dewy brow with the back of her hand. 'It's just . . . I – I knew Jane.' Her lashes fluttered shut. 'The way she died . . . it is

330

too gruesome.' She emitted an abhorrent groan. 'And to hear about that dead man –'

'Forgive me, I should not have allowed you to be present for the discussion.' His voice was laden with self-recriminations. Helping her to stand, he drew her against him and held her close. 'I'm sorry,' he murmured, kissing the top of her curly head. 'Crawford has been in the business for years. He's not accustomed to frail females,' he teased her.

'I am not frail,' she countered, slamming a playful fist against his chest. 'Really, I am not. At least, not ordinarily.'

'I think it is safe to say, that descriptions of dead bodies and rape victims are something entirely new to you and not at all pleasant.'

She leaned her head back to look at him. 'But I want to be a part of it, Simon. I want to help you find these vile men.'

He smiled and framed her ashen face with his hands. 'In future, madam, you may serve me best by not swooning.'

She pulled a face. 'I was sick, my lord. I do not faint.'

He grinned. 'I am relieved beyond measure to hear it,' he said lightly. 'I despise women who are prone to vapors and apoplexy.' His smile faded. 'Perhaps it would be best,' he said, smoothing her hair back from her forehead, 'if you retired above stairs until the interview is over. I am afraid these recent turn of events are a bit grisly.'

'No.' She shook her head. 'I am all right now. I promise not to turn miss-ish again.'

He gazed at her with a sceptical eye. 'You are sure you want to continue?'

'I must,' she said with grave sincerity, 'if I am to be of any help to you.'

He shook his head and sighed. 'You are a wonder.' His mouth covered hers, pressing a quick, hard, covetous kiss to her lips. Taking her hand in his, he lead her back to the library.

Mr Crawford shifted from foot to foot. 'Beggin' yer pardon, milady,' he said sheepishly, 'I ain't used t'women 'bout the place.'

Celeste offered him a kind smile. 'Think nothing of it. I assure you, I am not by nature squeamish. Pray, continue,' she advised, resuming her perch on the chair by the window, 'I promise not to swoon.'

He turned his attention to Simon. 'Like I were sayin', 'ard to prove Wilkinson's involvement in all o'this.'

'I don't need any more proof,' Simon muttered with contempt. 'I am satisfied he fathered Annabelle and is guilty of destroying the lives of God only knows how many other innocent young women.'

'Aye. But what are y'plannin' to do 'bout it?'

'Catch the bastard and make him pay.'

'But 'ow?'

To Simon's complete astonishment, his diminutive wife sat forward and cleared her throat.

'As to that, I have given the situation a considerable amount of thought. I have a suggestion to make,' she announced boldly. 'I wonder, Mr Crawford, if

332

you would be good enough to give your honest appraisal of my scheme?'

The Runner looked slightly less stunned than his lordship. 'I'll do me best, milady.'

'I recommend we set a trap for this horrid man, Wilkinson.'

Simon's eyes narrowed suspiciously. 'What kind of trap?'

'An amorous engagement, similar to the previous circumstances where he lured his victims. Only on this occasion, Mr Crawford, with your aid, of course my lord, will catch the villainous cad.'

'In the act, so to speak,' Simon supplied, his face set in stone.

'Precisely,' she said, smiling with pride.

Simon crossed his arms over his chest. 'And who, pray, will play the part of his willing victim?' he asked, his tone brusque.

She blinked at him. 'Why, me, of course. After all, we are fairly certain he founded the vile club that preys exclusively on defenceless young innocents. Poor Jane Greenly attended Almack's every Wednesday. Given that Lady Caroline met Shelton at Almack's and she is certain that is where Emily renewed her relationship with the very ungallant knight, we know, or can safely assume, Almack's is where these dastardly men approach their victims. Who better to play the part of a young, defenceless innocent than myself?'

Uttering a half-bitten oath, Simon vaulted to his feet. 'The *devil* you will! Have you taken complete leave of your senses?'

'Have you a better idea?' she challenged him.

His dark stormy gaze pinioned her to her seat. 'These men are killers,' he said, his tone grave. 'I don't intend to risk losing you through luring that villain into a trap, madam,' he ground out.

'She's may 'ave somethin' there, milord,' Crawford remarked, scrubbing his chin with his fingers. 'It's an idea.'

'My wife,' Simon gritted fiercely, 'will not, I repeat not, be bait for a man who seduces, rapes and ruins women on a whim. For God's sake, he founded the damned club where murderers and rapists figure largely as ranking members.'

The Runner nodded his head. 'Y'right, o'course. Still, I must admit, t'is one way to catch the blackguard.'

'Fine,' Simon fired back, wearing a path in the plush Aubusson carpet. 'We'll use somebody else.'

Mr Crawford etched a pensive frown. 'I doubt we'll find another woman brave enough –'

Simon gave him a quelling glance. 'Or foolish enough,' he intoned with meaning. 'You, madam,' he growled at Celeste, 'will do as you are told, or be brought to heel.'

Celeste pulled a face.

He glared at her with dark angry eyes.

Folding her arms over her chest, she looked away and arched her chin like a petulant child.

Swallowing audibly, Mr Crawford tugged at his collar and mumbled, 'I 'spect y'right, milord. 'Tis too dangerous.'

'No,' Celeste countered with energy, 'it is not. Simon,' she pleaded, getting to her feet, 'please try to be reasonable.'

Savage fury lit his silvery gaze. His mood was grim. He was closer than he ever dreamt he'd be to spanking his wife. He could not believe she'd proposed such a perilous scheme. It was preposterous.

'You know it is the only way to lure him. He's on to you. For heaven's sake,' she cried, throwing her arms in the air, 'you sent a Runner to investigate his secret club. He doesn't know me. You'll be a mere stone's throw away the entire time. What can he possible do?'

'No,' he snapped at her. 'It is out of the question. It is too dangerous.'

She uttered a derisive grunt of dissent. 'It is not,' she tossed back at him.

Stormy slate grey eyes threatened to impale her. 'I forbid you to do this.'

She gawked at him. 'Forbid me?,' she echoed with a look of incredulity on her face.

'Yes,' he snarled, 'forbid you.'

She expelled an annoyed sigh. 'You are just being stubborn. You know it is the only way to garner a confession from him.

'I don't need a confession,' he spat venomously.

'What is it you are after? If not the truth, then what?'

Wordlessly, he stared down at her, tall, darkly handsome and very angry.

'Do you not want justice? After all this time, why are you refusing to do the one thing that will result in his capture?'

His hand slid around her neck. He pulled her to him. Dark eyes, glittering with raw emotion, searched her face. 'I cannot bear the thought of losing you,' he admitted, his voice gruff with emotion.

Her heart swelled in her chest. Smiling up at him, she caressed his cheek with her palm. 'In that case, you never will.'

'Then you agree to abandon this foolhardy plan?' he asked, relief evident on his features.

'If you truly believe it is too dangerous,' she said on a sigh, 'I've little choice in the matter.'

His eyes narrowed on her face. 'Why are you willing to admit defeat so quickly?'

She traced the hard line of his jaw with her forefinger. 'I know when I am bested, my lord,' she said softly.

'Just like that?' he asked, eyeing her sceptically. 'You are relinquishing the argument? No attempts at persuasion? No wheedling for ground?'

She shook her head and locked her arms around his neck. 'When faced with an insurmountable foe, the only solution is to bow out gracefully, do you not agree?'

He arched a sooty brow. 'An insurmountable foe?' A sensual gleam lit his silvery eyes. His hands slipped around her waist, drawing her snugly against him. 'Is that what I am?' he asked her huskily.

Her heart tripped over itself. 'I don't want you to be,' she said softly. 'Please, Simon, let's not argue.'

His mouth twitched. 'I must confess,' he said with

a roguish grin, 'there are other things I'd much rather do with you.'

Two blotches of red stained her cheeks. 'I've the perfect solution to the problem,' she said, smoothing her palms over his well-made chest. 'If you are all that concerned for my welfare, I'll stay with Joy until this horrible mess is cleared up and Wilkinson is made to pay for his heinous crimes.'

Simon heaved an enormous sigh. 'If, as you say, he knows I am on to him, it might take some time to track him down. I would feel better knowing you were in safekeeping. Besides,' he said with a crooked grin, 'if I know the two of you, you'll need time to catch up on the latest *on-dits*.'

She blinked up at him. 'I do not know about that, my lord, you were the person we liked to speak of the most.'

He threw back his raven head and laughed. 'You flatter me, madam.' Kissing his adorable wife on the nose, he remarked in a dry tone, 'Pray do not plan any more weddings behind my back.'

She scowled up at him. '*I* never did.'

He leaned back and regarded her with a critical eye. 'I am still not sure you are being entirely honest.'

'My word is every bit as good as yours, my lord.'

His brow furrowed. 'What the devil is that supposed to mean?'

'Simply that I am as honorable a woman as you are a man.'

He looked at her askance. 'You are in a strange mood.'

'Am I?,' she asked airily.

'Indeed, you are. But we've a criminal to apprehend, have we not, Mr Crawford?' he asked, glancing over his shoulder at the red-faced man lurking in the corner.

The Runner cleared his throat. 'Aye, milord,' he replied with a lopsided grin, 'I was wonderin' when y'might get down t'business.'

'Immediately. I intend to pay George Wilkinson a visit he'll not soon forget. Will you accompany me?'

'Aye, that I will. T'will be a pleasure to make that bas – er . . .,' abashed, he glanced at Celeste, '. . . bloke's acquaintance.'

Celeste slipped away from her husband. 'I'll leave you two men to your planning.'

The following morning Celeste disembarked from the Barclay carriage to find her sister waiting for her at the door to Morely House with open arms.

'It is good to see you,' she said, giving Celeste a tight squeeze. 'I was dreadfully worried. You cannot imagine the horrors I have suffered, not knowing how you have fared this last month. You must tell me how you are finding marriage,' she said, linking her arm through her sister's. 'He has not mistreated you, has he?'

Celeste opened her mouth to reply, but her sister blustered excitedly,

'No. Of course, he has not. You look ravishing, dearest. Marriage clearly agrees with you. I must confess,' she intoned gravely as the two walked towards the blue salon, 'Simon looked positively vexed on his wedding day, poor man. I could have strangled Tony for divulging my little secret. Oh, but tell me, dearest,' she said, taking her sister's hands in her own, 'you are not terribly upset with me for playing cupid, are you?'

Celeste expelled a long breath. Retrieving her hands from her sister's grasp, she removed her blue beret with white plumes. That discovery seemed like a lifetime ago. So much had transpired since then. She'd been ready to commit murder when she'd realized what havoc her foolish, romantically inclined sister had wreaked. Since then, Celeste had become more forgiving. She was not sorry she'd been forced to marry the Dragon. Her only wish was that he cared for her, if only just a little. Smiling slightly at her sister's hopeful expression, she shook her head.

'No,' she said as her fingers undid the tassels and cords of her pale blue redingote. 'I am in love with him. Though I doubt he shares my feelings,' she said a little wistfully.

Joy sank down on the couch and drew her sister down beside her. 'You must give him time. Men need to adjust to married life. I dare say Tony was not in love with me at first. It took a full six months before he expressed any emotion at all. And then, he gushed like a schoolboy.'

Celeste gave Joy a rueful look. 'Joy, he asked for your hand the morning after you met.'

'That does not signify,' she said with a dismissive wave of her hand. 'He only did so because he thought I came from good stock and would bear him sons. He used those exact words the day he offered for me.'

Celeste was taken aback. 'You cannot be serious? Why did you never tell me?'

Joy shrugged. 'He was by far the most eligible bachelor of the Season. I was madly in love with him. And, I knew, with time, I could bring him around to my way of thinking.'

'Well,' Celeste replied sarcastically, 'he was right on that score – you have given him two healthy sons in as many years. He can find no reason to be unhappy with you.' Unlike Simon, she added silently.

'Mmm. But more importantly,' Joy said, a dreamy smile gracing her features, 'he has given me his heart and a promise of eternal devotion.'

Getting to her feet, Celeste wandered over to the window. 'I sincerely doubt I shall ever hear those words from Simon.' She gazed out the window at the elegant barouches rolling down the cobblestone street.

'You will,' came Joy's assurance from behind. 'I am certain of it. Else,' she teased, 'I should never have flung my arrow.'

Celeste cast a doleful smile over her shoulder. 'How can you be so sure?'

Joy blinked in surprise. 'How can you doubt it?'

Celeste turned away. Easily, she thought, very easily indeed. Only last night, she'd lain in his arms, after he'd made passionate love to her for the second time, and told him how deep her devotion went. He had remained silent. She was deeply hurt.

Her heart was heavy in her chest. She was a lovesick fool. Obviously, his feelings were not involved. Nor would they ever be. She'd long since given up on any possibility of refusing him her bed. For all she knew, she was already with child.

Like a fool, she'd fallen prey to his expert charm and roving hands. She was, it seemed, helplessly in love with her husband. While he found nothing to recommend his wife apart from fleeting moments of pleasure between the sheets. As far as he was concerned, she was simply a body with which to pleasure himself, an easily-replaced vehicle for an heir.

But there was a way to win her husband's favor. She need only give him what he wanted most. She bit her lower lip. How difficult could it be? After all, it wasn't as if she'd be doing something that was never done before – countless of women did it everyday. Why should she be afraid? She would not be alone. She'd make certain of that, in case anything unto-ward should occur.

She etched a bright smile and turned to face her sister. 'Let's go to Almack's tonight.'

Joy looked dazed and confused. 'But you detest Almack's,' she burst out.

'Detest is far too strong a word,' Celeste said mildly. 'Now that I am married, my attitude has changed.'

'Quite frankly, I do not know if I could convince Tony to escort us. He complained bitterly the last time I dragged him.'

Celeste flashed a conspiratorial smirk. 'Come now, Joy, I am certain there is precious little you could not persuade dear Tony to do.'

Joy gave her sister a sly grin. 'I collect you are right. I shall wear my lavender silk,' she said, springing to her feet. 'Now, where did I put that voucher?' she asked, flying from the room in search of the coveted social prize.

CHAPTER 17

Celeste's prophecy was entirely correct – in the end, Tony begrudgingly agreed to escort the ladies to Almack's.

'I still think you should have worn a more suitable gown, Celeste,' Joy remarked, eyeing her sister's drab white dress with disapproval. 'You are Lady Barclay now. Although, I dare say,' she lamented with sarcasm, 'anyone looking at you would not think it. Why did you not give those plain, old dresses to Fanny?'

'I hadn't thought of it,' came Celeste's noncommittal reply. A slow smile crept across her face. Everything was working out splendidly. If Joy thought Celeste looked like a novice, then Wilkinson was bound to agree. With a little luck, *he* would approach *her*, saving her a great deal of angst, for she had never actually seen him. All she knew was that he was blond and brown-eyed. She could not very well approach every tall, fair-haired gentleman on the premises in the hope of stumbling on to the culprit.

The carriage wheels ground to a halt before the large Assembly Hall on King Street. Tony shifted uncomfortably on the seat and tugged at his collar. 'I do hope Countess Lieven refrains from monopolizing all of our time this evening,' he grumbled to his wife. 'I was bored stiff the last time you forced me to suffer through one of this blasted evenings.'

'Yes, dear,' Joy replied, every inch the dutiful wife.

He glanced out the carriage window and groaned. 'Good Lord! What an abominable crush. I am still not entirely certain why I am here. The condition of the dance floor is appalling.' He gave Celeste a disgruntled look. 'Why the deuce didn't your husband take you, if you wanted to go so damned much?'

'Mind your language, dearest,' Joy admonished gently.

Tony grunted and turned his attention back to the long black row of carriages lined up outside the coveted hall.

Celeste pressed her gloved fingers to her lips to conceal her laughter.

Tony gave her a crooked grin. 'Where the devil is that rakehell husband of yours anyway?'

'He, um, had some pressing business to attend to,' came her somewhat vague reply.

Tony laughed. 'Simon Barclay would not be caught dead at Almack's.'

Joy patted her husband's arm. 'Yes, darling, we know. But you will be a charming escort, to be sure. We were so pleased you offered.'

'I did not offer,' he said sharply. 'I was coerced.'

'Hush now, dearest,' Joy remarked and descended from the carriage to blend in with the thickening crowd gathered by the entrance.

To Celeste's amazement, Tony muttered something unintelligible under his breath and fell silent. Climbing down after his wife, he extended a polite hand to help Celeste. He even offered to secure what promised to be weak tea and bland orgeat for the ladies.

As Celeste entered the huge spare room that passed for a ballroom, a surge of excitement rushed over her. The thrill of the unknown never failed to entice her. Tonight was no exception. How pleased Simon was going to be when she presented him with the villain.

Craning her neck, to survey the sea of pastel dresses and swarming bachelors, she tried to no avail to spy any and all tall, slender blond men with an evil look in their eye. Mr Crawford surely must have received her note by now. She chewed nervously on her lower lip. The difficulty was clearly going to be how to find Wilkinson. The rest of the details Bow Street could take care of.

Persevering in her search, she stood on her tip-toes and peered over the tops of the ladies' heads. To say the room was crowded would be an understatement. Tony was correct. It was a mob scene. This would never do.

'What *are* you doing?,' Joy demanded, her voice curt with reprimand.

Sinking down on her heels, Celeste replied lamely, 'I – I thought I saw someone I knew.'

'It is generally best to wait to acknowledge their address,' Joy muttered in a fierce undertone.

'You are quite right,' Celeste mumbled.

She caught her lower lip between her teeth. Oh, dear. This was more difficult than she had originally envisioned. She could ill-afford to appear obvious. Time, however, was of the essence. If tonight's scheme was going to be a success, she had to garner an introduction to Wilkinson and hope he found her worthy of his particular brand of charm.

It was not strictly necessary to dance the quadrille, or even elicit a waltz from the miscreant. She could just as easily win an introduction standing on the sidelines once she caught sight of him – if she ever caught sight of him. Oh, crumbs! It could take all night, provided he was actually in attendance *and* he found her worthy of his time.

On the other hand, she thought as she observed poor Tony cannoning his way through the throng of bodies with two cups of tepid tea in each hand, it might serve just as well to be formally introduced.

'I wonder,' she ventured to ask, after sampling the lukewarm libation Tony offered her, 'if you might do me the favour of pointing out a certain gentleman of whom Simon has spoken?'

'If I am able,' Tony allowed.

'Whom is it you wish to meet?' Joy asked, cringing at the tasteless contents of her cup.

'George Wilkinson,' Celeste remarked, looking at Tony from beneath lowered lashes. 'I do believe his property borders my husband's estate in Kent.'

Joy's ears perked up. 'Is Simon planning a visit to Kent?,' she asked, nearly bursting with excitement.

'A trip to the seaside would be divine at this time of year.' Her voice dripped with envy.

Ignoring her sister's comment, Celeste asked Tony pointedly, 'Are you, perchance, familiar with that most excellent family?'

'Yes. I am. I doubt there is anyone who is not familiar with the Earl of Greystone. It is probable,' Tony remarked casting his gaze around the room, 'that he is in attendance tonight. He is one of the regulars, I do believe.'

Celeste could barely contain herself. He was here. In a few hours, she'd have his confession and Simon would be proud and pleased with her cunning intervention.

'I am sure that if Tony sees him he'll be more than happy to point him out,' Joy interjected, patting her sister's hand. 'At present, however, I do collect my husband promised the first waltz to me,' she remarked, sliding her arm through Tony's and nudging him toward the uneven dance floor.

Celeste's face fell. If she knew Joy, it would be some time before the happy couple rejoined the sidelines. Celeste tried to cheer herself. Sulking against the wall might work in her favor.

Twenty minutes later, not a solitary soul had given her a second look. She was obviously not the proper lure for such a man as Wilkinson, or any man for that matter. Her heart sank. If only she were more attractive, Wilkinson would surely pick her out from among the crowd. From all reports, Emily had been a beauty beyond compare.

Celeste's mood soured. Simon would be livid when he discovered she'd involved Bow Street for naught.

She'd have sent poor Mr Crawford on a merry goose chase.

'Good evening, my lady,' a melodious voice murmured at her side.

Her head whipped around. Mutely, she stared in disbelief at the impeccably-dressed, tall blond man gazing at her with slumberous brown eyes.

She gulped. It was him. Gracious, what a stroke of genius!

'G-good evening,' she stammered.

He chuckled softly, apparently amused by her jitters. 'I do believe I have had the pleasure of making your acquaintance, have I not?'

She shook her head. 'No. We've never met.'

'Really?' he asked, cocking a dubious brow. 'I was certain, as I stood watching you, that you were by far the most beautiful creature on earth. I could not help feeling I knew you. But perhaps, it is because we were destined to meet.'

Gawking at him, she swallowed audibly. 'Destined to meet?,' she echoed stupidly.

An unfathomable emotion registered on his face. 'Mmm,' he said, his lips twitching. 'Fate has brought us together, would you not agree?'

She blinked up at him. 'Fate?' Good Lord, what a performance!

'You appear to be waiting for someone,' he remarked, studying her intently from beneath hooded eyelids.

She shrugged. 'No one in particular. This is my first time at Almack's. I must confess, I am a little nervous,' she prevaricated, dropping her gaze to the floor. 'I really should not speak to a gentleman without the benefit of a formal introduction.'

He gazed at her quizzically for a moment before he etched a bow. 'George Wilkinson, Earl of Greystone,' he said with a practised charm that grated on Celeste like chalk on a chalk board. She found herself wondering, if under different circumstances, she might have been his naive victim. The thought chilled her blood.

She drew in her breath and pressed her gloved fingers to her lips. 'Oh, my,' she crooned with admiration, 'not *the* Earl of Greystone?'

He smiled broadly. 'Pray, do not keep me in suspense. I am persuaded I have never gazed on such perfection. Whom do I have the pleasuring of addressing?'

Celeste fought the urge to be ill on the spot. The man fairly dripped honey. She forced herself to giggle like a nervous schoolgirl. At least, she hoped she sounded like a schoolgirl and not a complete imbecile. 'Well, perhaps . . . just this once, given your fine upstanding reputation . . . I don't suppose it would be wrong. My name is Camilla. My grandfather is –'

'Very charming, I am sure. But it is *you* who interests me at the moment,' he countered smoothly. He bowed and kissed her hand. 'May I say what a very great pleasure it is for me to make your acquaintance, Camilla?'

This was really too much! Celeste quelled the desire to roll her eyes. No wonder he was successful at seducing unsuspecting innocents. Even knowing what a monster he was, she could not deny his warmth and charm were disarming to a young woman.

'I do?,' she queried, essaying a wide-eyed innocent look.

'I am anxious to learn everything I can about you. You,' he said, his gaze drifting over her face with reverent appreciation, 'intrigue me.'

Celeste had to quell the urge to laugh. This was really too much to be borne. 'You flatter me, my lord,' she said demurely and batted her eyelashes.

'You must call me George and I shall call you,' he said, taking her hand in his and gazing deeply into her eyes, 'precious.'

The bounder had a penchant for absurd nicknames.

'You flatter me ... George,' she murmured, slipping her hand from his clutches, but not before he pressed a kiss to the back of her hand. It would be easier than she thought to arrive at an unpalatable end with this malevolent fellow.

'You look overly warm, precious,' he observed. 'A breath of fresh air will make you feel more the thing.'

Better and better, thought Celeste with a coy smile. 'It is a lovely evening. I am sure I would be only too glad to take a turn with you.'

'Capital idea,' he replied and secured her right arm firmly through his.

As they traversed the hot, stuffy room, which was filled to capacity, Celeste cooed like a lovesick dolt at the man beside her. Out of the corner of her eye, she caught sight of Joy tramping through the crush of guests in hot pursuit. Fixing her sister with a dark, menacing look, Celeste gave a stern shake of her head that effectively halted Joy in her tracks. Utterly perplexed, Joy stared blankly at Celeste and mouthed the words, 'What are you doing?'

Scowling, Celeste shooed her sister away.

'Is that woman an acquaintance of yours?,' George's dulcet tones wafted through the air.

Celeste cursed her meddling sister. She would ruin everything if she did not leave off. 'Er, yes, but I would much rather spend time with you,' she managed to say dreamily.

He glanced across the room. 'She looks rather intent on stopping you,' he observed.

'That is because she is jealous.'

He arched a golden brow. 'Is she, indeed?'

Celeste darted a glance at the doorway a few yards away. 'Can you doubt it?,' she asked, desperate to reach the exit before her sister ploughed her way through the crowd and demanded an explanation that might prove a trifle embarrassing.

He looked vaguely amused. 'I should think droves of young bucks would line up for your hand, precious.'

'Oh, no,' she hastened to assure him, 'you are the first.'

'I am so glad . . .,' he murmured. Taking her by the arm, he steered her outside, into the dark cover of night. '*Lady Barclay*.'

Iridescent moonlight cast the rows of black carriages in an ominous light. A small shiver crept up her spine. 'Why do you call me that?,' she asked, not daring to get a glimpse of the menacing figure at her side. A sense of dread enveloped her; the street was virtually abandoned save for the few carriage drivers who were still awake. But they would not dare gainsay a gentleman. She was horribly alone.

'It is your name, is it not?,' he replied quite calmly as he propelled her toward the road. Only the bite of his fingers on her bare flesh betrayed his anger. 'I was sure I recognized you. I watched you on the sidelines and waited for your husband to appear.'

Wincing, she tried to loose the grip on her arm, but it was no use. 'How did you know what I looked like?,' she asked, darting a frantic glance around her.

He sneered at her naïvety. 'Come, come, my dear, I make it my business to know everything about your husband since he saw fit to make it his life's ambition to ruin my life. It is only right that I should return the favour. Besides, there is not a person among the *ton* who does not know Barclay took a bride to avoid a scandal. Did you actually think if you played the part of the untried novice anyone would be fooled?'

Unaccustomed to being somebody of consequence whom anyone would take a second glance at, she had not considered her identity would be well-known. Talons of fear clawed at her heart. Simon was entirely correct. Her plan was anything but fool-proof. The problem was that she'd realized her folly too late.

Wilkinson's carriage was scarcely two feet away. Panic rippled through her; if she got into that carriage with him she was as good as dead. Letting

352

her legs go limp, she nearly collapsed to the ground. But he held her fast. His iron grip threatened to crush her bones.

'I suggest you put your legs to good use,' he remarked in a bored tone, 'or I shall be forced to hurt you rather badly.'

Grimacing from pain, she stood up. 'If you knew,' she asked, barely able to draw a steady breath, 'why did you go along with me?'

'Your husband is a rather tiresome fellow. He's cost me my club, caused me no end of difficulties with Bow Street, sticking his nose where it ain't wanted. I wonder how he'll feel now that the shoe is on the other foot, so to speak.'

Swallowing audibly, she cast a last furtive glance over her shoulder at the deserted dark street. Where was Joy when she needed her most? 'If you let me go,' she said, quaking with fear, 'I promise —'

'You'll forget all about this little incident?,' he chuckled nastily. 'I wonder when you chits will come up with a more compelling incentive.'

Her tongue darted nervously across her lips. 'My husband is a wealthy man. He'll pay you handsomely.'

'Ah, yes, Simon Barclay would pay a pretty penny for such a rare gem as yourself. Not that I'd ever ask for anything as vulgar as money. What a curious, difficult man he is, too. I wonder how he will feel when he discovers his wife has been used by another man. I must confess, I rather preferred his stepsister. But you'll do nicely for the present.'

His dark carriage loomed before her like the grim reaper of death. 'You . . . you cannot possibly hope to

353

get away with this. M-my sister saw you with me. It is only a matter of time before Simon discovers what you've done. You cannot possible think to get away with kidnapping me.'

'Once I am through with you, you'll wish I had decided to kidnap you and asked for a king's ransom.'

The color drained from her face. 'I – I am not worth the trouble, really I am not.'

'Nonsense, precious, it will be my pleasure. I do think it was extremely careless of your devoted spouse to use you to lure me in.' He tapped his chin with his long white finger. 'And, dare I say, out of character.'

'He does not know anything about this,' she blurted out, straining against his vice-like grip around her waist, but he hauled her forward. 'It was all my idea. Please,' she cried, desperation making her voice shrill, 'let me go. I swear I won't say a word. Why would I?,' she asked, unable to stem the wave of tears. 'You have done nothing untoward. If you let me go, I'll have nothing to report, nothing at all. I – it will be just a simple misunderstanding. No one need ever hear of it.'

He cocked a brow and threw open the carriage door. 'He doesn't know, eh?,' he remarked, dismissing her pleadings by ignoring them. 'How interesting.' He grabbed her chin and turned her face into the silvery moonlight. 'Then we have time to get better acquainted before he realizes what's become of you, precious.'

Repulsed, she squeezed her eyes shut. 'Please,' she sobbed, tears rolling unchecked down her face, 'you don't have to do this.' She darted a terrified glance into the black abyss awaiting her. 'You are a respected peer of the realm, not some lowly criminal off the streets.'

He cocked his head to one side. 'I reckon you are right. Of course, Paine was a rather vexing problem. Thanks to your meddlesome husband, I had to dispose of the pesky man. The poor devil talked too much. But I never actually tightened the noose. I mean to say, if kicking a chair out from under somebody is a crime, then we are all guilty of murder at some point, do you not think?'

Bile rose in her throat. Horrified, she stared at him. 'Y-yes, y-you are right. You've nothing to – to worry about. Paine hung himself. But I am nothing. Nobody. I could never harm you.'

'On the contrary, my dear,' he said with a chilling smile, 'you are married to the thorn in my side.'

Celeste never knew what hit her. The moment his fist collided with her face, the world went black.

'What do you mean, she's not here?,' Simon thundered at a tearful Joy closeted in the small boudoir of Morely House the following dawn. 'I left her with you for safekeeping.'

Seated on the pink velvet settee in her dressing gown, Joy blanched at his mordant tone. 'I saw her leave Almack's with George Wilkinson late last night,' she said, issuing a tearful sob. 'When I reached King Street . . . they'd gone.'

'Why the devil didn't you stay with her?,' he exploded with blistering fury.

'Be fair, Simon, you know how headstrong Celeste is,' Tony said, rubbing his distraught wife's arms. 'How could we possibly have known what she was scheming? It wasn't until Bow Street arrived that we suspected something untoward. As soon as we realized what had happened, we sent word. What could we have done? I had no idea this Wilkinson was a villain. You might have, at least, told me. Had I known, I never would have let her out of this house.'

Simon dragged his hands through his hair and drew a heavy sigh. 'Of course, you are right. Forgive me. The fault lies entirely with me. I might have known she'd try something like this.' He slammed his fists against the mantel. 'I was a blasted fool to trust her. Damned stupid chit will end up getting herself killed, or worse.'

Joy blinked up at him beneath tear-dotted lashes. 'What fate could possibly be worse than death?'

Tony patted her shoulders and said, 'There, there, now, don't fret. I am sure we shall find her. She'll be safe and sound in no time at all. You'll see.'

'I should have realized she was conspiring the moment she asked to go to Almack's. To think . . .' Joy blubbered into her handkerchief, '. . . I left her alone so that we might share a waltz, when all the time, that scoundrel was lurking on the sidelines waiting to pounce on my poor unsuspecting sister.'

Simon cast a disgruntled look over his shoulder. Her insipid caterwauling grated on his nerves. He was all too aware of the gravity of his current predicament. He could do quite nicely without her tearful reminders.

'Simon?,' Joy asked with a sniffle.

'Yes,' he growled impatiently.

'You don't hate me for tricking you, do you?'

'Hate you?,' he barked, his thoughts preoccupied with more grievous matters. 'What the devil are you taking about?'

'I tricked you. If not for my intervention, you might not have married my poor young sister,' she supplied with a gush of tears. 'I know it was terribly underhanded, but I felt certain you'd suit.'

He rolled his eyes heavenward. 'Good God, woman,' he snapped at her, 'how can you ask me such a question? Can you not see she is my life? I love her.'

She offered him a miserable, small smile. 'Well, even if she's . . . she's . . .,' she could not bring herself to say the word '. . . at least . . . you loved one another for a . . . short . . . space . . . of time,' she wailed, burying her face in her hands.

Simon grimaced. He refused to consider that grim possibility. Celeste was alive. She had to be. How he could still draw a breath if she were lying dead somewhere?

Pacing to the window, he planted his palms on the sill. 'Where the devil is Crawford? He should be here by now. We are losing valuable time,' he hissed vehemently.

'I am sure he is making a thorough investigation prior to presenting his report. Bow Street assured me, Runners are crawling the streets looking for her.'

357

'Mmm. I am sure. With the same competence as they responded to her note,' he muttered with a sardonic sneer.

'For all they knew, the note was a prank. After all, Crawford was on an assignment with you. Issuing a plea for men to come to Almack's is a bit odd, you must admit.'

Simon fixed Tony with a chilling glare. 'If this is your idea of helping matters, *don't*.'

Tony looked instantly contrite.

Joy sobbed even louder.

Rolling his eyes, Simon expelled a frustrated growl. Unable to endure another moment of her blubbering, he muttered, 'I need a drink,' and stormed from the room to await news downstairs.

'I'll join you momentarily,' Tony advised Simon with a curt nod and tried to calm his hysterical wife.

Shortly after Tony joined Simon's silent vigil in the library, Crawford made his appearance. He looked grim indeed as he informed Simon of his wife's whereabouts.

He shook his head. 'T'ain't good, milord.'

Simon's grip tightened around the glass, turning his fingers white. 'Well?,' he demanded, every cell of his body dreading the news that was to come, hoping against all hope that she was not dead and knowing if she were he would wish to die as well.

' 'E's taken her.'

Simon slammed his glass down on the table. 'Where?'

'To 'is 'ome in Kent, most like.'

358

Simon swore under his breath.

'Are you quite sure?,' Tony asked.

'Aye. Took a bit o' time, but we're fairly certain 'tis where 'e's 'eadin'.'

'Then we've not a moment to lose,' Simon averred with icy precision and headed for the door.

'Now 'old on a minute,' the Runner cautioned, stopping him at the threshold. ' 'E'll be ready and waitin', milord.'

'Good,' came Simon's clipped reply, 'I am more than ready to meet him.' His voice burned with contempt.

' 'E's got a good start. T'will be difficult to catch 'im.'

'I'll have the advantage of being on horseback. The carriage will slow him. You and your men follow, but Wilkinson is mine.' With that, Simon strode to the street door and wrenched it open. Calling to the groom, he issued orders to saddle his horse. He was about to descend the stone steps when Tony grabbed him by his jacket sleeve.

'Hang on, what are you planning to do?,' he asked, eyeing Simon warily.

Simon yanked his arm free. 'Kill the bastard,' he said through his teeth.

'That is a matter for Bow Street,' Tony insisted.

Simon shook his head, his dark eyes glinting with hatred. 'I am not about to stand by and let those bumbling idiots handle it while he rapes and murders my wife.'

Tony weighed the circumstance in his mind. 'Very well,' he said with a smile. 'If you are determined to kill him, at least let me lend a hand. You never were a decent shot,' he said with welcome levity and shouted to his butler to bring his pistols.

Simon clapped his hand on his friend's back. 'We must away for Kent. Every second counts,' he shouted and flew down the stone steps.

CHAPTER 18

Celeste felt the swaying of the speeding carriage, heard the creaking of the wheels and opened her eyes. Slowly, she regained consciousness. Gazing up, she tried to focus through blurry strands of hair, at the upside-down portrait of a man sitting diagonally across from her. Momentarily confused, she frowned and pushed the hair out of her face.

As the man's face became clear, the events of the last hour surged to the forefront of her mind with a vengeance. She sat bolt upright. Her head careened. The horrifying realization was visible on her face, eliciting a derisive chuckle from her male counterpart in this travesty of horrors.

A dull throb originated where her jaw had previously dwelt. Gingerly, she touched her fingertips to the side of her face, felt the swollen bruised protrusion and winced.

'Tender, is it?,' he asked in that hatefully dulcet voice of his.

She refused to honor that vicious remark with a reply. 'Where are you taking me?,' she asked pulling back the blind to peer out at the pitch-black landscape. 'What is it you are after – if not ransom money, then what?'

His hooded gaze drifted over her disheveled appearance, lingering over her snug bodice. He flashed a licentious smile. 'You are a single-minded wench, I'll give you that.'

'Aren't all your victims?' she asked, tossing him a hateful look over her shoulder. 'Or do you frighten them into submission?'

'Victims? Tut, tut. Victim is such an unattractive word. I prefer to think of them as playmates. After all, we are going to have such fun together, you and I. Who knows,' he said with a leer, 'you might even find you enjoy it, if you let yourself.'

'You're mad,' she hissed at him.

He pulled a face. 'You disappoint me, my dear,' his hatefully mellifluous voice condescended. 'Surely you can do better than that? Insanity would suggest that I was not in complete control of my faculties. And we both know that is not true.'

Her eyes glowed with burning enmity. 'You are a monster.'

He uttered a nasty chuckle. 'Don't delude yourself, I am no more a monster than your beloved Dragon. How many beds to you think he's graced over his lifetime, hmm? Too many to recall, I am sure.' He shrugged his shoulders. 'I merely have an unusual hobby; I like to deflower virgins,' he imparted with a lascivious smirk. 'And I am very good at it too.'

'How could you? You destroy innocent lives for a lark.'

362

He gave her a cynical amused look. 'It is quite easy, precious,' he drawled with heavy sarcasm. 'At first, it was a sexual challenge. Quite honestly, I wondered if it could be done. Then, of course,' he said, crossing his arms over his chest, 'it got boring, as these things do. After a while, we had to raise the stakes to make it more interesting. It was a deuced lucrative club before your husband saw fit to break it up.'

She glared at him, a spiteful glint in her eye. 'How nice for you and your friends,' she sneered contemptuously. 'Precisely how often did the gallant knight punch his favourite playmate, Emily Barclay, in the face?'

The smile slid from his face. 'I would never hurt little Em,' he imparted roughly. 'She was the most precious creature, the dearest thing in the world to me.'

'I suppose that is why you got her with child and left her to face the ignominies of scandal all alone?' Celeste spat with venom.

'Shut up,' he growled at her. His hands balled into fists. 'So he read my letter. I suspected as much. Damn him to hell! He had no right to delve into my private affairs,' he exploded, pounding his fist on the seat.

'My heart bleeds for you,' she mocked him.

He leaned forward. 'That's not all, my sweet,' he intoned with a vicious sneer. He grabbed a fistful of her curly hair and gave a hard yank. 'I wouldn't be anxious to arrive at our destination,' he remarked, smoothing his hand over the ivory column of her neck.

Gulping, she tried to lean away from him, but he tightened his hold. 'Why not?' she asked, fighting the urge to scream because of the pain he was causing by nearly tearing her hair from its roots.

He stuck his tongue out and licked her face. Recoiling, she closed her eyes in revulsion. 'I've a nice little cosy rendezvous planned for just we two.' His finger slid over her cleavage. She whimpered in disgust.

His hand splayed over her breast. She squirmed in protest.

'Take your hands off me,' she snarled.

Ignoring her command, he continued to maul her breasts. 'Should be quite a diverting exercise to bring you to heel. Of course, I don't normally sample used goods –' he gave her an evil smile '– but I'd be willing to make an exception in your case.'

Wriggling away from his repellent touch, she vowed fiercely, 'I'll kill myself before I allow you –'

'Allow me?' He threw back his head and roared with laughter. 'I don't require your permission. I take what I want when I want. But I dare say you'll learn to like it.'

As the carriage tore through the dark of night, Celeste sat curled in a miserable ball and prayed Simon would come to her rescue. Desperate to find an escape route, she glanced longingly at the door and debated flinging it open and leaping to her probable death.

Anything would be preferable to enduring what the man across from her had in store, she thought with a shiver. And she might survive the fall with only a few broken bones, if that. It was worth a try. She tried to inch her way across the seat. Her self-sacrifice was never realized, however, for her captor spoke up.

'Not much farther now. You can smell the sea,' he remarked, closing his eyes and inhaling deeply. 'I am always happiest in Kent.'

Her eyes flew wide. 'Kent? Why have you brought me here?' Her voice was taut with panic, for she now knew no one would come to her rescue. It was too much to hope. She was going to die in Kent at the hands of George Wilkinson.

Frowning, he gave her a derisive look. 'You are not overly bright, are you?' He sighed and flicked an imaginary piece of lint from his velvet-clad chest. 'None of you women are, I expect.'

The carriage slowed. Celeste darted a glance at the door. It was now or never. She threw herself across the seat. Jiggling the handle she shoved her weight against the carriage door. The door swung open. She fell from the carriage and would have landed face first on the hard ground were it not for the fact that she grabbed hold of the swinging door and hung on for dear life. Dangling from the speeding carriage, she glanced down at the ground narrowly whisking by her head. Her leg was caught. Wilkinson was holding her. She felt him tugging, trying to drag her back inside. Frantic, she kicked at his face with her free foot. She wished she'd donned her leather vamp boots instead of her soft kid-soled slippers. The result was the same. Uttering a string of furious oaths, he released her. She tumbled from the swaying carriage headfirst to the hard rough ground.

It took several seconds before she realized she had somersaulted into a rocky ditch. The breath was knocked out of her. Dazed by the fall, she sat up and tried to draw breath into her lungs. She caught a glimpse of the carriage grinding to a halt a few yards away. Catapulted by fear, she managed to get to her feet. She had not the slightest idea where she was going, but she ran as fast as her legs could carry her through the dark night.

She darted a glance over her shoulder. She could hear Wilkinson's angry growl. He was giving chase. She bit back the urge to scream and kept running.

The sounds of waves crashing against the rocks echoed against the craggy shore. In the distance, a yellow light glimmered through the darkness. Hiking her skirts above her knees, she ran towards the only possible safe haven. Heedless of the rough terrain and shrubbery that scraped at her legs, biting into her flesh, she ran. Her one thought was escape.

By the time she reached the enormous stone edifice, she felt as though she'd been running for miles. Exhausted and out of breath, she fell against the heavy wooden door and banged her fists, sobbing for help.

The door creaked open. A kindly-faced butler beckoned her to enter. Distraught and relieved beyond measure to have found succor, she stumbled into the dark hall.

'Thank you, thank you,' she cried, clutching the elderly man's arm for support. 'Please, you must help me. A man is after me,' she said, gulping for breath. 'He – he tried to kill me.'

'Is that a fact?' a horribly familiar voice drawled out from the dimly-lit staircase a few yards away. 'We cannot have the poor young woman fearing for her life now, can we Stevens?' George Wilkinson asked, coming into the light.

'No, my lord, we can't,' the butler replied with a malevolent smile.

Shaking her head, she backed away from him. 'No. No!,' she screamed. She covered her face with her hands. 'It cannot be!'

'Oh, but it is, my dear.' Regarding her with a cynical smirk, he cocked his head to one side. 'I must say, you are rather eccentric. I, myself, prefer the comforts of the carriage. Far be it from me to disparage the merits of a good tramp through the woods in the middle of the night. Invigorating, was it?,' he asked, mocking her.

'My lord,' a manservant said, entering the great hall from the shadows, 'I hate to interrupt you –'

Wilkinson's head turned. 'What is it?,' he snapped angrily.

'Begging your pardon, my lord, but two men on horseback have just entered the grounds.'

He turned back to her. His jaw clenched with rage. 'That would be your annoying husband, I should think.'

'Simon!,' she cried out, straining towards the door. But the butler held her fast.

'Take her to the tower and await my instructions. I'll handle these two interlopers.' He grabbed her by the chin. 'It won't be long now, precious.'

She spat in his face. Slowly, he raised his hand and wiped her saliva from his cheek.

He chuckled softly. 'You're a fiery little thing, aren't you?,' he said and slapped her hard across the face.

With a hard shove from behind, Celeste stumbled into a dank, cold room which she assumed was the tower. The creaking iron door swung shut behind her with a loud thud. As her eyes adjusted to the darkness, she saw quite plainly that the tower had large rectangular openings through which silvery moonlight streamed. Getting to her feet, she staggered over to look out. Far below, the ocean crashed against the craggy landscape with a thunderous rage.

No hope of escape unless she leapt to her death. Tears pricked her eyes. She hugged her arms around her waist.

Behind her, the door creaked open and then slammed shut. Someone else was in the room. But who? Oh, God, please God, let it be Simon.

She heard the rusty bolt slide into place, locking them both in. A flint struck and a tiny flame of a single taper flickered, casting Wilkinson's maniacal face in an eerie glow. Oh, where was Simon? She could hear Wilkinson's laboured breathing in the darkness. Obviously, he had hurried up the stairs that led to the tower room. Was her husband giving chase? Lord, she hoped so.

'Your husband is very persistent, precious. Do you think he intends to fight for you?' he asked as he traversed the darkened room in search of his prey.

Pressing her back against the damp wall, she held her breath and prayed Simon knew his way to the tower. She had no idea how many stone steps she'd been hauled up. Nor which direction the tower room faced. It was no use to try to call to him – the stone walls must be several inches thick.

The flickering light headed towards where she hid with her back against the cold, damp wall. 'I sincerely hope not; I, for one, find it hard to believe that any woman is worth a man's life.'

She slid her feet along the edge of the crumbling wall. The floor beneath her heel gave way and she gasped in surprise. Reaching out, her hand grasped the wall; it gave way beneath her clawing fingers. One glance over her shoulder at the white caps below and she vaulted away from the ledge. In her haste, she careened headlong into the arms of her foe.

'Here, now, I've got you,' his booming, amused voice cried out as he caught her around the waist. 'Where are you off to in such a hurry, precious?'

Desperate to be free, she kicked at his chins, shoving against his chest like a wild animal helplessly caught in a trap fighting for its life. 'Let me go, you vile beast.'

'Cheeky hellion!,' he burst out, amused by her pathetic attempts to wrench lose. 'You'll do nicely,' he told her with a salacious grin as he tightened his grip, nearly cracking her ribs.

'Celeste!,' Simon's shout echoed inside the stone stairwell.

'Here, Si –,' she tried to cry out, but Wilkinson's hand clamped down over her mouth.

Dragging her away from the insistent fists pounding at the door, Wilkinson whispered against her ear, 'It will take him quite some time to break down that door. Shall we pass the time with a favourite little game of mine? I am sure you'd like it.'

She could hear Simon calling to her through the door. Grimacing, she moaned against Wilkinson's palm. 'I don't imagine it would take you long to learn the rules,' he grated against her ear. 'I've a feeling you are the sort who'd rather fancy the pleasure and pain.'

Wriggling against him, she shook her head. It was no use. He dragged her along the tower edge into the damp cold darkness, farther away from Simon.

'I've particular tastes for your sort,' he said, caressing her smooth skin with his hand. 'How long do you suppose it'll take before you are begging for mercy?'

A small click sounded in the darkness like a pistol being cocked. 'Not long,' Simon's deep, menacing voice drawled from behind, 'but it won't come to that. And we both know it.'

Nothing had ever sounded as wonderful to Celeste's frightened ears. The Dragon had come to her rescue. Thank heaven. She wasn't quite sure how she was going to manoeuvre her way out of her current predicament without him. In fact, she was quite petrified.

Clutching her around the waist from behind, Wilkinson swung around to face Simon, using Celeste's body as a shield.

His pistol aimed at Wilkinson, Simon took a menacing step forward. 'Let her go.'

'Come any closer, Barclay,' Wilkinson growled, 'and your precious bride goes over the edge.' He motioned with his head toward the disintegrating ledge to his left.

Simon stopped short. 'It comes as little surprise to learn you'd hide behind a woman's skirts. This is between you and me. Leave my wife out of it.'

Wilkinson hauled Celeste's body hard against him. 'Look who's come to watch our performance?,' he asked, pressing his cheek to hers from behind.

Simon's eyes glinted silver fire. 'It's over, Wilkinson. There isn't going to be any performance.'

'You think not? You've pestered me long enough. If you still want her, when I'm finished with her, you can have her.' He sneered mordantly. 'But you'll not deny me the pleasure of making you suffer, Barclay.'

Simon's jaw tightened perceptibly. He shook his head and pointed the pistol at Wilkinson's chest. 'Afraid not.' His tight controlled voice held a note of lethal warning. 'She's a jewel well beyond your reach.'

'Damn you, Barclay. I loved Em, but you couldn't leave it alone. You had to dig it all up. Why the devil couldn't you keep your nose out of it? It was between Em and me. It was none of your concern.'

'You are wrong. It was very much my concern,' Simon countered, his tone hard and ruthless. 'It was stupid of you to insist club members wear that disgusting emblem. It was the one thing that linked the incidents together. I expected you to be more clever. You should have run away to India with

371

Everly when you had the chance. You cannot escape now. The grounds are crawling with men.'

Wilkinson darted a glance down below; flickering yellow torches could be seen traversing the grounds amid the distant shouts of men.

'Give yourself up, Wilkinson.'

'Never,' he snarled and threw Celeste at Simon.

Simon caught her. His pistol fell to the floor.

Wilkinson snatched it from the ground. 'Now who's got the upper hand?,' he asked pompously. 'I'll kill you. And have my way with the girl.'

'I wouldn't count on it,' Simon replied, pushing Celeste behind him. 'You haven't got the guts to put down the pistol and face me like a man.'

'Simon! No!,' Celeste cried, clinging to his arm. Ignoring her protest, he pushed her away. 'Simon, he'll shoot you!'

'That's right, my dear,' Wilkinson drawled amusedly.

'Only a coward would resort to raping a woman,' Simon taunted, taking a step closer.

Wilkinson burst out laughing. 'You are trying to goad me. Well, it won't work. I don't give a damn what you think of me. You think you are so superior,' he jeered contemptuously. 'You're not. We are very much alike, you and I – nothing wrong with celebrating male prowess.'

Simon shook his head. 'We are nothing alike,' he rebutted in disgust.

Wilkinson sniggered. 'That's what you think. Shall I tell you about your adorable little stepsister? Dear, sweet Emily was a whore. I did not have to seduce her. Don't kid yourself into believing it was rape. She wanted it. She even begged me to –.'

Snarling like a savage beast, Simon pounced on Wilkinson. As the two men fell to the ground in a death struggle, the pistol was thrown free. Celeste's frantic gaze searched the dark floor for the weapon. In desperation, she fell to her knees and felt the cold stone with her fingers. Distraught with fear, she scrambled across the floor on her hands and knees. In frenzied movements she searched until she felt the cold hardness of it. Her fingers wrapped around the smooth wooden stock. She dragged it from the ground. As she got to her feet, she did not stop to think about whether or not she could actually kill a man. She knew what she had to do. She had to save the man she loved.

'S-stop!,' she cried out, shakily, trying to get a clear shot at Wilkinson. But it was nearly impossible. No sooner did Wilkinson came into range, than Simon's fist collided with his jaw. Wilkinson fell backward, only to have Simon jump on top of him, pummelling his face with murderous fists.

'Stop, I say!,' she cried in frustration, aiming the large black object at the two men.

Footfalls sounded on the stone steps, the door was thrown wide and Tony rushed in. He darted a quick glance in Celeste's direction before trying to haul Simon off his adversary.

'You're killing him, man,' Tony shouted, dragging Simon away from the vile culprit. 'You cannot think to escape, Wilkinson, give yourself up,' he advised, holding Simon back.

Shaking his head, Wilkinson managed to get to his feet. He dragged the back of his hand across his bloodied face. Weaving to and fro, he turned to look at Celeste. His eyes traveled to the pistol in her hands. He threw back his head and uttered a hearty burst of laughter. Before anyone could stop him, he threw himself over the tower ledge and tumbled to his death on the rocks below.

Tony ran to the edge. Gazing down at Wilkinson's mangled body claimed by the rushing waves, he shook his head. 'He wreaked his own revenge in the end.'

'What about his victims?,' Simon asked Tony roughly. 'Where is their justice?'

Tony shrugged and stepped away from the rapidly disintegrating ledge. 'His death, I suppose,' he replied, his tone sombre.

Simon's mouth set in a grim line. 'His death won't bring back Jane Greenly, it won't erase Lady Caroline's pain, nor will it alter the fact that Emily died with a broken heart, believing herself in love with that villain.'

Tony released a heavy sigh. 'At least, you've put an end to their secret society of rapists and murders. There is some solace in that.'

'Not enough,' Simon said bitterly, 'it could never be enough.'

Celeste dropped the pistol on the dirt floor and rushed to Simon's side. Collapsing against him, she buried her face in his shoulder. 'Oh, Simon, Simon.'

His arms, strong and sure, closed around her. 'It's all right,' he assured her, the rich timbre of his voice calming her. 'He's dead. You're perfectly safe, now.

I've got you.' He turned his head and brushed his lips against her temple. He held her in his arms, running his hands over her. It took some time before he was satisfied she was still in one piece.

Watching the happy couple reunite, Tony smiled. 'I hope this has been a lesson to you, young lady?,' he teased Celeste, his tone sharp. 'You might have been hurt were it not for your heroic husband.'

Tears trickled down her cheeks. 'I know,' she cried, 'I've been such a fool.'

Simon cupped her face with his palms, the pads of his thumbs catching the tears as they fell. 'We both have.'

So engrossed in one another were they that they did not notice when Tony quietly slipped away.

Tenderly, Simon kissed Celeste's lips. 'I thought I'd go mad, not knowing if you were dead or alive or what that devil had done to you,' he told her, his voice thick and unsteady. 'It made me realize what an idiot I've been.'

'You? An idiot? I don't believe it.' She smiled dreamily up at him. 'It is beyond the realm of possibility.'

He smiled down at her, enjoying her teasing. 'I was damned selfish. When I thought I might lose you,' he said, caressing her cheek gently with his palm, 'I deeply regretted the time we'd wasted. Oh, my darling,' he said, pressing a gentle kiss to her lips, 'we can wait as long as you wish for a child. I have no right to press you.'

'Oh, Simon . . . Simon, you are magnificent, my love,' she gushed, showering kisses all over his face and clinging to her husband for dear life, 'truly, a splendid husband. Despite all your selfishness, I love you dearly.'

His arms tightened around her as he expelled a deep gruff laugh. 'You are quite an original, my dear. Thank heaven you are safe.' He hugged her to him, squeezing her tight to prove to himself she was really alive and well.

When at last he leaned back to look at her, he asked, 'Are you certain you are all right?' Brushing her tangled hair back from her face, he scowled at the bruise marring her porcelain skin and ran his fingertip lightly over the purple discoloration.

She nodded her head. 'I've never been better,' she said, fighting back the rush of tearful relief that was eager to flow. Rather than gushing like a river, she busied herself with the absurd task of straightening her husband's disheveled velvet coat and cravat. 'Where did you ever learn to fight like that? I was amazed by your agility, my lord.'

Simon gave her a rueful look. 'I'll give your regards to Gentleman Jackson when next I see him,' he drawled, locking his arms around her waist.

'Thank heavens you came when you did,' she said, adjusting his collar tabs with loving care, 'or I might have joined the ranks of his poor unsuspecting victims,' she added with a shiver.

'Mmm,' he muttered curtly and slapped her playfully on the bottom.

She gave him a startled look.

He fixed her with a stern look. 'I am still reeling from your deception. I suppose I should consider myself fortunate that the blackguard didn't stoop to killing my wayward wife prior to my arrival.' His tone was extremely sarcastic.

She colored slightly. 'As to that, I am so grateful you saw fit to follow. I do not know what I would have done had you not come to my rescue.'

'I cannot credit your stupidity. For God's sake,' he breathed, 'you might have been killed. And, I might add, very nearly were.'

'I know it was foolish. But I very much fear obedience has never been my forte, my lord.'

A grim frown ruffled his lips. 'Neither is sound judgement,' he countered brusquely.

'You mustn't be cross with me, Simon,' she said, gently tracing the hard line of his jaw with her finger. 'I did it for you.'

His brow darkened. 'For me?'

Lowering her gaze, she nodded her head. 'I wanted to make you happy. I thought if I managed to catch the villain, you might . . . .' Her voice trailed off.

'I might what?,' he pressed, his manner softening.

'Love me,' she said in a voice so low he had to strain to hear it.

'You little fool,' he said, his voice hoarse from emotion, 'don't you know you are my life, my love, my all? I love you. Oh, my darling Celeste, how could you doubt me?'

'Well,' she said blinking back tears of joy, 'you never said anything.'

'Was fighting to save your life not enough to impress you with the depth of my feelings?,' he asked, his grey eyes aglow with tenderness and deep abiding love.

She smiled coyly. 'I must confess,' she remarked with a rush of relief, 'I was never so happy to see any one person in all my life.'

'Neither was I,' he murmured huskily and pulled her close against him. 'If you ever do anything so stupid again,' he intoned fiercely, hugging her tightly, 'I'll lock you in the tower at Lindhurst myself.'

She leaned back to look at his face. Her forehead creased. 'Is there a tower at Lindhurst?,' she asked blankly.

'Yes,' he drawled out in a husky murmur, 'my bedroom.'

'I think I should rather like such a punishment, my lord,' she said on a dreamy sigh and pressed her softly-parted lips to his. He crushed her to him, smothering her mouth with a deeply possessive passionate kiss.

EPILOGUE

Two weeks later, a letter arrived for C.C. Dunhill at the Upper Brook Street townhouse address.

'Simon, you will never believe it when I tell you,' Celeste cried, bursting into the library where her husband was occupied penning his daily correspondence. 'I've received a letter from Mr Hammersmith at *The Chronicle*. He enjoyed my last article so much that he's requested I write another piece on Thomas Erskine, who has recently written *Internal Evidence for the Truth of Revealed Religion*.'

Seated behind his desk, Simon raised his brows. 'Has he really?,' came his uninterested reply as he continued with his business. 'Jolly good for him.'

Rushing towards the desk, she said with excitement, 'And there is more.' She hopped up on to the desktop, swinging her crossed ankles to and fro, and read aloud, 'The proprietor would very like to meet C.C. Dunhill in person on Friday, eleven o'clock at the Fleet Street office.'

Celeste's face fell. Slowly, she folded the crisp ivory paper and slid it back inside the envelope.

Simon glanced up at his wife who'd suddenly gone from jubilant to depressed. 'Why so glum?,' he asked, setting his quill pen aside and siting back to examine his wife's unhappy expression. 'I should think you'd be ecstatic.'

'I cannot possibly go,' she lamented, sliding off the desk.

Leaning back in his chair, Simon folded his hands behind his head. 'And why not?,' he asked, admiring the sway of her narrow hips.

She expelled an annoyed sigh and swiveled about to look at him. 'Vexing man,' she said, her tone cross, 'you know perfectly well why not. I am a woman.'

A wicked gleam shone in his eye as his dark sultry gaze roamed seductively over her. 'Mmm,' he drawled wickedly, 'I've noticed.'

She gave him a withering look. 'Simon, be serious,' she imparted on a forlorn sigh. 'It's important.'

His expression sobered. 'What has your being a woman to do with meeting the proprietor?'

'Once I meet him and he discovers my deception, I'll be through. No more C.C. Dunhill,' she muttered with a petulant frown, folding her arms at her waist.

'Not necessarily,' Simon allowed, getting to his feet. He crossed the room to where his distraught wife stood. 'The proprietor might have an open mind. After all, your stories have been well received in the past. C.C. Dunhill is gaining a following among readers. The proprietor could be persuaded to overlook your gender.'

'But consider the alternative? How will I ever be

able to indulge my intellectual side without C.C. Dunhill?'

Simon bit back a smile and hugged her to him. 'We'll think of something. In the meantime,' he advised, tilting up her downturned face to kiss her lightly on the mouth, 'you'd best send your reply.'

She did not look hopeful.

Framing her face with his hands, he coaxed gently, 'It will be all right, you'll see.'

Celeste's nerves were in tatters as she sat in the newspaper office outside the proprietor's door waiting for admittance. She had no idea how he would view her scandalous deception. Even if, as Simon suggested, her articles were well regarded, no proprietor in all of London would openly employ a female reporter. It simply was not done. Her only hope was that he agree to continue her subterfuge.

Mr Hammersmith appeared in the doorway and motioned for Celeste to enter.

Gathering all her courage, she got to her feet and marched into the proprietor's office. Her feet carried her across the threshold, then she stopped short. Not five feet from her sat her husband, happily installed behind a large walnut desk. Bold as brass, he addressed her, a look of cocky amusement on his face. 'Hello, my darling. Surprised to see me? I must say you look positively ravishing in that dress. Pink becomes you. Come over here and give me a kiss.'

'Why, you –,' she fumed, slamming the door in her wake, '– deceitful, dishonest, lowdown swine.'

He held up his hands to ward off her verbal attack. 'Now wait, I am not the one who pretended to be someone I wasn't.'

'No,' she stormed, slamming her palms down on the desk, 'you just neglected to tell me the truth. You knew all the time about C.C. Dunhill.'

Leaning forward, he shook his head. 'I had no idea. Hammersmith oversees the day-to-day operations. I am not all that involved with the paper. I merely own it.'

'Ooh,' she cried stamping her foot with temper, 'the performance you gave: "The proprietor might be open-minded." When I think of how I suffered,' she ranted with clenched fists at her side, 'and worried and agonized over this meeting, I could kill you.' She slanted him a dark look. 'And that ridiculous suggestion that I write about animal husbandry,' she complained. 'I've never been so humiliated in all my days.'

He threw back his head and roared with laughter. 'Never say Hammersmith actually agreed to print it? Well?,' he inquired his shoulders shaking with mirth. 'Did he?'

'I am not quite sure what he plans,' she confessed with a good deal of reluctance. 'I haven't actually received a reply from him as yet.'

'I shouldn't wonder,' Simon muttered, brushing the tears from his eyes.

She crossed her arms over her chest and drummed her fingers against her arm. 'Perhaps the proprietor would be so kind as to save C.C. Dunhill some embarrassment and pull the article?'

He inclined his head amicably. 'Agreed.'

'You are the lowest of the low. I shall never forgive you.'

His hand snaked out and caught her by the wrist. 'Darling,' he said, dragging her down into his lap, 'I wasn't serious when I suggested you compose an articles on ewes and rams.'

'Well,' she grumbled, piqued by his amusement at her expense, 'how was I to know? You can be rather moody and difficult from time to time. I never know what to think.'

His finger brushed a lone curl back from her forehead. 'Has life with me been a trial for you, then?' he asked in a husky undertone.

Scowling, she gave him a disgruntled look. 'You are a beast.'

His compelling grey eyes gleamed with concern. 'Have I truly made you miserable?,' he asked gently.

'Oh, no, Simon,' she cried, throwing her arms around his neck and hugging him, 'I do love you. And I am happier than I ever dreamed possible.'

'Except for when I'm moody and difficult and keep things from you?,' he teased, retrieving her arms from around his neck to look at her. 'Like the future of your sacred C.C. Dunhill? Which, by the way, promises to be long and fruitful. You may write for the paper as long as you are inclined.'

'Thank you, Simon. But I very much suspect my journalism days are numbered.'

He gave her a quizzical look. 'What do you mean?' he asked, his voice a velvet murmur. 'I thought I married the girl who'd be happy to while away the hours in the country, provided of course, she had her intellectual pursuits to occupy her time?'

'Well . . . you did. I felt that way then.'

A questioning gleam lit his silver gaze. 'And now?'

She heaved a deep sigh. 'Now . . . I am not so sure.'

'Not so sure?,' he echoed incredulously. 'I don't believe it.'

She laughed. 'Strange but true. I've found something more . . . interesting to occupy my time, shall we say.'

He cocked one ebony brow. 'Such as?,' he queried silkily.

'You. And . . .'

'And?'

'Our baby.'

He stared at her, a blank look on his handsome face. 'Our baby?,' he whispered softly. 'What are you saying?'

Beaming from ear to ear, she said her tone dry, 'I should have thought it would be quite obvious.'

'So soon?' he asked stupidly.

'I am afraid so,' she said with a deep sigh.

Gazing deeply into her eyes, he asked, 'You don't . . . mind?'

She cupped his face with her palm. 'How could I mind? The child is yours, isn't it?'

'Celeste,' he breathed. His hand slid over the top of hers and he pressed a kiss on her palm, 'you are a treasure.' He wrapped his arms around her and kissed her deeply. Pulling back suddenly, he frowned slightly and lifted her chin to look at her. 'How long have you suspected?'

384

'A few weeks.'

A dark scowl clouded his features. 'You mean to say you risked your safety and that of our child,' he intoned gravely, 'on a ridiculous folly with Wilkinson that might have meant your death?'

'Well, no, at the time I wasn't positive I was actually carrying your child.'

His eyes narrowed on her face. 'When *precisely* did you know?'

'Last week.'

'And you waited until now to tell me?'

She gazed up at him with artless blue eyes that were always his undoing. 'When did you want me to tell you?'

'The moment you suspected,' he snapped.

'Why?'

'Why?,' he repeated, gawking at her. 'Well,' he spluttered, 'so that I could take care of you. Good Lord, I made love to you last night.'

'Yes,' she said with a dreamy smile and rested her cheek against his shoulder, 'I remember.'

He looked disconcerted. 'You should have told me you were with child,' he said awkwardly.

She lifted her head to look at him. 'So that you could see to my every need?,' she queried, arching a dainty brow. 'Make certain I did nothing too strenuous?'

'Yes.'

She sighed and laid her cheek against his shoulder once more. 'In that case, I wish I had waited to tell you.'

He looked slightly taken aback. 'Don't you want me to care for you during your confinement? Think

385

of all the long difficult months that lie ahead. The agonizing hours upon hours of birth –'

She pressed her fingers to his lips, silencing him. 'I'd rather not consider that at the moment.'

He smiled. 'You need me to look after you,' he said – his voice, like his expression, was warm and deeply tender – 'to see to your every need and prevent you from doing anything that might cause you discomfort.'

'Making love to my husband does not cause me discomfort.'

'Are you sure?'

'Mmm. Hmm. Quite sure,' she said, locking her arms around his neck.

One end of his sensual mouth curved upward. 'Well, in that case my beautiful, wayward wife,' he murmured in soft seductive tones, 'I think you need more bed rest.'

His eyes held a dark velvet promise that made her grow warm. 'So do I,' she purred. Tugging his head closer, she pressed a kiss to his lips. It was an all-encompassing embrace, full of love.

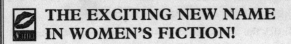

THE EXCITING NEW NAME IN WOMEN'S FICTION!

PLEASE HELP ME TO HELP YOU!

Dear *Scarlet* Reader,

I have some wonderful news for you this month – we are beginning a super Prize Draw, which means that you *could win an exclusive sassy Scarlet T-shirt!* Just fill in your questionnaire and return it to us (see addresses at the end of the questionnaire) before 31 November 1998, and we'll do the rest! If you are lucky enough to be one of the first four names out of the hat each month, we will send you this exclusive prize.

So don't delay – return your form straight away!*

Looking forward to hearing from you,

Sally Cooper

Editor-in-Chief, *Scarlet*

QUESTIONNAIRE

Please tick the appropriate boxes to indicate your answers

1 Where did you get this Scarlet title?
Bought in supermarket ☐
Bought at my local bookstore ☐ Bought at chain bookstore ☐
Bought at book exchange or used bookstore ☐
Borrowed from a friend ☐
Other (please indicate) _____

2 Did you enjoy reading it?
A lot ☐   A little ☐   Not at all ☐

3 What did you particularly like about this book?
Believable characters ☐   Easy to read ☐
Good value for money ☐   Enjoyable locations ☐
Interesting story ☐   Modern setting ☐
Other _____

4 What did you particularly dislike about this book?
_____

5 Would you buy another Scarlet book?
Yes ☐   No ☐

6 What other kinds of book do you enjoy reading?
Horror ☐   Puzzle books ☐   Historical fiction ☐
General fiction ☐   Crime/Detective ☐   Cookery ☐
Other (please indicate) _____

7 Which magazines do you enjoy reading?
   1. _____
   2. _____
   3. _____

And now a little about you –
8 How old are you?
   Under 25 ☐   25–34 ☐   35–44 ☐
   45–54 ☐   55–64 ☐   over 65 ☐

cont.

9 What is your marital status?
Single ☐ Married/living with partner ☐
Widowed ☐ Separated/divorced ☐

10 What is your current occupation?
Employed full-time ☐ Employed part-time ☐
Student ☐ Housewife full-time ☐
Unemployed ☐ Retired ☐

11 Do you have children? If so, how many and how old are they?
_____
_____

12 What is your annual household income?
under $15,000	☐	or £10,000	☐
$15–25,000	☐	or £10–20,000	☐
$25–35,000	☐	or £20–30,000	☐
$35–50,000	☐	or £30–40,000	☐
over $50,000	☐	or £40,000	☐

Miss/Mrs/Ms _____
Address _____
_____
_____

Thank you for completing this questionnaire. Now tear it out – put
it in an envelope and send it, before 28 February 1999, to:

Sally Cooper, Editor-in-Chief

USA/Can. address
SCARLET c/o London Bridge
85 River Rock Drive
Suite 202
Buffalo
NY 14207
USA

UK address/No stamp required
SCARLET
FREEPOST LON 3335
LONDON W8 4BR
*Please use block capitals for
address*

HESEN/8/98

Scarlet **titles coming next month:**

FINDING GOLD Tammy Hilz

In this, our second *Scarlet* hardback, Jackson Dermont is on the trail of a thief! If he doesn't find her he will forfeit the business that he almost lost before, through someone's cunning and deceitful behaviour. Rachel Gold is high on his list of suspects . . . and Jackson is determined to do *anything* to save his beloved company. Anything . . . except fall in love and learn to trust – again!

SEARED SATIN Vickie Mohr

Security guard Tess Reynolds is a woman to be reckoned with. Boss of a successful security firm, she doesn't need any man's help to do her job. Until, that is, she meets gorgeous Ethan Booker who reluctantly joins forces with her to solve a deadly mystery. But isn't the real mystery how he's gonna persuade Tess to stick around once the case is closed?

A WOMAN SCORNED Kathryn Bellamy

Reeling with shock as a man from her past walks into the cafe, Tessa Grant grabs her daughter and makes a run for it – straight into the path of a passing bus! She wakes in hospital to discover that Max is back, and has taken over her life and her daughter. Now that he knows he is the father of her child, will they be able to make a life together? And why is someone else trying to destroy Tessa?

JOIN THE CLUB!

Why not join the *Scarlet* Readers' Club – you can have four exciting new reads delivered to your door every other month for only £9.99, plus TWO FREE BOOKS WITH YOUR FIRST MONTH'S ORDER!

Fill in the form below and tick your two first books from those listed:

1. *Never Say Never* by Tina Leonard ☐
2. *The Sins of Sarah* by Anne Styles ☐
3. *Wicked in Silk* by Andrea Young ☐
4. *Wild Lady* by Liz Fielding ☐
5. *Starstruck* by Lianne Conway ☐
6. *This Time Forever* by Vickie Moore ☐
7. *It Takes Two* by Tina Leonard ☐
8. *The Mistress* by Angela Drake ☐
9. *Come Home Forever* by Jan McDaniel ☐
10. *Deception* by Sophie Weston ☐
11. *Fire and Ice* by Maxine Barry ☐
12. *Caribbean Flame* by Maxine Barry ☐

ORDER FORM

SEND NO MONEY NOW. Just complete and send to **SCARLET READERS' CLUB, FREEPOST, LON 3335, Salisbury SP5 5YW**

Yes, I want to join the ***SCARLET* READERS' CLUB*** and have the convenience of 4 exciting new novels delivered directly to my door every other month! Please send me my first shipment now for the unbelievable price of £9.99, plus my TWO special offer books absolutely free. I understand that I will be invoiced for this shipment and FOUR further *Scarlet* titles at £9.99 (including postage and packing) every other month unless I cancel my order in writing. I am over 18.

Signed ....

Name (IN BLOCK CAPITALS)..

Address (IN BLOCK CAPITALS)...

....

Town... **Post Code**..............................

Phone Number ....

As a result of this offer your name and address may be passed on to other carefully selected companies. If you do not wish this, please tick this box ☐.

*Please note this offer applies to UK only.